To Avril, thank you for your support.

1

THE DIAMOND LADY

The sound of bagpipes echoed through the streets of Glasgow as Beryl Diamond's horse-drawn funeral carriage passed through. On one side of the carriage 'Nana' had been spelled out in beautiful red roses and on the other side was simply 'Diamond' in yellow ones. People came out of shops and stopped whatever they were doing to say their last farewell to the matriarch of Thistle Park Estate.

Patsy looked out of the window of the sleek black car that followed the carriage and saw the burnt-out remains of what had once been her car, and was now the last resting place of Natasha, Nick Diamond's mistress. The car had burst into flames following a well-timed explosion from Patsy and her newfound friends in the name of justice. Patsy had discovered that Natasha had killed Nick out of jealousy and had been prepared to let his beloved nana, Beryl, take the blame for it.

'This is so touching Patsy; no one would ever give me a send-off like this. Look, there are hundreds of people lining the streets.' Nick's mother, Victoria, brushed away a tear from her eye, feeling the emotion of the day building up inside of her.

'Well, it would be touching if it wasn't for the sound of those bagpipes. Christ, I can't hear myself think. It sounds like cats fighting. But I know what you mean Victoria, she might have been an old cow at times, but this is real community spirit. They have known her and her family for years; she was one of the old matriarchs of Glasgow and it's just a shame she isn't here to see it, although she would have found something to moan about.' They smiled at each other and Patsy reached out for Victoria's hand, squeezing it comfortingly.

'She was my mother-in-law Patsy, so today, for her last procession through Glasgow, we only speak well of her. I'm so pleased that no one knows that she made that silly confession on her death bed about killing Nicky. All everyone knows now is that the police have come to a dead end and put the case on hold until new information turns up, which we both know it won't.' Victoria cast Patsy a knowing look. 'She did it to protect her family, her great-grandson and even Natasha.'

'Natasha got her just desserts Victoria. Whatever you feel inside about what I did, you know I did it for Beryl and for Nick. He was my husband, and although he was going to leave me for Natasha, he didn't deserve to be shot because of her jealousy. Beryl and I started getting on well at the end, even if it had taken fifteen years for us to do so. So let's smile and have a drink to send her on her way.'

'And what about Natasha?' Victoria spoke in a hushed whisper so that the chauffeur who drove them couldn't hear anything.

'What about her? She had her own cremation, and we can't exactly sieve through the ashes of the car to bury what's left of her. She brought it on herself. She lied and deceived all of us. Good riddance to her Victoria, that's what I say.'

'Are those the words of a scorned wife or her murderer Patsy?' The stern look Victoria gave her made Patsy shudder.

'I had accepted Nick was going to leave me. That was my fate and there was no changing his mind. Natasha was young and offered him a bright new future. I was the past. But it all came to nothing, and he died for what? I shudder when I think that the last face he saw on earth was the woman he loved pointing a gun at him.' Tears brimmed on Patsy's eyelashes when she thought about that awful night.

It was now Victoria's turn to comfort Patsy. 'I know. The shock and confusion he must have felt in those last seconds of his life must have been more painful than the bullet that killed him. But Natasha was staying at my house and was almost part of the family; we have to sort something out for a funeral.' Victoria looked out of the window of the car at the crowds of people bowing their heads. It pleased and saddened her at the same time.

'Let's just get today over with shall we Victoria, before you start planning your next funeral.' The silence that followed made Patsy wish she hadn't snapped at Victoria. She was trying her best for all of them and she knew having a funeral for Natasha made sense, but having to pay her respects to the woman who had almost destroyed her family single-handedly? It made Patsy's blood boil to think about it.

Finally, the hearse stopped as they reached the cemetery and they made their way inside the church. 'Thank god those bagpipes have stopped,' Patsy whispered in Victoria's ear as Beryl's coffin was placed at the front by the bearers.

Victoria put her finger to her lips and gave a furtive glance behind her to the next pew where Maggie and Sheila sat.

Sheila leaned forward, her head almost resting on Victoria's and Patsy's shoulders. 'You two wee lassies okay? I've brought

Angus with me... I bet you didn't recognise him without his bright orange rescue service jacket on. I suppose the beard gives it away.' She giggled. They all looked up when they saw the vicar take his stand on the podium.

Once the vicar had spoken, Victoria got up and spoke about Beryl and her little ways which made everyone laugh. Instantly the mood seemed lighter, as people recalled their own memories about being on the sharp edge of Beryl's tongue.

'Jerusalem', Beryl's favourite hymn, led the procession out of the church and into the graveyard. Linking arms with each other, Patsy and Victoria walked across the grass to the plot.

'My heels are going to be ruined with all this mud. It's supposed to be summertime, for Christ's sake,' Patsy moaned.

Standing in the graveyard, Patsy lowered her dark glasses and looked up at Sheila. As their eyes met, a small grin appeared on both of their faces. It wasn't that long ago that they were both nearly killed in this very cemetery and Beryl's body wasn't the first body that they had buried here.

Victoria threw a rose and a thistle onto Beryl's coffin after it had been lowered into the ground and Patsy did likewise. Patsy surprised herself as a lump rose in her throat. She and Beryl had become better friends before she died and she respected Beryl's loyalty to the family, which had meant everything to her. Yes, as silly as it might sound to everyone, she was going to miss her.

Everyone soon made their way back to their cars, leaving only Patsy and Victoria standing next to the graveside. Clearing her throat, looked down at Beryl's coffin. 'I hope you feel justice has been served Nana. Me and Victoria will take care of little Nicky, you know that. I am so sorry you suffered the way that you did. God bless you Beryl Diamond and rest in peace love.'

Coughing slightly to clear the lump in her throat from Patsy's words, Victoria looked around at the dwindling crowd walking away to their own cars. 'Is that your mum and dad over there, Patsy?' Victoria nodded to the couple. 'I haven't seen them since they bought that villa in Greece. I must pop over and say hello. You never said they were back in England.' Curiously, Victoria looked at Patsy. 'You're not ashamed of us are you Patsy, considering how things have been recently?'

'Don't be silly Victoria. I sent them an invite but I didn't know if they could make it, which is why I never said anything. You know what it's like since Dad left the air force; they've taken their retirement seriously and have travelled everywhere. He had so many air miles logged up and they've used the lot of them.' Patsy felt uneasy but was also glad her parents were there. Looking up and following Victoria's eye line, Patsy smiled and waved to the couple opposite them.

'Who is that with them?' Victoria enquired. 'She's beautiful.' Victoria thought the little girl was about five or six years old. She wore a red tartan kilt and white blouse. Patsy's parents had made a huge effort with their young charge for Beryl's sake, which touched Victoria's heart. The young girl's long, sandy coloured hair trailed down her back, while her fringe was swept back from her face with a tartan headband. The little cherub face showed two dimples on either side of her cheeks when she smiled. Holding a small posey of flowers in her tiny hands, she ·held them up excitedly to show Victoria.

Frowning, Victoria looked at the little girl again. She felt a fleeting flash of recognition. It was as though she had met her before, but she knew she definitely hadn't. Suddenly Victoria felt cold, but she didn't know why. It was as if someone had just stepped over her own grave. 'Who is she, Patsy?' Victoria pressed again, while not taking her eyes off the little girl. 'I didn't know there were any small children in your family.'

'Oh, that's a long story Victoria and not one for today,' Patsy replied, pleased that she was wearing her sunglasses and could avoid Victoria's stare. Patsy waved to them all again and blew a kiss. 'Come on, people are starting to leave and make their way to the community centre. I'm glad we had that place cleaned up for today and got the caterers in.'

Brushing a tear away, Victoria agreed. 'It was the only place I could think of that she would approve of. The community centre meant everything to her and it's a good place to hold her wake. Although it does seem to be surrounded by death and corruption, Beryl loved it and that's all that matters. You never know, I might even throw in a round of bingo!' They both laughed at the memory of Beryl's beloved bingo nights. That's what had started Nick's idea to renovate the place and use it as his drug emporium. It had seemed the perfect smoke screen.

As they made their way back to the funeral car, someone else caught Patsy's eye. Larry was stood in the disappearing crowd, looking towards her. 'Just a minute Victoria.' Walking over to him, she smiled. 'Thank you for coming Larry. Are you joining us for a drink and a well curled sandwich?'

Patsy was pleased to see him. Larry was her lawyer as well as her lover. He was kind, gentle and by all accounts, a one-woman man, which was more than she could have said about Nick Diamond.

'No Patsy, not if you don't mind. I just wanted to make sure you were okay and to pay my respects.'

Patsy stroked the black jacket of his suit. 'You look taller in a black suit Larry, and very handsome. Maybe we could meet up later and do something?' She grinned and pecked him on the cheek.

Smiling at her and showing a perfect row of teeth, he stroked her face. 'And you, Patsy Diamond, look like Jaquie Onassis in those dark glasses. Ring me or pop around when you're free.'

After brushing away some imaginary fluff from his shoulder, Patsy walked back to the car. Glancing behind her, she could see Larry smiling. Lowering her glasses, she gave him a slight wink.

The community centre was already filling with people by the time they got there. It looked more like a birthday party than a wake, but that was what Victoria had wanted. For everyone from Beryl's estate, young and old, to come and give her the best send-off ever.

Sheila sidled up to Patsy, and offered her a glass of whisky, as Victoria played the dutiful hostess and mingled, thanking everyone for coming to pay their respects. 'I see Larry was sniffing around like a helpless puppy again. Poor laddie; I wish you would throw him a bone now and again. After all that business with Natasha, he made the police drive past the estate to check on you. He really cares about you Patsy. Be kind.' She winked.

'I know, but having the police hanging around on a regular basis and me having to play the scared victim didn't help matters. But you're right, it did clear us all of any suspicion,' Patsy replied.

'Us?' Sheila laughed. 'Since when did what you organised become "us"?'

'Well, I thought we were like the musketeers, all for one and one for all. Isn't that what they say? No matter who makes the decisions.'

'Oh, stop being so touchy Patsy. You know me and Vicky are backing you all the way. I take it she's going to keep young Nicky, then? What about Natasha's other son, Jimmy? Where does he come into all this?'

Jimmy was the son Natasha had had before she'd met Nick. By a tragic accident, Jimmy had shot Sheila's husband, Steve, with a real gun he had found, thinking it was a toy one from his play box. The boy was now in foster care and undergoing all kinds of counselling, although Sheila felt it was pointless. He didn't know what he had done; all he knew was that he was being punished by being kept away from his mummy.

Taking a sip of her whisky, Patsy nodded. 'I believe social services have approached Victoria. They would like to keep the siblings together if at all possible. After all, little Nicky is Victoria's grandson and half-brother to Jimmy. I see their point and she seems willing enough to take him on. You know Victoria, she'll keep the brothers together and social services will be glad of one less case load for them to bother with.'

'You're right there, lassie; there are loads around this area that aren't brought up by their real parents. Anyway, what about that other matter? Your new partner, or Nick's old one.' Sheila laughed. 'Yes, Patsy, the French lassie with her nose in the air, like we're just some bad smell underneath it. What are you going to do about her? She's trouble, I can smell it.'

'I have Larry on the case with that one. His jaw nearly hit the floor when I told him Karen Duret was alive and well. I have a meeting with her next week. Or rather "we" have a meeting with her. I don't understand it, Sheila. She has a headstone in the cemetery. To all intents and purposes she is dead, but here she is, as large as life, claiming half of everything Nick left me. Well, I don't mind saying, he left me with a lot of shit to clear up!' Angry and frustrated, Patsy's face flushed. 'I have wracked my brain about her Sheila, but I don't remember Nick ever mentioning her name.' Patsy sniffed back the tears she felt forming on her lashes. 'Yet she has legitimate bank accounts in her name taking half the takings from the pizza shops. How can that be Sheila?' Exasperated, Patsy threw her hands up into the air. 'I feel like I'm drowning sometimes. Well, fuck Nick, and fuck her! She's not getting one more penny out of me!' Picking up her whisky, Patsy gulped it back in one.

Sheila shook her head and looked around the room. 'I don't know Patsy. This is one mystery even Miss Marple would have problems solving. Personally, I don't understand why she's come now. She didn't turn up at Nick's funeral, or contact you through a lawyer after his death – isn't that what other people would do? Why has she decided to show her face now? None of this makes sense. You can't bury someone without a legal death certificate and you can't just go putting up headstones where you feel like it. I smell a rat, a rat wearing French perfume. She wants something Patsy, and badly enough to leave Paris and come to Glasgow for it.' For a moment the two women stared at each other. They were full of questions but had none of the answers.

Dismissing Karen from her mind for the moment, Patsy looked around at everyone toasting Beryl and sighed. 'Let's just get all this other stuff sorted first. You know, Victoria wants some kind of ceremony for Natasha.'

'For Natasha? Well, I'm surprised...' Sheila trailed off.

'She thinks it makes sense considering Natasha was living with her and had become part of the family. She has a point.'

'And how do you feel about that?' Sheila asked tentatively.

Patsy's nonchalant shrug was all the answer she needed. 'Look, I'm sick of being jostled around in here. I'm going to get Victoria; two hours in here is more than enough. They won't even notice we've gone.'

Walking over to James and Fin, Patsy shook their hands and then gave James the keys. 'Will you lock up for me when this lot have gone? I'm going to go back to Beryl's for a well-earned coffee and to get out of these black clothes.' She smiled at them both. They had become good friends, even though a year ago she would never have believed it. They were an unusual mix. Judgemental people would say the dregs of the earth, but she had learnt over the last few months that you can't judge a book by its cover. Fin was the Glasgow estate drug dealer and thief, hence his name, 'Fin', for fingers. He was around thirty and hadn't had many opportunities in his life. He'd been abandoned and brought up by his ill grandmother and had been in and out of prison most of his life, but strangely enough, Patsy found him loyal and honest. He had saved James's life when the man was going to be murdered by his Albanian business partner, Noel, and had hidden him at his aunty Maggie's flat, who didn't want anyone to know she was related to Fin. She came over as a cold woman but, in fact, she was very decent and had been Beryl's best friend. James was around sixty, she guessed, a local gangster, bank robber and drug dealer. He too had done his fair share of prison sentences. He was handsome and had kept himself fit, but he had also worked for her husband, in the gangland world of Glasgow. Now, here she was, Patsy Diamond, friends with criminals, and to be honest, she was grateful for all of their help.

James took the keys from her. 'Sure thing, Mrs Diamond. Me and Fin here will see to everything. I think they've had their fill anyway. Chucking out time before they all get pissed, I'd say.'

Fin took the lead and clapped his hands loudly, gaining everyone's attention. 'Right, you lot, Beryl's buried, you're all pissed, now fuck off and take that potato salad with you. Go on, piss off!'

Patsy and Sheila both burst out laughing.

'Not exactly the words I would have chosen, but my sentiments exactly,' said Patsy. Within minutes, everyone headed for the exit, but not without taking what was left of the buffet with them.

'There you are girls; if you want something done properly, just ask,' Fin shouted towards them. Wobbling slightly and all the worse for drink himself, he seemed very pleased with himself for getting rid of the guests in the only manner he knew. Fin rubbed his hands together and walked around the room, helping some of the guests out of their chairs and herding them to the door.

Patsy, Sheila and Victoria left him to it and made their way to Beryl's flat. It had been a long day and their feet ached. It had been a great farewell to Beryl, but now it was time for a well-earned cup of tea and a biscuit.

2

NEW BEGINNINGS

'Well, I'm glad that's all over and done with. I'll put the kettle on while we discuss what we are going to do about Natasha and the children.' Victoria walked into Beryl's kitchen, leaving a sneer on Patsy's face and a puzzled look on Sheila's.

'What does she mean?' Sheila whispered as they followed her.

'I told you earlier: she wants to do right by Natasha and have her cremated.' Patsy felt disgusted at the idea that Victoria wanted to pay for Natasha's funeral.

Ignoring Patsy's look of disdain, Sheila carried on, louder now, so that Victoria could hear. 'And the wee kiddies?'

'As I said before, they don't want to part siblings unless it's absolutely necessary. They can see that Victoria is self-sufficient and wealthy enough to look after both children – that is if you want that, Victoria.' Cocking her head to one side and raising one eyebrow, Patsy waited for the one answer she knew Victoria would give.

'Of course I will take the brothers. Why wouldn't I? I don't think Jimmy has any other family, and none of what has happened is his fault. Why should he spend a lifetime being punished? How would you feel Patsy, if your brother lived in the lap of luxury and you didn't have a penny to your name?'

Looking directly at her, Patsy shrugged. 'You mean like Nick and Fin? Are you sure you're not just trying to compensate for the past, Victoria? Believe me, we were all shocked that the very man who drugged and raped you, making you pregnant with Nick, is also Fin's father. Even Fin didn't know that his feared boss was actually his brother!'

Victoria blushed and cast a glance over at Sheila. 'I can't compensate for something I didn't know about Patsy. I never knew Billy Burke even had a wife. But, yes, a little money can make a lot of difference. And one day Patsy, that sharp tongue of yours will catch up with you.'

Sheila looked at them, stunned. 'Nick Diamond was Fin's brother?'

'Half-brother,' Victoria corrected her. 'We found out the night at the cemetery. It seems Billy Burke has probably fathered a lot of siblings out there who don't know each other.'

Raising her voice and wiping the spilt coffee off her black trousers, Sheila sat forward. 'Jesus Christ; are you going to tell Fin?'

'Absolutely not,' Patsy butted in. 'What would that serve now? Fin has nothing to gain from it. If anything, it could make him feel like shit. No, Fin has been brought to us through fair means or foul and somehow, he is part of the family again. Fate has worked its magic; let's leave it at that, shall we.'

They all nodded in agreement. Victoria took a big sigh and laid back on the sofa. 'I'm tired and I'm too old to keep going to funerals! Before long I will be attending my own. Right ladies – to business.'

Sheila and Patsy frowned. 'What business?'

'This place of course.' Victoria laughed. 'What on earth did you think I meant?'

'This place? What about it?'

Shaking her head at Patsy and Sheila's ignorance, Victoria let out a deep sigh. 'Well, what are we going to do about this place? It was Beryl's, lock stock and barrel, which means we own it now. I suppose we could put it up for sale...' Victoria trailed off. It was a lovely flat and in pristine condition; only the area let it down.

Sheila burst out laughing. 'Who the fuck would buy a flat on a shitty estate like this? A blind man, with no hearing and no sense of smell, wouldn't buy this. For crying out loud, you would have to be a moron to spend good hard cash in a place like this. Even the people who get their rent paid by benefits don't want to live here. You don't choose to live in Thistle Park, Victoria!'

Angered by Sheila's outburst, Victoria sipped her coffee. 'How dare you Sheila! My husband bought this flat and there is nothing wrong with it!'

'No Vicky lass. Your husband bought his mum her home. I'm sure time and time again he wanted her to move, but this place was her roots. Christ, I think they built it around her. There is a difference. Nothing would get her out of here and so he bought her what she loved.' Sheila could see she had upset Victoria, so she did her best to justify her outburst. But she was right and Victoria knew it.

'Oh, for goodness' sake,' snapped Patsy. 'Who cares? We are saddled with a flat we can't sell. We might as well have just buried Beryl inside here and sealed up the door.' She laughed. 'Although, I might have an idea...' Patsy's business brain was starting to work. She had an idea, but not one she wanted to share yet. Or at least not all of it. 'Maybe we could rent it out.'

Pondering on her words, Sheila snapped her fingers. 'There

is a shortage of housing around here; what if we offered it to the council so they could sublet it?'

Victoria nodded and agreed.

Patsy on the other hand had other ideas and smiled sweetly as she mentally began hatching her own plan. 'Well, that's one thing sorted.' Patsy grinned like a Cheshire cat. 'Now what's next on the itinerary?'

'That bloody French woman Karen Duret! Who the hell does she think she is?' Sheila barked. 'Patsy, we have stood at her graveside, yet here she is waltzing around, with her airs and graces. She is seriously pissing me off. How do we even know she is who she claims to be? She could be anyone. What else do you think she knows? Just having her around makes me nervous. Let's find out what she wants and get rid of her.'

Victoria shook her head. 'I really don't know what to think. Don't you find it strange that no one has ever met her or seen her before? What is her involvement with Nick?' Victoria could have bitten her tongue, when she said that. She knew Nick hadn't been a faithful husband and now there was another woman on the scene claiming to know him.

Patsy surveyed them all and narrowed her eyes. 'Do you think they were lovers Victoria?' Before Victoria could answer, Patsy sighed. 'Maybe they were, I really don't know. All I do know is that my marriage has been a sham and I have been a fool. With regard to Karen, I think we play for time and play her at her own game. She wants something and she wants it badly enough to come back from the dead for it. I've asked Larry to look into it for us. There is more to her story than she is letting on and I want all the details. She must want something very badly to come looking for us and my gut instinct tells me it's not just money. She doesn't look like a pauper to me, on the contrary.'

In unison, they all nodded their heads. What Patsy had said made sense.

Patsy continued. 'I intend to find out her story. Where has she been all this time? She has another name, I'm sure of it. Karen Duret is just the name on the bank accounts Nick set up just before his death, while he was planning on leaving me. I presume Nick's accountant, Tom, could tell us more, but apparently he's having a holiday. Who else was in on this plan with Nick? Maybe Natasha?' Patsy pondered. 'But I doubt it. We all know to Nick's cost she was a jealous woman, so I doubt she would have put up with snooty Karen.' Patsy's head was spinning with questions about this mystery woman who had just popped out of nowhere claiming to be Nick's partner. 'I told her I needed time to sort things out with Beryl's funeral and stuff. We're playing for time, until the truth comes out, but then we'll meet. Not here as she suggested, but at Larry's office. All legal and above board.'

'Okay, okay I agree, but just one last thing that no one has mentioned,' Sheila added. 'What about all those drugs we dug up at the cemetery? What are we going to do with them? Christ lassies, I thought Fin was going to have an orgasm when he saw the mixture of bags and boxes buried in that grave.' Taking a breath, she looked at Patsy. 'I have a feeling those other marked graves on Nick's little map of secrets are full of the same. Christ, no wonder they all called him the Undertaker. Everything he did was in graveyards; he would give Dracula a run for his money!'

Standing up and clapping her hands, Patsy smiled. 'Firstly ladies, there is no point in talking to Fin or James right now. They will both be drunk. Personally, I think we need to find a good restaurant and have something proper to eat. I'm starving, I don't know about you two.'

'Me too,' moaned Sheila. 'My stomach thinks my throat's

been cut. And I'm sick of wearing black! I need to get out of these clothes. Let's order a taxi and I'll just pop across and check on the girls. Maggie took them home earlier for me.'

'Bring them along too, Sheila, and ask Maggie if she wants to come,' Victoria chirped up. 'Let's eat, drink and be merry. It's been a bloody long day and I feel we have a few more ahead of us. So tonight, we relax... Deal?'

Patsy agreed. 'I want to get out of all this black too. I've had my fair share of funerals. I'll patch up my make-up and change my clothes. Something that makes me look more human. What about you Victoria?'

'I'll have a quick shower if you don't mind. I won't be long ladies; I just need to freshen up.' Victoria walked to the bathroom.

Once alone, Patsy picked up her mobile. An idea was forming in her brain, and she needed James's help to sort it out. 'James, it's Patsy. Will you meet me tomorrow? I have a proposal for you.'

'That sounds ominous coming from you Mrs Diamond. But, yes, I'll meet you. Let's say around lunchtime at the cemetery where we last met? I know it may seem weird, but your husband had a point – there are no ears or eyes at a place like that.' Patsy agreed and James ended the call. But a sinking feeling in the pit of her stomach made her feel sick. She was just like Nick arranging a meeting in a cemetery.

Just then Sheila returned to the flat with her two young daughters, Sharon and Penny, in tow. 'Here girls, go and spray yourself with Victoria's perfume and then we're off. Where are we going for dinner or is it that good old Scottish restaurant McDonald's?' Sheila laughed. 'Well, that's what Steve used to call it when he was taking me out for a meal. Closest I got to a steak and chips...'

'I wouldn't let the Americans hear you say that Sheila, but I'm a fish out of water here. Do you know of any good restaurants nearby?'

'Aye lassie, never been in them though, so I can't tell you about the food. The local steak house seems a safe bet, not that far either. By the way, Maggie is coming she's just changing from her funeral cardigan. Apparently it's a special black one that she always sets aside for those things, but now she's going to change into her regular old black cardigan!' Sheila laughed.

Sheila had left the door ajar, and no sooner said than done, Maggie tentatively walked in. 'Evening Patsy, Victoria.' She nodded. They could see that she seemed uncomfortable and slightly nervous. None of them had been the best of friends, but the olive branch had been offered and she had taken it.

As everyone piled into Patsy's new six-seater Range Rover, Sheila burst out laughing yet again. 'Be careful when you turn the key Patsy; this could be an explosive night!'

'Tut tut. Bad taste Sheila,' Victoria snapped. 'I think you had one too many sherries at Beryl's wake.' Sitting in the back with Maggie and the girls, Victoria gave Sheila a stern look.

The drive to the restaurant went without further issue, and once seated at their table, even Patsy had to admit, it was a nice place and the food looked good.

Sheila looked around. 'I've heard about this place, just never been inside. Everyone talks about it, don't they Maggie?'

'I've never been either Sheila, but you're right, it's well known and now I can see why. I hope I've brought enough money with me; I didn't realise we would be going anywhere so posh.'

Victoria scoffed and reached out her hand to Maggie's across the table. 'You're my guest Maggie and Beryl's best friend. Let's not talk about money; friends don't do that.'

A faint smile crossed Maggie's face. For Patsy, it was as

though a light bulb had just switched on in her head. Maggie! She was just what she needed. When she spoke to James tomorrow, she would mention Maggie.

'You're not just our guest, you're our family Maggie. Families are not made by biology. Some families hate each other, but we have all chosen each other.' Patsy smiled, oozing with charm and politeness as she filled Maggie's wine glass up. The softly, softly touch was the best way of getting Maggie to do her bidding. Maggie liked to be needed, Patsy realised that. Why else would she have put up with James on the run from the Albanians and hiding out in her house for so long?

Raising her own glass of soda water in the air, Patsy made a toast. 'To Beryl Diamond.'

Chinking their glasses together, they all smiled. 'To Beryl!' they all said in unison.

3

A NEW ENTERPRISE

'So, we meet again, even if it is pissing it down with rain.' James was standing in the cemetery under an old oak tree, holding his newspaper over his head to stop himself from getting wet. The wind was howling, and the rain was bouncing off the ground.

Noticing how wet his jeans were, Patsy shouted out to him, 'Dear god James, get in my car. Come on, you're drenched.' Patsy's shoes sank into the sodden grass as she beckoned him towards her. As she held her umbrella high for him to shield himself, James pulled the collar of his jacket up and ran towards her. Once inside the car, Patsy handed him some tissues to dry his face with, then lit two cigarettes.

James brushed his wet hair back from his face and wiped the raindrops from his face. 'So Mrs Diamond, what is this proposal of yours?'

Patsy liked James; he was business-like and got straight to the point. He was quite a handsome man, too; around sixty, but he still had dark hair with some grey bits in. Now he had got rid of his beard, he looked younger and not so drawn, especially now the bruises had disappeared. 'You're looking a lot more human these days James, have you got over your ordeal with near death?'

Patsy had felt responsible that James had turned on his own partner in crime Noel, the Albanian ice-cream vendor, to save her skin and help her. He had been beaten to a pulp and had been about to be buried under a tonne of cement by his own associates for his betrayal. Thankfully, he had been suspicious of Noel's invite to meet him at the warehouse and had asked Fin and his friends to follow him, which in turn had saved his life. Fin had saved James and buried the Albanian henchmen instead. After a short spell in hospital, it was presumed by everyone that James was dead and that was why he had to hide out at Maggie's house. James was a man with a contract on his head, but he was also full of knowledge about how things worked in the gangland world, unlike herself who knew nothing. He had become her right-hand man and Fin had become her left.

'I'm doing okay, Mrs Diamond. You can never trust a partner in crime, never let your left hand know what your right is doing.' He chuckled.

Exhaling the smoke from her cigarette, Patsy smiled, and changed the subject. 'Those prostitutes who were working from the community centre, where are they working now?' she asked.

Puzzled, James stopped drying his hair and looked at her. 'Well, I must say, I wasn't expecting that. To be honest, as far as I know, there are a few nail salons that Noel was in charge of. Some of the girls work there. Some find it cheaper to work on street corners, where there are no overheads. But that's usually the girls from the estates; I believe they still work the cemeteries. Your husband had a good ring of prostitution, Mrs Diamond. They owed him money for their drugs and their credit and had to pay him back somehow. Maggie took pity on a lot of them by all accounts. But the Albanian women who were forced to work for Noel owe him a lot of money. They can't work the streets; if they were ever arrested, they would be deported. That's the fear that hangs over all their heads... Why do you ask?'

'I wondered where they had all gone to, that's all and well, someone has turned up and declared themselves my business partner, or rather Nick's, so I just need to make sure I know exactly what's going on around here.'

'I take it you knew nothing about this partner then? Do you need any help?' James's genuine concern made her feel almost humble.

Patsy shook her head. 'Not yet. I need to find out more first.' The weak smile she gave betrayed her true anxiety about the situation.

'Has it got anything to do with those unopened bank statements that Nick wanted put safely away until he returned?' James gave her a knowing look.

Patsy knew she had dropped the hook to catch the fish and that James would know something about Karen Duret, however small. Maybe he had even met her. 'What do you know about them? Do you know who I am talking about James? If you do, tell me. Tell me everything you know.'

'I know that kettles let off steam and steam opens envelopes Mrs Diamond. Your husband was adamant those letters needed to be kept safe and that made me suspicious. I'm a criminal after all and old habits die hard.' He smiled. 'That's all I know really; I've never met the person in question if that is what you mean.'

'I see.' Patsy felt deflated, although she couldn't be sure James wasn't holding something back. Maybe he knew Karen Duret had been Nick's lover and didn't want to hurt her feelings, she thought to herself. She wasn't looking forward to her meeting with Karen Duret, but she did want answers.

'And I know how this woman feels Patsy. I have to declare myself alive again too. I've been dead long enough and I would have been for real if it hadn't been for Fin and his mates. I'd have been buried under concrete, curtesy of Noel and that would have been the end of it. It's time I told the police I'm alive and that way my frozen accounts will be available to me again. And I can see what kind of a dent my wife has made in my savings.'

'I remember you saying you were married. It's going to be one hell of a shock for her.'

'Not that much of one. She turned her back on me when I was at the hospital. I don't blame her; I just want what's mine.'

'And what about you and Maggie?' She nudged him playfully with her elbow. 'Will you be staying there? Is there love in the air James?' Patsy laughed to try and lighten the mood. She could sense facing his wife was one task James wasn't looking forward to, but she could see he didn't want to discuss it.

'Maggie is a good friend with a good heart, and she has done her best looking after me and the prostitutes, but she can't do it forever. Keep her on board Patsy; I know you're not her super fan, but sometimes we all have to start afresh.'

Nodding at his wise words, Patsy decided to get on with the business in hand. 'Which brings us to the reason I have asked you here today. I have a flat to let; Beryl's to be precise. Me and Victoria now own it. There are two options, rent or sell. Selling will take forever; the building will fall down before we find a buyer and even if we did, we would hardly get a penny for it. To rent it out is also a risk; some bloody junkie might move in who wants to wreck the place and strip it bare.' Patsy took another draw on her cigarette, nervously. She knew what she was going to suggest would shock James. Opening the window slightly to let out the smoke, she turned back to James. 'So, a few prostitutes who need somewhere to work from and are prepared to pay the rent and look after the property seems like a good proposal – that is, if they want it.'

Stunned, James rested his head on the head rest. 'So you want to be a madam now Mrs Diamond?' A choked laugh escaped him.

'No James, I want to be a landlord.' Patsy's voice instantly changed. She wasn't going to let him laugh at her. It was a good idea, or she had thought so at the time. 'And I don't want some junkie trashing the place. God knows the women would probably treat it better. It was just a thought. Never mind, my mistake.' Patsy sat up straight and started fastening her seat belt.

'Hey lassie stop. We're having a conversation and we're both entitled to our opinions. What do you need me for? You seem to have skipped that part.'

'I don't know the women in question. How do I contact them? I think they might think it strange if I approached them and offered them a flat to rent, don't you? Maybe you could plant the seed in Maggie's mind. After all, you said yourself, she likes to help them where she can...' Patsy trailed off, hoping James would catch her meaning.

James laughed. 'What are you implying, Mrs Diamond, that I hang around with prostitutes?' He gave her a cheeky wink. 'I'm sure Maggie would think it was a good idea, but you don't want her to think such a sordid idea has come from you?' When she said nothing, he continued. 'So, you want the Albanian girls who worked for Noel at the community centre. Am I right? You do know, or rather, I presume you know that most of them are illegal immigrants. They have no means of renting anywhere or getting council housing.'

'I thought as much.' What Patsy had seen of the Albanian women were clean shy women who had been dealt a shitty hand. 'But unlike the local prostitutes, the Albanian women

Noel had don't look like a load of junkies to me. Out of curiosity, why can't the foreign women sell their wares back home?'

'They don't get much for the odd blow job here, but they would get even less in their own country. Most of them do it to send money back home to keep their families. After a few months some go home, and others take their place. And some that come don't even know they are going to be prostitutes. They are offered jobs as maids or to work for Noel in his ice-cream business. It all sounds very glamorous when you're penniless – that is until you get here.'

Now it was Patsy's turn to be confused. 'If they travel back and forth all the time, then they must have passports?'

James let out a sigh. 'Containers.'

Their eyes met and James could see the shocked looked on Patsy's face.

'They come across hidden inside big shipping containers. That's how they are smuggled in. Some people call it trafficking. The women earn hardly anything. Firstly, they have to pay off their passage for being brought over in the container and then there is the cost of living etc. You know what I mean.'

Patsy tried to hide her shock. 'When you say containers, do you mean those big iron things? How do they breathe?' The very thought of being trapped in a metal container for god knows how long chilled her to the bones.

'Who are they going to complain to? They are promised a life of milk and honey when they come here and find out they have been tricked and all their money has gone. Some end up on the streets; they can't afford to go home. It's a mean business Patsy.' He smiled. 'Personally, I think if you are willing to put a roof over their head, they would bite your hand off. They had Noel's protection and since he and his associates don't seem to be around any more, it's become a free for all. Most of the women are fleeing anyway because they don't know when Noel is going to turn up again. But of course, we both know that isn't going to happen.'

Pausing, Patsy remembered that night when Noel, the Albanian gang boss and his men had turned up at the graveyard threating to kill them all. That is, until Fin had turned on his flame thrower...

'His ice-cream vans are sitting outside the warehouse. I presume his brother or his wife's family will take over. Fin has gone past a few times, but the place is deserted. His family will have to do something. The police will maybe be looking into it, but they also know Noel had a lot of enemies. Fin has been quite clever. I must admit I never thought of it. Because of Noel's swift departure, Fin took his debit card and credit card out of his wallet. You can use it contactless four of five times, which makes everyone think he is still alive somewhere. Noel's account hasn't been frozen or closed. That's good for us, because that means he didn't die with us in the cemetery that night.'

'Fin has been using his card to buy stuff. What the hell is he thinking?' Stunned by this revelation, Patsy couldn't stop herself from shouting. 'For Christ's sake, James, he will hang us all.'

'Calm down Mrs Diamond.' James held his hands up to stop Patsy's outburst. 'Fin has gone to shops and bought food and stuff and paid contactless. No big deal. He knows how to avoid CCTV cameras, he's a burglar. The fact is, as far as anyone is concerned Noel is still alive. His card has never been reported lost or stolen. Fin has bought us time.'

'And now what happens when his contactless spree ends. What has he done with all this stuff he's bought?' Intrigued, Patsy couldn't believe that something as simple as that could keep a man alive. There was definitely more to Fin than met the eye. He played the fool, but he seemed far from it. Mentally,

Patsy admired Fin and James. She had a lot to learn, and she was determined to be a good pupil.

'Well, he's kept it local. He's filled up Maggie's freezer and that has paid for my keep. He's kept us in cigarettes and a few beers. He also bought me some underwear.' James grinned. 'Nothing untoward. He hasn't bought Rolex watches or anything. Noel's wife probably thinks he's lying low somewhere, or that he has a mistress on the side; it's not unheard of. Either way, Mrs Diamond, she hasn't reported him missing.' Letting out a deep sigh, James sat back in his seat.

'I'm sorry for shouting James, I didn't mean to snap. We just need to cover our tracks, especially as you're still in hiding. If you need to tell the police where you've been, say you've been staying with me. My reputation is tarnished enough; one more stone thrown at me won't make any difference.' She laughed.

'No links Mrs Diamond. We are not linked in any form or fashion and let's keep it that way.' Pointing at her seriously, he looked her directly in the eye. 'Now that is good business. I have a flat in London, if my wife or the police haven't already been there, that could be where I've been. I need to find out first.'

'You have a flat in London?' Surprised, a frown crossed her brows.

'Yes, Mrs Diamond. I think when you get to my age, you should own something, don't you? You're not the only one with money lassie. I'll find out what I can about your new venture into the world of vice and get back to you. It shouldn't take too long. I presume you want to meet these new tenants of yours.' He chuckled and then indicated for her to start the engine.

'Yes, I would like to meet them and lay out some ground rules regarding the property. I'll drop you off just outside the estate and then no one will see us together.'

'No, like I said, I have something to do and the sooner I get it over with the better. Start driving and I'll give you instructions.'

Patsy was surprised when James told her to stop near a semi-detached house. Once again she could have kicked herself for making assumptions about where people lived. She had done it before with Larry and knew she'd offended him. Parking up, she put her hand on James's arm. 'If you need anything, James, call me.'

Without a word, he nodded and opened the car door to get out. She watched the back of him slowly walk up the path. His shoulders seemed to droop as he knocked on the door. Revving up the engine, Patsy drove off. She felt genuine concern for James. It was time for him to go home and see his wife and let the world know he wasn't a missing person any more. God knows what kind of welcome he would get. But it had to be done, he knew that. All the time he was a missing person, he was a ghost. As Patsy thought about him, Karen Duret crossed her mind again. Was she a missing person like James? A ghost, with no background? Maybe that was an avenue to go down. She must remember to tell Larry.

4

ANXIOUS MOMENTS

Fin, Spider and Beanie sat in the local greasy spoon eating their fried breakfasts. It was their usual morning meeting place, because it was easier than cooking. This was where they discussed the day and put the world to rights. Fin wanted to keep a low profile since the massacre at the cemetery and didn't want another stint in prison. He had a gut feeling his life would take a turn for the better if he stayed straight with James who seemed like a solid bloke. Spider and Beanie had been nagging at him for days now, always the same conversation, and to be honest he had almost run out of answers.

'Fin, when do we get our hands on some of those drugs? There's a market out there and people keep asking me. After all, that Diamond lassie was going to get rid of it all. What is the fucking difference!' Beanie was agitated; money was running low even though Fin had shared his spoils from doing a job in London for Patsy, when she'd had him break into Nick Diamond's office at the law firm where he'd worked.

'You're in your thirties Beanie, you have a girlfriend, which is more than Spider's got. Christ, he hasn't had a blow job in months, and he isn't complaining. I've given you some cash, what else do you want?'

'Gear to sell, that's what. This cash isn't going to last forever. I see the other mob trading their shit on the streets and it sticks in my throat. Come on Fin, where is it? I know you've moved it because I looked,' Beanie spat. He was sweating and Fin could tell he needed another hit of drugs himself. His addiction had clearly got the better of him and these few days of cold turkey were killing him. His hands were trembling, he was sweating, and he couldn't sit still.

'I told you, James has them stashed somewhere. He didn't want me getting my hands on them. They are Patsy's. She'll share, but we just have to wait. Just hold fire, you will get your spoils.' Fin reached into his jacket and took out his wallet. 'Here; there's fifty quid. Go and buy something to snort, you're getting on my fucking nerves.'

Picking up the money, Beanie stood up, purposely pushing the wooden table with his thigh, and stormed out.

'He's got a point though Fin. We saved her life; I think a little payment in return is due don't you?' Spider tried being more reasonable. 'Other distributors are out there; it's like the whole world has stopped and is waiting for that Diamond bird to give the orders and a few crumbs to us. The nightclubs are going dry and those foreign lot are selling god knows what. Someone said they're importing it.'

'Who's importing it? We know the main man is dead,' Fin whispered. 'So who is in charge of their distributors?' Fin was curious now. He knew there was always someone out there with something to sell but this seemed like a well-run operation and it was up to him to find out who was behind it.

Spider shrugged.

'Find out what you can Spider.' He smiled at Spider, to reassure him. 'And don't worry, it will come, but I ain't stealing it. If it's given to us, then there will be more given won't there. If we steal it, it dries up and we don't get any more.'

Knowing he made sense, Spider nodded. 'Five more days, Fin. Sort it. Joe and Midge need stock for the mobile shop or they don't get paid. Speak to James and let him know how serious this is while that Diamond bird is sat on her designer arse!'

Fin carried on stuffing his mouth full of bacon and eggs as he listened to Spider. He knew exactly what they both meant and he was tired of waiting too, but what other option was there? 'I'll speak to him Spider mate. I just can't promise anything. Now, can we just leave it while I eat? I must be hungry cos even Lardy's bacon tastes nice.'

'No idea why they call him Lardy; his name is Dave.' Spider looked over his shoulder at the man behind the counter. Lardy, as he was known, was leaning on his unwashed counter, smoking a cigarette through his yellow nicotine-stained fingers, flicking ash on the floor behind the counter. Now and again he would mop it, but he hadn't changed the water in the mop bucket for months and it was dirtier than the floor itself. He was bald on top but had remnants of greasy lank strands of what remained of his hair around his shoulders. If anyone complained about him smoking behind the counter, he just told them to fuck off and not come back.

Fin looked at Spider and leaned in closer to whisper, even though the yolk of his egg had dribbled down his chin. 'They used to call him the mechanic cos of his greasy hands. He picks his nose, and then butters your toast.'

'Well, it doesn't have cockroaches or anything like that, does it? There's worse around here.'

'Christ, if there was an apocalypse his bacon would survive the fallout.'

At last, Spider grinned then looked over at Lardy again.

'You lads meeting some chicks tonight?' Lardy shouted towards them. 'Or are you a pair of poofs? Never see you with any chicks?' Lardy laughed; he thought it was so hilarious he started coughing and spluttering.

Puzzled, Fin looked at Spider. 'Chicks? What era does that come from? Oy lardy, if I was gay, I wouldn't meet you in the showers! You ugly bastard.' Fin stood up, picked up the sausage left on Spider's plate and shoved it into Lardy's mouth before he left.

They were both leaving in opposite directions, but before they separated, Spider shouted towards Fin, 'Don't forget Fin: five days.'

Fin held his hands up in submission. 'I get the message; I'll speak to James.' Fin had no idea what to do. He could see it from both sides, but his friends were getting agitated and impatient. Inwardly, he felt like he was betraying them but he also knew that if he played for time, Patsy would come good and James would see they all had something to sell. He didn't know which way to turn and felt helpless. His friends were looking to him for support and he didn't have anything to offer, just hollow words. Mentally, he prayed for a miracle to solve all of their problems, but taking a deep breath, he knew his life had been pretty short of miracles in the past and nothing was going to change now. With a heavy heart, he walked down the street, preparing what he was going to say to James when he saw him.

* * *

'Hello Kathy, I thought you might be in this time of day.' James stood on the doorstep facing his wife. So much had happened to him over the last couple of months, but Kathy looked exactly the same.

'Why are you here James? I've moved on and it's time you did too. Just bugger off. Were done!' Kathy was about to shut the door in his face, but James pushed his way into the hallway.

'Is that it? We haven't seen each other in ages and that's the best I get? I know you recognised me when you came to visit me at the hospital, but you told the police you didn't. Thanks for that!' James spat out. He'd known this reunion was never going to be easy, but this wasn't the best of starts.

'Kathy! Kath love are you okay?' James followed the sound of a man's voice coming from the lounge and looked back at Kathy.

'Who is that?' Walking into the lounge, James saw a man sitting in his armchair drinking a cup of tea.

'Who are you?' the man shouted at him.

'I'm her fucking husband; who are you?' James turned towards Kathy for an explanation.

Glaring at him, she pouted. 'Pete lives here. With me. He lives here with me.' Kathy's matter-of-fact way shocked James. She seemed so cold and disinterested. Suddenly, the cold light of day dawned on him. This wasn't a new affair; she had obviously been seeing this man for a while. His eyes darted around the lounge, and he could see photo frames perched on the mantelpiece showing photos of them both with James's kids. It seemed as though everyone had celebrated his absence. She must have been pleased when she'd seen him half dead in the hospital bed and denied it was him. She didn't want to be the dutiful wife nursing him back to health, and with him missing, presumed dead, she could do what she liked, even move in this waster.

'You've moved in some bloke the minute my back is turned.

For Christ's sake, after all of these years of marriage?'

'All these years of a shit marriage! The only good thing was the kids. I've spent my life wondering when the next visiting order from prison would come from you. Pete lives here now, and you don't.' Kathy stood with her arms folded.

Stunned, James looked on as Pete got to his feet and put his arm around Kathy's shoulder to prove a point. James decided not to make a fuss; there was no point. He was desperate to punch Pete, but his next port of call was the police station and the last thing he wanted was to turn up there with a split lip. Mentally he cursed them both, but he would wait until the time was right. Anyway, he mused, Kathy was right; he had been in and out of prison. She had brought the kids up almost single-handedly. Maybe this was the end of the road and she had found something better.

'I'm going to the police station now. I have to officially let them know I'm still alive and then they'll give me access to my bank account again. I'm no longer a missing person after all.'

'Where have you been living anyway?' asked Kathy. 'I know for sure it isn't that flat you had stashed away in London.'

Kathy's last retort, with her grinning boyfriend beside her, made James's blood boil. 'What's that supposed to mean?'

'Me and Pete have sold it. It surprised me how quickly property sells in London. I'm your wife, I'm allowed to sell it. What is yours is mine, isn't that right?' She laughed.

Pausing to gather his thoughts, James tried to keep calm. He could see Kathy was spoiling for a fight, and she wasn't worth the effort. Keeping his voice low to hide the anger, he said, 'So now you've made me homeless too. Where is the money from the flat Kathy? What have you done with it?'

Looking very pleased with herself, she cuddled up closer to Pete, putting her arm around his waist. 'We had a lovely holiday.

A cruise in fact. Pete took over the financial side of things. All that mobile banking and stuff online isn't my thing. Anyway, you were never homeless; I'm sure there's a prison cell with your name on it. Now get out. This is my house – leave!'

Avoiding her glare, James looked towards Pete. 'So you're in charge of my money, are you? You're not only ripping me off but you're ripping her off as well. You can have Kathy, I really don't care about her any more, but I want my money back.' Standing in the lounge, James felt sick. Kathy was the golden goose to this fat, unshaven man. Kathy was at least ten years older than Pete and obviously flattered by this younger man's attentions. 'When was the last time you did a day's work? I presume you still let her work at the supermarket?'

Standing up straighter to make himself seem taller, Pete grinned and rubbed his chin. 'I'm a security guard at the supermarket Kath works at. Or rather I was until they had some cutbacks. Don't worry, I'm looking for something, but there's no rush, is there? You've made that possible. I've become a house boyfriend and soon to be husband. I look after Kath and make sure her meal is on the table when she comes home every night.' He laughed.

James swallowed down the rage that was building up inside of him. 'Fair enough; it's your funeral.' James forced a grin. 'Good luck Kathy, because I feel you're going to need it.' With that, he headed for the door, leaving a very confused Kathy behind him. It was pretty clear to him she had expected him to make a fuss and she seemed disappointed that he hadn't. If anything, he felt he had won the war without even having had a battle.

He wanted to scream when outside but calmly walked away and punched his hand with his fist. The police station wasn't far away and so he made his way there. He knew there would be a lot of questions, especially as he had no ID to prove who he was, but he was prepared for it. They had his fingerprints from a life-time of crime and he knew they would ring Kathy for her to confirm his identity. Taking his mobile out of his pocket, he dialled Patsy's number. She answered instantly. 'Are you okay?'

'Things didn't go as planned; I'm on the way to the cop shop now to let them know I'm alive. I want no link with you or Maggie, and I don't want them thinking I've been lying low because of some job I've pulled off. But I need to tell the police where I've been. Any ideas?' he asked hopefully.

After a pause, Patsy said, 'Oh my god, yes, it's looking me straight in the face. Victoria. You've been in Dorset living the life of Riley with her. You met her at the community centre and fate lent a hand. She's single and shit happens.'

Shocked, James stopped walking. 'Do you think she'd back that up? She seems pretty prim and proper to me. You know they'll check.' He didn't know what to say, but he hadn't expected that for an alibi.

'You saved her life James; it's the least she can do, isn't it. It's not going to cost her anything. And of course, I didn't know anything about it. What my mother-in-law does in her spare time is her business. You do what you have to do, and I'll text you Victoria's mobile number so they can call her. Give me five minutes.'

Outside the police station, James looked up at the stone-grey building and took a breath. Lighting a cigarette, he stood outside for a few minutes and watched police come and go. Suddenly his mobile started vibrating. Looking at it, he could see it was a message from Patsy. Inside was what he presumed was Victoria's mobile number. Adding it to his contacts, he felt like a weight had been taken off his shoulders. The perfect alibi. Sweeping his hair back and straightening his clothes, he opened the doors of the police station and walked inside.

5

A NEW BOSS

After a few beers, Beanie had sat brooding all day. Things weren't happening quickly enough for him. The very thought that there was a stash of drugs hidden somewhere made him drool. He had also purposely forgot to mention to Fin that he had been getting drugs on credit from the Albanian mob who he'd bumped into at a nightclub one night. That was how he knew they were importing it. It wasn't very good cocaine; in fact, on a scale of one to ten it was bloody rubbish. Their heroin just gave you diarrhoea, but he'd been using more lately since the split up with his girlfriend, although that had been another thing he had kept to himself. He had lashed out one night and beaten her up. He felt ashamed now, but he had been off his head on drugs, and she had annoyed him by wearing a short skirt while other blokes had smiled admiringly at her. He had blown his top and couldn't remember much about what had happened, until he had seen her the next morning. She'd left and her dad had called the police. Beanie had been arrested, charges made and there was an injunction for him to stay away.

All of this had made him take more drugs. He hadn't used heroin before, but it had made him feel better and helped him forget.

He looked at his watch. It was nearly nine in the evening. Going to the bathroom, he threw some cold water on his face to wake himself up and then headed out to the nightclub to try and score. When he got there it was already in full swing.

The music was loud, and the lights were flashing. Everyone was enjoying themselves and the alcohol was flowing. Standing at the bar, Beanie took out a twenty-pound note and handed it to the barman. Instantly the dealers he owed money to stood on either side of him.

'You seem to be rich tonight, Benny.' The foreign voice at the side of him made Beanie smile. For whatever reason they couldn't say Beanie and always called him Benny. 'Mine is a large whisky and my friend will have one too.'

Beckoning the barman over, Beanie knew he had no choice but to buy them a drink. 'Of course, laddies, good to see you, Endrit. Let's all have a drink together.' He smiled.

'It's good to see you too Benny, especially with money in your pocket. You owe us one thousand, so let's see what you have.' Taking the whisky that the barman had handed him, Endrit gulped it back in one and then turned to grab Beanie by his shirt. 'Pay up or pay the price. We asked you where that Fin boy was and you keep telling us you don't know. Well, I know. He was seen today – with you in that shithole of a café. Have you come tonight to tell us?' Endrit's eyes were nearly bulging out of his head. His closely cropped blond hair seemed to make his face bigger. He always wore a tight T-shirt, even in the coldest of weather, which showed off his muscular frame.

'Yeah,' Beanie lied. 'That is why I've come tonight. I thought I might find you here.' He was frightened and trying to free himself from Endrit's grasp. He could hardly breathe. Beanie felt something sharp in his back. It was Albi, with a knife.

'This is what happen when friends stab you in the back Benny; they fucking bleed.' Endrit's cold, Albanian accent seemed to emphasise his meaning. 'I fucking kill you, you addict. Pay up now.'

Beanie knew he was cornered. He was frightened, and he started sweating. His mouth went dry and he could barely speak. Moistening his lips, he spied his pint glass and bottle of lager on the bar. Reaching out, he picked it up and smashed it over Endrit's head, freeing him from his grasp. Instantly, Endrit put his hands to his head and saw the blood. Swiftly, Albi jerked forward and plunged the knife into Beanie, making Beanie gasp in pain.

With all of his might, Beanie thrust the jagged glass bottle into Endrit's face and hearing his cry, pushed him out of the way. Beanie ran for it, pushing his way past everyone in blind panic, almost tripping over people in his wake. As soon as he got out, he could feel a wetness dripping down his back and his shirt was stuck to him. He could feel the knife but left it there for the time being. He knew from experience not to take it out as it would make the bleeding worse. Touching it with the palm of his hand, he saw that it was in deep. His hand was soaked in blood, but he carried on running. He needed to get to a hospital, but he knew time was not on his side. He could hear the Albanians shout to each other further down the street and he knew he had to get out of there no matter what. He felt sick and faint; his head was spinning and, leaning over, he vomited in a shop doorway.

Wiping his face, he continued towards the subway. There, he ran through the barriers, ignoring the shouts of the men that worked there and not noticing the trail of blood he was leaving behind him. He was panting and almost out of breath; only adrenalin was keeping him on his feet. The sharp pain in his side from running was almost as bad as the one in his back. Sweat dripped down his brow, blurring his vision, and he wiped it away with the back of his sleeve while blood seemed to be soaking through his jeans. He felt weak and was trembling, but he knew he couldn't stop. His life depended on it.

Nearly falling on the elevator stairs that led to the tube trains, he spotted someone who looked familiar. The man was out of breath from running and Beanie presumed it was one of his assailants.

'We know you here Glasgow boy. You're leaving a trail behind you!' the man shouted in the air, and laughed. The man's voice echoed across the platform.

Lying as flat as he could, Beanie crawled to the train. Fortunately, there was one coming. He didn't care where it was going, he just needed to get away. His body was awash with pain, and narrowing his eyes to look behind him, he saw the tell-tale signs of the blood trail. It had led them straight to him.

The doors opened and he threw himself into the carriage. Panting, he looked around but there was no one to help him. He tried hoisting himself up when he saw a pair of feet before him. Looking up, he saw the man take out a knuckle duster and slip them on. The large grin on his face said it all. 'Have you stopped running now Glasgow boy?' he snarled. Then he heard the door in between the carriages open and turned to see if it was a saviour, but to his dismay they shouted in Albanian. Out of breath and out of luck, Beanie closed his eyes as a dark curtain engulfed him and he passed out.

* * *

'Patsy, it's Larry. Everything is arranged for the meeting with this Karen woman tomorrow. I'm interested to know more about her, and I have a few questions for her too, if you don't mind.'

'No, of course not. Anything you can come up with will be a big help. I have no idea what this is about but it has to be some kind of scam, don't you think?'

'My main question Patsy is how she knew Nick was dead. This was local news, not international. Of course, it could have been on social media,' Larry argued the point with himself. 'Maybe someone posted it on Facebook or something? But how did she know where to find you? Why did she go to Beryl's flat and not yours in London? I think she has someone on the inside. There are too many coincidences here.'

Frowning, Patsy took in Larry's words. It made sense. 'I hadn't thought of that; my mind is all over the place at the moment. Tomorrow then.' As an afterthought, with a feeling of guilt, her voice softened. 'How are you Larry love? Sorry, I didn't mean to sound abrupt. Like I say, I just have a lot on my mind. I seem to be juggling balls in the air at the moment when the ones I would like to be juggling are yours.'

His warm laughter on the end of the telephone convinced her she had said the right thing. Poor Larry; he always seemed to come last in her plans. She didn't mean it to be like that, it's just that each day she had something more pressing to deal with.

'So you haven't forgotten me altogether then?' he asked. 'I'm more concerned about your safety. Have you had any more threats towards you? That Natasha business was awful. I know I shouldn't say this but I'm so pleased it wasn't you in that car bomb. That's a horrible thing to say, isn't it? Natasha didn't deserve to die like that.'

'I know what you mean Larry love; believe me, I have thought the same thing. It could just have easily been me. After all, it was my car, and it was intended for me. The very thought of it makes me shudder.'

'When can I see you?' he asked tentatively.

'Soon. At the moment I'm organising maybe getting some tenants into Beryl's flat. There's no point in putting it up for sale.'

'Make sure you get a good agent. Do you want me to help with the paperwork or anything? Oh, and make sure you get some money up front. A good deposit makes people think twice about wrecking the place. Have you advertised it yet?'

'Kind of; people have asked us rather than the other way around. It seems there is a housing shortage in Glasgow,' she laughed, through gritted teeth. 'If I need you, I'll let you know, and thanks for the advice about the deposit.' As an afterthought, she realised she did want to see him. 'You can see me tonight if you want; maybe I could drive over to your house and you can cook me something in that fancy kitchen of yours. What do you think?'

'I think that sounds very interesting. Would 8 p.m. suit you? Come earlier if you want and then we can catch up, but I will have dinner ready for eight.'

'And what about afters?' she asked seductively.

'Believe me, there will be plenty. I feel like I haven't seen you properly in ages, and my hand is beginning to ache,' he joked.

'Later then – bye.' Taking a sigh of relief, she felt that was one job off the agenda.

Suddenly there was a knock at the door, and when Patsy opened it, she saw Maggie standing there in her usual tell-tale black cardigan, and sour face. 'You have visitors at mine,' she said and walked away. Curiously, Patsy watched as Maggie disappeared from view down the landing. She was obviously meant to follow her. Victoria was busy in the kitchen wrapping Beryl's beloved China in bubble wrap. 'I'm just popping out.' Patsy didn't wait for an answer but grabbed her coat and went to Maggie's flat. Seeing Maggie stood outside it intrigued her even more. Was this some kind of trap? Patsy followed Maggie into her flat.

'Is that you Mrs Diamond? We're in the lounge.' Hearing James voice put her at her ease, and she walked through to see James sat in an armchair opposite three beautiful young ladies on the sofa. Two of them were no more than nineteen, possibly younger. The one in the middle seemed older, possibly in her twenties. 'Sit down Mrs Diamond. I have mentioned to the ladies here that you're looking for tenants for Beryl's flat. I've told them she didn't die there or anything,' he joked, 'but you're looking for decent tenants who won't trash the place and will pay their rent on time.' He winked. Now Patsy knew what he meant. These were the prostitutes they had spoken about yesterday.

Patsy walked across to them, smiled and shook their hands. She could see they seemed nervous at the gesture and a little confused. She felt old enough to be their mother; they were just young girls being taken advantage of and this annoyed her. One looked barely seventeen; she still had that schoolgirl glow about her, but her eyes were full of fear. With a heavy heart, Patsy looked at them all, and instantly the maternal side of her rose to the surface. These were someone's daughters and their families thought they were happily working and living in Scotland, that is if they even knew where they were. But, the fact was, they were someone's babies.

Maggie came through with a tray of tea and biscuits. 'Here you are everyone, help yourselves.'

'I'm Leandra, I speak for all of us. Why do you want to rent your flat to us Mrs Diamond? Our last meeting was you throwing our clothes out into the street; now you want our money.'

Shocked at the abrupt way the foreign woman spoke to her,

Patsy took the cup from Maggie. 'We all have our off days... Leandra, is it? I don't like my property being used without my knowledge. Yes, I have a flat to rent at the moment, but that is the only money I want from you. If you don't want it, then I will hand it over to an agent.' Lighting a cigarette, Patsy blew the smoke into the air with a carefree attitude.

Leandra turned and spoke to the other two ladies in their own language and they seemed to nod their approval. 'My friends are living above the nail parlour; they share a mattress and use a cardboard box as a bedside table. Their clothing is beside them in a suitcase. They share the room with six other girls. More would live there if we took your flat. It's not just us. Do you understand that?'

Stunned, Patsy stared at the three women. Once she looked past their young fresh faces, she could see the dark circles around their eyes. They were tired and their spirits seemed to have disappeared. She was giving them hope, and as much as she wanted their money and Beryl's flat off her hands, she also felt like she was handing them a lifeline.

'All I want is my rent and a guarantee you don't trash the place. That is why James and Maggie thought you would make good tenants. The flat is fully furnished. I would want a month's deposit and a month's rent in advance. The rent is a thousand pounds a month without bills. I am prepared to trust you; now it's your turn. Take a look at the flat first, see if it's to your liking.'

Again, Leandra spoke to her friends in their own language. Patsy could see their pensive looks, but they nodded their approval. 'My friends want to know if you intend being our pimp and take a share of what we earn. We want no heavy-handed thugs supposedly taking care of us with their fists, we have had that. We want to come and go as we please.'

Getting a little annoyed, Patsy looked at James and saw him

nod. 'The ladies here want reassurance that they are not being tricked as they have been so many times.'

Patsy took another drag on her cigarette. 'I want tenants. I don't want to know what goes on there and if anyone complains about you, that is your fault and your business. All I have done is rent my flat out. Can you pay what I ask?'

'I'm not sure about the bills. There is no record of us being here and we haven't had credit with the companies. Maybe if we paid extra, you could pay them in your name.' Eyeing Patsy suspiciously, Leandra carried on. 'Between us we could scrape together what you ask. What about protection? Once we leave where we are working, they might come looking for us.'

'I'll sort that out if needed,' James butted in. 'And Maggie is on hand too,' he reassured them.

'Protection costs money,' Patsy intervened. 'I thought you didn't want anyone hanging around with their fists? If you want someone to fight your battles for you then that is another matter.'

James shot her a look of surprise.

Taking a deep sigh, Leandra nodded. 'So you are like the others then, you want payment for helping us?'

Shaking her head, Patsy laughed. 'You asked me about protection love. I never mentioned it. But if you want someone to be on hand if needed they are not going to do it for nothing. I would have thought you realised by now, no one does anything for nothing.'

James intervened before it went too far. 'I will see that you're settled in,' he suggested. Then he saw Patsy's stare and decided not to undermine her. 'But, if it becomes a regular thing and you need bouncers, so to speak, then that in itself is a job and that is what Mrs Diamond means.'

'Can we see how things go first? They might be glad to see

the back of us, although, I doubt it, and when Noel comes back he will go crazy. Let's put that on ice for now.' Leandra smiled. Mentally she was concerned how much this was all going to cost. They would have to pool all of their resources and possibly steal what they could off the customers, but it would be worth it in the end. Freedom had its price it seemed, and she and her friends were prepared to pay it.

Patsy felt sorry for them, for all of their matter-of-fact ways, they were frightened women who had been used and abused since they'd left home, hoping for a better life. 'Come and take a look at the flat.' Patsy stood up to leave. The best way was to be business-like about it. That would make it more official. 'We can sort something about the bills, but don't go running out on me,' Patsy warned.

'Run to where, Mrs Diamond? If we had that option, don't you think we would have done it by now?' Leandra shrugged. The three women stood up and followed Patsy.

'Victoria! We have visitors,' Patsy shouted. 'Some possible tenants for the flat.'

Peering through from the kitchen, Victoria brushed herself down. 'For goodness' sake Patsy, I look a fright.' Then she saw the three women and looked across at Maggie.

'These are friends of mine looking for somewhere to rent Victoria,' Maggie explained.

Instantly, Victoria had an idea who they were and what they did for money. 'I'm just packing a few of my mother-in-law's personal possessions. Photos and things; I'm sure you don't want those.' Victoria smiled.

Each in turn, the three women nervously wandered through the three-bedroomed flat. Their excitement made Patsy smile. They would take it and her rent would be assured. They would work around the clock to make sure they had a roof over their heads, she was convinced of that. Somewhere to call home.

'There would be nine of us in total, Mrs Diamond,' Leandra explained, and was a little confused when she saw Victoria's face drop.

'I'm sorry ladies, there are only three bedrooms. There isn't room for nine,' Victoria said apologetically.

'There is room,' Leandra assured her. 'We can share.'

While they continued looking around the flat, James found the opportunity to speak to Victoria. Lowering his voice, he moved closer to her. 'Thank you for yesterday, I'm sorry to have put you in that position.'

Victoria touched his arm in a friendly fashion. 'That's what friends are for James, to call upon when you need them most. Did everything get sorted out okay?'

'It may take a few days, but it seems okay. I owe you a drink, and possibly a meal for helping me out of a sticky situation.' He smiled and then moved away as the women all came back into the lounge.

'It's very modern and clean,' Leandra commented, 'when Maggie said it was an old lady's flat I presumed it would smell of piss and be full of old-fashioned furniture.'

Victoria giggled at their presumptions. 'No, my mother-in-law was the gadget queen, she loved modern things, including her fifty-inch television. As for cleanliness, Beryl was a stickler for tidiness as you can see.' Victoria's eyes glazed over when she remembered how her husband and Nick had always made sure that Beryl always had new carpets, furniture and every kitchen gadget. Nothing was too good for her.

Leandra spoke to her friends and then to Patsy. 'We will take it, but we won't have your money for a week or so. When will the property be vacant?'

'It will be vacant as soon as you have the money Leandra, plus I want 400 for the bills. When we see what the first quarter is we can go from there, but I am not being left with debts. I have rented in good faith. Do you understand that?' Patsy emphasised.

The two women shook hands. 'It's a deal Mrs Diamond.' With that, she ushered the other two women out.

James sat down once they had left. 'Phew! That was more nerve-wracking than I imagined, but I think it will work out well Madam Diamond.' He smiled.

Patsy punched him playfully on the arm. 'Madam Diamond indeed. I am their landlord. It's up to them now.' Everyone seemed pleased with the deal in their own way and Patsy was glad to have this millstone taken from around her neck. These women were desperate for some place to call home. She knew she had done the right thing.

'Well, I had better get on with sorting things out,' Victoria exclaimed. Turning, she raised her eyebrow and gave Patsy a stern look. 'I do know they are prostitutes, just in case you thought I was stupid and naïve. I also realise now, that you had this plan boiling in your brain the moment you suggested renting. That's just for the record, okay.'

Blushing slightly at the reprimand, Patsy shrugged. 'Prostitutes, junkies, criminals. Who else would pay a thousand pound to stay on this estate? Even the council don't charge that much. That's one problem sorted. Next plan is to sort out Karen Duret.'

6

TROUBLED TIMES

On their way back to Maggie's, James spotted Fin running through the estate. 'Whoa Fin, where are you going in such a hurry?'

'Hospital!' Fin shouted back, without stopping.

'Fin, stop! Wait a minute. What's wrong? For god's sake, slow down.'

Catching his breath, Fin stopped and waited for James to catch up with him.

'Why are you going to the hospital? You don't look hurt.' Puzzled, James waited for an explanation.

'It's Beanie,' Fin panted. 'I've just heard through the grapevine he's been beaten up and is in hospital. I need to go and see him. He was acting weird yesterday; something is wrong, I can feel it.'

'I'll come with you. No doubt Beanie has just got into a fight, and he'll be home before we get to the hospital. I thought he was a lover not a fighter.' James laughed, but he could see Fin was worried.

Fin nodded. 'Okay, if you want to, but I'm going now.'

'Let's get a taxi off the high street. Stop panicking Fin, we'll get there in good time.'

Relieved to have James with him, Fin gave a weak smile. The rest of the journey to the taxi rank was in silence, and even in the taxi, James noticed Fin wasn't in his usual jokey, flippant mood.

Once in the hospital, Fin marched up to the desk and asked about Beanie, obviously giving his real name, which took him a moment to remember. Looking around while the nurse checked her computer, Fin took a sharp intake of breath. 'James,' he whispered, 'that's Beanie's parents. I'm sure it is. I haven't seen them for years, but I'm sure it's them,' he stressed.

'Okay, well, let's pop across and introduce ourselves. We'll get more information out of them than we will out of that nurse, especially as you're not family.'

They could both see Beanie's mum's red, tear-stained faced. Beanie's dad looked as if he had been crying too, but was trying to hold it back while consoling his wife.

'Sorry to interrupt,' James began, apologetically. 'Are you Beanie's mum? Sorry, we're friends of his and we just heard he's in hospital.'

'I know you.' Beanie's mum pointed at Fin. 'You're Fin, you were always getting him into trouble. My boy was a good boy until he got mixed up with you and your fucking drugs.'

Fin was about to retort and remind her what a bad mother she had been in the past to Beanie, when James stopped him. 'Sorry, we only came to see if he was okay. We didn't mean to interrupt. Come on Fin, it's time we left these good people alone.' Pulling Fin by the arm of his jacket, James pulled him away.

'He said it was you they were looking for. You're to blame for all of this!' shouted Beanie's mum as they headed back down the corridor.

Angry at being yanked away by James, Fin pulled his arm away. 'What are you doing? We never even found out how Beanie is.'

'We'll find out more from the nurse. Follow my lead and do as you're told. Didn't you hear her? She said it was you they were looking for – *who* is looking for you? And more to the point, what does she know? It sounds like they've already spoken, so Beanie can't be that bad, can he.'

James's words sunk into Fin's brain. He wasn't thinking straight and was glad James had gone with him. God only knows what argument he would have had with Beanie's mum in front of all the hospital staff if he'd opened his mouth.

James calmly walked up to the desk and charmingly enquired as to Beanie's whereabouts. Looking up, the nurse had noticed that they had spoken to Beanie's mum and was about to say something, when a nearby doctor standing on the desk raised his head. Hearing Beanie's name, he looked puzzled. 'Hasn't his mother told you yet?' he asked.

'Told us what, doctor? As you have probably noticed we don't get on well with the parents; we're more interested in Beanie.' James laughed. 'Or rather, that is what we call him. I'm his real father and it's been a long time since I've seen my ex-wife and her husband,' James lied, much to Fin's astonishment.

'Oh, I see.' The doctor seemed to understand and ushered them aside out of earshot. 'Your son Beanie is no longer in the hospital as such.'

'He's not here?'

'When I say he is no longer in the hospital, I mean, I'm afraid he is in the morgue.' Looking at James with sympathy, he said, 'Your son died about an hour ago. He was badly beaten up, what with that and the stab wound to his back, he was near to death when he was brought in. We took him straight down to surgery, but it was too late. I'm sorry.'

Stunned, Fin listened, but he wasn't taking it in. He felt sick inside.

'I don't suppose there is any chance we can see him, is there?' James asked tentatively.

Shaking his head, the doctor apologised. 'That's up to his mother. The police are here to speak to her, but there isn't a lot she can tell them.'

'Please doctor. I know she won't agree. There is no love lost between us. I just want to see my son. I doubt she will even invite me to the funeral. I'm his father and this is his brother,' James pleaded. Tears were already forming in Fin's eyes and spilling on his cheeks. Taking all of this into consideration, the doctor nodded.

'Go into that side room, I will see what I can do,' he said and walked away. After a few minutes, the doctor walked back into the room. 'Five minutes, follow me.'

James could see the doctor looked worried, especially as he was probably breaking every rule in the book, but linking his arm through Fin's, he followed the doctor to the lift which took them down to the morgue. They all stood in silence as the lift seemed to take forever going down. James swallowed hard and squeezed Fin's hand. They both didn't know what to expect. It wasn't as bad as he thought it would be when they got there. Two men in white coats walked James and Fin to the metal slab that held Beanie's body. When the men pulled back the sheet, both James and Fin stood back in horror.

Beanie's body had been battered to death. There wasn't a part of him without a bruise; you could hardly recognise his face and one ear had been cut off. Fin turned his head away and bile rose in his throat rose. He was about to vomit on the floor when one of the men working there handed him a sick bowl. 'Take this son,' he said nonchalantly.

Fin couldn't stop himself vomiting; tears ran down his face as he emptied the contents of his stomach into the bowl. Meanwhile, James calmly pulled back the sheet further. He reached for Beanie's hand and noticed his murderers had cut off his fingers. This was what he was looking for. He now knew who they were.

Doing his best to keep his self-control, he looked up at one of the attendants. 'They said there was a stab wound; where is it? And I notice his ear and fingers are missing.'

'The stab wound is in his back; he had lost a lot of blood. And his ear had been placed in his mouth. It was impossible by all accounts to save him. I'm sorry for your loss.'

Fin was almost hysterical; tears flowed and there was no more in his stomach to bring up. Almost throwing himself on top of Beanie, he cried his name. 'I will find them Beanie, I promise,' he vowed in anger. 'I will torture these bastards for you. I promise you Beanie and I am so sorry.' He shouted hysterically, over and over again until James pulled him away.

The doctor who had brought them gave a polite cough to let James know that their five minutes were up.

'Say goodbye Fin,' James whispered. 'We have to leave now.'

Wiping the snot from his nose with the back of his hand, Fin raised his head and nodded. Walking over to Beanie he leaned down and kissed his forehead. Then a thought occurred to him. 'Where is his Beanie hat? He always wore it. I would like it if possible,' he asked the doctor.

'I presume it will be in his possessions.' The doctor shrugged. 'His mother will be given those.'

James put his arm around Fin's waist. 'Come on Fin, it's time to go home.' Thanking the staff and the doctor, James almost carried Fin back to the lift. Once inside, Fin fell to the floor and sat in the corner sobbing, while James looked on helplessly.

'Our floor is next Fin; wipe your face. You can do what you like once we're out of here.' James reached out his hand to help Fin back to his feet, while Fin mopped up the tears and snot from his face.

'I knew something was wrong, but I didn't do anything,' Fin croaked as they walked out of the lift towards the exit.

Once outside and in a taxi, James took Fin to Maggie's. He knew she wouldn't turn him away in this state whatever their history was.

'Dear god, what's happened?' she exclaimed when she opened the door.

'Let's just get in, shall we,' said James, giving her a knowing look. 'Maggie, go and make some sweet tea; Fin has had a bit of a shock. We both have.' Doing as she was told, Maggie instantly busied herself in the kitchen. James sat with Fin on the sofa and opened his arms, letting Fin fall into them and sob his heart out.

When Maggie came back through, she wasn't sure what to say. Offering him the mug of tea, she winked at him. 'I've put a little something in it. It might help.'

James was surprised at Maggie's soft and comforting tone. She and Fin always seemed to be at loggerheads, but not today.

She looked up at James. 'Am I allowed to ask what the matter is?'

'Beanie is dead, Maggie. We've been to the hospital, but he had been beaten, tortured and stabbed. You would have had to be a miracle worker to save him.'

'It's that Patsy's fault!' Fin spat out. 'It's all her fault. All Beanie wanted yesterday was some drugs to sell. He was running short of cash and she has a shitload of it and has never offered us anything to sell. Everything is drying up because of her; the

Albanians are taking over the world while that bitch is doing nothing.'

James and Maggie looked at each other. There was nothing they could say. Half of what he said was right; Patsy hadn't let them get their hands on anything.

'Me and Spider had breakfast with him yesterday. He was in a right state, looked like he was going cold turkey. I gave him fifty quid to buy something. For fuck's sake, James, who did that to him and why?'

'From what I can piece together Fin, he has been hanging around with the Albanians. Chopping one ear off and stuffing it in your mouth is their trademark. I've seen it before. Gruesome.' James winced. 'My guess: he's got in too deep with them. Was he working for them do you know? Was he selling their stuff?'

'Are you saying he was a back stabber?' Fin shouted. 'He might have been crooked but he was loyal to his mates. We've known each other since school.' Suddenly, Fin's eyes widened and he raised his hand to his mouth. 'Oh my god, Spider! We never saw him at the hospital. I'd better give him a call.'

Fin checked his mobile; he had a message from Spider.

I heard. God rest our Beanie. One of the musketeers. Not up to talking now. Speak soon.

Fin shook his head. 'Spider knows... but why hasn't he called me?'

'Because,' soothed Maggie, 'he feels exactly the same way as you. He needs time alone, like you do. Drink your tea,' she urged.

'Why are you blaming Patsy Diamond?' James was intrigued by Fin's outburst.

'Midge, Joe, me and Spider, we've had nothing to distribute. If there is none fair enough, but we both know she has it stashed away, so what is she going to do with it? She could have stopped Beanie from dying James.'

'Patsy Diamond hasn't done anything with the drugs because I told her not to. I want the street littered with that Albanian crap and then we are going to flood the market with the good stuff at a much better price. All we have to do is lie low for a while and then we make our move. She doesn't know what to do with it, Fin. Christ, Victoria wanted to burn it! They have no idea about how much that stuff is worth or how to get rid of it.'

Feeling a little stronger now, Fin looked at James. 'You told her not to share it? Why? We're mates, or I thought so.'

'We are mates, Fin. I owe you a lot, but there is too much of a spotlight on us all at the moment. The police might not be making it obvious but they will be sniffing around. Things have gone too quiet and on top of that, Natasha has been blown up. Noel and his men seemed to have disappeared. Do you really think the police haven't noticed any of this? Why would we bring attention to ourselves by running out onto the streets selling stuff? Now was not the time.'

Fin nodded and sniffed. 'That was what I said at the café when we was arguing but he wouldn't listen.'

'It's not your fault Fin. Beanie was a grown man, and he knew what he was doing. The only thing is, this time it turned around and bit him on the arse. He was beaten like that for a reason. Let me have a word with Patsy and we'll sort something out. My main concern Fin, is why are they looking for you?'

'Don't know James, I really don't. Although I suppose, they know I know that Diamond bitch and I hear things on the estate. Do you think I should be worried?' A look of horror washed over Fin's face. 'Are they going to do to me what they did to Beanie?'

'Possibly. I'm not going to lie. I just don't know why they want you, but I have a feeling we're going to find out.'

* * *

Patsy arrived at Larry's house earlier than expected. She was looking forward to seeing him and a smile crossed her face.

Larry met her at the door, quickly pulling his apron over his head. 'I heard your car pull into the driveway.' His face beamed with pleasure and his heart skipped a beat. For once he had her all to himself; the very thought of that made his body tremble.

Locking the car, Patsy walked over to him seductively. 'Well, if you heard my car, why aren't you already in bed?' Reaching up, she put her arm around his neck and pulled him closer to kiss him. It was slow and lingering, and Larry almost stumbled as he pulled her into the hallway.

'I've missed you Patsy.' He kissed her again excitedly.

'Don't tell me Larry, show me. Show me how much you've missed me.'

He led her up the staircase and into the bedroom. Patsy giggled like a schoolgirl as she undid the buttons on his shirt, while kissing him. Eagerly, he pulled at his shirt and ripped open the front, letting the buttons fly into the air. Then sliding his hands under her blouse, he cupped her breasts and freed them from her bra. Patsy put her arms in the air and let Larry slip her blouse over her head.

Picking her up, he laid her on the bed. The desire built up inside of her quickly as Larry playfully flicked his tongue across her hardened nipples. Her body trembled as she arched her back, thrusting her breasts towards him. As he mounted her, she gasped and their sweaty bodies met in rhythmic pleasure as one. His need and urgency matched her own, and soon they were both crying out in ecstasy as they reached their peak. As they laid in each other's arms, a satisfied grin crossed Patsy's mouth. Mentally, she thought, as she stroked him, they were like lovesick teenagers who couldn't get enough of each other, but the next time would be slower. Letting her hand roam over his dark, hairy chest she playfully entwined her fingers in it. She couldn't help but admire the firmness of his body. He made her feel safe and she liked that feeling – she liked it very much. As she stroked him she could feel his arousal again as he turned to kiss her once more.

Later, as they sat in their bathrobes at the dining table eating lasagne, Larry took a sip of his red wine. 'Will you be staying the night or fleeing off as usual?' He wanted to hold her and wake up with her but she always seemed to have somewhere to go or someone to see.

Smiling at him, Patsy nodded. 'Well, I've drunk too much of your lovely red wine to make a run for it, so I guess you're stuck with me.' Giving him a naughty wink, she could sense the nervousness leave him.

'Good, well here's to red wine,' he toasted.

'No Larry, here's to red wine, lasagne and most of all, good sex.' She laughed. Together they toasted and savoured the moment and chinked their glasses together.

Waking up in Larry's bedroom felt disorientating and looking at the clock she could see it was just past 6.30 a.m. She could hear the shower running and picking up her phone, she saw there were already some messages from James. She chose to ignore them for now. Not only could she not answer them with Larry there, she wanted to have this moment to herself a little longer. Lighting a cigarette and wrapping her bathrobe around her, she went downstairs to make some coffee and brought it back upstairs.

'Leave the shower running Larry,' she shouted through the door and followed him into the bathroom, dropping her robe on the way.

Following her, James waited until they got in the flat before he said any more.

Victoria was already up and having a coffee when she saw them both come in and smiled. 'Well, I never.'

'If you think we spent the night together, then think again Victoria. Did you know Beanie had been murdered?'

The smile disappeared from Victoria's face. 'Fin's Beanie?' Not quite able to comprehend what Patsy was saying, she looked at James.

James told them all of the gory details word for word; once or twice he saw them both wince when he told them about Beanie's horrific death and how his ear had been cut off and put in his mouth. Victoria felt sickened by it all and held a tissue to her mouth, catching the bile that rose in her throat. Ignoring her, Patsy glanced at James. 'Why do they want Fin in particular? They know where to find him. And you say this is an Albanian message. This is their trademark?' She felt shocked and angry at the same time. It was disgusting. 'Can his parents pay for a decent funeral?'

'I don't know. Personally, I wouldn't like to ask; they didn't seem too happy to see Fin.' Swaying his head from side to side, James reasoned, 'Although, you wouldn't be pleased to see anyone would you, especially when your son has been murdered.'

The room fell quiet as James carried on, informing them about Fin swearing vengeance and blaming Patsy. 'What has it got to do with me?'

'Patsy, don't play the silly schoolgirl; you're up to your neck in this. They know how much of the drugs you took from the grave and yet you've never offered them a packet of pills to sell. That is their job, like it or not. You're sitting on a fortune, but never once did it cross your mind to reward them for their bravery. The

Albanians are still working everything, supposedly until they hear from Noel. Take the community centre – you own the place and you're doing nothing with it. Wise up lassie; they won't wait forever and if they take the law into their own hands I would say that you're top of their list to get rid of.' As the last of his words sunk in, the room fell silent.

'You're right James, there is none so blind as those who don't see, and I didn't see it. My mind has been elsewhere and I have let them down.' Thinking about it, Patsy cursed herself. Of course they were dealers and needed something to sell, even Sheila and Victoria had mentioned the drugs, but she had dismissed it and wallowed in Karen bloody Duret! 'What do you suggest James?' she asked.

'You need to sort it Patsy, and fast, or don't say I didn't warn you.' James took another sip of his coffee and was about to leave when Patsy pondered his words.

'But I still don't understand why they want Fin,' she said.

James turned. 'Isn't it obvious? They have an idea that he has been doing some work for you and my guess is that someone else was at that graveyard that night, or possibly watching Fin and the laddies when they saved me. Whatever it is, there is a death warrant out on him. Sort it out Patsy. Help them, the way that they helped you.'

'Organise a meeting James. Tell them all to come to the community centre in a couple of days. Let us see what they have to say when they are faced with me. That includes any of those Albanian mobsters. I don't fucking care James. I am sick of being Patsy, Nick Diamond's posh wife.' Pointing her finger at herself, she stressed her words to James. 'I am Patsy Diamond, and I will show them who is in charge here. I am sick of all of this cloak and dagger shit, let them crawl out into the sunlight and face me, or haven't they got the balls? I have a pile of mobile phones with hundreds of confessions from those stupid bastards Nick recorded. They couldn't wait to grass each other up, including the Albanians. You should listen to them James, it puts Netflix to shame. All of them begging for help from Nick to help them get a lighter sentence. They are weak. I am not weak, and you can tell them from me, if any of them start their threats, I will have their balls cut off and use them for earrings. Enough is enough. It's time they learnt to respect me as a business woman and their bloody boss! They all want to use my premises and want something from me, well, it's time they started earning their keep. I am *Mrs Diamond*!' Patsy's face was flushed with anger and her eyes were almost bulging out of her head; even James was shocked at her outburst.

'Are you fucking crazy Patsy?' James sat down again and put his head in his hands. 'You want all of those men, some of whom hate each other, in the same room as you? Do you realise what these men are like? They are not businessmen in suits Patsy. They are murderers, thieves, drug addicts. Look at Greek Paul, he is mentally insane. For god's sake Patsy you will be lucky to come out of there alive.'

'I realise that.' Although frightened, Patsy felt the only way to sort this out was to face it head on. Moistening her lips, she looked across at James. 'But let's see what they want from me. I want Fin there too. I know he hates me, but he needs to hear it too and we are probably stronger together. Can you do it, James?'

Shrugging in disbelief, wondering if Patsy was also insane, James nodded. 'I can try. I'm sure once we mention it to a couple of them, they will tell the others. I'll see what I can do.' As the door behind him slammed, Victoria and Patsy looked at each other. There were no words to say. Soon would be judgement day and neither of them knew what they would be facing.

Breaking the silence, Victoria changed the subject. 'Sheila will be here soon.'

'Good. I want us all to go to the meeting this afternoon and we need to tell her what's happened. I know she'll be upset because she's known Beanie for years. But let's start with one thing at a time.' Patsy rolled her eyes up to the ceiling. 'Bloody hell, what a day this is going to be and I'm knackered already!'

'Away lassie, trouble's here!' The sound of Sheila's voice echoed down the hallway. When she saw Victoria and Patsy, she said, 'Good god, who died? Your faces are as solemn as could be.'

Patsy and Victoria gave each other a knowing look. 'Well, actually, funny you should say that. I have some bad news, Sheila. Beanie is dead,' Patsy blurted out. There was no easy way to say it, so she got straight to the point.

Sheila nearly staggered back when she heard the news. 'Beanie... dead, but how?'

Patsy told her the whole sorry story and as predicted, Sheila burst into tears.

'What about Fin; how's he coping? He's already lost Steve and now Beanie. What the fuck has been going on Patsy. Why didn't you ring me the moment you knew? Has anyone been to see if Fin is okay?'

'James only told us this morning Sheila, and no I haven't been to see Fin yet; it was early and I didn't want to wake him.'

Looking up from her tear-stained face, Sheila glared at Patsy. 'Shit scared, more like. You don't want to face him, do you? You're a fucking coward Patsy Diamond!' she shouted. 'Well, I'm going now, and you are coming with me whether you like it or not. You're going to take any shit he throws at you. Come on you coward.' Almost dragging Patsy by the arm, Sheila marched out of the flat and towards Fin's flat.

Patsy paled as Sheila rained insult after insult at her; she had never spoken to her like this before, but then she and Fin had been friends long before herself and Sheila had ever met. Patsy bit her bottom lip and contemplated Sheila's insults, realising that maybe she was afraid of facing Fin on her own. He already blamed her for everything, and this was the icing on the cake. She felt ashamed hiding behind Sheila like this. Swallowing hard, she stood beside Sheila once they reached Fin's flat.

The windows were blacked out and Sheila shouted through the letterbox and banged on the door. 'Fin! Fin!'

They both heard footsteps and bolt after bolt slid across the door as Fin opened it half an inch.

'What do you want Sheila?' he muttered from behind the door.

Sheila pushed the door open and barged past him into his flat. 'What the hell do you think I want Fin? I've just heard about Beanie; are you okay?' Seeing his swollen eyes and his shaking hand as he raised his cigarette to his mouth, Sheila grabbed hold of him and threw her arms around him, holding him close. 'I'm here Fin, let it out.'

After a few minutes of sobbing and incoherent words, Fin raised his head. 'Why have you brought her here? It's all her fault.' Glaring at Patsy, he walked through into his sparsely furnished flat. Patsy looked around and couldn't believe what a shithole it was. Christ, she thought to herself, squatters lived better than this.

'She had nothing to do with cutting off Beanie's ear you prat. I'd say I'd make some tea, but I doubt you have a clean mug.'

'I'll find whoever did this Sheila and I will kill them. I won't let Beanie die for nothing. I will shoot the bastards!'

'Oh well, that's just dandy; they don't kill you on the outside, but you get twenty years for murder and get stabbed by someone on the inside. Listen to yourself. Anyway, you can't shoot straight.' She laughed. Instantly, they both saw the grin appear on Fin's face.

'That's a fair point.' He chuckled and brushed away the remainder of his tears.

Feeling braver now that Sheila had broken the ice, Patsy spoke up. 'Fin, James has told me that you've been keeping everyone going out of your own cash. Why didn't you ask me for help?' Shaking her head, she waved her hand in the air. 'I'm sorry Fin, I've let you down. But I'm going to get some cash for you to distribute, and from now on you're in charge of finances. I'll also put five thousand pounds in an envelope so that you can put it through Beanie's parents' letter box for a decent funeral. Then I want you away from here for a while.'

'I don't want your shitty payoff. Is that all you think Beanie was worth you bitch?' he shouted. 'Get out of my house. Go on, get out!'

Seeing how angry he was, Patsy looked at Sheila and she indicated for Patsy to leave. Now was not the time; he was too upset. Patsy felt guilty that Fin should feel like this about her. Is that all she did? Throw money at people to make them feel better?

Once Patsy left, Sheila asked about Spider and Fin told her he was in hiding. 'We're shit scared Sheila!' Throwing his arms around her again, he sobbed. He didn't want to admit that he was afraid, but he knew Sheila wouldn't tell anyone.

'Aye, course you are Fin. You would have to be crazy if you weren't. But don't bite the hand that feeds you. Let Patsy pay for the funeral; she owes Beanie that. And you sort out your debts and look after the laddies. That is the wisest thing to do.'

Fin nodded his head and agreed when suddenly Patsy came charging back into the lounge, having left the door ajar once she'd left. 'Here, ignore me if you want, shout at me if you want. But in this bag is twenty thousand pounds. Pay for Beanie's funeral and pay your friends what they are owed, but you're in charge of the money Fin. Victoria wants to know if you want to get the train today or go back to Dorset with her tomorrow. And for the record Fin, this is not a payoff. I know I must come across as an uppity selfish cow at times, but you're my friend Fin, please believe me.' Almost out of breath having said her piece, Patsy waited for Fin's outburst.

'What am I going to do in Dorset? Where the hell is it anyway?'

'It's away from here and safe. Countryside and stuff.'

'What about Spider?'

'What about him. Is he hurt, too?'

'No, but he's in hiding. Could he come too? That is, if I agree to go. Not sure about the countryside; it's all cow shit and fields.'

Patsy gave a slight chuckle at his description, but she presumed a lot of people from the city felt the same.

'Besides, if I run, it looks like I'm scared, doesn't it?' Fin felt uneasy about it all, but looked down at the bag full of money Patsy had brought with her. 'Anyway, how can I look after the lads if I'm in Dorset?'

Patsy shook her head in dismay. 'Scared is better than dead and I'm sure it won't take you long to hand that out to your mates.' Following his eyes to the money, she grinned. She still had plenty of Nick's money stashed at Beryl's house. He had brought millions with him to start his new life with Natasha. At least now it would be going to a good cause. 'James is spreading the word to some of the men that worked for Nick, including any of those out-of-work Albanians who worked for Noel. I want a meeting with them all; let's get the ground rules sorted about who is running this. If they want you, they will have to get past me first. I have enough evidence to put them all behind bars for years. Let's play it Nick's way; blackmail the bastards. Let them be forever looking over their shoulders in fear. Maybe we can sort something out, but I need you too. We know there are other graves out there stuffed full of drugs and whatever else Nick wanted to bury. We need to check them out.' Now, Patsy was back on form; her mind was back on the job in hand. James had been right; she hadn't worked out what to do and to be honest to herself she was winging it.

Surprisingly, this idea pleased Fin more than going into hiding in Dorset. She realised he wanted to be in the thick of it all. He didn't want to miss out on an adventure like this.

Sheila spoke up. 'Well, you have business to sort out Fin and so we're going to leave you alone. We have to be somewhere, so we'll speak later – and don't think of running off with that money or the Albanians won't be the only ones looking for you!' Sheila paused. 'Wait, did you say some of the Albanians are coming to the meeting? Surely these are the very people Fin needs to steer clear of?'

A fleeting thought passed through Fin's mind. 'Are you selling me down the river Patsy, and handing me over to them to make peace?' He looked at Sheila for reassurance.

The smile dropped from Patsy's face. 'I wish you two would stop doubting me. I'm a silly woman as far as they are all concerned, which means my authority is worthless. The word, according to James, is that a lot of the Albanians are skint without Noel, but the Albanian ghetto is looking after them. All of the people who worked for Nick are now waiting for a hand-out; well, they are not getting one. I'm not a free bank. Let's see how brave they all are when they are called out on it, shall we? At least we have the balls to face them. What do you say Fin, do you have the guts to face these cowards who killed your friend?'

Fin's voice was more of a whisper when he answered. 'I do, Patsy. I have nothing to lose and I owe that to my mates. Yes, I'm game if you are.' He laughed and Sheila nodded her head to Patsy to leave Fin to his own devices.

* * *

Arriving at Larry's office earlier than expected, Patsy was annoyed when it looked like he was about to lean towards her and kiss her on the cheek. Giving him an icy glare, he stood back. The last thing she wanted was for this meeting to look unprofessional. This was business and Larry should know better. She wanted to be in that state of mind when Karen turned up and not have Larry fawning over her, making a mockery of this meeting.

'Afternoon Mrs Diamond; ladies,' he said in a more professional manner, offering them all a chair. Patsy was dressed in a black trouser suit with a cream silk blouse underneath. She looked very much the businesswoman. Victoria wore her Chanel suit, while Sheila wore her jeans and T-shirt. They sat while Larry went through his papers until the secretary popped her head around the door and announced Karen Duret had arrived. Larry indicated for her to be shown in the office. Patsy's hands felt sweaty and sticky. She didn't know what to expect, but felt this woman had the upper hand, although she didn't know why. All she could do was wait and see what unfolded.

Almost floating, Karen walked into the room. All three women looked up as her perfume wafted in the air. Wearing a red skirt suit and shoes, which heightened her long, wavy blonde hair, she sat down in the chair Larry proffered her.

'*Bon après-midi.*' She smiled at them all, displaying a row of perfect white teeth.

Sheila leaned into Patsy and whispered, 'God, she glides like she's on ice. Do all posh lassies walk like that?'

Patsy nudged her with her elbow to silence her. 'If you're going to speak in French, then I suggest we leave.'

'My apologies, habits die hard. Good afternoon, ladies.' Reaching out her hand, she shook each of their hands and then stood before Patsy. 'Will you not shake hands, Patsy?'

'Mrs Diamond to you.'

Victoria and Sheila looked at each other. They both knew this was going to be an interesting meeting.

Patsy was about to speak when Larry interrupted her. 'Ms Duret, you have claimed to be Mrs Diamond's business partner, when in fact you were partners with her husband, not Mrs Diamond. And given the headstone in the local cemetery with your name on it, I think we would all like to know where you have been. It seems a very big coincidence, that the lady in the graveyard has the same name, date of birth and even middle name as yourself. Maybe you could enlighten us.' Once he had finished, Larry sat back in his chair and waited.

'Of course! I have been living in Paris these past few years. I knew Nick for a long time; we met approximately seven years ago. I am sorry I missed his funeral and couldn't pay my last respects.'

'So you want the money you think you're owed?' Patsy asked, blunt and straight to the point. She didn't want to hear any more. Mentally, she was shocked that this woman said she had known Nick for so long. How could that be possible when she had never heard her name before?

Sharply, Karen turned to Patsy. 'I don't want or need your money. The partnership carries on, that is what Nick would have wanted. You have seen my bank statements. They are all recent. I haven't come for a bitch fight Patsy, I have come for what is mine, what your husband felt was mine, and I won't be swindled by you!'

Patsy got out of her chair to slap her, and Karen did likewise, until Sheila stepped forward. 'Time out ladies. We're not here for a cat fight.'

Patsy's face was flushed and she was angry. She wanted to tear this woman's hair off her head. Another bloody blonde Nick had known.

A glance from Sheila made her sit back down.

Exhaling deeply, Larry rubbed his forehead and pointed out that court proceedings in this matter would be a very long and costly case and even then she might come out with nothing.

'Indeed,' Karen agreed, 'which is why I have come here today to try and sort things out between us.' Turning to Patsy, she looked her up and down. 'If you think myself and Nick were lovers of some kind, you would be right. He would fuck anything if he thought there was something in it for him.' Although her voice was raised, she wasn't shouting.

The sinking feeling in the pit of Patsy's stomach made her feel like crying. Nick had been playing her all along. For years he had cheated on her, if what this woman was saying was right. She felt humbled and humiliated in front of another one of Nick's lovers. It made her wonder why he had stayed with her all of those years.

'We would need your accountant's address and details Ms Duret,' Larry intervened. He could see the wind had been well and truly taken out of Patsy's sails and felt sorry for her. 'I don't seem to have any paperwork from them.' Searching through the paperwork on his desk, Larry frowned. 'Surely you must have a printout for tax purposes.'

'I will see what I can do about that for you.' She grinned, trailing her tongue over her glossy red lips.

Larry noticed how she evaded the question about her accountant. Ignoring her provocative smile, Larry closed his file. 'Well, we can't do any more Ms Duret, until I have all of the paperwork. I don't seem to have the original partnership contract either. Does your solicitor have it?'

He found it suspicious considering she had come for a business meeting, that she wasn't prepared at all.

Opening a gold cigarette case, Karen first asked Larry if it was okay to smoke and then passed around her cigarette case to the rest of them.

Patsy sighed. 'Look we are getting nowhere here. You don't have any paperwork. You don't have an accountant, because you won't say who he is, but you have been taking a chunk of my money for a so-called partnership you have no proof of! How did you know Nick, where did you meet him?' Questions buzzed around Patsy's head. She wanted to know everything, but she could see that Karen was on her guard.

'I have the same accountant as you Mrs Diamond. I am sure he can come up with any paperwork you may need.'

Shocked, Patsy leaned forward. 'Tom? Your accountant is Tom Walker?' Bewildered, Patsy sat back in her chair. 'Well he never mentioned you to me – not ever. I think you are lying. So why don't you just get out of here, you scrounger. Take your cheap suits, your bad French and fuck off!' Patsy screamed.

Karen stood up. 'Don't push me, Patsy. You really don't want to. I know everything about you, you foolish woman. You stayed loyal to that piece of shit you were married to. Well, that was your problem. The best thing that could have happened was him getting shot.'

'That's my son you're talking about!' Victoria's face was flushed with anger.

'That is your problem, Mrs Diamond. You brought him up, maybe you should have slapped him more as a child. He was beautiful, yes. But he was rotten through and through.'

The resounding noise as Victoria shot up and slapped Karen stopped them all in their tracks. Karen staggered backwards and instantly her hand went up to her bright red cheek. Her face glowed red and tears stung at her eyes.

Victoria blew on her hand. It was hot and stinging. Sheila and Patsy sat there stunned.

'You've had your fun Ms Duret, now I suggest you leave. Don't ever lie about my son again. Come on girls, we're leaving.'

Smarting, Karen glared at Victoria and then Patsy. 'Me, lie? I think your liar is closer to home Mrs Diamond, isn't she Patsy?'

Patsy was about to speak but Victoria stopped her.

'Tell her, Patsy Diamond!' Karen shouted, 'This is your opportunity to do the right thing at last. Tell them the truth. Tell them about Nancy Nicola Diamond...'

Patsy's face paled. Her body began trembling and her face burned with shame and anger. How did this woman know everything about her, but she knew nothing about Karen Duret? Who the fuck was she?

Patsy knew her long guarded secret was out, and she felt frightened and vulnerable, and after all these years she had to face the consequences of her deceit. She felt sick to her stomach. This was not the way she wanted them to find out about Nancy, but either way the truth was out and she had to open the door to the skeleton in her closet.

Patsy could see that all eyes were upon her and that they

wanted answers. Calmly she collected her thoughts and composed herself as they all sat in silence waiting. Clearing her throat, she looked at Victoria. 'Nancy is mine and Nick's daughter... your granddaughter. She is six years old and lives with my parents,' she confessed, leaving Sheila and Victoria stunned.

The sound of Karen's laughter rang in Patsy's ears as she stumbled her way towards the exit.

8

SKELETONS

Sobs wracked Patsy's body. She had lied for years, and the longer it had gone on, the harder it had been to tell the truth. Some of her tears were of relief. At least it was out in the open now and there was no turning back. Victoria would hate her, but she was prepared for that. She had robbed her of her granddaughter for years. Patsy just hoped she would give her a chance to explain her impulsive action. The other part of her damned that bitch Karen into damnation. She hated her, but couldn't help wondering how she knew. Nancy had been a top-secret operation and yet, Karen knew. She had waited for the opportunity to throw it in her face, the bitch!

Passers-by could see Patsy crying in her car, but she didn't care. Brushing away her tears and reaching for a tissue to wipe her sodden face, she felt the only thing she could do now was to go back to the flat, collect her things and leave all of this behind her.

She wanted to go back to London, to hide her face in shame for the wrong she had done to everyone, including her beloved little Nancy. Realising she had been sat there for half an hour, she turned the key in the ignition and drove off. Hopefully, she would get to the flat before Victoria, but she doubted it now.

As she turned into the estate, her heart sank, because Larry's car was there. Taking out her compact, she tried making the best of a bad job, patching up her ruined make-up. If she was to face the Spanish inquisition, she wanted to do it looking good.

As she walked into the flat, Sheila, Victoria and Larry all looked up. She could see that Victoria had been crying and another wave of emotional guilt overwhelmed her. 'I'm just collecting my things,' she muttered and was about to walk away when Victoria called her back.

'Don't you think you owe us all an explanation Patsy, before you wander off into the sunset? I'm not only your mother-in-law, I thought we were friends. You have deceived me and my son; maybe things would have been different if he'd known he had a child. *Sit down, right now!*'

Patsy gulped. She didn't know what to expect, but she did as commanded.

'Sheila's right; you are a coward Patsy. All this bloody show of what you can and can't do is a load of bollocks. You were just going to leave without a goodbye. Larry has convinced me, although I don't know why, to listen to you and give you a fair hearing. So come on, let's have it. It had better be good.'

Looking down at the carpet and wringing her hands, Patsy avoided Victoria's glare. Glancing across at Sheila for support, she was surprised when her friend held her hands up and shook her head. 'This isn't my business, Patsy. I think I should leave you all to it, but Vicky here thinks I should stay.'

'I'm waiting!' Victoria drummed her fingers on the arm of the sofa. 'Don't you think I'm hurt? I have feelings and I am pleased that you had a daughter because when she shits on you then you will have some idea as to how I feel. You're talking about my granddaughter, my blood. Are you ashamed of us? I always stood by you Patsy, I always defended you, but I feel like you have torn my heart out. I want to know the truth and I want to know why anyone would hide their own child from its family?' Victoria felt sick and confused. 'My god Patsy, you never fail to shock me. And you are the one that complains about Nick's double life. I swear you two were made for each other.' She was in no mood for excuses or lies. She wanted the truth. 'Are you sure it's even Nick's baby you have hidden?'

'Yes!' Patsy shouted. 'Yes, she's definitely Nick's. I loved Nick and you know it, but he changed and I was frightened. I don't know what happened Victoria, but I started putting on weight. If you think back you might remember when I kept being sick and you suggested that I should see a doctor because maybe I had an ulcer?' Patsy looked up at Victoria.

Victoria's mind wandered back and she could recall that time. Patsy had looked shocking. 'Go on,' Victoria encouraged.

'Can you imagine my surprise when they told me I was pregnant? It was impossible, but it was true. I wanted to rush home to tell Nick, but he had been in Scotland and was tired and irritable. He'd changed lately and already he had me laundering money through the salon. If I asked him about the money or the time away, he would just say it was none of my concern.'

Everyone sat in silence as Patsy poured out her story. 'He hinted about his new friends. He had become Jekyll and Hyde, Victoria. Wasn't that around the same time that he was distant from you? Suddenly he hated you and I had no idea why. He started having night terrors and hot sweats, and was always disappearing. I had an awful feeling that my news wouldn't please him. If anything, he would only feel that our baby would get in the way. I really don't know what went through my mind. The one thing I did know, was that Nick would use Nancy against me. She would be his weapon to keep me in place. I was frightened and couldn't tell anyone, not even you.' Patsy cast Victoria a furtive glance and looked down at the carpet again. 'I was mixed up and having my dream baby, but I felt it would be a disaster once Nick got his hooks into her. That was when I hatched my plan. Why should Nick even know I was having a baby? He was away all the time, sometimes for weeks on end. Now we know why, Victoria, don't we? He was playing Scottish cops and robbers with his new so-called friends,' Patsy spat.

Victoria's voice softened somewhat. 'Tell me what you did; I'm curious.' A frown crossed her brows and she looked directly into Patsy's eyes. 'Was this really all Nick's fault? I don't think so, because you never even gave him the chance to find out.'

'I did Victoria,' Patsy confessed. 'It was my last shot before I made my decision. We had dinner together one evening and I brought up the subject of us having a baby. I told him what a good father he would make. He laughed Victoria; his sneering laugh haunts me now. *"Shit, vomit and crying,"* he said. *"We've coped all of these years without one, why rock the boat now? Anyway, a baby wouldn't fit our lifestyle Patsy. Who would launder the money through the salons if you weren't there?"* That was all he cared about and so I decided on plan B. I knew the one place Nick never went was my parents' house. I could hide my baby there and no one would ever know.'

Sheila took a sharp intake of breath, and without thinking, butted in, 'But for how long, Patsy?'

'I don't know Sheila. I hadn't thought that far ahead and the more time passed the harder it got to tell anyone. All I did know was that I wasn't going to let this new Nick get his hands on something precious and use her as the stick to beat me with.' Burying her head in her hands, Patsy began to sob. 'I'm sorry

Victoria, I really am. It's time I left now.' As Patsy stood up to leave, Victoria stopped her.

'Is she the pretty little girl I saw with your parents at Beryl's funeral?'

Patsy turned sharply. 'Yes. I wanted Beryl's great grand-daughter to be there.' Although the mood was solemn, somehow Patsy felt better. At last, she had got it off her chest, although she had never expected to have it blurted out like this. But maybe it was for the best.

Victoria spoke softly. 'What you did took a lot of planning. Do you see her often?'

'I see her all the time, Victoria. We spend the school holidays together and some weekends. My parents have their villa, but I fly out for long weekends and see my baby.'

'And what does she think about her father?' Victoria asked bitterly. 'It must be a relief to you that he's dead. But you've robbed me Patsy, and you robbed Beryl too. What you have done is bloody evil on both sides.'

Feeling braver, Patsy couldn't stop the sarcasm dripping from her mouth. 'Well, we can't all be like you and pass off your illegitimate baby as your husband's child can we? And you think I'm a scheming bitch.'

Victoria lost her temper and strode towards Patsy, raising her hand to strike.

'Don't even think about it Victoria, or I swear to god I will slap you back!' Patsy shouted.

Stopping herself, Victoria looked at her. 'Don't ever compare yourself with what I did to what you have done. I was raped and you're just a liar.'

'You could have easily let the truth come out, but no, you wanted an heir to your Diamond palace and it pleased your husband and his mother. I protected my child in the only way I could think of and kept her safe.'

For a few moments the two women stood and stared at each other, contemplating what to do next. 'So what now?'

'I want her to come and live with me. I will do everything I can to keep her safe Victoria, and so will you... if you want to meet her, that is?' Patsy's voice softened.

Nodding her head, Victoria put her arms around Patsy. 'Yes, we will. Together.'

Rubbing her hands together, Sheila smiled. 'So, Patsy, when do we get to meet the wee lassie? Do you have any photos? Larry can put the kettle on, and I think we could all use a drop of something in it. And I want to know what we're going to do with that smarmy bitch Karen. She has got her head right up her arse and she isn't getting one over on me.'

Patsy shook her head. 'I'd almost forgotten about her. Yes, I have photos of Nancy on my phone, come and see.' Patsy's face illuminated when she passed around her phone for them to see pictures of her daughter.

'Nancy,' Victoria mused, 'I like that. What does she know about her father Patsy?' Holding her hands up, she continued, 'I'm just asking. I would like to meet my granddaughter and I want us to sing from the same hymn sheet.'

'To be honest, I haven't said anything. She's never asked and my dad has always been there for her.'

Larry came through with the mugs of tea. 'Here you are ladies, and it's time I left you to it. But I will say one thing and I am glad Sheila brought it up. Karen Duret; where do we go from here? Personally, I think there is another story and I aim to find out what it is, and secondly, how could she have known you have a daughter, Patsy? It's been well hidden. But we'll talk properly soon.' Picking up his battered brief case, he walked to the door. Patsy followed him to show him out.

Giving her a knowing look, he shook his head. 'You don't trust anyone, do you Patsy? You have built a brick wall around yourself and we're all paddling about in the moat. Try being open and honest for a change; it takes a lot of planning deceiving people like that for years, but you have to live with it. Maybe Nick would have made a great father and packed his life of crime in? After all, he was going to do that for Natasha and their baby. He might still be alive if you hadn't lied. That's on your conscience. But it doesn't matter now, does it? It's all worked out in the end.'

Larry's words stung her. She had never thought about it like that. Maybe Nick would have changed. She would never know now. 'You sound like you're saying this is the end of us Larry. Is that what you want?' Patsy frowned; she couldn't understand why he had taken all of this personally, especially as he already knew.

'I love you Patsy, much to my own stupidity I think some-times, and I believe I always will, but at the moment I just don't like you very much. The way you have treated Victoria and Nancy and brought your parents into this web of lies disgusts me. Let's just deal with the business in hand. Sort out your domestics and be kind to Victoria, she has had one hell of a shock. Christ, her life has been turned upside down lately. The bottom line is that you have lied to everyone, including your daughter. I'll be in touch if I have any news.' Leaving Patsy standing on the doorstep, he walked away and got in his car.

Sheila walked up behind her and put her chin on her shoulder. 'Well, that went well! He'll be back Patsy; he's just hurt and he can't understand your way of thinking. Jeez, I thought I was a devious cow, but you blow me out of the water. Oh my god, Patsy, do you see what I see. I don't believe my fucking eyes!'

Patsy looked up and her jaw almost dropped. Seeing the blonde woman float down the landing towards them stunned her. Karen Duret carried on walking towards them. She wasn't wearing the usual, designer stuff. It looked like she aimed to blend in and was wearing denim jeans, a T-shirt and a leather jacket. Her make-up and hair looked the same, but she had a different air of determination about her.

Folding her arms and on the defensive, Patsy stood there ready for a fight. 'You have no business here, you evil bitch.'

She was about to slam the door in her face when Karen said, 'Patsy, we need to talk. I have waited all this time for that lawyer of yours to leave and this jacket is barely keeping my tits warm. I have things I need to say.'

All kinds of emotions ran through Patsy. She wanted to wring Karen's neck, but she was also curious as to why she was here. Turning, Patsy looked at Sheila. 'Well, do you want to listen to what she has to say or not?'

'Definitely.' Sheila nodded. They both stood back to let Karen enter.

Victoria walked out of the bathroom after washing her face and freshening up. Surprised, she looked at Karen and then at Patsy and Sheila. 'Have you come to tell me how many other grandchildren I've got stashed away?'

Karen blushed, and bowed her head. 'I'm sorry about earlier Mrs Diamond. I shouldn't have done that, but at least the truth is out now. No more secrets.'

'I don't know why you bothered letting her in, Patsy.' Victoria walked away to the kitchen but Karen followed her.

'Let her say her piece Victoria.'

Composing herself, Victoria walked back into the lounge. 'Sit down. You have something on your mind and you have taken a risk coming here.' All three of them were puzzled, but curious to hear what she had to say. The silent pause in the room as they all sat there waiting for Karen to speak seemed to go on forever.

'My brother faked my death,' Karen blurted out and swallowed hard to collect her thoughts. Tears brimmed on her lashes, but she sniffed hard and squared her jaw to stop herself and carried on. 'In my grave is my best friend. We were both junkies; she was unfortunate to take an overdose of bad shit. My brother identified her body as me. We both knew it was my only escape out of Scotland. Yes, I'm from these parts.' Her voice was barely above a whisper and they strained their ears to hear better. 'I was that fat junkie lassie.' Giving a fake laugh, she swept her hair back from her face, and met Victoria's eyes, pointing her finger at her. 'Your son made me like that. It wasn't the drugs I was running away from. It was Nick Diamond, the charming suave sophisticated lawyer who paid me attention when I was his office junior. I was flattered and he used me until my only way out was to overdose or escape.' Letting out a deep sigh, and lost in another world, and another time, she stared at the fireplace.

Patsy, Sheila and Victoria sat there in silence, not believing what they were hearing. This sounded like some horror story. Patsy had presumed she had been just another one of Nick's affairs, but this went far deeper than that, and she wasn't sure if she wanted to know. This woman would rather fake her own death and live a lie than be in Nick's clutches?

Victoria went and sat on the arm of the chair Karen was sitting on and stroked her hair sympathetically. 'You're a very good actress Karen, and it's easy to blame a man who is not here to defend himself. That was a really nice, rehearsed speech, now take your scrawny arse out of this flat and fuck off to wherever it is you crawled out from.' As she stroked her hair, Victoria yanked it back sharply, pulling Karen's head backwards, making her cry out and reach her arms up to defend herself.

Patsy thought about what Karen had said. 'Wait, Victoria! Karen – if that is your name – prove who you are and that you worked for Nick and maybe… just maybe… we will listen to the rest of your pitiful story. Now do as my mother-in-law says and get out.' Victoria released her grip on Karen's hair, and immediately Karen reached up to smooth it down and rub her aching head.

'I will and when I do you will listen to my proposal. You and your family owe me that!' With that, she ran for the door and left.

9

REVENGE

Once safely back in her hotel, Karen took a shower and poured a large brandy to calm her nerves and anger. She was outraged at her treatment from those bloody Diamond women. Sitting upright in her bathrobe on the bed, she picked up the telephone and made a call. A satisfied grin appeared on her face as she waited for an answer.

'Are you okay? You have been ages. What's happening? Has she agreed?' The man's voice on the other end of the telephone seemed nervous and agitated.

'Calm down for goodness' sake,' she snapped. 'It's me having to go through all of their interrogation and violence, not you. Just sit tight and carry out the plan. I've met up with them and spilt the beans about Nancy. It took the wind out of their smug sails, that's for sure. But that lawyer of hers could be trouble. She's definitely screwing him. Anyway, how are things at your end?'

Giving a half-hearted laugh, he couldn't help himself. 'Much easier than I thought. No one is any the wiser. Your main problem is the plantation. Another field has been set on fire. It's chaos, so you need to get those women on side and soon. You will have nothing left if you don't...'

'I've tried the soft touch with those women, but now it's time for business. I'm going back there tomorrow and I swear to god, if her mother-in-law touches one hair on my head again I will beat her to pulp. You said she was the reasonable one. Well, she's not. She is a crazy bitch!'

The man on the other end of the phone chuckled. 'Be nice, Karen.'

'Oh, stop calling me that. Karen was a stupid ignorant girl from the estates. I don't intend to be her for much longer.' Taking one last gulp from her glass, she swept away the wet hair from her face. 'Nick Diamond brought me back to life like Franken-stein's monster. He made me her partner and I intend to make the most of it. This is their undoing. Now just carry on as you are, and I will be in touch.'

'Time is not on our side. You need to act fast; you are losing thousands of pounds every day.'

Karen put the phone down. She felt uneasy. She had expected the women to feel sorry for her but it had backfired. Her back was against the wall and she knew it. This time she would go and play her ace hand.

Pouring herself another drink, she walked to the mirror and looked at herself. She didn't recognise herself any more, and coming back here brought nothing but bad memories. 'I swear I will bring all of you Diamond bastards to your knees. I have waited a long time for revenge and the longer it's been the better it will taste.' She grinned and raised her glass in the air to toast herself.

* * *

Pacing up and down his flat, Spider kept punching his fist against his hand. 'Someone has to avenge Beanie. He was my best mate.' The atmosphere was tense and he was angrily mouthing off to anyone that would listen. Paranoid from drugs and alcohol, he had lost all sense of reason. Empty lager cans were scattered all over the floor. The overflowing ashtray full of roll up cigarettes smelt of the marijuana they had smoked. Spider opened another can of lager and took a large gulp. 'No one cares, no one has done anything. Fin's gone soft, I swear. Somebody out there knows who killed Beanie and I intend to kill them so that he can rest in peace.'

'Sit down Spider. Take a snort of this; it will help you to relax.' Joe drew a line of cocaine down the cardboard box that served as a coffee table. His eyes were glazed and most of what Spider was ranting on about didn't sink into his brain. 'The way I see it Spider mate, is that these people are looking for Fin. Well, that's it. That's the answer. Fin is going to be our bait and we're going to hook them in. They know where to find him, but they want him somewhere secluded to torture him just like our pal Beanie.' Between their drugged up brains they hatched their plan.

Wiping the excess powder from his nose, Spider felt braver and nodded. 'You're right. It's up to us now. Fin won't do anything about it. We'll make sure he wishes he had.'

The more Joe and Spider sat sniffing their cocaine, the more their self-confidence grew, until they felt that they could fight the world. The coded knock at the door made them forget their bolshiness and answer it. Midge stood there with a carrier bag, while Joe let him in.

'Here you are lads. It's the best I could get at short notice.' Looking very pleased with himself, he emptied the contents of the bag onto the floor before them. Four handguns came tumbling out. Smugly, Midge stood there and folded his arms. 'And yeah, before you ask, I have the ammunition for them too.' He laughed, taking the boxes of bullets out of his pockets. Joe's and Spider's eyes lit up. They would go to that Albanian club tonight and shoot it to pieces. They all knew that it was them who had killed Beanie, they didn't just know exactly which one of them it had been. But it didn't matter; all they wanted was a shootout and a bit of excitement.

Swaggering with excitement and adrenalin, Spider picked a gun up and loaded it. Stupidly, he pointed at the wall and fired. The plaster fell from the wall onto the ground, making them laugh out loud.

'Come on laddies, let's show those bastards who owns this town!' Midge knelt down and sprinkled some cocaine onto the back of his hand and snorted it.

The three of them put their loaded guns into the waistbands of their trousers and swaggered to the front door.

* * *

The nightclub on the other side of town was in full swing. It was Albanian territory and no one else went there unless invited. The bouncer on the front door stopped the three of them as they approached. 'Fuck off Glasgow boys; you're not welcome here.'

'Well, this is fucking Glasgow you fat bastard, where else are we supposed to be?' Midge snarled.

Spider laughed and swayed. 'Be careful laddie. If Midge could give you a Glasgow kiss he would but he can't reach.' Turning to Joe, he burst out laughing while the bouncer looked at them, still barring their way.

'I can't reach, but this can.' Midge took out his gun and pointed it at the bouncer. 'Now get out of my way.' Stunned, the bouncer stared down the barrel of the gun and then at Midge, while mentally calculating how to get the gun out of his hands. As he stepped forward, Midge fired a bullet into his forehead. He staggered backwards, crumpling to the ground.

Spider kicked him away from the door and spat down at his dead torso. 'Nice one Midge. You showed that bastard like David and Goliath.' He laughed. The drugs had got the better of all of them. They were bloodthirsty and worked up into such a wrath, they felt untouchable.

'That fucking showed him, didn't it laddies?' Midge laughed, stepping away from the bouncer's dead body and into the club.

The laser lights flickered and the music was loud. Everyone seemed to be dancing and having a good time. No one noticed them enter.

'We have to act fast now laddies; some do-gooder will have reported that gun shot by now. Fucking busybodies! Just shoot as many as you can of this lot; they make me sick and it's time we showed them who was boss in Glasgow.' The sneer and glazed look on Spider's face with all of his bravado spurred the other two on, like some shoot out in a western movie.

Midge pushed his way through the crowd and went to the bar, and didn't care how many people he annoyed in the process by pushing them out of the way. Looking up at the bar, he shouted to the barman, 'Whisky!'

The blond Albanian barman looked at him and shrugged. 'Are you sure you're old enough? You look pretty small to me to ask for a whisky,' he joked.

Without a second thought, Midge took his gun out of his waistband and pointed it towards him. 'Do I look too young for one of these?' He grinned.

Stunned, the barman picked up a glass and turned to the optics to pour his whisky. The few people that were standing at the bar waiting for their turn to be served, looked at Midge in horror when they saw the gun. Immediately, three men walked up to Midge and one whispered in his ear, 'Put that fucking thing away and do not point it in here or I will show you mine.' His angry, thick accent didn't seem to seep into Midge's brain, nor did the other two men flanking him.

'What's that?' Midge laughed. 'I'll show you mine if you show me yours. Was it you who killed my mate Beanie?' Spider and Joe immediately joined Midge at the bar and stood behind the three men. Spider took out his gun and shoved it into one of their backs. Without a second thought, Spider bit the man's ear and sunk his teeth so hard into it the man screamed and elbowed Spider in the ribs to shake him off, winding him in the process. Blood from his ear spurted out and poured down his neck. He flew at Spider, punching him to the ground, one after the other until he was barely conscious. Joe fired his gun and shot the man beating Spider. Spider's face was a bloody mess. His nose was flat, and you could hardly see his face for blood. The other two men grabbed hold of Midge but Joe fired his gun again and shot one of them in the back. Women screamed and ran, pushing and shoving each other, climbing over people who had fallen to find cover under tables or in the ladies' toilets. Joe laughed when they saw the man sway a little and then fall. A pool of blood poured onto the floor from his back near Midge's feet.

'Benny was a fucking junkie; he owed us money!' one man shouted and then threw a punch at Joe, knocking him backwards. The gun fired out aimlessly in the room and from behind them they heard someone cry out. A group of people ran forward to where the scream had come from. A woman had not been lucky enough to escape the bullet. People fell to their knees, trying to help the innocent bystander, but it was too late: she was already dead.

The manager of the club ran up to two of his friends. 'Make sure no one leaves this place. Go and block the doors.' Nodding, a group of them ran towards the exits, barring panic-stricken people from leaving. Fights broke out as people tried retaliating, but it was futile. The whole place was mayhem. Men and women crouched down or sat on the floor, waiting for this nightmare to be over. Tears ran down their faces as they wondered if they would get out alive.

The once crowded dance floor was now deserted. Everyone had headed for cover. With the lights flashing, Joe took centre stage and fired his gun into the air. 'We're here because you fucking lot killed our mate Beanie. You want blood on your hands you can have it. You said you wanted Fin.' Joe glared. 'Well, you can fucking have him.' Suddenly Joe stumbled, and loud gunfire shot out. The manager appeared, holding an automatic rifle. Bullets fired one after the other into Joe, and his body bounced around the dancefloor until the manager stopped.

Midge paled, the realisation of what was about to happen waking him from his drugged up state. Knowing there was no way out, he fired what was left of his bullets towards the manager who dodged them. The manager stood up, knowing that Midge's gun was now empty, and with both hands, pointed his rifle at him. Midge tried to run, but it was too late. Sparks from the gun lit the place up as he fired at Midge's back and killed him.

Everyone in the exit corridors fell silent, for fear of being the next target.

Three men stepped forward and dragged Spider off the floor and perched him on a stool. Barely conscious, and finding it hard to see, he tried mopping the blood away from his eyes with his sleeve. His body felt limp, and he could barely hold himself up. The manager cleaned his finger prints off the automatic rifle with a cloth. Then he walked up to Spider and, picking up his limp hand, placed the rifle into it, making sure his fingerprints were all over it.

'Call the police,' the manager ordered to one of his men. The manager knelt beside Spider's broken bloody body on the stool. 'Don't try and fire it. I have taken the cartridge out for now.'

Through the slits of his eyes, Spider saw that the manager was holding the cartridge of the automatic. Blood poured from Spider's mouth as he tried to speak, but he couldn't; his jaw was broken. Frisking him, the manager found Spider's mobile and took it out. He took three photos. One of Midge, one of Spider and the other of Joe. Then searching through the numbers on his phone, he found what he was looking for and pressed send.

Within minutes, there was a loud banging and shouting at the club doors. Policemen making their presence known. Within seconds, they burst through the doors. Seeing people sat on the floor, terrified and screaming, the police shouted for them to get out, while another group of armed police ran past them.

The manager slid the cartridge back into the automatic. Spider was swaying on the stool, and with the last breath left in him, Spider held the automatic tightly and pressed the trigger, firing aimlessly, emptying the cartridge in all directions. The manager lay face down on the floor with his hands behind his head to show that he was a victim. Before Spider closed his eyes, and his heart stopped beating, he heard a shout and then nothing. The armed police had been given the order to fire. What had been a happy, lively evening out at a nightclub had now become a blood bath.

* * *

Fin was sat in his flat with the curtains closed, drinking a can of lager, when his mobile vibrated. Looking at it, his blood ran cold, and he began to tremble. Tears ran down his face and saliva spilt from his mouth. Like some horror movie he didn't want to watch, he couldn't help but look at the three gory photos of his friends that had been sent to him. Rushing to the bathroom, he vomited. Flushing the toilet and gathering his thoughts, he picked up the mobile again and ran to Maggie's; he didn't know what else to do.

He barged past Maggie when she opened the door and made his way into the lounge. Hearing the commotion, James stood up. A frown crossed his brow. He could see Fin visibly shaking. Tears and snot rolled into one down his face.

'Sit down Fin, come on,' James ordered, trying to get Fin to move his feet. Maggie stood behind them both. She could see Fin looked scared to death and he thrust his mobile into James's hand and kept repeating for him to look at it. Snatching the phone from him, James almost threw Fin on the sofa. He looked up at Maggie. 'Get us something strong to drink,' he ordered.

James looked at the mobile. Stunned, he couldn't take his eyes away. One photo was of Midge face down in a pool of blood. James couldn't make out where he was and so swiped to the next photo. He exhaled deeply at the gory sight of Joe also dead. In the background he could see a barstool. The dim surroundings made him realise it was a club and he knew who it belonged to as he had been there himself with Noel. The third photo brought the bile up in James's throat; it was a badly beaten Spider holding an automatic rifle. 'Where the hell would those three get an automatic from and why would they take photos? They didn't take those photos Fin, the people who killed them did. Did you know where they were going?' James shook him hard to make him listen. 'Stop fucking crying and listen to me. Those bastards who did this could be on their way here now. *Listen to me!*'

Calmly, Maggie handed James and Fin a mug containing whisky. 'Drink it,' she ordered before taking a sip of her own whisky to ease her shock. She looked at the mobile James held. 'What's on it?'

Without thinking, James passed it to her and saw her eyes widen with horror.

'Are these photos real?' she asked, not wanting to believe what she was seeing. 'Are the laddies dead?'

James snapped at her, 'Of course they're real Maggie and it's quite clear they didn't take them. This is a turf war now. They have all the soldiers, and we have me and Fin. We're fucked. God knows how those three got into that state or why they were in a club with the Albanians.'

'It will be because of Beanie. James, they wanted revenge. They have gone looking for trouble and by god, they found it. Poor souls.' Sitting down, Maggie put her arm around Fin and comforted him. With Fin's head buried into her shoulders, Maggie looked at James. A sense of foreboding swept over them. They both knew this was only the beginning.

10

BARGAINING

Opening the door and half smiling, Sheila looked Karen up and down. 'Well, well, well, if it's not our old friend Karen. What do you want? Didn't yesterday tell you anything?'

With a stubborn stance, Karen stood there. 'I'm not here to see you, whoever you are. I need to see those two.'

Patsy stuck her head around the lounge door to see who was there and her face dropped. 'No lady. You have had your say. Enough is enough. Leave... now.'

'I need to speak to you.' Furtively, she looked around to make sure no one was listening. 'Believe me, this is important.'

Out of curiosity Patsy nodded to Sheila. 'It's okay; let her in.' Although Patsy hated the very sight of Karen, she was still intrigued by her. She had all the answers and Patsy was still ignorant to all the facts.

Karen walked into the lounge and faced Victoria, who was about to open her mouth when Patsy stopped her.

'I need to speak business with you both. Firstly, I am going to tell you a story, you deserve that. And then the business. Please don't interrupt.' Walking to the sofa, Karen picked up a cushion.

'This is the talking cushion. You can only speak when you are holding it.'

Sheila wanted to burst out laughing, but bit her tongue.

Intrigued, Patsy motioned to them to all sit down.

Each of them nodded in silence as Karen sat down with her cushion. 'I was a young office junior when I met Nick. I was still at college and the law firm was my work placement. I adored him from our first meeting, but he never noticed me. I was fat and still had acne and my dress sense was worse. As time went on, I saw him glancing towards me now and again and I was flattered. On occasions he even said "hello" and "goodbye".' She smiled. 'After a while, he asked me to photocopy things for him. Some of the things I photocopied were not from the office. They were passport forms and confidential stuff about prisoners. I had no real idea what they were to be honest, but Nick said it was our secret. He always wanted me to stay behind when everyone had left and, being young and naïve, I did as he asked. He bought me presents for my hard work, and asked me if I would do other things for him too.' Karen looked around the room at the women listening to her. 'He used to get boxes of deliveries and wanted only me to sign for them. I found out later, those boxes were full of drugs. Men of all shapes and sizes came to see him when the office was closed and I was there to let them in. There would always be shouting and arguing, but I never asked any questions. Stupidly, I went along with it. One day, he asked me if I wanted to try a drug that would possibly help clear my acne. I had no idea what it was.' She sighed and rolled her eyes up to the ceiling, almost laughing at herself. 'Of course it was speed. It was strange, but for a while it did work. Some of my friends asked me if I could get some for them. I thought Nick would be angry, but no, he seemed very pleased. He flashed that famous smile of his and said he would sell it to them. One day, he said he had something even better, but he wanted a favour from me. He told me about a friend of his who was in prison who wanted some form of female company. Nick said he would pay handsomely and give me this new product if I would let the man touch me up a little while Nick interviewed him. I didn't like the idea, but I was eager to try something better. The man was old, fat and bald. No sooner had I sat down, he had his hand down my blouse. I was frightened and looked to Nick for support, but he laughed it off, telling me everything was okay. I felt uncomfortable trapped in that interview room. Solicitors are allowed to be on their own with their clients, which made it much easier for that man to grope me and make Nick laugh in the process. The man was called Billy something; I can't recall.' Karen looked towards the ceiling, trying to remember the name while Patsy and Victoria stared at each other and knew exactly who she meant. This bombshell made them realise that this time she was telling the truth. Tears rolled down Karen's face, and she looked like she was reliving this haunting nightmare in her mind once more.

Sniffing and brushing away a tear, Karen continued. 'Anyway, I tried his new product which I now know was cocaine and very quickly I was hooked. I soon realised I was his guinea pig. If I didn't foam at the mouth and drop dead, then he would sell the coke on. I went on a few more visits with him to see other prisoners and after a while, coked up to the eyeballs, it didn't seem to matter who touched me any more. I thought we were partners, that he might even love me, but I know now I was a fool.' Raising her eyebrow, she gave a sarcastic grunt. 'I soon brought my friend in on the deal. It's easier when there are two of you; somehow you don't feel so alone and it was an easy way to feed our habit – she had already been selling herself for her addiction. Sometimes, we had to go on our own if Nick was busy and as far as the guards at the prison knew, I was his secretary and going alone wasn't that unusual as I was working on his behalf. Nick liked that and decided that he would have some fun. So my name became his own secret code word.'

Puzzled, Victoria shook her head. 'What do you mean Karen? What secret code word?'

'I'm sure you've worked it out. K-a-r-e-n D-u-r-e-t... Undertaker.' Karen smiled.

'You're right Karen; our late friend Natasha and ourselves worked out the anagram, but we couldn't be sure,' Patsy confessed and looked at Victoria.

Victoria squirmed inside as she listened. It was a horrible story and a year ago she would never have believed it of her son, but now, knowing this different side of Nick, she accepted it without argument. He had silently groomed and smugly prostituted this woman, without her realising it at first.

'Anyway...' Karen shrugged. 'Nick eventually got me to try heroin and I became hooked. Only now, I started turning up late for work and people in the office were noticing. Nick fired me without a reference. I threatened to tell his partners and the police, but that was a stupid, stupid thing to do. He had me arrested for drugs, imprisoned and beaten up by his friends. The stupid thing is you can still get drugs in prison and I was an addict. My brother did his best to look after me and always bailed me out when necessary; he even sent me to rehab. We both knew things had gone too far and that Nick wanted to silence me once and for all. I had a friend, another addict, and we used to meet at a squat and either smoke or inject any heroin we could get our hands on. She led me into prostitution, but as I had done it for Nick, it didn't matter. I had no self-respect any more. One day, she stole a batch that I should have had. It killed her instantly. I knew that it had come from some guy they called the Undertaker and that it had been meant for me.' She shrugged. 'When my brother was alerted that two women were found in a squat and one was possibly me, he identified her as me. He had tried his best to get me clean, and I suppose this was his golden opportunity. It had become more serious now. Nick wanted me dead because I knew too much.' Karen paused. 'It was the wake-up call I needed. I knew it was time to get clean and make a fresh start. I would never get a job here; everyone knew I was a junkie and I wouldn't get a reference from Nick, would I?' Her sarcastic laughter filled the room.

Stunned, Patsy was about to speak but Karen stopped her. 'I have the cushion.' Patsy nodded and sat back. 'I knew Nick forged passports and I knew who did them. I told them I was on an errand for Nick and got myself a fake passport. My brother helped me get away to Paris. I have been there in hiding ever since.'

Sheila let out a slow whistle and stopped when they all turned to look at her. 'Okay, I don't have your bloody cushion but a story like that deserves a reaction. What happened in Paris?'

'Cutting a long story short, I got clean and I have been ever since. My brother got me references and I got a job being a nanny for a widower and his young daughters. Armand and I became close and then lovers, you know the story. Anyway, he has a chateau and farmland. Quite a lot of it actually. He left it all to me and his daughters when he died. There has been some trouble lately. You see one of our biggest outlets... and its legal' – Karen laughed – 'are black diamonds.'

'Okay, cushion over. What are black diamonds?' Victoria butted in.

'Truffles. That is our logo. Black diamonds because of their colour,' Karen explained.

'You sell chocolate truffles?' Sheila was puzzled. 'You can get them in any chocolate box. What's so good about yours?'

Tutting, Karen shook her head. 'Not chocolates. Truffles, like mushrooms. They are very exclusive and very expensive. Believe me, the high-class restaurants pay a fortune for them. But it is a delicate operation. They grow where it is shaded and moist under certain trees. They used to get pigs to sniff them out, but that was useless because they ate them. Dogs are the new truffle finders because they don't eat them. You can get a thousand pounds for one single truffle.'

Sheila burst out laughing. 'A thousand pounds for a mushroom, are you joking? So you own a mushroom farm!'

Victoria stopped Sheila. 'She's right. The ones she speaks of are very expensive. I have eaten them in the past. They have an earthy taste of their own.'

Satisfied with Victoria's input, Karen smiled and gave Sheila a sneer.

'What has all of that got to do with us? So you have a mushroom farm,' Patsy echoed Sheila's words, making it sound less than it was. 'Does that mean I am your partner in that too? Because I doubt that very much,' she scoffed.

'I hear you have new friends... violent friends. I have people trying to destroy my farm, setting fire to it and causing mayhem. Trying to steal my business. I have lost a couple of contracts because they have poisoned the truffles and made people ill. The police are all over the place. They want to take it all from me, so I want you and your friends to help me.'

'Why should we protect your *mushrooms*?' asked Patsy. 'I have "friends", but why should I help you? Their work costs money; are you going to pay them?' Feeling in a stronger position, Patsy grinned sarcastically. 'They will do as I tell them, but for a price. You haven't made an offer yet and I am a businesswoman, so if you want my help let's talk business.' Patsy was very matter of fact about it all. 'You were Nick's problem; I don't owe you anything.'

'Yes you do Patsy Diamond. You've got your hands dirty more than once. I know you were money laundering. And I am desperate. I hate to admit it, but I am. These men are trying to steal my farm, my business and my money. You have to help me. Your family owes me, and we are partners, Nick saw to that.'

Sheila cocked her head to one side. 'Aren't there any hit men in Paris? This is ridiculous.' Letting out a deep sigh, Sheila looked down at the floor. 'I'm sure you could find someone closer with your own money lassie.'

Karen shook her head. 'Money is running short and I will do whatever it takes to save my land. Your family owes me,' she shouted. 'Otherwise, I will ruin your reputation and spill my guts to the police about your activities and your friends.'

Patsy felt angry and sick to the stomach. Nick had dropped her in it again. 'What the fuck! No way lady. Don't blackmail me. What happened to you is your problem, not mine.'

'Have you spoken to your daughter today, Patsy?' Karen interrupted.

Looking at her through narrowed eyes, Patsy suddenly felt scared for Nancy's safety. She didn't like the smarmy look on Karen's face. It was obvious she had a secret and what was more, she had the upper hand.

'She and your parents are having a lovely time in my chateau.'

Outraged, Patsy stood up. 'You have kidnapped my daughter and my parents, is that what you're saying?'

'It's not kidnapping if they come willingly. If you want to see them again, then I suggest you come to Paris with your friends. I don't have much time.'

Patsy flew at her like a hellcat and pulled at her hair, kicking and screaming. 'If you touch one hair on my daughter's head, you will be using that grave with your name on, you malicious cow. Where is she?'

Although frightened at Patsy's outburst, Karen still knew she had the upper hand. 'Get off me and I'll give her a call to show you she's safe.' Gathering herself together, she stood up and brushed herself down, panting slightly from the onslaught. She took out her mobile and pressed a number. Instantly a man answered.

'Bring Nancy to the phone to say hello to her mummy,' she ordered. Everyone stood in silence, waiting.

Patsy winced, but took the phone when Karen offered it to her and put it on loud speaker so the others could hear. 'Nancy, is that you? Are you okay?' Patsy asked, trying not to alarm her. She needed to sound in control. The little girl's chirpy voice on the other end of the mobile almost broke her heart and tears brimmed on Patsy's lashes. Trying to hide her distress, she listened as the little girl told her she had been swimming and playing on a big farm. Satisfied, Patsy told her she loved her, then Karen took the mobile off her and ended the call.

'I could have you arrested for kidnap.'

'If you do that, you will never find her, will you? I need your help and I had to do something drastic to get it. Fortunately, your family know my brother well and when they bumped into each other, it was easy to arrange a trip.'

'Who is your brother? How do my parents know him?' Patsy ranted on. Her only thought was for the safety of her daughter. 'You fucking low life. Nick was right, you should have died in that squat that day.'

Karen gave her a smug smile, ignoring her outburst. 'We can leave for Paris tomorrow.'

'Or we can leave tonight, you fucking witch,' Patsy snarled.

'Do you think I'm leaving my daughter in the hands of your kidnappers one more night?'

'It's too late now and once in Paris we have a long drive ahead of us. We will leave tomorrow. She is my bargaining chip. Why would I ruin that?'

Knowing she was beaten, Patsy agreed to her terms; she had no choice. 'Tomorrow it is, although I don't know if I can get any of these friends you mention to come. What do you expect us to do?'

'They will come if you ask them. And something is better than nothing. I want my life back and you want to see little Nancy again, don't you?'

Patsy grimaced, but agreed. 'Tomorrow it is.'

Once Karen had left, Patsy paced the room. Her face was flushed, and she was angry. 'I will kill that bitch.'

Trying to calm the situation, Sheila shook her head. 'You do nothing until she leads us to Nancy and your parents. We need to find out who this famous brother of hers is too. Keep calm Patsy, she is your only hope of seeing Nancy again.'

As the words sank in, Patsy sat on the sofa and buried her head in her hands. Sobs wracked her body. She was helpless. Karen held all the cards and she knew it.

Sheila went into the kitchen to make a cup of tea. She didn't know what else to do and tea cured everything, didn't it? Running back into the lounge, she was panic-stricken. 'Have you heard the news? The radio is on in the kitchen, and they're reporting a shootout. They've given the names and one of them is Spider!' Sheila was in shock and her hands were shaking. Victoria and Patsy sat stunned at the news.

'Put the television on Patsy,' Victoria ordered. 'Let's see if anything is on there.'

Turning on the news channel, they listened as the reporter

told the world about a shootout at a Glasgow nightclub. Pictures of the men came up. Sure enough, they were photos of Spider, Joe and Midge who were all dead. People that were interviewed told the reporter how the three of them had come in with guns and started shooting at people and that it had been a massacre. Numbly, the three women watched the screen without a word said between them.

Suddenly Patsy jumped off the sofa. 'I need to see James and Fin. Surely, they would have come to tell us this. I wonder if they even know,' she pondered.

Banging Maggie's door down a few minutes later, Patsy waited. Eventually Maggie opened it. Cocking her head, she indicated for Patsy to come in. 'You've heard then?'

'James!' Patsy shouted as she ran inside. James was calmly drinking a mug of tea. 'Have you heard? Have you seen the news?'

'Of course I have lassie. We're fucked. They've killed the whole of our team and now it's just me and Fin. What those stupid bastards thought they were doing is anyone's guess.'

'It's unbelievable, James. Why would they walk into an ambush like that? What about Fin, is he okay?'

James's voice was low and calm; it seemed like all the life had been kicked out of him. 'Of course he's not okay. He's frightened and knows he's next. They want rid of us all, and I don't want to point out the obvious but that means you as well. You have been nothing but a thorn in their side. This is turf war, Patsy. So have you got any bright ideas Mrs Diamond?'

Sitting in silence opposite each other, Patsy thought of a million things but nothing seemed appropriate. Then a thought occurred to her. Mentally, she wondered if it would work. It would certainly kill two birds with one stone. 'Actually, I do have an idea,' she started. Seeing James's head shoot up, she moistened her lips. 'I have a little trouble I need to sort out.' She poured out the whole story about Karen kidnapping Nancy.

His jaw dropped; not only did he not know she had a child, but the very fact that she was in Paris being held prisoner astounded him. It was unbelievable. 'That's one hell of a story Mrs Diamond. What about that lawyer bloke? Can he help you?'

'He would involve the police. I can't have that. If we frighten her, god knows what she'll do.' Throwing her hands up in the air, Patsy stood up and walked around the room.

'Was that the blonde woman I saw on your doorstep earlier?' Maggie asked. Patsy nodded. 'Something in the back of my mind tells me I know her. I don't know where from, but she seems familiar.'

'You know her?' Patsy asked. 'She did say that she had lived around here once, years ago, and knew Nick. Maybe she knew Beryl, too? She calls herself Karen Duret. Do you know her, Maggie?'

Shaking her head and shrugging, Maggie said, 'I'm not sure; the name doesn't ring a bell. The only Karen I know around here is that prostitute who overdosed in the squat by the skips, but it can't be her, can it?' Maggie shrugged. 'But she is familiar, I am sure of it. Hopefully, it will come back to me.' Maggie trailed off and went and put the kettle on.

'Let's hope Maggie's memory comes back soon.' If Maggie could remember her name, they would have a trail to follow. Patsy looked at James and got back to the matter at hand. 'Why don't you and Fin come to Paris with me? It gets him out of harm's way, and you, too.'

'Aye lassie, and it also could get a French bullet through our brains. You have no idea what you're facing out there. Whoever wants to take her land seems to be making a good job of it, because she's running scared and has no one to turn to.'

'What's the alternative?' she pleaded. 'An Albanian bullet in your brains. You've seen what's happened to Spider, Beanie and the others. This lot are merciless. Some chance is better than no chance at all.'

Although he didn't like the idea, James agreed it was an option.

'Do you have a passport? Does Fin?' Patsy asked. She didn't want to be pushy, but she needed to know.

'Yes, I do have a passport, although it's still at my wife's house so I'd need to collect it. I don't know about Fin.'

'You don't know what about Fin?' Fin asked as he walked into the room. He didn't seem pleased to see Patsy but wanted to know why they were discussing him. James asked him if he had a passport.

'No,' he said, 'but I know where to get one if I needed one and I don't mean the passport office. Why?'

Impatiently, Patsy looked up. 'How long would that take? When could you get one I mean?'

'Couple of hours I suppose, but it would cost. Nothing like that comes cheap. *Why*?'

'I need you to come to Paris with us. It will get you away from here and there is something I need you to do.'

As bad as Fin felt, he couldn't help laughing. 'There is always something with you, isn't there? You're not helping me, you're helping yourself. Is this some golden opportunity for you that my mates are dead and I am a dead man walking?' Annoyed that Patsy would try and manipulate him when he needed support, he glared at her.

'It gets you away from here, doesn't it? Are you going to sit around waiting for them to come to you then? What other plans do you have up your sleeve?' Patsy snarled through gritted teeth. 'I'm offering you a way out and yes, I do need help.'

James told them both to calm down and filled Fin in on Patsy's dilemma. 'I have contacted a few friends already Fin, who might be able to help you. Mrs Diamond asked me the other day to round up anyone from the Undertaker's crew and any of the Albanians that wish to talk terms.'

Puzzled, Fin looked at Patsy. 'Why do you want to meet the blokes that worked for your husband?'

'It's simple Fin; because I want them to work for me. They know the score; same job, different boss. I have an angle that might just sway them. Blackmail isn't always the best way. If we have them in our corner, our battle with the Albanians is half over and I don't intend working with the very people that killed your friends. They would double cross me and I know it. Maybe some of the people that worked for Nick just want to make a living, be it honest or otherwise. If any of the Albanians come willingly, well, we will think about it, but at least we will get a look at the spies in our camp.'

'That makes sense, but why should anyone work for you Patsy? You're no crime boss.' Fin laughed.

'Oh yes I am Fin, and they had all better get used to it. I will make the Diamond empire bigger and better than Nick ever did. We're going to flood the market with our good stuff and make a fortune, and if Nick's old crew have any sense, they will jump at the chance. I'm going to be as two-faced to the Albanians as they are to me. We will have talks, but I will kill every one of them that harmed your friends and I will take their business from under their noses, including their fucking ice-creams!'

'You really mean business don't you?' Fin asked.

'Yes, I am the head of the Diamond business now. In fact the Queen of the Diamond empire and that lot will quake in their boots when they hear my name. I demand respect from these low lifes, especially if I'm paying them!'

James looked at them both and gave a lopsided grin. 'I have arranged a meeting this afternoon at the community centre. Let's see who comes.' Turning towards Patsy, he wagged his finger in warning. 'Be prepared Mrs Diamond. None of these men had any real loyalty to your husband and they hate you in name already. There will be a lot of animosity. These are rough men who have spent most of their lives in and out of prison. They won't just sit calmly and listen to you. Do you understand?'

Seeing her nod, James felt he had made his point and only time would tell.

11

NETWORKING

'Well, ladies, after all that packing, I need a cup of tea. Any idea when we'll be able to take these few boxes home with us, Patsy? We can't leave the place cluttered up with your new tenants moving in.'

Patsy looked at the pile of boxes without much interest. 'Maybe Maggie would let us store them at her flat. I'll ask her.' Smiling, Patsy held Victoria's hand. 'That's a nice gesture; you're wearing Beryl's wedding rings.'

Blushing slightly, Victoria was going to pull her hand away, but explained she felt it was the right thing to do. What good were they sat in a drawer somewhere? 'She didn't have much jewellery, not her thing. Just her watch and some stud earrings. I've put her jewellery box away. You take what you like.' Suddenly an idea came to Victoria and made her grin. 'It's something to give your daughter and my granddaughter.' Leaning forwards, she hugged Patsy.

Sheila came in bearing mugs of tea. 'This is all very touching ladies, but forget your hugs and your tea, I need some sex.' Sheila blushed. 'If this is our last night of freedom before we fight the Frenchies, I am going home to have the very best Angus can give me.'

'Don't forget your passport,' Patsy warned. 'You'll need it.'

Hesitantly, Sheila cocked her head. 'Are you sure you want me to come?'

'Not if you don't want to. It's up to you. I understand Sheila, I really do. I suppose it's wrong of me to just assume that you'll be at our side. If it's about leaving Sharon and Penny, bring them if you want. Let them see what Paris has to offer.' Patsy smiled. She really wanted Sheila with her and did her best to make it sound like some holiday.

Sheila burst out laughing. 'Are you taking the piss lassie? Take my girls to the French firing squad who want to fight over mushrooms?'

'Well, I would like to go and see my granddaughter. I don't care about anything else.' Victoria seemed to lift everyone's spirits by being so adamant that all they were going to do was go to Paris, collect Nancy and come home.

A thought crossed Patsy mind. 'I have an idea, although it's not brilliant. If you want them to stay around here, we could always ask Maggie to watch the girls.'

Sheila thought about it for a few moments before saying, 'Actually, Patsy lass, that isn't a bad idea. I'm sure Angus could do his shifts around school time and make sure the girls are at school and Maggie could look after them when he is at work,' Sheila said, tapping her fingers on her chin. The more Sheila thought about it, the more she liked the idea. And secretly, she wanted to go to Paris. 'Right, well, I am going to rip off Angus's trousers and you will hear my orgasms from here. You're going to see your bunch of maniacs this afternoon with James and then I suggest you give Larry a call and get your rocks off, too. You could do with a little unwinding. You're tense.' Winking at Victoria, she laughed. 'What about you Vicky lassie? I've seen the way that James looks at you, all puppy eyed. Why don't you have a drink with him? Might do you both good.' She grinned.

'You sly old thing Victoria, I had no idea. Has he said anything to you?' For the first time that day, a genuine smile appeared on Patsy's face.

Victoria blushed to her roots, and emphatically denied anything was going on between her and James. 'Absolutely not! Only a few days ago the man was going back to his wife, or has that slipped your mind?'

Playfully, Sheila nudged her. She was enjoying winding Victoria up. She could see how embarrassed and uncomfortable she felt. Like a schoolgirl caught out about a boy she fancies at school. 'No Victoria, he was going back to his wife so that he could get his hands on his accounts again. He knew it was all over.'

Stubbornly, Victoria stuck out her chin. 'Well, there's nothing between us, so there's no point talking about it.'

Patsy and Sheila watched as Victoria left the room, and winked at each other. Sheila leaned forward and whispered, 'Time to play cupid Patsy.'

* * *

Later that afternoon, after Patsy had telephoned Larry and grovelled, he had agreed to see her, although it hadn't taken much grovelling.

James arrived and, looking at Patsy, he shook his head. 'Go and change. This is a business meeting, not a day at Ascot. Do you still have that black trouser suit you wore at the funeral? Wear that.'

Perplexed, Patsy looked down at herself. She had tried hard

to make a good impression, but, apparently too hard. Taking his advice, she went to change. Looking at herself in the mirror, she could see what he meant. She looked like a feminine woman who was going to dinner. But this was business. Walking back into the lounge, James gave her the thumbs up.

Once in the community centre, they waited. There was no one there and no one seemed to be coming.

'Be patient,' James said. 'These men don't know what to expect either.'

'Did you bring the things?' Patsy asked and nervously watched James tap the holdalls on the floor.

Suddenly the side door opened, and a man peered around it. James beckoned him to come forward. Furtively, the man looked from side to side before sitting down.

'Who's the bitch?' he asked, pointing at Patsy.

Under the table, James put his hand on Patsy's leg and squeezed it to stop her retaliation. 'This is Mrs Diamond. She has a proposition for you.' James turned to Patsy. 'This is Danny Toothpick...'

Patsy looked at the man in front of her and the very sight of him frightened her. Even though he was wearing jeans and a T-shirt, she could see there wasn't a part of his shaved head or arms that weren't tattooed. Patsy felt as though he looked like something out of a circus. Slowly but surely, men of all shapes and sizes filtered through the door. Some were young, some old. The biggest surprise of all was when a woman walked in. Her dyed black hair was shaved on one side of her head; on the other side, it hung to her shoulders. She looked around late forties, Patsy guessed, and she was surprised when a younger woman walked up behind her and held her hand.

'You just got out Bernie. How long this time?' James joked.

'Fuck off Jimmy laddie. Only two years; mistaken fucking

identity.' She smiled. 'Who's the pussy? If you don't want to screw it, I will!' She laughed. The strong Scottish accent made it hard for Patsy to understand, although she caught the gist of it. Blowing Patsy a kiss, Bernie and her partner walked away and sat down in one of the many chairs that had been set out for them.

Patsy's stomach was doing somersaults, but she knew she had to brave this out and not look weak. Although she had practised what she was going to say to these criminals, she now realised it all sounded ridiculous. These people had been around the block so many times and knew every trick in the book and they were probably laughing at her. One man she recognised walked through the door and Patsy half smiled and then stopped herself. He was a man known as Greek Paul, the chef at the community centre.

James spoke to them all in turn, and they laughed and joked with each other like old friends. Mentally Patsy decided she had to gain the same trust that James had with them. It was going to be hard, but she was ready for that. Although she was loath to admit it, she needed them to help her with Nancy. She didn't even know what they could do, but desperate times called for desperate measures. And she would do anything, whatever it took, to keep Nancy safe. Patsy didn't want to think about it now; it made her feel sick knowing that her daughter was in the hands of strangers and she was helpless. Patsy desperately wanted to hold her little girl in her arms again, and smell the lavender scented shampoo Nancy loved to use. Clenching her hands together, Patsy could feel her nails biting into her palms and swallowed hard. She knew she had to get as many of these men and women on side and save her beautiful daughter, and she was determined to do that whatever the cost.

Four swarthy men turned up in very expensive suits, donned

with jewellery. Patsy cast a sideways glance at James.

'Dealers,' he muttered.

Patsy tried her best to get her head around all of this. 'Did Nick know them all?'

'Oh yes.' James nodded. 'And he blackmailed them all. They've come to listen to what you have to say out of courtesy to me, that's all, and to see what is in it for them.' He grinned.

Standing up, James felt now was the time to get the meeting started. 'Ladies and gentlemen, we all know why we're here. The Albanians are flooding the market with whatever crap they can get their hands on. Three of our mutual colleagues have been murdered and we are now in a turf war. This is Mrs Diamond.'

Sat there with their arms folded and their legs crossed, they muttered and almost heckled Patsy. Their sneering looks annoyed her. It was time to have her say.

'Right, everyone, I believe James has told you most of the story. Now it's my turn,' she began.

'What the fuck do you want lady?' one man shouted from the back of the room.

Feeling braver than she felt, Patsy looked towards the back of the room to see where the voice was coming from. 'If you don't want to hear what I have to say then you can fuck off,' she shouted, much to the surprise of everyone in the room.

James looked down at the table. This wasn't a good start to the meeting, but Patsy could see that she had sparked interest.

'If no one is interested in what I have to say, then leave, but first I have something for you all.' Turning to James, she nodded. Sitting down, Patsy lit a cigarette and turned her head away nonchalantly. None of them knew what to expect as they saw James unzip the holdall.

Inside the bag was a bunch of envelopes with names on the front.

'Mackie,' James shouted out, 'come over here.' Everyone looked around the room as Mackie stood up and walked towards James and Patsy. 'Mrs Diamond feels this belongs to you. She inherited them from her husband.'

Puzzled, Mackie opened the envelope and inside was a SIM card. Blankly, he looked at James, who laughed. 'Well, it's not severance pay, but on that is a confession you once told your lawyer, otherwise known as the Undertaker.'

For a brief moment the man stood staring at James and Patsy and his face drained of colour. He knew what was on that confession and he also realised so did James and Patsy. Mackie had given the names of his associates after a bank job to reduce his sentence. James and Mackie both knew that if any of the men in this room knew that, he would be killed.

James called out another name and another. Each in turn they came forward and opened their envelopes containing a SIM card.

'Are there any copies Diamond lady?' asked the woman Patsy had seen earlier.

'Not as far as I know. Well, I don't have them anyway, but who knows?' Patsy shrugged.

'Why are you doing this? What do you hope to achieve? Do you think we're all going to slap you on the back and have a party? Where did you even get them from?' The woman was full of questions, and seemed to be the spokesperson for the rest of the group.

Pausing to gather her thoughts, Patsy glanced at James who was still busy sorting through the envelopes and handing them out, then she looked back at the woman. 'Those SIM cards were from my husband's office,' she replied. 'They are yours. Each and every one of them has you introducing yourselves by full name and date of birth.'

Patsy could see some of the men in the room were uncomfortable and were wringing their hands, waiting for their name to be called out. Each one desperately wanted the recording Nick had made of their confession. This was how he had blackmailed them to do his bidding for years. Each one of them had committed a crime and confessed to their trusted lawyer, Nick, who just happened to have recorded all of these confessions on his mobile. And they had told him the truth in the hope he would get them off going to prison or at least get them a lighter sentence. Even Patsy knew what happened to a grass – it was sure death.

The Scottish woman tore a piece of the envelope and lit it with her lighter and put it in the ashtray. On top of it she put the SIM card and watched the plastic burn. Satisfied, she beckoned to her partner. 'We're leaving.'

'What are you doing for a living now that you're out of prison?' Patsy shouted to their backs.

They both turned their heads towards Patsy and glared hatefully at her. 'We're getting by, don't you worry.'

'Is that enough? To get by?' Patsy's sarcastic voice boomed in the direction of the women. 'Will you be working for the Albanians? Will they make it worth your while, or will they sell you down the river and betray you when things go wrong? How long will it be before you're back in prison?'

The burly woman walked up to Patsy while all of the men in the room looked on. 'You got five minutes lady. Whatever it is you have to say, get on with it.' Clenching her huge fist and punching the palm of her other hand, she coldly stared at Patsy.

Standing up to meet her eyes, Patsy moistened her lips. 'Don't try and intimidate me, whatever your name is. I don't need your five minutes; go and use them elsewhere. What I do have is a proposal. And jobs for you all. I intend taking over my husband's little drug ring, but I want people to work with me because they want to, I don't want to use blackmail and hate. Some of the jobs will be legitimate. I presume some of you have probation officers? Don't they want to know how you are doing on the outside? I can provide that, but I want employees I can trust, not people who hate me.'

Hearing her speech, the Scottish woman and her friend took their seats again. Everyone was now intrigued by Patsy's offer.

'Look, Mrs Diamond,' a younger man shouted. 'It's okay you sitting there in your designer blouse, but what do you know about us? You have no fucking idea what it's like to wonder where you're going to sleep tonight or if you'll eat. You live on another planet. We've all made money in the past and we have all served our sentences for it. You have no idea what it is like to scratch your arse for a living while constantly being a suspect to the police.'

Patsy fully understood their reluctance. This young man reminded her of Fin and his friends. 'You're right Mr...' Patsy waited for him to introduce himself.

Sitting there with his legs crossed and full of self-importance, he said, 'I'm Harry Meatballs. I'm a hacker, not a drug dealer. You give me a computer Mrs Diamond and I have the key to the world. Social media is a crime ring of its own.'

Patsy liked his frankness. He was young, bolshy and clearly took pride in what he did. 'Well, it's nice to meet you.' Patsy smiled. 'I understand that you all think I am playing at gangsters, but rest assured I mean business and I'm prepared to learn. So now, I will lay my cards on the table; if you don't like it, leave.' Patsy waited for them to stand up and leave, but surprisingly they didn't.

'Firstly, we have drugs to sell if anyone is interested. And yes' – Patsy turned her heads to the dealers – 'we do have samples.'

James had schooled her earlier on the way to the community centre that they would want samples of what they were selling and that they should take some with them to the meeting. The dealers stepped forward and waited for James to unzip another bag. They were amazed when they saw it was full of blocks of cocaine covered in cellophane.

Without a word spoken, one of them took a pen knife out of his pocket and stabbed the packet, making a small dent. With the end of his knife he scooped a little out and held it to his nose and sniffed. His eyes watered and he shook his head, laughing. 'Fuck that is good. It stings like hell. Lady that is the real thing; it's never been cut.' Wiping the excess powder from his nose, he grinned at his friends and nodded.

'What else you got in the bag lady?' another one of them asked.

James answered their question. 'We haven't done a stock take, but there is a variety of meth, uppers and downers and of course heroin. You name it, we can provide it... at a price of course,' James emphasised.

Narrowing his eyes at James, the dealer turned to his friends and nodded. 'We will talk later James.' Then he turned to Patsy. His hand was heavily donned in gold rings and he held it out to her to shake hers. While she shook it, he gripped it hard. 'Don't fucking cross me lady, and yes that is a warning. I will put your severed head on a spike.'

Patsy nodded. For the first time, she noticed the crazy faraway look in his eyes. Her mouth felt dry, and she swallowed hard to moisten it, as they walked away and took their seats again. James nudged her with his elbow to bring her back to reality and resume her conversation. Snapping out of it, she carried on. 'I will be closing all of the pizza parlours and this community centre for refurbishment.' Now she got to the point she needed to. 'I have been in talks with someone who has been having trouble in Paris. It seems they need protection. They have been having trouble on their land over black truffles, which are worth a lot of money. Someone is trying to infiltrate their business and is making life hard for them. You would need passports for Paris and of course all expenses would be paid. If you're interested, let myself or James know. We leave tomorrow morning.' Secretly crossing her fingers, Patsy hoped someone would want to come with them. She didn't mention she was emotionally involved. This had to sound like business.

'Protection?' another man shouted. 'That's Freddie's business. He and his many cousins sort that out.' They all looked around to see if Freddie was there, but he wasn't, much to Patsy's disappointment. Inwardly sighing, she looked around for any more volunteers.

'Truffles?' Greek Paul shouted excitedly. 'You mean the proper ones that restaurants use?' His face beamed and he was almost licking his lips.

James nodded and smiled. Turning towards Patsy, he explained that Paul was a qualified chef.

'Yeah, and he's also fucking insane,' the Scottish woman said, causing everyone to laugh and lightening the mood slightly.

'Okay, let's wind this up. If any of you are interested in the Paris operation, or you want to ask Freddie to join us, be our guest, but we leave tomorrow. You have a few hours only to decide.' Turning towards the dealers, James addressed them. 'If you would like to stay behind, we can discuss things further.' Addressing everyone else in the room again, James continued. 'There is work if you want it, but it's up to you. Mrs Diamond is in charge of things. I am the operations manager; come to me if you want anything. Fin will handle sales and distribution.'

'We have our own distributors James; why would we need that loud mouth Fin?'

'Because he is part of the deal. He knows the nightclubs and we come as a package. No Fin, no deal.' James waited as the four men spoke to each other and nodded.

'We will allow him to sell his own stuff, but we want 30 per cent of his takings.'

James nodded. 'That sounds reasonable.'

Patsy lit another cigarette. She felt like a chain smoker, but needed something to calm her nerves as James walked over to the four dealers. Everyone was leaving now. Straining her ears, she could hear that James was bartering with the dealers over the price of the cocaine. It all looked very heated and she decided to leave James to it, until he called her over. 'Mrs Diamond, Angel and his friends here are offering two million for the bag we have with us. There are four blocks of cocaine in there and an assortment of other things. Would you accept that in good faith?' James's eyes bore into her, almost pleading with her to accept.

Stunned at the price and trying to hide it, Patsy held out her hand. 'Gentlemen, you have a deal.' She smiled.

Angel, who seemed to be the spokesman, took out his mobile phone and turning his back for privacy, started talking. Within minutes, a man came walking through the door with a holdall and put it down beside Angel.

The man unzipped the bag and inside were rolls of bills held together by elastic bands. Angel kicked the bag towards her and told the man to collect the other bag containing the drugs.

'See you next week Mrs Diamond,' they shouted as they were about to leave.

'You forget Angel,' Patsy began, 'I will be in Paris.'

'Just make sure you deliver on time. Don't let me down now,' he shouted as they disappeared through the exit.

Worried and confused, Patsy looked at James. 'We might not be back next week, and that man is going to put my head on a spike. And how the hell did he have that kind of money outside with his driver?'

'They are dealers Patsy. Believe me, there would have been a lot more money in that car. And anyone can drop a bag of drugs off Patsy. We will sort it. Stop panicking and count your spoils. They are prepared to do business with you, which will seriously fuck the Albanians up. Their imports are worthless now and that will cause a war in itself.'

Looking down at the bag, Patsy realised her fatal mistake. 'Fin was right wasn't he? He said we were sitting on a gold mine, and I was dragging my feet. I'm sorry James.' She frowned. 'And what about this war?'

James laughed loudly. 'Believe me Patsy, those guys have enough guns and street soldiers to silence anyone if they think they have a better supplier. Better goods make better money. They can put their prices up. We're the suppliers, the rest is their problem. Come on, I could do with a drink.'

Locking up the community centre, Patsy had an idea. 'Talking of drinks James, have you thought about asking Victoria out for one? Me and Sheila have plans for tonight and she'll be on her own.'

James blushed slightly. 'Now that is seriously punching above my weight Patsy. No man likes rejection and I have had enough to last a lifetime.'

'It was only an idea, but, if you don't ask you don't get, and I think she would like it,' she prompted.

Saying nothing, they walked together, but Patsy could see that she had planted an idea into James's head and hoped he would act upon it.

12

NEW FRIENDS

Patsy's mobile was ringing and, waving at James, she took the call and walked in the opposite direction. She could hear Sheila's distraught voice.

'I walked in from the shops to a burglar. It was bloody scary. As I came down the path, I noticed the front door was ajar. I thought it might have been the girls playing out or something. When I walked in there was a man in his twenties, obviously drugged up to the eyeballs, rifling through my kitchen. I asked him what the fuck he was doing here; god knows why I said that Patsy, what a stupid thing to say. It was clear why he was there, wasn't it. He was burgling my fucking house!'

'Sheila, are you all right?' Patsy interrupted. 'Are the girls okay? Where's Angus?'

Sheila tried laughing it off. 'I confronted him Patsy, bloody stupid really, he could have had a knife. He could have had a mate upstairs. You say stupid things when you're in that position, don't you?'

Patsy wanted to know what happened next.

'I saw that he had the spare door keys in his hand, which

meant the bastard obviously intended coming back! I punched him in the face and when he staggered back, I grabbed hold of his hoodie and dragged him to the front door and threw him out. He didn't get the chance to steal anything; I think I caught him just in time, although I don't have anything worth pinching. My window is broken, but the council will sort that out. Angus is on his way. Thank god the girls weren't in Patsy, it would have terrified them.' Patsy heard the choke in Sheila's voice. 'Do you think it's got anything to do with that gang stuff? They know we're friends...' Sheila trailed off.

'No Sheila, it sounds like some drugged up opportunist. He was no professional by the sounds of it and he definitely was no hit man. Do you want me to come over?' A cold feeling washed over Patsy. She couldn't be sure this had nothing to do with her.

'Nah lassie, the police are on their way, although there is nothing they can do, is there? Nothing has been taken and I'm okay, although when I think about it now, he could have pulled a knife on me or anything. It never crossed my mind at the time.'

'Sheila, I'm on my way. Sit tight and lock the doors until the police get there.'

Patsy ran indoors to tell Victoria what had happened. Instantly Victoria picked up her jacket. 'I'm coming with you; god knows she would come to our rescue.'

When they arrived an hour later, the police were there and Patsy could tell that Sheila was relieved to see her.

'Patsy, have you seen this?' Sheila opened Facebook on her mobile phone. It seemed Sheila's burglar had been travelling around from street to street looking for empty houses. One of the neighbours had CCTV and had caught him on camera and posted it all over social media. Other people were commenting that they had seen him in the area and he had tried door handles and been chased off. The police went about their business and walked down the street, knocking door to door to see if anyone else had seen or heard anything.

Sitting beside her, Patsy put her arm around her shoulders. 'They are definitely going to catch him now love. The main thing is, you're okay and he didn't get away with anything. Maybe it's time you took up my offer Sheila and took the money from the sale of my house to buy something in a better area with more security.'

'Are there better areas Patsy? I didn't think poor people bothered robbing poor people's houses. They always go to the posh houses where they know there will be something to steal.'

Smiling, Patsy could see the logic in that; the better the area the bigger the spoils. 'Take the offer Sheila, let's buy you something nice. Your home has been violated and you're supposed to feel safe in your own home. I feel the same way about my London flat after that guy nearly killed me in there.'

Sheila looked up at Patsy and nodded. 'Maybe you're right Patsy, thank you.'

Suddenly, Angus barged through the doors, his face full of concern and panic. 'Sheila lassie, oh my god, are you okay?' Almost lifting her off her feet, he hugged her.

'I will be when you stop squeezing me to death,' she protested, but smiled and kissed him. Then she looked at Patsy and Victoria while Angus described what he would do if he ever got his hands on Sheila's intruder.

'Why don't you and the girls come away for a few days? I'm going to Paris. I'm sure Angus wouldn't mind.' Raising one eyebrow, she gave a little grin. It was the perfect opportunity to suggest a break away. Angus instantly agreed it would be good for Sheila and encouraged her to go.

Sheila gave her a knowing look, shaking her head in disbelief. 'That's a nice idea Patsy. Thank you. But I couldn't take the girls out of school,' she muttered. As Patsy predicted, Angus assured Sheila that he would look after the girls. Everything had slotted into place perfectly and Sheila could leave Angus without too much explanation.

Satisfied, Patsy hugged Sheila. 'Don't forget your passport love.' Knowing Sheila was safe with Angus, she beckoned to Victoria. It was time for them to leave.

* * *

No sooner had Patsy got back to the estate than she saw James stood on the balcony, waving at her to catch her attention. Patsy's face dropped. What a bloody day it had been. She hadn't had time to catch her breath.

Patsy and Victoria entered Maggie's flat. 'What's wrong James?'

Without saying a word, James pointed into the lounge. Her eyes followed the noisy chatter and curiously she walked over to the door. There were six men lounging around in poor Maggie's flat like they owned the place.

'This is Mrs Diamond,' James introduced her. Even though these men were not burly or brutish looking, they had an aura about them that made their very presence frightening.

'Diamond, pearl, who cares? Names don't interest me,' said an older man. He was very flippant in his manner. 'You need a job doing I believe. What do you want?'

Slightly confused, Patsy looked at James.

'This is Freddie. He deals in security.'

Patsy nervously sat on the edge of the sofa opposite. Freddie had grey, greasy hair slicked back in a ponytail. The butt end of a roll up cigarette was perched on his lower lip. He wore a denim waistcoat, which had obviously been cut from a jacket, and nothing underneath it. His jeans had seen better days and as she looked down she could see he was wearing army boots. Looking around at his friends, she noticed they were dressed likewise. They all had the usual tattoos which Patsy was now becoming accustomed to seeing in the criminal world. All in all, they looked like a bunch of rough hooligans, and they put Patsy's teeth on edge. As she looked up at Maggie, she could sense her uneasiness, too.

Moistening her lips and swallowing hard, Patsy stammered through her story of being offered a security contract in Paris. James had insisted she say nothing about this being a mission of mercy for her daughter, well, not yet anyway. Looking at her through his thickset brows, Freddie listened to her and he looked almost bored. After a while, Freddie spoke.

'Are you paying us James?' he enquired.

'No, this is Mrs Diamond's job,' James answered politely. 'I'm just the middle man.'

Smacking his lips together, Freddie looked around at his friends. 'Well James, I only speak to the organ grinder and not her monkey. He who pays the piper and all, no offence.'

Freddie interrogated Patsy some more about the why and where. She admitted she had no address yet, because she hadn't agreed to anything. This was all enquiries, but if they were interested they were all to leave tomorrow, she explained.

'No fucking way.' Freddie laughed and nudged one of his friends who grinned at him. 'Who else is going on this mystery tour to Paris?'

'Victoria and my friend Sheila. We are business partners.'

Freddie raised his eyebrows and pouted somewhat. Then without warning, he spat at Maggie's fireplace. Patsy was disgusted but said nothing. 'Sorry Lady Diamond, but sometimes the tobacco gets stuck in my teeth when I chew it. Got to spit. Okay, let's talk money, because there's more out there than a few mushrooms lady. Now why don't you tell me the truth and we will talk properly. Let's cut the bullshit. Be damned straight with me or we walk!' He banged his fist on the arm of the chair.

Pondering slightly, Patsy felt it was time to be honest, because if he found out after they arrived, he would possibly put a bullet between her eyes. So she poured out the whole story about Nancy and why Karen had kidnapped her in exchange for protection from her friends. This time, Freddie seemed to relax.

'What do you think boys, do you feel like a shoot up in Paris?' He smirked. All of his friends nodded and grinned. 'Now Lady Diamond. No one travels together. We all take separate flights. You going with the girls is okay, but James, you travel alone; it looks less suspicious. You pay all expenses, and me and the boys here want you to rent some cabin or something for us nearby. We like our own space and we like it stocked up, if you get my meaning.' Picking up a bottle of beer, he waved it in the air. 'If we agree to this and I get my payment in advance and in full, even if you die in the process, we continue until the job is done. There is no mind changing, we have agreed on a deal and that is the end of it, just so you're sure. You want us to rescue, murder and protect. That's one hell of a mission you have set yourself Lady Diamond.'

'Well' – Patsy smiled nervously – 'I never mentioned murder, did I?' Wringing her hands, she waited for an answer.

Freddie and the rest of his gang sat up straight and burst out laughing. 'You sure fucking did, Lady Diamond. How do we protect and save your kid without killing someone? I reckon we're talking around two million plus expenses. We will keep you safe and bring your little girl home. I swear to that.' Freddie held his hand up as though swearing an oath in court. 'What you're talking about is war Lady Diamond and with a war there are always casualties, possibly even one of us, but we're used to it.'

Darting her eyes around the room at James, Maggie and Victoria, Patsy felt uneasy. She was being pushed into a decision. She knew she had no choice; this could save her baby and she would donate an arm and a leg or both if it meant seeing her little Nancy again. She had to trust them, there was no one else.

'Do you have the money Lady Diamond?' Freddie asked slowly. He was in no mood for playing games.

Emotions swam around in her brain. This gang was her only hope of getting Nancy back. They were brutal, that was for sure, but they seemed professional she supposed, whatever a professional looked like. They could take her money and run, but they were her only lifeline. 'Yes, I have the money, but I want to leave tomorrow; I haven't time to hire you a cabin or something. I presumed you would want a hotel.'

Again, they all burst out laughing. 'Now what the fuck would we be doing in a hotel when you're on a farm somewhere in the middle of nowhere. We don't want to check in anywhere and leave a paper trail. If you agree, just give us the address and we will sort it. We come the day after you.' Freddie had full authority now and was dictating his terms. 'We want our money transferred to this account.' Freddie rummaged through his jeans pocket and gave her a piece of paper. 'You get more interest on those Swiss accounts Lady Diamond.'

Feeling on firmer ground, Patsy couldn't help herself. This Freddie had played with her long enough. 'Don't call me Lady Diamond. This is not a joke, it's business. You can call me Patsy or Mrs Diamond, I don't mind either. But don't mock me.'

Nodding to Patsy, he agreed. 'Fair play Patsy, you do have balls after all. We'll also need twenty mobile phones; we'll get them and bill you for them. Obviously, there are no receipts so you just have to take my word for it.'

'Why twenty?' Patsy was now curious, but she was impressed by Freddie's professionalism. She had to admit, he seemed in charge of the situation already.

'No trace or tracking. After a couple of calls, we get rid of them. I suggest you do the same. We will stay in contact, don't worry; we will find you. Don't even bother looking for us.' Freddie sat back, crossing his arms.

Puzzled, Patsy looked at him and then the others, not knowing exactly what he was waiting for.

'Make the payment Patsy,' he prompted, 'and add another 50,000 for expenses.'

Patsy took out her mobile and started transferring the money to Freddie's account. She felt uneasy about this and wondered if she would ever see him again now the money had gone through. She had to confirm the payment because of the amount, but as soon as Freddie saw the payment go in he seemed satisfied. Urging his friends to stand up, he reached out his hand to Patsy. 'Nice doing business with you. Safe journey.' As he led the way, all of his friends trailed behind him without a care in the world.

Maggie swiftly shut the door behind them and let out a deep sigh. Holding her hand to her heart, she started to breathe heavily and after sitting down for a few minutes her breathing became normal again.

'Do you think we will ever see them again?' Patsy asked. She felt she had made a blunder giving over two million away to a bunch of strangers.

'They are a rough bunch, but you will get your money's worth. He's a businessman believe it or not. As he said earlier, once it's taken on there is no turning back.' He looked at Maggie.

'Sorry about the mess, Maggie, I didn't know he was just going to turn up out of the blue like that. I'll help you clean things up.'

'Don't worry James; I've known worse,' Maggie scoffed.

James looked Patsy directly in the eye. 'Freddie's reputation is built on trust. If anyone ever found out he hadn't carried a job out he'd be finished and his name wouldn't be worth anything.' James shrugged. 'It's a done deal now, Patsy. No turning back. I suggest you book the other tickets and like Freddie said, different airlines and different times. Oh, and use different credit cards or pay for them in cash.' For a few moments they all sat in silence, not knowing what to say and letting the events sink in. It was the second deal Patsy had made that day.

Strangely, a warm feeling swept over Patsy's body. She liked the feeling of control and power it gave her, being the boss lady. It excited her in a strange way she couldn't explain, even to herself.

'Right everyone, let's get started. James, go and buy yours and Fin's ticket to Paris in cash. I'll pay for mine, Victoria's and Sheila's. That just looks like a girlie trip to Paris. Maggie, I believe Sheila would like you to help with the girls while she is away. Angus will be working and maybe you could lend a hand. Of course, you will be paid, I can't keep taking advantage of you.' Patsy walked towards Maggie and put her arms around her. 'Let's start again Maggie. You are part of us. I am sorry.'

'Beryl would have liked that.' Maggie smiled and let go of Patsy. It was a genuine hug between friends who had depended upon each other every step of the way without realising it. 'Of course, I will take care of Sharon and Penny, and it's not about money, Patsy. It's about friendship.' Moving closer to Patsy, Maggie whispered, 'Look after Fin for me; he's an idiot but he's family.'

This sentiment made Patsy smile. She turned towards James and saw he was holding a bag.

'This is what I owe you Patsy. This is the amount you gave me when I first got here. Now we're even.' James kicked the bag towards her.

Puzzled, Patsy looked down at the bag and back at James. 'Are you bailing on me?'

'That's up to you. You have your contacts now. You've rented the flat, you've got your dealers and you have the wild bunch going to Paris. I need to move on.'

Panic rose in Patsy; she couldn't believe James was deserting her. 'Move on to what? I thought we were partners in all of this.'

'If that's the case Patsy, then take the money. That makes us even. Except for one last favour...'

Patsy frowned.

'My wife,' he began, 'and her new boyfriend have made a mockery of me.'

Patsy was surprised to hear the bitterness in James's voice. He had always acted so calmly, but whatever his problem was it had hurt him to the very core.

His eyes met Patsy's. 'My wife has sold my flat in London and that bastard is living off the spoils of my ill-gotten gains she complains so much about. I haven't been the best husband,' he confessed. 'I've been in and out of prison most of my life, which is how I know most of those people we met today. But I need to get my own revenge. I need to make that man suffer. He made me leave my own home. What is more humiliating than that? Talking of the people we met today' – James leaned closer to Patsy's ear – 'I know you've made copies of those recordings, haven't you? I'm no fool, just don't let them find out,' he warned.

Patsy blushed so much her face burned. She had indeed

taken a leaf out of Nick's book and given herself some insurance should they turn against her.

'Come to Paris with me, James. Help me. I'll help you sort out your family problems. That is what partners do, they help each other.'

'I don't want my wife hurt. I don't hurt women, that's not my thing. It's him, laughing at me the way he did, knowing I couldn't fight back.' His voice was low and almost sad. It was obviously eating him up and had taken his male pride away.

'We'll sort it, James. Maybe not today, but we will sort it. Come to Paris, take some time away from this place. Please don't leave us now, when we need you the most. I need to get my daughter back and preferably alive without Rambo and his mates storming in there with all guns blazing.' As an afterthought, she added, 'We all need some time out. Why don't you take Victoria out for a drink tonight? I'm sure she'll agree; trust me.' Patsy had dangled the carrot she knew he secretly wanted.

'I'll come to Paris with you Patsy and we are partners. Take the money. I had better go and see how Fin is getting on and sort out our flights.' James clapped his hands and smiled. 'You're the very devil Patsy Diamond and I am glad I am on your side. If there was an apocalypse, you would be the only survivor... I swear it.' He laughed and walked out of the door.

13

PARIS

Patsy's lips met Larry's again. Their sex had been feisty and passionate and now fully satiated, she lay in his arms and kissed him. Reaching out for her cigarettes from the bedside table, she lit one and inhaled deeply. 'Larry darling, I'm leaving for Paris tomorrow. I have to go there if I want to get Nancy back.'

Larry sat upright in bed. 'What do you mean, if you want to get Nancy back?'

Patsy mentally went through what she was going to tell Larry, leaving out the parts he didn't need to know. Slowly, she filled him in on Karen's kidnapping of Nancy and her parents on the condition that she go to Paris to help her for something or other. 'She probably needs money Larry, to fix up some shithole she's bought. It's a game, but I have to go... You see that, don't you?' Patsy bit her bottom lip and paused.

'No, I don't see that. We're going to call the police and have that woman arrested! She's luring you out there.' Turning towards her, he rested on his elbow and looked at her. 'You can't do her bidding Patsy. God knows what could happen to you.'

His genuine concern touched Patsy and made her feel guilty

about lying to him. 'We can't call the police Larry. Nancy is in Paris somewhere and I don't even know where. If that bitch thinks we're going to have her arrested, she could kill my family. For now, I have to go along with her and her crazy plans. I need to find out where Nancy is first.' Without realising it, tears fell down Patsy cheeks. For the first time, she let her emotions take over. She always had to be strong and in charge, but with Larry it was different. He understood her and took care of her in his own way.

Larry brushed away her tears with his hand and then kissed her cheeks. 'I understand Patsy, but this kind of thing has to be reported. Anything could happen to you if you go to Paris. I think maybe I should come with you.'

'No!' Patsy shouted in panic. That was the last thing she wanted. 'No, Larry, I need you here.' Sitting upright, she stubbed the cigarette out in the ashtray and tried her best to think on her feet. She hadn't expected this. 'You are the only person who will know where I am, and I will tell you as soon as I get there. I need you on the outside looking in, not with me where you can do nothing if that bitch turns on us both. I need you to be strong for me and help me from this side of the Channel. To start with, I need to know more about her. Have you come up with anything yet?' she questioned, trying to change the subject. 'Do you know who her brother is?'

'It's taking time, but we're looking into it. She's covered her tracks well, but I guarantee if it's the last thing I do I will get to the bottom of this my love. And Patsy, you are my love.' Gently, he kissed her, and a wave of emotion washed over her. She had feelings for Larry that she wanted to bury deep inside her, but each time she lay in his arms her heart ruled her head. She liked Larry more than she dared admit, even to herself. He was handsome, caring and an excellent lover who knew his way around a kitchen. What more could any woman want?

'Swear to me that you will keep in phone contact while you're there. Take photos of the area you're staying, which will make it easier to recognise if I need to. Signs, landmarks, anything to help me find you if I need to.'

A smiled crossed Patsy's face. 'I promise Larry, cross my heart.' Patsy made the sign of the cross on her chest. 'I'm leaving tomorrow. The longer I hang around here, the longer my daughter and parents are out there somewhere in danger.'

Larry couldn't believe his ears. 'You're leaving tomorrow? So you've already made your plans and you're telling me after the fact. This is not a discussion Patsy. Christ, you probably have your ticket in your handbag.' Larry jumped out of bed and promptly started getting dressed. 'So was that what the sex was about? Soften Larry up before you tell me you're pissing off and dumping me again?' Larry shook his head in disbelief. 'I always fall for it, don't I? Here I am worried and concerned about your welfare and you have already made your mind up.'

'No, wait. I meant what I said. Yes, of course I have made my mind up. Wouldn't you if it was your son someone had had hidden away somewhere? I need you here, Larry. I need to be able to contact you and for you to keep me safe from afar, while you're digging up whatever information you can on that bitch. I need you to work with me, not against me.'

It seemed mentioning Larry's son had struck a chord. Half-dressed, he sat on the edge of the bed and reached out for her hand and squeezed it. 'I suppose I should be grateful you haven't already left and at least came to see me tonight. You need to find your daughter and I will be your man on the ground, so to speak. But keep in contact with me regularly Patsy. I don't know what I would do if I lost you. I'm not going to say it Patsy, because I know you don't want to hear it, but you know how I feel.' The tenderness in his voice made her swallow hard.

'I have strong feelings for you too Larry, but I can't commit to anything right now. My head is not in the right place. You know how I feel about you; can't you feel it in my kisses and the way I hold you?' Patsy moved closer to Larry and stroked his hair. An overwhelming feeling of desire washed over her. Grabbing his hair tightly, she pulled his head back and kissed him ardently, while pushing him backwards onto the bed. This time she was in charge, she was the dominant one and by god, for her last night of freedom she was going to damn well enjoy it!

* * *

As they approached Charles de Gaulle airport, Patsy's stomach was in knots.

Sheila seemed excited as she looked out of the window. 'Ochs lassies, this is great; it's like going on holiday.'

Victoria smiled and patted her hand. 'Paris is a beautiful place Sheila, and full of romance and passion; wouldn't you say so Patsy?'

'It is Victoria, but it's also full of kidnappers and extortionists!' she snapped.

Victoria nudged her. 'Keep calm Patsy, people can hear.'

Sheila instantly picked up on the tense body language between Patsy and Victoria. 'Hey Vicky lassie, how did your night of passion go with James? Did he stick his tongue down your throat?'

Instantly, smiles appeared on Patsy's and Victoria's faces. 'No Sheila. We had a very nice evening in a nearby wine bar. Personally, I didn't even realise there were any wine bars around there.

Then we went to a nearby Indian restaurant. James is very good company.'

'Yes, yes Vicky, but what we want to know is, is there a smouldering hot bed of passion lying beneath that cool exterior?' Sheila eagerly waited for Victoria to spill the beans but was quickly deflated when Victoria shook her head.

'It was just two friends enjoying a drink and a meal. Then he walked me home. He's a gentleman; none of that tomfoolery.'

Sheila burst out laughing. 'Walked you home? He lives across the other side of the balcony. I take it you didn't invite him in for coffee?' Sheila gave a shiver and grimaced. 'I suppose you couldn't shag him in your mother-in-law's house, and I suppose you couldn't go to his with Maggie the watchdog sitting there with her arms folded, glaring at you. Well, maybe you'll bump into him somewhere romantic.' She winked.

After landing, they picked up their suitcases, which included Sheila's hurriedly bought zebra print one. As they walked outside, there was a car waiting for them. Nervously, they watched the driver put their bags in the boot of the car and then got inside. They didn't know what the driver knew, if anything.

'Where are we heading?' Patsy asked innocently.

'My instructions are simply to drop you off,' was all he said. It was clear to all of them he had been instructed to say nothing else, so there was no point in pushing the point any further.

Sheila patted Patsy's arm. 'We'll find out soon enough lassie. All this cloak and dagger stuff is getting on my nerves. Let's look for that Eiffel Tower place before we go to Chateau Duret. And you' – Sheila tapped the driver on the shoulder – 'I know you can understand every fucking word I say, but I don't give a fuck. I'm going to smoke in your car. Don't try stopping me baldie or I will stub it out on your head – got it?'

Sheila lit three cigarettes and Patsy laughed as the chauffeur coughed and opened the window, but not for one moment did he tell Sheila she couldn't smoke in his car!

Victoria took one cigarette and nudging Patsy, she laughed. She was glad Sheila was there; she always seemed to ease the tension.

After a short while, the driver stopped outside a train station and promptly got out. Making his way to the boot of the car, he took out their suitcases and handed them three train tickets. 'Platform three; it leaves in fifteen minutes.'

Puzzled, Patsy looked at the tickets. 'These are train tickets to Brittany.' She handed over the tickets to Victoria to check. 'I thought we would be staying in Paris. What about Nancy?'

'Sounds like a fucking paper trail to me Patsy. This is to throw whoever knows where we are off the trail. My god this is real James Bond shit. Oh well, let's go and see what's there, possibly another fucking train to Moscow. We have fifteen minutes; let's grab a shitty coffee and an overpriced sandwich.' Sheila marched forward, wheeling her suitcase behind her.

A worried frown crossed Victoria's brow. 'How will James and Fin find us? They think we're in Paris. Brittany is an hour and a half away by train.'

A grin appeared on Patsy's face. 'That is why we have trackers on our phones Victoria. They will know exactly where we are. This is the twenty-first century and big brother is always watching.' Patsy paused, pondering. 'What did Karen call that company of hers again?'

Victoria rolled her eyes to the ceiling. 'I know I am an old woman, but you're dragging me kicking and screaming into this tech world. Black Diamonds, that's what she said it was called.'

Patsy nodded, remembering what Karen had said about her expensive truffle farm. Surely there would be evidence of the company online. Larry had said there was no trace of Karen, but maybe they were looking in the wrong place. Black Diamond truffles is where they needed to look first. 'Come on, before Sheila picks the best sandwiches for herself.'

The train journey was short and scenic, and as soon as they got off the train, Karen was waiting for them by a car. You could cut through the tension with a knife, and no one spoke as they climbed into the vehicle. Eventually, after rows of green fields, they turned into a large drive with a huge manor house. Confused, Patsy looked out of the window as the house loomed towards them. 'Is this yours?'

'*Oui* Patsy, this is my home and farm.' Karen smiled smugly, knowing she had impressed them all. Her ego and pride doubled as she saw the astonished looks on their faces. 'I will give you a tour of the land first; I am sure you will find it interesting.'

'No, you won't,' Patsy warned. 'First, you will show me my daughter and parents. We have followed your little plan and you have had your fun. Now I want to see my daughter.' As the car stopped, Patsy got out and strode to the front of the house and waited for Karen and the others to catch up.

'Your side of the bargain isn't finished yet Patsy. I have asked you to get some of your newfound friends to help me save all of this.' Karen waved her arm in the air and towards the house. 'Where are they?'

'Do you really think I would let my friends walk into the unknown? What other traps do you have in mind Karen. Don't take me for a fool. Where is Nancy?'

Angrily, Karen opened the door. The shaded hallway and cool marbled floor were a warm welcome from the sunshine and heat. They had been travelling all day and Patsy and the others were tired and weary. Tempers were beginning to fray and Patsy's agitation was beginning to show.

'I assure you, they are all safe,' Karen whispered. 'They are going on a little trip today. As far as they are concerned, you will be joining them, but you have business to attend to first. Don't fuck with me Patsy Diamond; it has taken me a lot to get you here and agree to help me. This is the only way I could do it. I want to keep all of this. I want my life and you want to keep what you have with your family. That makes us even, I think. So for now, I would appreciate you going along with the story, no hiccups, if you know what I mean.' Karen gave Patsy a knowing look and raised her eyebrows, waiting for a reply.

Stubbornly, Patsy stuck out her chin. 'What is to stop me walking in there and taking my family home?'

'You really don't think I have a backup plan? You stupid bitch. I am sending your family away for their own safety, but the people who will be with them will be waiting for my calls. Let's tell your family about your newfound friends, and your drug scam. Money laundering and surrounding yourself with the scum of the earth. I'm sure your parents would love to hear about that. Let's tell your daughter how you have hidden her away like some dirty secret, when her father was blackmailing and killing people. That is your legacy Patsy, and I can ruin you in minutes,' Karen spat out. 'Believe me, if you don't help me, you won't like the consequences. I'm angry and I'm desperate, and desperate people do desperate things. Now go and say hello to your family and tell them you will join them soon after you have finished your business. Don't try anything clever; every possibility has been thought of and killing you and your entourage here and now would make no difference to me. I hate you as much as you hate me, but we're partners Patsy; Nick saw to that. I own half of everything you have, thanks to your loving husband. I could clean you out and sell my shares to anyone for a pound and you would be fucked!'

Patsy felt deflated. She knew for the time being she was

beaten. It seemed the odds were against her, and she had to go along with this charade. Apart from Victoria and Sheila, she was on her own.

Inhaling deeply, Patsy let out a huge sigh. 'Okay, have it your way – for now. I want to see my daughter.'

They all followed Karen down a long hallway, and past many rooms before eventually stopping at a door. 'Smile everyone.' Karen's red lipstick seemed to enhance the wide grin on her face and with her long red fingernails, she brushed aside her blonde hair from her face and smoothed down her red jacket before opening the door.

Patsy's heart nearly broke as Nancy ran to her, full of excitement and surprise, and flung her arms around her neck as Patsy bent down. Victoria looked at the happy reunion and tears brimmed in her eyes. This was her granddaughter, Nick's daughter, whom she had never met. It was so obvious she was Nick's daughter, with her emerald-green eyes highlighting her face. She was the very double of him; only her hair was darker, like Patsy's.

The sun shone through the windows into the lounge, highlighting its expensive furniture and gaily coloured ornaments. It was a bright and airy room scattered with toys. There were two other girls in the room and Patsy's parents were sat having tea and watching the girls play, but Victoria sensed an uneasiness in the air.

Patsy's mother stood up. 'What's going on Patsy; why are we here? We've been told to wait for you and the doors have been locked.'

Patsy looked at her mother. 'Why did you agree to come here?' She tried keeping her tone light in front of the children, but inside she felt like screaming.

'We came because we were already in Paris and when your

friend spotted us in a café he said that you were also in Paris and to come and see you. That is why we're here. We haven't been able to leave,' she whispered between gritted teeth.

'Are you hurt? Have you been threatened? What friend?'

'Not directly,' intervened her father, 'but they have taken our mobile phones. We couldn't call you or the police. And the friend in question was that friend of Nick's, Tom. We met him only once, but stupidity comes with age, Patsy and that is how I feel. Bloody stupid and bloody old. We haven't caused a fuss for Nancy's sake.'

'Tom?' asked Patsy. 'Tom who?' Patsy waited for an answer, but her mind was swimming. The last time she had heard the name Tom, was when Karen had said they shared the same accountant. Tom Walker. How on earth could he be involved in all of this? It couldn't be, could it?

Her father suddenly stopped talking, and he looked over her shoulder. Following his eyeline, she watched as Victoria walked slowly to the other side of the room where Nancy was playing.

'Hello Nancy.' She smiled. She wasn't sure what to say, but given how shaky the ground was below their feet, she wanted to say something; it might be her only chance.

The little girl, dressed in jeans and T-shirt with a *Frozen* character on the front, turned and smiled. Emotion overwhelmed Victoria and she couldn't stop the tears from falling down her cheeks. There was a flash of memory and she could see Nick stood there at that age, with the same grin, same eyes.

Victoria knelt down. 'I'm your other grandmother, Victoria. It's nice to meet you at last,' she croaked. She knew she shouldn't have blurted it out like that, but she couldn't help it.

Nancy's green eyes flashed and she looked towards Patsy at the other side of the room. 'Mummy?'

Patsy nodded. 'This is your grandmother Nancy; she's come to say hello.'

Feeling safer, Nancy walked up to Victoria and smiled shyly.

While everyone seemed to be engrossed in their own conversations, Sheila sidled up to Karen and whispered, 'I hope you're pleased with yourself lassie, because when this is over you're mine.' She walked away to join Victoria.

'Right everyone!' Karen clapped her hands together to get everyone's attention. 'The train leaves in two hours; it's time to get ready and packed. Come, come now. Time to go!'

Confused, Patsy looked around the room. 'Where is everyone going?'

'Were going to Disneyland Mummy, don't you remember?' Nancy shouted and giggled.

Patsy's mind was spinning; she felt sick and angry although she knew she had to remain calm. She felt as though everyone's eyes were burning into her, waiting for answers.

'Will you be going to Disneyland Mum? Dad?' Patsy asked her parents hesitantly.

'Of course we are. Do you think that bitch will let us out of her sights until she gets whatever she wants from you?' her father spat out.

Patsy hugged her father then looked him directly in the eyes. 'I want you to have a lovely time in Disneyland with Nancy. Do nothing Dad; I mean, do nothing,' she emphasised.

Fortunately, her father seemed to understand that Patsy had all of this in hand. Whether it be his military training, or just trust, he nodded his head and agreed. 'When will we hear from you?' he asked.

'Soon. Come on; I will help you all pack.' Linking her arm with his and her mother's, she walked past Karen, casting her an icy glare.

Victoria was with Nancy, packing her dolls, while Sheila was talking to the other girls. She was laughing and joking with them. Suddenly there was a beep of a car horn and Karen announced it was time to leave. There were two men in the car and Karen informed Patsy they were friends of hers who would be looking after her parents.

'Why don't you get these men to fight your battles for you?' Patsy snapped. 'Or is it just old people and children they frighten?'

'Nobody is hurt, Patsy! I have let you see them; they are going to Disney for Christ's sake. The sooner you do your bit, the sooner this nightmare will be over. Now stop fucking about and say goodbye.' Karen turned from the door and walked back inside.

Patsy went up to her father and put her arms around his neck, straightening his collar and hugging him. Once closer to his ear, she whispered, 'I have put a tracker down your collar. You're not alone Dad.' Kissing him on the cheek, she smiled and waited until they all got into the car before waving them off.

Sheila rubbed her hands together in a matter-of-fact way. 'Well, that's it, lassies. They are all safely out of the way. Let's find out what Karen shitbag wants and take a look at this shitty farm. I thought farms had cows and sheep; there's none to be seen here. It's just woods and it's fucking eerie.'

Patsy surveyed the huge manor house and rows and rows of fields and forestry. The place was enormous and she smiled. 'So ladies, do you reckon half of this place is mine?' Raising one eyebrow and grinning, Patsy took out a cigarette and lit it. Maybe there was more than one way to skin a cat. Especially a cat called Karen.

14

THE BITTER TRUTH

Patsy couldn't sleep; she had tossed and turned most of the night. After everyone had left they had all eaten and been shown to their rooms. Then they had all handed in their mobile phones and been given walkie talkies. The only amusing thing of the evening was Sheila insisting she speak to Angus and her girls, so as not to cause suspicion. Karen had no choice but to agree on the condition that she put the call on speaker phone. After five blood-curdling minutes of Sheila describing what she would do with Angus when she got home, Karen had quickly left them, saying she wanted an early start in the morning and would show them around the farmland.

The wind was blowing through the open bedroom window in the darkness. Patsy got up to close it. As she moved the curtain, a hand flew out and covered her mouth. Shocked, Patsy gave a muffled scream.

'Patsy,' the hooded figure whispered in her ear. Her heart was racing and she was about to struggle when she saw her assailant remove his hood with his other hand. In the bedroom, lit only by moonlight, she made out Fin. Pushing his hand away, she exhaled deeply, and sat on the bed.

'Where is James? Is he here?' Patsy whispered into the darkness.

Fin nodded. 'Go for a walk around the farm tomorrow; we will find you. We can talk then. In the meantime, close your windows; it's not safe.'

He handed her a piece of paper and then, in the blink of an eye, he had climbed out of the window and disappeared. Even when Patsy looked out of the window, she couldn't see him. Patsy went into the en suite bathroom and put the light on, looking at the paper Fin had given her. On it were basic symbols of sign language. Patsy studied the page closely and tried imitating the symbols on the page. She couldn't even remember them her brain was so tired, but she was pleased that help was at hand and Fin, the famous burglar, had found her.

* * *

The next day they ate breakfast alone until Karen appeared. 'It's time to go *mon amie*.'

Sheila stood up and stubbed her cigarette out in the croissants that were laid out for breakfast. 'Fuck the French shit; you're a wee Glasgow lassie who has fucked her way into a farmer's bed. Now lead on lassie and show me the mushrooms.'

Patsy giggled as the smile disappeared from Karen's face.

As they drove along in the Range Rover, Patsy was struck by the beauty of it all. As they went deeper and deeper into the forest, the smell of the wood bark and dampness of the soil was overpowering.

'Can you smell the truffles? The smell of the moisture can be a little much, but they are here somewhere.' Karen smiled.

'Hang on a minute,' Sheila butted in, 'are you saying that you don't know where these mushrooms are?'

'Not entirely, that is why we have these chaps.' Karen pointed in the distance and there was another open truck with a cage full of dogs, barking and wagging their tails excitedly. The drivers of the truck opened the cages, and the dogs ran off in different directions. 'The dogs sniff the truffles out that are hidden by the trunks of trees. Once picked, they have to be delivered quickly. The restaurants in Paris pay a fortune for them and we already have contracts with most of them...'

'I think it's time you were straight with us Karen. Who exactly are you fighting with? How can your land be taken away from you if you own it?'

Hesitantly, Karen began. 'I didn't know it, but although the house is Armand's and now mine and his daughters, the land belongs to the Milieu. They had an agreement with Armand, but now he has gone they say the land is theirs and whatever is grown and sold is also theirs. They have truffles to sell, but they are not the real thing. They are dyeing normal large truffles black. The inside of the dark truffles have a black powder in them or white if not mature. We also have found white truffles recently. They are very rare, and you can name your price. The Milieu are ruining our reputation, as they are selling their fake truffles under our logo and now two people have died. Poisoned. They are poaching my business and it's all I have left.'

'Are a few mushrooms worth risking your life for lassie?' Sheila jumped in.

'This is my home, don't you understand? I was prepared to give up and walk away until I found out Nick had died and had made me his partner. It was like a gift from the gods. It's another chance to fight back. I will win this battle and I will keep what is mine.'

Suddenly there was a gunshot in the air. Everyone looked at each other, shocked.

'It's okay. That is how they alert us they have found truffles.' Karen drove off and with great interest, Patsy, Sheila and Victoria watched ten barking dogs wagging their tails and running around old oak trees. Farm workers were on their hands and knees carefully digging up the truffles. Others rushed forward with small crates and laid the truffles flat, leaving lots of space between each one. Patsy and the others found it intriguing. It was strange to see the military precision involved.

Seeing the excitement in Karen's face and seeing how proud of the place she was, Patsy could understand why she would resort to such measures. Patsy knew she too would do anything to keep her salons. She admired Karen's determination, but she could also see how desperate she was. She also felt this grand plantation with its enormous chateau was wasted on someone like Karen who didn't know how to look after it. The potential of this place was mind boggling and Patsy could understand Karen's passion for it... She was beginning to have a passion for it herself and was determined to keep her eye on the prize in hand. This place was the only proper home Karen had known and she wasn't going to give it up easily.

'It's fascinating, isn't it?' Karen smiled. 'The fresher, the better and once the chef smells the freshness of those he will pay double.'

'How much are you looking at?' Patsy couldn't help but ask.

'For those three small crates, around seven thousand euros, possibly more.'

Sheila let out a slow whistle. 'Jesus Christ lassie. No wonder you want to hang on to the place.'

'That's the point; I need to sell those before the landowners take their cut. I have overheads, wages to pay but they want 50 per cent.'

Victoria shook her head in dismay. 'It's a sad story dear, but so is kidnapping for greed.' Her short sentence brought everyone back to reality. 'Where do we find these people? This Milieu you keep talking about.' Victoria waited, but Karen kept quiet and continued driving.

After their tour of the extensive farm, they drove back to the house, where, to their horror, the sky was filling with black smoke and they could hear people shouting. The chateau was on fire. As they got nearer, they could see the front windows were shattering as flames and black smoke filled the air. Karen stopped the truck and ran around the grounds, shouting for the farm labourers who were already doing their best with buckets and hosepipes to put the fire out.

A short while later, fire engines arrived and got to work. But all that remained were wet, smoking embers at the front of the house. Once everything had been checked, the fire brigade left. Karen walked over to the truck and sat in it. Sobs wracked her body and she couldn't stop.

Still shocked and watching the mayhem before her, Patsy walked over to Karen. 'This was no accident, was it?'

'No, this is the third time. Before it was one of the fields, now it is my house. Will you help me or not? Where are your friends to scare these bastards off?' she screamed. 'If I don't make that call, the people in charge of Nancy and your parents will presume I am dead and they will kill them.'

Anger raged inside Patsy. She flew at Karen and dragged her out of the truck. She'd had enough of being under this woman's thumb. She threw punch after punch. It was as if a red curtain had dropped before her eyes and all she saw was hate and anger. Karen's screams alerted the farmers and Sheila and Victoria.

They ran towards Patsy and tried dragging her off Karen who was covered in blood. Patsy was like a wild woman scratching and punching. Karen was lying on the floor, trying to fight her off, but now Patsy was sitting astride her, pinning her to the floor. Venom spewed from her mouth as she put her hands around Karen's neck, strangling her.

Sheila couldn't pull Patsy off; her anger was making her stronger. In the end, Sheila punched Patsy in the face to bring her out of this trance of hate. 'Patsy! Stop it! She has to make the call. Get off her!' Sheila screamed. Eventually, Patsy ran out of steam and fell to a heap beside Karen, her hands scraped and covered in blood. Victoria looked around and saw a discarded bucket of water left by one of the labourers. Picking it up, she threw the water over Patsy and Karen, almost making them choke. Drenched, coughing and spluttering, Patsy sat up, shaking her head to get rid of the excess water. Karen was too weak to sit up, but she was panting heavily. Patsy had beaten her badly; it looked as though her nose was broken and her lip was cut and she was semi-conscious.

'Get them both inside,' Victoria ordered to one of the labourers nearby.

Karen was cleaned up and put to bed. The cook wanted to call a doctor but Victoria wouldn't allow it. She said she would tend to Karen herself.

Sheila popped her head around the bedroom door. 'How is she, Vicky lassie?'

'She'll be okay Sheila. There will be bruising and some discomfort, but she'll live. Let's leave her to rest.' Victoria ushered Sheila out of the room and they both left Karen to sleep. 'How is Patsy doing?'

'I've cleaned her up Vicky; she's still trembling with anger but a couple of large whiskies have solved that, plus a bucket of ice for those hands. They are mighty swollen; she looks like a prize fighter. She would have killed her Vicky. God knows what that Karen said to her, but I've never seen her so angry. It looks like the fire was a warning, but that Karen is in deep shit if you ask me and these people mean business. Come on, Florence Nightingale, you deserve a wee dram yourself.'

* * *

Washed and changed, Patsy tried lighting a cigarette. Her swollen hands trembled as she held the cigarette to her mouth. Strangely enough, it was as if something had changed inside of her. She felt strong and in charge again. Walking out of the bedroom, she pushed past the men who lived in the house with Karen.

'Give me my mobile phones back. I know you understand me and if you want to get out of this with your life, do as I say. As far as I'm concerned, this Milieu can string you up outside and leave you for the rats.' The men looked at each other and nodded. In no time at all, Patsy had all of their mobiles back. It seemed only fear bred loyalty as far as Patsy could see.

Her first thought was to call Larry to see if he had come up with any new information about Karen. She was surprised that he was so cheerful to hear her voice.

'You little minx; what have you been doing?' He laughed.

Puzzled, Patsy apologised for not calling sooner, but she was confused even more when Larry informed her it didn't matter, because he'd enjoyed her texts.

While he was talking, Patsy looked at the messages to Larry on her phone. She couldn't believe it; there was nothing on her mobile and nothing deleted. She found this odd. 'Are you sure it was me texting you Larry?' Patsy's first thought was maybe Karen had been playing games.

'Oh it was definitely you my love, your number, your name, although I think you must have been a little drunk because the spelling was off or the predictive text had gone mad.' He laughed again.

Patsy shrugged and told Larry about her meeting with her parents. 'They said they had met a friend of Nick's called Tom, who had got them to bring Nancy here. The only Tom I can recall is my accountant. We share the same one, but he's never mentioned a sister in Paris.'

'Let me look into that. I think I already know, but I don't want to say anything until I have checked it out. Oh my god,' Larry groaned, 'why didn't I see it? I'll call you back Patsy. Just bear with me.' Larry hurriedly ended the call and a frustrated Patsy felt like throwing her phone at the wall but thought better of it.

Needing some air, she walked outside to a nearby field. It was almost dusk now, and the day had passed in a blur. 'What the fuck is happening!' she shouted to the trees, venting her anger once more.

A voice from behind her spoke, almost making her jump out of her skin. 'For Christ's sake Patsy, stop being so dramatic.'

Quickly, Patsy turned around and nearly fell into James's arms. 'Where have you been James? Oh Christ, it's a mess here! Nancy is in Disneyland. My parents hate me and this Milieu or something is waging a war. I feel like I'm in a nightmare! And I've nearly killed Karen.'

'Busy day then?' He laughed. 'Come sit on the grass. Let's talk.'

Doing as she was told, Patsy sat down.

'Firstly, the Milieu are the French gangland bosses. That name is like the mafia. It's a group of businessmen and thugs who all know each other. I've heard of them, but I don't know much about them.'

'This is worse than I thought. We can't fight people like that.'

James showed her a photo on his phone. 'Do you know this man?'

Patsy held the phone. For a moment she couldn't speak. 'Yes I do James. Is that the man who met my parents and convinced them to come here?' Devastated, she looked at the photo again. Patsy felt crushed; her suspicions were confirmed. It was her accountant, Tom. 'How does he know Karen? What involvement does he have with her? He knows everything about mine and Nick's finances.' Angry and upset, almost to the point of tears, Patsy was sick of betrayal. It seemed everyone went out of their way to betray her. Could no one be trusted?

'I think he is Karen's brother. Either way, he's been keeping her updated about your affairs and Nick's death of course.'

Patsy's mind swam. 'I want him dead James. I want him silenced for good.' Suddenly, a thought occurred to her. 'Where are you staying?'

'There's a bed and breakfast up the road. Fin's a bit disappointed, but I've promised him a night in Paris so he can enjoy the nightlife, the women and the sights, but business first. I've organised Greek Paul to oversee the closing down of the pizza parlours. As predicted, some of the others have come on board. Money is money and they think you have done right by them.'

Patsy nodded then looked back at the photo on James's mobile. 'How did you get this photo?'

'The computer hacker. You know, the one you met at the meeting. He found him.'

'Can we get a meeting with these Milieu people? I would like to get their angle on things.'

'I doubt it. Although maybe Karen could organise it. She

knows who they are and who to contact. What are you thinking Patsy?' Frowning, James was concerned. He knew Patsy was impulsive and hot-headed and all of this stress wasn't helping. 'You're not going to do anything stupid are you?'

'I'm not sure yet. I haven't thought it out.'

'Just don't do anything hasty. I know of this Milieu gang; they are mobsters. They are not just going to let you waltz in there, asking questions.' James could tell his words were falling on deaf ears. Even though it was dark, he could see her mind plotting.

'Thank you James; you have given me a lot to think about. You're a good friend and partner.' Patsy looked into the vast open space of Brittany. 'This is a nice part of the world, isn't it? Do you know those dogs they use to sniff out those truffles are worth five to six thousand each? Probably more. Karen has twenty of them and they are all insured. She even breeds them. I was thinking about Greek Paul.'

'Greek Paul? What are you talking about Patsy?'

'He's a chef isn't he? A properly trained chef, I mean. I wonder what he would cook up with those lovely truffles. He could really be worth his weight in gold.'

James couldn't help shrugging his shoulders and laughing. He had no idea what Patsy was talking about. It was as though she was having a conversation in her head, and he was only hearing half of it.

'I want you and Fin to come here tomorrow. I want her to see I have the backup she so desperately needs. In the meantime I will convince her to contact these people. It's time we put our cards on the table, but we don't show our hand James.'

'I'll walk you back; come on.'

Kissing James on the cheek, Patsy smiled. 'I'll see you tomorrow morning James and in the meantime I will convince Karen to call these people and set up a meeting. Make sure you put your best bib and tucker on; Victoria will be very pleased to see you I'm sure.'

'Patsy Diamond, you are a very mischievous woman, but you're no matchmaker. Don't forget, after all of this, you owe me one.' Seeing that she was safely at the door, James walked away.

'Where the hell have you been lassie? I was going to send a search party.' Frantic, Sheila was almost shouting.

'I've seen a friend.' Patsy winked. 'Is that bitch upstairs awake yet? Never mind, I'll go and see for myself.' Marching up the staircase, Patsy pushed open the bedroom door. She could see Karen was asleep in bed and shook her awake.

Dazed, Karen sat up, quite alarmed at seeing Patsy.

'Have you made the call?' Seeing the confused look on Karen's face, Patsy slapped her to bring her around. 'Make the fucking call now!'

Karen pressed the number on her mobile, and Patsy told her to put it on loud speaker so she could hear for herself and say goodnight to Nancy.

'If she isn't awake, my parents will be. I want to talk to them.'

Karen looked uneasy and cast a glance at Patsy through her swollen eyes.

Stunned, Patsy heard what she wanted to hear. The man's voice on the other end of the mobile confirmed who she had seen in James's photo. It chilled her to the bones, but she did her best to hide the recognition of the man on the other end. Karen told him she was okay and asked if Patsy's parents were around, then there was a silence. After a brief period, which seemed like forever, Patsy's father spoke. He told her all was well, and Nancy was enjoying herself at Disney. Satisfied, Patsy ended the call. Her mind was troubled, and her blood was boiling. She wanted revenge and she was damn well going to have it.

15

THE MILIEU

Patsy had had all night to think her plan through. She didn't have all the answers but the outline of it seemed just fine. Walking into Karen's bedroom in the light of day, she was surprised by the bruising on Karen's face – more so that she'd been responsible for it.

'I've brought you some coffee and croissants Karen; you need to eat something.'

'You bitch; I can hardly move my face, let alone speak. Why do you come now with these offerings of kindness? Just wait until I video call the men who are looking after your family and show them what you have done. Maybe they will want to retaliate, eh?'

Biting her tongue, Patsy smiled. 'Sorry about that, but all's fair in love and war Karen. Anyway, enough of that.' Patsy sat down on the bed. 'I like your farm and as you say, we are partners, and I would like to be a partner in this place. I could help you keep it safe and also put money back into the running of things. Therefore, I would like you to call this Milieu you keep talking about and set up a meeting. Maybe we can sort something out if he thinks you have a partner. Call them Karen; let us meet with them today.' Dramatically, Patsy drummed her fingers on her chin. 'Of course, they might want to see the paperwork. If we're partners, there has to be proof of our partnership, doesn't there?'

Karen tried taking a sip of her coffee through swollen lips, and staring at Patsy through the slits of her eyes, she thought about what she was saying. 'How do I know this isn't some kind of trick? You want my farm, don't you?'

'Absolutely not, although I am prepared to invest. You will live here and run things. But what about your enemies? Perhaps if they are paid off for the land, they will leave you alone. But if you're not interested that's fine by me.' Slowly, Patsy started to stand up to leave. She knew this was the sprat to catch the mackerel.

'Wait! Would you really want to invest in this place and become partners?'

Patsy nodded, waiting.

'I will call them,' Karen muttered under her breath. 'But I want to see the colour of your money first.'

'My, my Karen where is the trust? No Karen, my money stays where it is until proof of our partnership is in my hand. I don't trust you, but at the moment you have no choice but to trust me.' Patsy could see Karen pondering over her offer.

Mentally, Karen couldn't believe how stupid Patsy was. Patsy was prepared to buy the land off the Milieu, and when all of this was over she would get rid of Patsy and then she would own the lot! This was better than even she had expected. She would own the Diamond empire, the very thing that Nick loved most in the world. Vengeance was sweet and she had waited a long time for this. Well, she would bring his world crashing down around Patsy's ears. Once she had served her purpose, Patsy Diamond would meet her end. Of course, she would give the order to kill Nancy and her grandparents, too. They were just a bargaining ploy and the last thing she wanted was for Nancy to inherit half of the partnership. No, the decision was final. They all had to die, and Karen's secret would be safe forever.

'Okay, I agree to your terms. I will make the call and hopefully we can get an appointment today.'

Each of them smiled at each other sweetly, both of them plotting each other's end.

* * *

'When are we leaving this place Patsy? And what is happening with Nancy and your parents?' Victoria fired question after question. She was sick with worry; nothing seemed to be happening. 'I could lose my granddaughter before I've had the chance to get to know her.' Victoria was still smarting over Patsy's secret but there were more important things to deal with.

Suddenly the doorbell rang. Patsy pointed towards one of the labourers helping out in the kitchen. 'Answer it and let whoever it is inside. I am expecting someone.' Victoria and Sheila looked at each other and then at Patsy. 'Don't worry you two; it's a nice surprise.' She laughed.

James and Fin walked into the kitchen area. Without thinking, Victoria stood up and threw her arms around James's neck. 'Oh my god, it's good to see a friendly face James.'

James smiled. 'If I had known I would get this reception I would have come sooner.'

'Blimey Vicky lass, he's only been through the door a minute and you're like a dog on heat.' Sheila laughed.

Victoria stood back, blushing.

'Do I get a hug like that?' Fin chimed in, and was taken aback when Victoria hugged him too.

'It's good to see you too, Fin. Now I know we'll all be safe.'

Shying away, Fin looked down at the floor. It had been a long time since he'd been hugged like that by a motherly figure. He'd forgotten how good it felt to have family. There was Maggie, but she always kept her distance, and this felt different, like he was part of something.

'Oh my god Vicky, you're a cougar! If you're going to have one of those threesomes, I suggest you leave it for the bedroom.'

'Sheila, your mind is always in the bedroom. I think Angus will be glad of the break,' Victoria retorted.

They all laughed; it was a welcome relief to the stress.

Suddenly the house was full of alarms going off and they could hear gunshots and barking dogs. It was deafening and they all put their hands to their ears. Karen's farm labourers ran through the doors; some were blood-stained and bleeding.

'What the hell is going on?' demanded Patsy. 'And why are all those alarms going off?'

They all ran towards the front door, missing a round of bullets by inches. Frightened, they ran to the front windows. All they could see was a cloud of smoke from the gun fire and two open-backed jeeps driving off.

As best as she could, Karen held on to the banister and struggled down the stairs, shouting orders at the farm labourers to get outside now the coast was clear.

Sitting on the stairs, Karen was crushed when minutes later, a couple of them came back and informed Karen the dogs who sniffed out the truffles had all been stolen. Tears rolled down her swollen face. 'That's it. My business is over. You, Patsy Diamond, are all I have left!'

Patsy just smiled at Karen. 'I'm sure we can sort things out; that's why you've brought me here isn't it?'

James cast Patsy a furtive look; she was up to something but wasn't sure what. He knew in time he would find out though.

16

JOURNEY'S END

'Hi Lady Diamond, I bet you thought I'd forgotten all about you.'

Patsy and the others had decided to take a walk around the grounds to assess the damage, and so they could talk between themselves before their afternoon meeting with the Milieu. Karen had made the call and told them her partner was here to talk things through and it seemed they were just as eager to talk.

Now hearing Freddie's voice made her panic. She thought to herself that he would only call her if something had gone wrong. Excusing herself, she walked away from the others.

'Freddie! What's wrong? Have you found Nancy? Do you know where they are staying?' Her heart was beating in her chest.

'Calm down Lady Diamond.' His easy nonchalant drawl annoyed her. 'We have been with your daughter every step of the way.' Freddie's voice seemed offhand and easy-going as they spoke which irritated Patsy even more. This was the most important thing in her life, and he was taking it all in his stride.

'Well, what's happening? What are you going to do?'

'Well, that's up to you and the reason why I'm calling. Do you want your daughter and parents bringing to that chateau or do you want them all put safely on an aeroplane home? It will be today, because we have other commitments.'

Patsy's first impulse was to say bring them to the chateau, but there were things to sort out here and she didn't want her parents and Nancy dragged into it. 'Take them home. Or rather see that they get home. Today you say?'

'Yes lady, we're on it. Just a couple of things to clear up first. Karen's brother is in charge of things here. Did James show you the photo? I know you know who he is and I wondered what you wanted doing with him?'

'I want him to know that it was me who sent you to him. I want his side of the story and then I want him tortured and killed. I also want proof that you have done this. It's not that I don't believe you,' she stammered, not wanting to upset him, 'I just want the satisfaction.'

'Fine with me Lady Diamond. Now, you do your bit and smash this phone up as soon as we have finished this conversation.'

'But how will you contact me?' Patsy felt her stomach churning.

'I'll find you lady; now do as I say.'

The slow drawl of his voice didn't convince her, but she decided to go along with his plans. As an afterthought, she asked, 'Freddie, just a thought. Have you ever heard of the Milieu gang?'

'Milieu? Why do you ask?' Now Freddie sounded cautious. He obviously wasn't expecting this.

'I have a meeting with them this afternoon. They are involved in this in some way. They are causing all kinds of problems apparently.'

'I know them, and what you say sounds about right. You're

having a meeting with them? Well good luck with that. When you get there, say hello to Charles; we used to do some work together; that should grease your path a little.'

Patsy took a sigh of relief. 'Thanks Freddie. Keep in touch, eh?' But Freddie had already ended the call. Feeling stronger now, she opened up the back of her phone, took out the SIM card and taking out her lighter, she held it close and watched the plastic melt.

James came walking up to her and smiled. 'Was that call from Freddie?'

Patsy nearly jumped out of her skin. 'As a matter of fact, it was. It seems everything is in hand. The boot is on the other foot now James. I am in charge and I will sort this bitch out once and for all.'

She joined Victoria and Sheila again. Sheila stood with her arms folded. 'Well, that seemed important. Are we allowed to know what it was about?'

'No, but according to my source, I think Nancy and my parents may be going home today.'

'My god lassie; you mean all of this is over and we can go home then?' Sheila grinned.

'Absolutely not!' Patsy snapped. 'The fun has only just begun and I want answers and lots of them. Not a word now; let's continue playing her game and let these farm workers and would-be security guards watch us. After all, if they were any good, she wouldn't need our help would she?' Patsy laughed out loud, almost maniacally. Everyone was safe now; she had nothing to lose.

Victoria and Sheila looked at each other; Patsy's crazy ways were starting to worry them. They didn't want to ask too many questions for fear of the answers.

* * *

There were many cabins in this fancy Davy Crockett ranch-style holiday park near Disneyland. Nancy and her grandparents were living in one, while guarded by minders. The one next door was where Tom and the rest of his men were living. Two minders took it in shifts to watch Nancy and the family which was why Freddie had delayed tactics and put himself and his men on surveillance.

Fortunately, it wasn't peak season and most of the other cabins were empty. Freddie could see why it had been chosen – it was desolate, apart from the caretaker-cum-holiday rep, whose office was a cabin at the far end. Freddie had watched them change shifts and knew when it was their break time. He wanted no witnesses. Freddie had seen Nancy and her grandparents being taken out, and knew it was time to make his move.

Going around the back door, he let himself in, and once he saw the coast was clear, the rest of his gang joined him in the luxurious cabin, while patiently waiting their return. On hearing a car pull up outside, Freddie peered through the blinds at the window and grinned to himself, feeling for his gun on the inside of his green army jacket. 'Here they are boys; battle station.' Freddie lounged on the sofa with his legs hanging over the end of it, lighting a roll up cigarette. One of his associates stood behind the door leading into the lounge area opposite Freddie, while another two were around the back entrance looking out of the window.

The guard in charge of Patsy's family walked into the room first. Startled at seeing Freddie, he shouted in French to raise the alarm to the man behind him. Instantly, Freddie's man behind the door grabbed him from behind and put his hand over his mouth and with his other hand held a knife to his throat.

Freddie took out his gun and pointed it at the other man behind Nancy and her grandparents. 'Shut your mouth Frenchie and don't even think about bolting through that door.'

'What's going on?' Patsy's dad shouted. 'Who are you; what are you going to do to us?'

Patsy's mum burst into tears. 'Please! Please don't shoot us. She's only a child.' Gripping Nancy's shoulders, Patsy's mum squeezed her tightly.

Freddie shrugged and smiled. 'I am a friend of your daughters. I think it's time you went home.'

Pointing his gun at the man behind Patsy's parents, Freddie smiled. 'I can shoot the wings off a fly Frenchie, so you just stand there like a good boy and I might let you live.'

The man pushed Patsy's parents out of the way and made a grab for Nancy, making her cry out. Without flinching, Freddie fired his gun and shot the man between the eyes. Fortunately, the silencer on the gun hid the noise of the bullet entering the man's head. Patsy's parents paled. They stood there, stunned, wondering if the next bullet would be for them, but Freddie smiled. 'Collateral damage.'

'Bloody hell, Freddie; I thought you said no killing in front of the kid?' Todd said. 'If I would have done that, you'd have shot me!'

'Best laid plans boys. He can't say he wasn't warned. Sorry about that,' Freddie said to Patsy's parents. 'She's young; she'll get over it. Time to get you out of here.'

Patsy's dad followed Freddie's lead and smiled weakly. 'It's okay Nancy, this man is a friend of Mummy's.' It was all he could think of to say; he was still stunned by Freddie's accurate gunshot. Nancy started to shake and tears fell down her face. Patsy's mum took hold of her and lifted her up.

'It's okay Nancy love. It's all make-believe. Look, they are playing soldiers. No one is hurt.' Looking at Freddie for reassurance, she smiled weakly and clung to Nancy, burying her head in her shoulders.

Todd was busying himself taking the jacket and the flat cap off the dead man and dressed himself in this would be his disguise if anyone from the cabin next door looked out of the window. Once dressed, he stood up and nodded at Freddie.

Freddie grinned and put his gun back into the inside pocket of his jacket. 'Now listen to me. Todd here, is going to walk you to the car. You act as normally as possible, as you did when that piece of shit was escorting you out. You've got to pretend Nancy. This is a secret and you have to be quiet and fool the bad guys eh?'

Nancy lifted her red, tear-stained face from Patsy's mum's shoulder and looked at Freddie. 'Are we playing hide and seek?' she croaked and rubbed her face.

'We are Nancy, and you're going home.' Once Freddie saw the smile appear on Nancy's face he nodded to Todd to walk them to the car. Taking the car keys out of the dead man's jacket pocket, Todd stepped over him in the hallway and opened the door, furtively looking around in case any of the other men in the cabin next door were hanging around outside.

Patsy's dad picked Nancy up. 'Close your eyes Nancy and count to twenty to let them hide,' he instructed, so that she wouldn't see the dead man on the floor. Blood had started to pour from the bullet hole in his forehead and was leaving a puddle on the floor.

Slowly, Todd, Patsy's parents and Nancy made their way to the car. As they got in, the door of the cabin beside theirs opened.

'Paul, where are you going?' shouted a man. He started to run towards the car, but Todd drove off. Relief washed over Patsy's parents as they turned to see their prison, the cabin, disappearing into the distance behind them.

Patsy's dad gripped Patsy's mum's hand. 'Are you okay?'

Frightened and shaken, she nodded and pulled Nancy closer to her for comfort. 'You can open your eyes now sweetie; we're well hidden.'

Patsy's dad reached out and ran his hands through Nancy's hair. She had quicky recovered and was smiling. 'I counted to twenty Grandad!'

* * *

Freddie stood up and walked up to the man held at knife point. The small cut on his neck from the razor sharp knife that was dug into his flesh had started to bleed and droplets of blood dripped onto his jacket. Freddie stuffed a soiled handkerchief into the man's mouth. Reaching into his pocket, he took out some plastic garden ties. 'Bind his hands and slit his throat if he struggles,' he ordered. Still with his roll up perched between his lips, he walked to the front door and locked it. He walked to the back entrance where his friend was still watching out of the windows.

'That bloke who ran out has raised the alarm boss; I can hear shouting. I reckon they will come in a minute.'

'Good, because the coast is clear now; I don't have to make excuses to kids. Bolt the door quickly; I want them around the back entrance.'

Three men ran around the back door and kicked it in, knocking it flying and making Freddie stand back for fear of being hit by it. Quickly, Freddie fired his gun twice then stopped and slowly pointed it at the only man alive. 'It's you I have come for. Are you the lover or the brother?' Freddie laughed. 'Either way, you're the last man standing.' Freddie smiled and gave him a wink. Freddie's friends were putting all of the bodies into one room in the cabin, then dousing them with petrol.

The man looked around at his dead friends wide eyed and shaking with fear. He fell to his knees, clutching at Freddie's legs and pleading for his life. 'I have money; you can have it,' he shouted. Tears ran down his face and spit dribbled from his mouth, as he begged and pleaded.

Freddie shook his head and tutted. 'Hey boys, this kidnapper of little kids is crying. Do you think he gave a fuck when the little girl was frightened? Let's show him some sympathy boys.'

They all burst out laughing as Freddie shook him off his leg and each in turn, Freddie's men beat and kicked the man kneeling on the floor.

'Wait, don't kill him; we should deliver him,' Freddie said, hitting him on the back of his head with his gun, knocking him out. 'Fucking loser. Right lads; burn this place to the ground and the next cabin too, including the cars.' In no time at all, the cabins and cars were blazing away like an inferno.

Freddie and the boys drove off, with their special parcel tied and gagged in the boot.

* * *

Patsy, Sheila and Victoria looked at James and Fin. Each in turn, they raised their eyebrows in surprise. Patsy had expected the meeting to be in an office, but instead Karen was pulling up at a bistro. Patsy was the first to speak up. 'I thought we had a meeting with this French mob of yours; what are you doing stopping for dinner?'

'This is the meeting place,' snapped Karen. They could all see how nervous she was, and to be honest they all felt the same.

None of them knew what they were walking into, not even James.

The bistro was empty when they entered, but the shade was a welcome change from the sunshine.

A man appeared from behind the kitchen area, walked to the door and pushed the bolt across to secure it. He beckoned them with his hand and they followed him to an open hatch in the floor behind the counter. He pointed, indicating for them to go down. Patsy looked down first and could see there were stairs. She took the initiative and carefully climbed down. To her surprise, the space below was an office. Four men sat at a table smoking cigars and playing cards. They quickly glanced at Patsy and the others, and then they saw Karen and smiled. Two men came from nowhere and stopped James and Fin going down the staircase. James made a fight for it, but the two men pointed guns in their faces and they had no choice but to stay put. Victoria asked to stay with them, as she didn't want to go down, explaining it was claustrophobic. Nodding, they let her stay with James and Fin.

A lump rose in Patsy's throat and her mouth went dry when she saw the hatch close and heard the bolt locking it. James had warned her they may be frisked, and they had come without weapons... But now she regretted it.

One of the men at the table poured a round of whiskies. 'Please sit down, *madames*.'

Patsy looked around the office cellar. There were no windows. It reminded her of some illegal gambling club.

Her knees felt weak as the men pulled back chairs for them to sit on, but she had to show courage she didn't feel for the sake of the others. She looked around at these suited men. They were a mixture of ages. One, Patsy noticed, looked around sixty with white hair; another was balding but around late forties she guessed. Her heart was in her mouth. These could be the last faces she was ever going to see.

Folding her arms like a spoilt child, Karen sat down. 'This is my partner, Patsy Diamond. She owns half of the chateau and farm and wants to know why you are burning down her land and stealing off her. I want my dogs back! I know it's you who has stolen them.'

Patsy and Sheila raised their eyebrows in surprise at Karen's outburst.

'We are not the thieves Karen, you are. As for your partner, how come you have never mentioned her before?' the white-haired said.

'We have a partnership in lots of businesses in England and Scotland. Name your price and call your dogs off!' Karen screamed again.

One of the younger men raised his hand and slapped Karen, almost knocking her off the chair. The white-haired man offered Sheila a chair, with all of the charm of a Frenchman, and he handed them a glass of whisky each.

The bald man began making his introductions. 'This is Jules,' he said, pointing at one of the younger, handsome men. 'He is the great-grandson of Jules Bonnet, our founder.' He smiled. 'I am Jacques, this is Pierre and lastly, Manon.' Then he looked at Patsy. 'We have checked you out, Mrs Diamond, and we know who your husband was. Why would you be playing around with Karen?'

Taking a gulp of her whisky, Patsy smiled. 'Why do you keep burning down land and dyeing truffles? Surely that's not good business. You're poachers and you're murderers. You have already poisoned people while using our logo. Surely, when this is investigated, you will be incriminated?' Patsy knew she was winging it here. The four men looked at each other and spoke in

French. Mentally, Patsy wished she had paid more attention at school.

Sheila shifted around in her chair. She'd had enough. 'I can't take any more of this,' Sheila snapped. 'Fighting over fucking mushrooms, when you're supposed to be grown men! I don't even eat mushrooms. Look, being dragged into some cellar with some blokes doesn't intimidate me and I am sick of this shit. Are you going to stop harassing Karen, and if not, why not?'

Patsy smiled to herself. As much as they were confused when the men spoke in French, the men were doubly confused when Sheila's Glaswegian accent flowed. They looked dumbfounded.

'Firstly *madame*, it is our land and Karen knows this,' Jacques explained.

'Its's not true! That land and house is Armand's and mine. I don't care who you are. You are not taking my land,' Karen shouted. Her face was nearly as red as her lipstick.

Ignoring her, Jacques, who was obviously the spokesman, looked at Patsy. 'How much have you put into this so-called partnership? Did you know she's broke...?' When Patsy said nothing, Jacques continued. 'We have taken the dogs Karen, but that doesn't put a dent into your husband's debts.'

Patsy and Sheila felt out of their depth. There was a story here that they didn't know. Patsy wasn't sure if they would even get out of there alive. Sooner or later, these men would get tired of Karen's outbursts and possibly shoot them all. She decided it was time to play her trump card. 'A friend of mine said to say hello to Charles. I just thought I would mention that before you kill us all.'

Instantly, the bald man narrowed his eyes and looked piercingly at her. 'Who is this friend, who says hello?'

'My good friend Freddie.' Patsy fiddled with her hands under the table. Her smile got weaker the more he looked at her, then he turned and spoke to the others in French. They seemed to be arguing amongst themselves while the women watched them.

'Get out Karen; we have spoken enough.'

A man from a corner of the room walked up, grabbed Karen by the arm and pulled her out of her chair. She screamed and kicked out as he pushed her towards the staircase. Gripping her wrists in one hand, the man knocked on the hatch twice and it opened.

'Patsy Diamond, you owe me,' Karen shouted as she was escorted out. 'Sort these bastards out!'

The white-haired man poured them all another drink and straightened his tie. 'Now Mrs Diamond, you have my attention. Why are you in France really?'

'Why don't you tell me your story first, Jacques?' she replied with more courage than she felt.

Nodding, Jacques smiled at the others and motioned to an unseen man in the furthest darkest corner of the room. Swiftly turning, Patsy and Sheila looked on as the man pulled at a sheet covering a large piece of furniture, the size of a wardrobe. As the sheet fell away, they could see it was a cage and cowering and half beaten to death was Karen's brother.

Shocked, Patsy turned back to Jacques and the others. 'You already know why I am here, don't you?'

'Of course, but we had to make sure. After all, you and Karen could have kissed and made up by now.' He grinned. 'But I presume those marks on her face and swollen lips she didn't do herself.'

Patsy looked on as Freddie stepped out from behind the cage. 'Well, Lady Diamond, you did say you were coming here.' He laughed. 'You also wanted proof I killed this bastard, but you want answers first, is that right?'

Dumbstruck, Patsy nodded and stood up, slowly walking

towards the man in the cage. He was covered in blood and was trying to speak to Patsy through his gag.

'Take his gag off; I want to speak to him.'

Opening the cage door, Freddie did as she asked. The man seemed to give a sigh of relief as he took a large gulp of air to fill his lungs. He thought Patsy would save him!

Looking at Jacques, Patsy made her own introduction. 'This is Tom Walker, my trusted accountant, and he was also my husband's. He knew about the money we laundered through my business and covered it well, but now I know he was taking his fair share at the same time even though he was very well paid. Karen is his sister by all accounts, and she is supposed to be dead – did you know that Jacques?'

The four men drank their whisky and listened stony-faced.

'She has a very nice headstone in Scotland. I know now that Tom is the man who hatched this plan once he knew there was a bank account in Karen's Duret's name. He kidnapped my daughter and parents. He did his homework; there is an account for a Nancy Diamond. I told him it was a trust for a family member.' Shaking her head, she couldn't take her eyes off the caged man. 'My parents know him, and they have been to his office with me at times. They have also met him at my house when Nick and I had a party.' Patsy walked around the cage, letting her fingers trail along the metal, while Tom's deafening pleas filled the room. He was visibly trembling as tears rolled down his face, and urine wet through his trousers as he repeated how sorry he was again and again.

'People are always sorry Jacques when they are caught. But he would willingly have followed Karen's orders and killed my family. So what do you suggest we do first?' Patsy grinned like a Cheshire cat. She hated Tom more than ever. She had trusted him, and he had offered tea and sympathy after Nick's murder, yet all the time he had been hatching his plan. 'Why did you do it Tom?'

His mouth seemed to be foaming with spit as he spoke. 'Nick Diamond used my sister. I had to lie to get her to safety. She is my family, just as Nancy is yours, and yet he turned her into a junkie. He didn't know she was my sister,' he spluttered, 'but I knew, and I vowed I would kill him but someone got there before me.' It seemed to them all that Tom had found his strength and voice through his hatred for Nick.

'But I am not Nick, am I Tom?' Patsy saw Tom sit back on his haunches in defeat. 'Well Jacques; I have dealt with people claiming they are not criminals, but this honest accountant was prepared to kill my family and possibly me simply to get his hands on my money. What about you Jacques, are you and your friends honest criminals?'

'We are businessmen. Karen's husband was an avid gambler and mortgaged the land to us a long time ago on the condition that he continued to manage the place. He got greedy too. The truffle business is a good laundering prospect; no one really knows how much you can get for them. They are like drugs; you can name your price. Karen is a greedy woman and once she found out about Armand's debts, she caused a lot of trouble for us. We can run our own land, but not with her around.'

'I'm prepared to pay whatever it is you are owed, by Armand, but for myself. I have my own ideas about those fancy mushrooms and that land. It's a pot of gold in the right hands and I'm a businesswoman.' For a fleeting moment, she thought about an idea she had had earlier. She remembered how excited Greek Paul had been about those truffles. Now she had seen the chateau and the land, she liked it and it would be easy to sort a restaurant out here with a chef who knew his stuff. It made good business sense, but she wasn't sharing it for the moment.

Jacques turned to the other men and they spoke in French to each other. We he turned back, he said, 'We are prepared to go into partnership with you Mrs Diamond. We are all crooks, but honest ones until we're double crossed. Freddie here, is your guarantor.'

'And the money laundering, I would need to do that here, too?' she asked hesitantly. She knew she was taking a big risk and could lose everything, but it was worth a try.

'We will shake on it, Mrs Diamond. You do what you will as long as we get our percentage. What about him and Karen?' He pointed to the man in the cage.

'Burn his balls!' Jules shouted. 'Fry them. He threatens to kill children for money.'

They could all see the horrified look on Tom's face as he screamed and kicked at the cage in wild panic.

Jacques gave Patsy a wry grin. 'Do you have the stomach for that Mrs Diamond?'

'Yes, but Karen is mine. I will take her back to Scotland, away from you. Then we will be even.'

The men seemed satisfied with that. Jules stood up and walked away walking back to the cage with a car battery. 'Take his pants off Freddo; I will fry his balls.'

Sheila let out a gasp of horror and they all turned towards her. Patsy had almost forgotten she was in the room. 'This won't take long,' Patsy assured Sheila. Sheila held Patsy's crazed eyes and almost vomited as they attached wires to a battery and held them against Tom's balls and sent electric shocks through him, making him almost dance in the air. His screams were deafening, but Patsy stood there watching the man's pain. She enjoyed it.

They could hear banging and shouts on the hatch in the ceiling, but Patsy ignored them. Manon wheeled a table forward and took off the covering. To Patsy's surprise, it was a smaller version of a guillotine. 'Do you think he has had enough Mrs Diamond?'

'Yes, don't let him pass out.' Looking at Jacques, she smiled. 'I take it this is your torture chamber Jacques. I must remember that if I am ever invited here again.' She grinned. Taking out her lipstick and mirror from her bag, she applied more.

'My my Mrs Diamond, what an ice queen you are.' Jacques returned her smile. 'We will enjoy doing business with you.' Manon grabbed hold of Tom, and still with his trousers around his knees, dragged him forward towards the guillotine. Once Tom regained his senses, he gave out a piercing scream, but knew it was futile. Manon grabbed him from behind and thrust his neck under the sharp steel blade and pulled the chord to let the blade drop, slicing Tom's head off and letting it roll along the floor. Satisfied, Patsy took out her phone. Everyone looked at her in puzzlement as she tiptoed past the blood and held out her mobile and took a photo of Tom's head.

Sheila couldn't stand it any more and vomited. This Patsy sent cold shivers down her spine and frightened her. She was cold and ruthless.

'When do you want your money Jacques for my half of the truffle trade?' Patsy's voice was cold and steady.

Jacques poured her and Sheila another whisky. 'That is for your stomach.' He nodded at Sheila, who was now trembling and deathly pale. He turned back to Patsy. 'Mrs Diamond, let's say the end of the week. Sort out your business first, and Karen of course.'

Patsy picked up her glass and toasted the air. 'To business, Jacques.'

17

SOLID GROUND

Patsy led the way through the hatch with a trembling Sheila behind her. She could hardly climb the stairs her legs felt so weak.

James ran forward. 'What the hell was that all about? We heard muffled screams; I thought it was you.'

Patsy waved him off nonchalantly and headed for the door. 'They had someone down there, possibly one of your farm labourers Karen. He was just beating him up. That was for our benefit. He was putting on a show, to let us know what would happen if we double crossed him.'

James looked at Sheila, who for once was quiet; he knew it was a lie.

'So,' said Karen, totally oblivious to everything but her own selfishness, 'is he going to accept your terms and leave us alone?'

'Yes, he is Karen. Everything is sorted now, he just wanted to speak business with myself to make sure I had the funds. Without your shouting. The farm will not be touched again, the dogs will be returned, and you can rest in peace that it's sorted.' Patsy smiled to herself. *RIP*, she thought.

No one spoke apart from Karen on the drive home. She couldn't stop cursing the mob and how they had used her and tried robbing her like Nick had. Then, without thinking, she said, 'I knew it was the right thing to kidnap your daughter to make you see sense.'

Patsy could almost hear James and Fin sucking their breath in waiting for an outburst from her, but none came.

Arriving back at the farm, Patsy smiled and saw it through new eyes. This was half hers now and she had the protection of the Milieu.

'You will need to come back to Scotland with me tomorrow, Karen. My lawyer is there to draw everything up professionally and so is my accountant to send the funds to your French mob.'

Sheila almost choked on the goulash they were serving, or stew as she had called it.

Karen's eyes sparkled. 'Yes what a good idea. I would like to meet your accountant.' She grinned. 'I will make the call to make sure your daughter is okay.' A shudder ran through Patsy; she had overlooked that. Tom was dead. He wouldn't answer the phone.

Sheila and Patsy watched as Karen dialled Tom's number and waited, then she tutted and moaned that he wasn't answering. Suddenly her phone sprang into life and vibrated, indicating there was a message. Karen showed it to Patsy. 'He may not be answering but look.'

The message puzzled Patsy. It simply said:

It's too loud in the Disney park to talk. All is good here.

Then it dawned on Patsy. Good old Freddie had thought well ahead of her and was keeping Karen's game alive. He had taken

Tom's phone and texted Karen back with this cock and bull story.

'I'm messaging him back to let him know I am going to Scotland with you in the morning. Maybe he could meet us there with your family.'

'That is a good idea. What about your stepdaughters?'

'I don't know, they are not my business. They always were spoilt brats. They were being dropped off at some old aunties of theirs. I told them it was for their own safety as we were having trouble here.'

Patsy felt sick; this woman knew no mercy. She didn't give a toss about anyone but herself.

For the time being, Patsy avoided James; she knew he would be full of questions and at the moment didn't want to discuss what had happened in the cellar. Sheila wanted to go for a walk to clear her head and James decided to go with her. Patsy presumed he would press Sheila for information, but she knew Sheila well. He would get nothing out of her.

Fin stayed behind with herself and Victoria while Karen went and packed for their trip. Patsy had already booked the tickets; she couldn't wait to get back.

Victoria chatted away to Fin while she made him a proper cup of tea. It had crossed her mind many times, but now there was no one around, she decided to ask Fin about his father, Billy Burke. 'How did you get to know him Fin? It was in prison you said, wasn't it?' She didn't want to push in case he thought she was being nosy cow and clammed up.

'Yes, he was on remand. Christ, I nearly shit myself when they showed me into his cell. A bloody big brute of a man.' Victoria laughed, but she remembered Billy Burke well, and could imagine Fin's horror.

'He used to make and drink that hooch.' Seeing Victoria's

puzzled face he explained, 'It's an alcohol you can make out of fruit or veg. Anyway, Victoria, he got pissed one night and was boasting about how many women he'd had and then he slurred his way into telling me he had been married and then he showed me a photo of his wife. I don't know why he carried it around, or even kept it. I tell you Victoria, I nearly wet myself. It was the same photo my nan had of my mother. I asked him again if that was his wife and he confirmed it, which meant he was my dad.' Fin sat there, wide eyed, stressing the fact to Victoria. 'Can you imagine that Victoria? That big bastard was my father!'

Victoria laughed. 'What was he inside for?'

Fin shrugged. 'Billy had spent more time behind bars than an animal at the zoo, but he seemed to be angry that a partner he'd had had grassed him up to lessen their own sentence. Fuck he was blazing with what he was going to do if he ever got hold of them!'

'Oh dear, that doesn't sound good. What did he say when you told him you were his son?' she pressed further.

'Well, it took me a few days and I wasn't sure if I should. Anyway, I said it when we were laid in our bunks one night. I had to prove it though, so I told him who my nan was and stuff and that seemed to satisfy him. At least he stopped robbing off me after that.'

Victoria reached forward and patted his hand. 'It sounds awful Fin. How do you survive in a place like that?'

He shrugged and kept his hand near hers. 'I knew a few of the lads in there. Some treat it like home from home. Even when they get out, they can't cope so they steal something to get arrested. It's three meals a day, no rent or council tax, and you can still get your drugs.' Sheepishly, Fin looked down at the table. He knew that didn't sound good, especially to a lady like Victoria. And she was a lady, he decided. She never had a cross word with anyone. He enjoyed someone giving him attention for once. He was always 'good old Fin', but no one took him seriously enough to really talk to him like this. He was thirty now. Most of his life, he'd ducked and dived stealing or selling drugs. He suddenly felt the pain of losing his friends Spider and Beanie again. He told Victoria all about the daft things they had done together, making her laugh in the process.

Victoria couldn't help but ask, 'What were you in prison for Fin? Was it drugs?' Catching herself, she shook her head. 'No, sorry Fin, it's none of my business.'

'No, it's fine really. I tried killing myself.' Fin shrugged. 'As you can see, it never worked.'

Victoria was horrified. 'They put you in prison for trying to kill yourself? That's awful. Oh my god Fin, you must have been feeling terrible to do something so drastic.' Victoria laid her hand on his to comfort him.

'I had a girlfriend, really liked her I did, but then she dumped me. She said I was common because of the cretins. Anyway, I'd had a few beers too many and I went to the cemetery and used my belt to hang myself from a tree. The problem was, the bloody branch snapped and I fell to the floor and broke my ankle when I fell on one of the headstones. Bloody hurt too. My back was scratched to fuck and I was half choking from the belt around my neck. Gasping for breath I was...' Suddenly Fin looked up at Victoria and blushed. Victoria was a lady, and he had just sworn in front of her.

'Go on Fin,' she urged. 'What happened?' Totally absorbed by Fin's story, she didn't want to ask why his girlfriend thought he was common because of the cretins, but she felt the need to ask. Mentally she presumed the cretins were his pals, Spider and Beanie.

'I was at her brother's wedding and we had soup for our

starter. I loved them cretins, and had never had those crusty, sprinkly things on top of my soup before. They have them in cuppa soups as well now,' he boasted, quite pleased with himself. 'Anyway, I ate loads of them, and when I asked for some more, that's when she called me common and an idiot.' He shrugged sadly, and sat up straight.

Puzzled, Victoria tried making sense of the conversation. Suddenly, a light flicked on in her brain. Crusty things on soup? 'Oh, you mean croutons. Is that what you mean?' She half smiled to herself.

'Aye, that's them Victoria. Little toasted square things on your soup, lovely they are. Saves you dipping your bread in the soup. Anyway.' Fin took a deep sigh. 'Somebody heard my screams and called the police and that was when they took me to the hospital and arrested me. When I fell, I'd broken one of the headstones with one of those little angel things on it and I had broken its wings. I got charged with vandalism in the grave-yard, and got six months in prison and put on suicide watch. That's how I met my dad, Billy. He thought it was hilarious; he didn't care one hoot about my broken heart. Never saw that woman again. She didn't even visit me in prison.' Gloomily, Fin looked down at the table and sniffed, while remembering his lost love.

Despite the sadness of his story, Victoria wanted to burst out laughing. It was the funniest thing she had heard in years, but she could see it was a deadly serious matter to Fin, and did her best to stifle it.

Changing the subject, Fin looked at her hopefully. 'Do you think Patsy will be able to get those Albanians back for killing my mates, Victoria?'

'I'm sure she will Fin. She just needs to sort things out here first, but at least we're going home tomorrow.'

'I was going to stay to have a look around Paris, but to be honest I'm sick of France now. I just want to go home.'

'Just think Fin, this time tomorrow, we will be back in Glasgow. One more sleep darling and home. Now then, I am sure there is some decent whisky in this large house, and as Sheila would put it, you sound like you could do with a wee dram.' Victoria stood and walked towards the lounge where the drinks cabinet was. Fin couldn't stop grinning. At last, he'd found a friend.

Patsy joined Victoria in the lounge. 'Well, well, well, Victoria, rifling through the drinks cabinet.' She laughed. 'I'll have whatever you're having.'

Victoria poured Patsy a whisky. 'I'm going to take this through to Fin. I suppose I had better take the decanter. One will not be enough.'

Victoria disappeared and then came back. 'I was asking him about Billy Burke and how he found him.' Victoria explained everything that Fin had told her. Although Patsy was listening, her mind stopped when she heard Victoria say that Billy Burke had been grassed up by his partner. Somewhere in the back of her mind, something was nagging at her. It rang a bell somewhere and she couldn't remember where she had heard it.

'I'm going to have an early night. And I suppose I had better ring Larry. He must be frantic. Goodnight Victoria.'

She made her way to her room, dialling Larry's number as she went.

'Where the hell have you been Patsy? I was almost tempted to come to Paris to find you!' Larry shouted down the phone. Patsy waited while he let off steam. She knew this would happen and felt it would be better to get it out of the way before she returned to Glasgow.

'I'm coming home tomorrow, Larry. The phone signal is

terrible here.'

'Did you know that Karen Duret's brother is your accountant Tom? No wonder she didn't want to discuss accounts. He has betrayed you, Patsy.' Larry rambled on like a steam train.

'No, I didn't know that, Larry. Thank you for telling me. Everyone is okay and we're all coming home. Karen is also coming so that you can draw up some paperwork regarding our partnership.'

Again, Larry went on about how foolish he thought she was being entering into a partnership with Karen, but Patsy stopped him. 'It's to dissolve the partnership, Larry. And I wouldn't trust anyone to do it but you. I will text you what I want. I am also sending some photos I have taken. I want to invest in the chateau and farm.' Hearing Larry's deep sigh, Patsy added, 'It's a good investment Larry, and I am not paying a lot.'

Larry seemed to breathe a sigh of relief. 'I've missed you Patsy, have you missed me?' His voice softened.

'You know I have and I'm coming home tomorrow. I can show you how much face to face.' Patsy felt happier now that Larry wasn't panicking. She'd missed him, missed his arms around her, even though it had only been days. The more she thought about him, a tingling feeling ran through her body. Larry made her feel like a woman again, a sexy, desirable woman.

* * *

'Am I glad to be going home.' Sheila rested her head back on the aeroplane seat and sipped her drink. It had only been a few days, but she was drained. She hadn't had time to talk to Patsy alone about their meeting, and every time she closed her eyes, she saw Tom's head rolling on the floor with his eyes wide open. It was like a horror movie continuously on replay. A fleeting thought passed through her mind, that if she was ever going to turn to drugs again, it would be now. But no, she decided. She was clean now and she would stay that way.

Victoria smiled. She too was glad this stressful time was over, but none of them could speak openly with Karen there. 'Angus will be pleased to see you I'm sure Sheila. I bought some T-shirts at the airport for the girls with the Eiffel Tower logo; I thought they might like them.'

Giving her a weak smile, Sheila looked down and felt ashamed. She had been so glad to leave Paris, it had never crossed her mind to buy souvenirs.

Patsy looked across at James and Fin sitting together; they seemed to be in deep conversation, and she wondered what could be so interesting that they had their heads locked together liked that. Karen was sat beside her; she had made sure of that. It was a direct, short flight to Glasgow and once there it was a hop and a skip home.

Larry was waiting for them at the airport gates. Patsy breathed a sigh of relief when he wasn't standing there with a bunch of flowers and instead, he had his business head on and called her Mrs Diamond. Mentally, she thanked her lucky stars that she had told him she was bringing Karen back to Scotland to sign some papers, which had put him on his guard. She could say a lot about Larry, but what she loved most was his professionalism.

Angus was there with Sheila's children. Her face lit up as she ran towards them all for a group hug. Turning swiftly, Sheila caught Patsy's eyes. 'I'm going home Patsy. We'll speak later, okay?'

Victoria handed over the carrier bag containing the souvenirs for the girls. 'Take a break Sheila and enjoy your family. You've been very quiet; are you okay?' Victoria had a feeling it was something to do with the muffled screams they had heard from the cellar, which surprised Victoria. She thought nothing frightened Sheila.

Sheila cast a glance at Patsy then back at Victoria. 'Aye Vicky lass, just homesick you know.' Her explanation seemed to satisfy Victoria.

Patsy sidled up to Victoria. 'Karen and I are going directly to Larry's office. Do you want to come or would you rather get a taxi and head off home?'

'What I want to know,' Victoria snapped at both herself and Karen, 'is where my granddaughter is.'

Karen seemed to blush slightly beneath her long flowing blonde hair and her skilfully applied make-up. 'Everything is okay. I have spoken to the people looking after Nancy and your parents and they assure me she will be home, today or tomorrow.' Karen shifted uneasily from one foot to another.

'Just make sure it's today, Karen, do you hear me? Nancy is my granddaughter, and if I don't hear she is in England by the end of the day, I will inform the police. Do you understand?'

'I guarantee it will be today Victoria.' Patsy grinned. 'Everything is sorted out now.'

Victoria knew there was more to this than met the eye and accepted Patsy's word.

Patsy was pleased when Larry took the lead. 'Come on Victoria, I'll get a taxi for you.' Taking her bag, he walked ahead with Victoria, leaving Patsy and Karen to follow.

Patsy cast Karen a sideways glance. 'So you've spoken to your contact looking after Nancy and my parents and they will be coming home as soon as possible then?'

Karen nodded her head, which made Patsy smile more. Karen hadn't spoken to them at all and she was lying her head off – not unless she could speak to the dead! Patsy knew that Freddie would see that Nancy was home. Safe and sound.

Once they had waved off Victoria, they were in Larry's car and on their way to his offices. Patsy sat in the front with Larry while he chatted about the weather and other immaterial subjects. Patsy pulled down the visor to check her lipstick in the mirror, all the while she could see Karen frantically texting on her mobile. The sheer feeling of satisfaction warmed her. Now the boot was on the other foot, and this was only the beginning.

No sooner did they get to the solicitors than they were jostled towards his office. It was time to call Karen's bluff. 'Before you sign these legal papers I have prepared giving me a share in your property in return for payment to the landlords, as promised, I would like to speak to Nancy.' Patsy grinned.

'They are still all having a good time in Disneyland, but I assure you they are safe. After all, we are partners and there has to be some trust. Are you going to transfer the money now?' Patsy and Larry could sense Karen's nervousness. She seemed agitated and kept checking her phone.

As if by magic, Patsy's own mobile burst into life, indicating a message. Quickly glancing at it, she smiled. It was a photo of her parents and Nancy in their living room. Patsy recognised it instantly. Even better was the fact that her father was holding up his own mobile phone with the date and time on it. Patsy breathed a sigh of relief. Her family were safe, and this bitch before her was lying her head off to save her own skin – again.

'Sorry about that, just Victoria letting me know she is home safe and sound.' Patsy smiled. 'Right then, to business. Make sure you read all of the small print Karen and you're satisfied with everything.'

'Can we just sign and get it over with?' Karen snapped. 'I have to get back home and there is a flight in a couple of hours.

Can we just speed things up please, this legal jargon is boring.'
Drumming her fingers on Larry's desk and continuously
checking her mobile, Karen looked bored.

'You shouldn't sign anything without reading it Ms Duret,'
Larry explained.

'Look, just get on with it will you!' she snapped again.

Patsy took delight in watching Karen squirm. She then
turned to Larry. 'Is my accountant here yet?' Again, Patsy had to
restrain herself from laughing.

Larry shook his head. He felt Patsy was playing a dangerous
game and avoided her eyes and shuffled the papers around on
his desk.

'Never mind, he will turn up soon; maybe he is stuck in
traffic.'

'Look, can we just sign the paperwork. Surely you can sort
out the finance side of things. It's only transferring money.'

Looking at them both, Larry sighed and handed over two
pieces of paper, one to each of them. 'This is to confirm that Mrs
Diamond is paying for half of your business and will become
your business partner in your truffle business. Do you understand that?'

Karen sat swinging her crossed legs; she was agitated and
nervous, and Patsy thought she saw sweat appearing on her
brow. This was the best game of poker Patsy had played and she
was enjoying it.

'Yes, yes, Larry. That is why I'm here, isn't it? Just give me the
pen.' Snatching the pen out of Larry's hand, Karen signed the
bottom of the paperwork and almost threw it at him. Patsy
signed her own slowly and then prompted Larry, 'The other
paperwork Larry.'

Casting her a furtive glance, Larry handed the paperwork
over to Karen that dissolved their partnership in all of her busi-

nesses that Nick had set up. Patsy had text him her instructions, that as Karen had no money, she wanted to dissolve the partnerships as long as Patsy paid off her debts. Patsy almost rubbed her hands with glee. In a matter of seconds, Karen would own no shares in her pizza parlours or the community centre.

Larry stood up and opened his office door and asked his secretary and receptionist to step in to witness the paperwork being signed.

'Why the hell do I have to sign twice for god's sake?'

'You know what lawyers are like, Karen; everything has to be in duplicate.' Patsy laughed.

Larry's face was deadpan. He didn't like deceit and continued against Patsy's wishes to urge Karen to read what she was signing, but it was futile. She didn't even look at the heading which clearly indicated the paperwork was about dissolving the partnership. Karen turned swiftly to the back pages and signed them and waited patiently for the paperwork to be witnessed. 'Have you transferred the money yet Patsy?' Karen asked.

'We're doing it now.' Patsy brought her account up on her phone and typed in the account number the Milieu had given her. This was the sting in the tail. Karen and her brother had been so meticulous with their plans but when it came to the paperwork Karen couldn't be bothered.

Patsy felt like jumping in the air. She was free of Karen Duret and everything she stood for. More to the point, she was free from Tom and he had been silenced forever. It felt like a huge weight had been lifted from her shoulders.

'Can we not have dinner or a drink together Karen, before you go back to Paris? I feel the occasion needs something, don't you?' Patsy could see this cat and mouse game was getting to Karen and she was trying to remain calm.

'Yes, I suppose we could on the way back to the airport Patsy, but we have to be quick about it.'

Patsy's heart warmed with glee. This was just what she wanted and now she could put her plans in place.

'Has the money gone through? Show me?' Karen leaned over Patsy's shoulder to see her online bank account.

'Yes Karen look.' Patsy held up her phone and showed her the amount of money that had been paid out of her account and to whom.

Faltering slightly, Karen looked at Patsy. 'That is more than I expected. Is that what they wanted to speak to you about? More money?'

'Something like that; they knew they had the upper hand, but it's sorted now, isn't it?' Although everything had been signed, Patsy began to feel nervous. She didn't want Karen asking questions now, especially in front of Larry. 'Like I say Karen, maybe we should have that drink before you leave.'

A puzzled frown crossed Karen's brow and she nodded. 'Yes, I think we should.'

To change the subject, Patsy said, 'I'm also in a hurry; I need to get back to London to see my daughter. You did say she would be home today, didn't you?'

Stammering slightly, Karen nodded. 'It will most likely be tomorrow, because it is getting late, but I will check for you.'

Larry stood there watching these two women battling it out. They were both strong women who hated each other, and they both liked the upper hand. Personally, he didn't like any of it and now it dawned on him that Patsy had not only tricked him but Karen too. Patsy had given him the impression that all was well, and that Karen wanted to dissolve the partnership and take the money to invest in her own home and business. Now he knew this was not the case. He loved Patsy and deep inside him he felt he always would, but could he ever trust her?

18

A FRESH START

Patsy shook Larry's hand and thanked him. Turning towards Karen, she urged her to do likewise and then they shook each other's hands to seal the deal.

Larry gave a little cough to clear his throat. 'Could I have a word with you on another matter Mrs Diamond?' he asked politely. He hated playing this game. He hadn't seen her for days and the closest he was getting to her was across from his desk as a client. He wanted to hold her in his arms.

'Not just now Larry. As you heard, Karen and I are going for a drink to celebrate. I am sure whatever it is can wait, and don't forget I will be leaving soon myself to go to London to see Nancy.'

Patsy suddenly hated herself when she saw the crushed, disappointed look on his face. It made her feel like she had just kicked a puppy. There was nothing she could say in front of Karen, and she looked at Larry almost pleading for him to understand.

'If that is what you want Mrs Diamond. Enjoy your evening.'

Larry stood up and opened the door for them both. His face was grim and he avoided Patsy's eyes.

Karen walked out first. Patsy turned to Larry and mouthed the words 'sorry' and blew a kiss, making the sign with her little finger and thumb like a phone, indicating she would call him. She knew this was little consolation and she wanted to have some time alone with him but she had loose ends to tie up.

'We need to call a taxi or something, if that lawyer of yours isn't driving us.' Karen's snotty attitude annoyed Patsy. Suddenly she had become self-assured and arrogant again now she thought she had beaten her.

'I've already thought of that and I have Fin picking us up. You remember Fin don't you?'

'You expect me to get into a car with that scruffy idiot? I would rather call a cab.'

Patsy smiled through gritted teeth, almost biting her tongue. What right did this ex-junkie have to sneer at Fin? She was no better than him. In fact, she was worse.

Fin had done as instructed and brought Patsy's car. She opened the car door for Karen, and Fin looked at Patsy for instructions. 'Are we going home Mrs Diamond?'

'Karen and I are going to have a drink and a chat together and I have found the perfect place for us to talk in peace.'

Karen looked puzzled. 'What have you planned? Where are we going?'

'For a ride, for a drink. You have some unfinished business to attend to while you are here.'

'I have no business here; I have to get home. Drive me to the airport Fin,' Karen commanded. Faltering slightly, Karen tapped Fin on the shoulder. 'Actually, I need to go to the hotel I was staying at the last time I was here. I left something there and I need to pick it up. They are expecting me.' Fin waited for Karen to tell him which hotel and he drove off.

'So, what is it you left that is so important?' Now Patsy was intrigued. 'How were you going to collect it if you had no plans to come back to Scotland?'

'They were going to post it, but I may as well pick it up.'

A cold chill ran down Patsy's spine. She hadn't expected this turn of events. Why would Karen need to go back to her hotel if they could post something? Why hadn't they posted it already, whatever it was?

'Wait here, I will be five minutes,' said Karen, getting out of the car.

Patsy rolled down the car window. 'Actually, Karen, we could have a drink here. After all, they have a bar, don't they?'

Fobbing her off and waving her hand in dismissal, Karen shook her head. 'Five minutes Patsy. I would rather have a drink nearer the airport if you don't mind. Anyway,' she scoffed, 'the service here was crap.'

A frown crossed Patsy brow; she felt nervous. What was Karen hiding?

'Do you think she'll come back Patsy?' asked Fin, while lighting a cigarette. 'Maybe there's a back door; she seemed pretty eager to get rid of you.'

'Give me one of those will you?' Taking a cigarette from Fin, she lit it and blew the smoke out of the open window. 'Did you do as I ask?'

'Sure thing Patsy. James thinks I've gone to bed. He said he wants you to make his wife disappear – is that right?'

Shocked, Patsy looked at him, her eyes wide with horror. Suddenly she remembered the conversation she'd had with James, before they'd left for France. He had said he wanted a favour and that Patsy owed him. Could this possibly be it? Patsy sat back in the seat and inhaled deeply on her cigarette. 'I honestly had no idea about this crazy scheme of his. It's not my argument Fin, not my marriage. If he has problems with his wife, then he needs to sort it out himself.'

Fin lowered his head. 'Is that how you feel about Spider and Beanie? Like they're not your problem?'

'Absolutely not Fin. They were fighting my battles, although they did jump the gun a little. That is a different matter entirely.'

'Are you sure about that Patsy, because I'm putting myself on the line for you. If James knew I had lied to him he wouldn't be happy. What is all of this about?'

'Fin, I never agreed to anything about his wife disappearing. What does he think I am, a bloody magician?' Surely, James knew all of the right people. Why would he need her to make his wife disappear? It didn't make sense. 'I appreciate you thought I already knew. This conversation stops here. I am killing no one's wife. If that is James's intention then let him do it. Is that what you were talking about on the aeroplane?'

'Something like that,' Fin muttered. He knew he had said the wrong thing and didn't mean to drop James in it. He presumed by what James had said that it was all agreed. James had told him on the aeroplane that he would need an alibi because he needed to be as far away from his wife as possible while Patsy made her disappear. That was all Fin knew. He didn't know when or where this was supposed to happen.

Patsy took another drag on her cigarette. This was the time to sow her seed of doubt in Fin's mind about James. 'Is his wife another partner he wants rid of? It seems he is known for it, either grassing partners up or disposing of them. You're a loyal friend Fin and never forget, it was you who saved his life. He owes you more loyalty than you do him.'

'What do you mean? James has been good to you; why would

you say that? What do you know about him?' Puzzled by Patsy's manner, Fin waited. Patsy admired him for defending his friend, but she knew sooner or later Fin would have to make a choice and she wanted herself to be that choice. As much as she liked James, things didn't add up. Why would he tell Fin she was going to make his wife disappear? And more to the point, who else had he mentioned it to? James obviously had a plan he hadn't told her yet, and it made her feel uneasy.

'Oh, nothing Fin, just mouthing off. Don't worry about it. Although, it does make me wonder why he doesn't just divorce her or get Freddie's help. Do you know what I mean?'

Fin fell silent, and she could see she had given him a lot to think about. She liked Fin; he wasn't the brightest of men, but he had his own talents and she respected that. He just needed a push in the right direction.

Karen looked around the hotel room she was still paying for. It was clear that no one had been there since she had left. She had expected Tom to be there or that he might have at least left her a note, but there was nothing. She wondered if he had already taken Nancy and Patsy's parents to London, but when she had last text him, she'd told him to meet here so that she could hand them over personally to prove she hadn't double crossed Patsy. Even though he hadn't answered his phone, she knew he would get her message and she checked her phone again to make sure the message had gone through. She felt satisfied that it had, but where the hell was he? Picking up the hotel phone, she telephoned reception asking if there were any messages for her, but there were none.

She knew Patsy didn't want to be partners with her, and more to the point, Karen didn't want a partner. Now that she had seen Patsy pay the gang bosses, that meant, for the time being, she had the Milieu off her back and she would own the chateau again. All she needed to do was get rid of Patsy, but where the hell was Tom?

Ringing his mobile again, she was frustrated and frantic when nothing happened. His phone was dead. There was no connection and Karen's mind was spinning with explanations of what could have happened. She knew she had to leave soon as Patsy would be getting restless waiting for her and would probably come looking for her.

Running her hands through her hair, she sat on the edge of the bed and kicked her shoes off. She didn't know what to do. She realised that something could have gone badly wrong, and that Tom and Patsy's family were possibly dead. Maybe Patsy's parents had attacked him? Tom and the others had guns, and maybe Patsy's father had found one. Apparently, he had been a military man of sorts. Karen wracked her brain; she didn't know who to contact or what to do. Tears of frustration brimmed on her lashes. She felt trapped. At least if Tom was dead, it would mean she wouldn't have to share anything with him, she mused. There was always a bright side she supposed, and she would never be under his watchful eye ever again. He had been a good, loyal brother, but a fleeting thought crossed her mind, that Tom could have double crossed her and was now on Patsy's side. Maybe he had taken a bribe and was leaving her to take all of the blame? Her mind spun as all kinds of possibilities crossed her mind.

Lying full length on the bed, Karen looked up at the ceiling in the hope that Tom would come sailing through the door any minute. Her mind wandered back to that awful time in her life when she vaguely remembered waking up in the hospital after her near miss with a drug overdose. Tom had thought quickly and identified her dead friend as herself, and when she had come around he had prompted her to use her dead friend's name. She remembered being too ill to argue and had just gone along with it. Tom had urged her to do this and had then got her into a rehab programme. It had been hard, and Tom had sent her to Paris away from Nick and the rest of the world. Getting her away had been the answer to Tom's prayers... but not hers.

The thorn in her side had always been Patsy Diamond. From the very beginning, Karen had always felt that if it wasn't for her, Nick would have loved her. She remembered seeing Patsy Diamond float into Nick's office one day with her designer clothes leaving a waft of expensive perfume in her wake and happily Nick had gone to lunch with her, laughing and joking as they had passed her by. It had stung like a knife in her heart, although Nick assured her afterwards, that it was all a pretence. He was playing the long game and he had to keep it up for fear of Patsy taking all of his money and he just needed to find the right time to tell Patsy he was leaving her. What a bloody stupid fool she had been!

Sweeping her hair back from her forehead and brushing away a tear that had fallen down the side of her face, Karen cringed when she remembered the girl she had once been. She had always vowed vengeance on the Diamond family and then out of the blue after all of these years, they had discovered that Nick had arranged an account in the name of Karen Duret. Ironic really. He really did like that name and what it stood for, but it had been the answer to all of her prayers. The Milieu were bleeding her dry. Armand had been a useless piece of shit, and he hadn't realised she had known what a sad, lonely drunk who gambled too much he was. But now he was gone.

Karen realised that the only thing she could do now was go home. If Tom was alive, he would contact her there.

'Fuck!' Karen shouted at the ceiling in anger and frustration. Her palms were sweaty and as she got up from the bed, she caught sight of herself in the mirror and winced. She opened her bag and applied some more make-up. She realised she had to see this charade through. The contracts were signed and Patsy would go ape when there was no sign of her daughter, but she would cross that bridge when she came to it.

Remembering her plan B, Karen pulled back the small chest of drawers. Taped to the back of it was a gun that she had managed to smuggle into Glasgow. She would let Patsy and that fool drop her off at the airport car park and shoot them both in the back of the head before she left for Paris. This would be her last goodbye to Scotland and the Diamonds.

Taking a deep breath, Karen smoothed down her hair and picked up her bag. Looking around the room once more, she closed the door behind her. She still had the faint hope that maybe Tom would turn up. It wasn't so much him she wanted to see but Nancy. Nancy was her golden goose and she cursed herself for letting the girl out of her sight.

Leaving a message at reception for Tom, she paid the bill and painted a smile on her face as she walked back towards Patsy and Fin.

'Did you get what you needed? You have been gone over half an hour,' Patsy snapped. Her and Fin had been clock watching. They had sat in silence and waited, wondering if Karen had found some way out of a back door. Patsy was prepared to wait another five minutes and then drive to the airport. They both knew that was where she would run to and they wanted to be there when she did.

'Yes,' replied Karen, 'but so much red tape proving who you are and so forth. These people are thorough.'

Patsy cast a glance at Fin. Neither of them believed the lies that dripped out of Karen's mouth.

'Well, let's go for that drink shall we? Time is getting on.' Patsy's smile was as false as Karen's as Fin drove off. He had an uneasy feeling about all of this, especially when he knew what surprise Patsy had planned for her...

Patsy was growing tired of Karen's complaints, especially when she'd realised they were driving in the wrong direction. Fin mumbled something about road closures and traffic and she had no choice but to go along with it. Disgruntled, Karen sat back in the seat of the car and gripped her handbag containing the gun close to her. She was beginning to become impatient; she wanted rid of these two clowns and to be safely back home. Nothing was going as planned.

When they turned up at the cemetery, Karen was startled. 'Why are we here?' she demanded, gripping the back of Patsy's seat.

'I thought as you were tying up loose ends Karen, you might like to say goodbye properly to your friend. You never did get the chance to pay your last respects, did you? I have some flowers in the boot of the car for you to put on the grave, if that's okay.'

Wide eyed and horrified, Karen protested. 'Do you realise that name on there is mine you stupid bitch! Why would I want to do that?' She was about to open her handbag and reach for her gun when Patsy handed her her mobile. Karen looked at the image on the screen. It was a photo of Nancy with her grandparents at home safely. 'Thanks for this Karen; I now know you are a woman of your word, and we can put the past behind us and concentrate on business.'

Looking at the image, Karen was stunned, but it reassured her that Tom was still in charge of the situation and Patsy was happy with the outcome. Mentally, she decided to go along with Patsy's stupid game and lay a bunch of flowers on her junkie friend's grave. What a stupid idea! The only thing she had in common with the woman was that they had shared the same syringe. What did she care? Although the idea of seeing her own grave made her skin crawl. She had never seen it and never wanted to, but if Patsy wanted to do this, she couldn't object. At least she knew that Patsy was now on her side and would not suspect what was coming. The very idea of Patsy Diamond near a cemetery with a bullet hole in the back of her head made her smile.

'Yes, let's do that Patsy, but, then I really must go.'

Fin got out of the car first and went to open the door for Karen. As he glimpsed Karen putting on her red leather gloves, a frown crossed his brow. Keeping calm, he saw her safely out of the car and then walked around to the boot of the car and took out a bunch of flowers Patsy had instructed him to buy and handed them to her. Walking over to Patsy's side of the car, and through the half open window, he lowered his voice and whispered *gun* under his breath and then coughed while opening the door.

Remaining calm, Patsy got out of the car and linked her arm through Karen's and walked ahead of Fin. Fin wasn't sure if she had heard him; all he could do was cross his fingers and hope.

As they walked, Patsy looked around; the cemetery was empty and peaceful. She realised now why Nick liked them so much. They were solitary places.

Once they stood beside the graveside, they were both solemn. Not knowing what to expect after Fin's revelation, Patsy knelt beside it. 'Come Karen, let's arrange those flowers properly.'

Karen had no choice but to kneel beside her. Patsy handed her some flowers from the bouquet and started putting the others in the small vase in front of the headstone. Leaning over, Karen did likewise, while Fin looked on. He felt nervous and wondered who would pounce first.

Avoiding her stare and concentrating on the flowers, Patsy felt this was her time. 'I know you hate me Karen, and whatever you and Nick got up to is not my fault. If anything, yet again, I am the wronged woman. It seems he was forever fooling around with other women and god knows how many others there are.' Patsy sighed. 'But he's dead now and you have had your revenge. But kidnapping my family has made you my enemy, I'm afraid. Do you really think I would let you get away with it?'

Cocking her head to one side, Karen smiled. 'You already have you fool. I own half of your Diamond empire and you have paid up and bought into mine. Your accountant is my brother Patsy. He organised everything and what a bloody good job he has done.' Karen reached into her bag and took out her gun, pointing it at Patsy. She didn't care now. This was as good a place as any. Looking up, she smiled at Fin. 'Don't try anything silly, because the next bullet is yours.'

Stony-faced and quietly spoken, Patsy looked at the gun and then at Karen. 'Are you going to kill me Michelle, and take my identity too?'

Karen's face paled, and a frown crossed her brows. 'What are you talking about you stupid bitch?'

'You are Michelle Walker, now Mrs Devall.' Patsy smiled and shrugged. 'Most of your story wasn't a lie Michelle, and Victoria even felt sorry for you at times. But you were, and are, just as bad as Nick. Karen Duret was one of the prostitutes who worked for Nick. You befriended her. True, you were a junkie, and besotted with Nick, doing his bidding, but she was a young woman, with no background to speak of and you were her friend. Did you help her? No. You used her. When Nick had had enough of you, you stole her identity and claimed it as your own. That grave is actually correct in an ironic way. That is Karen Duret's grave, isn't it? That is why my friend Maggie couldn't recollect you. She had seen the two of you hanging around and drinking vodka while sniffing drugs and shooting up around the back of the estate where the skips are kept, but the face didn't match the name, that's what confused her. You're Michelle, your friend was Karen. The junkie Glasgow lassie done good eh?' Patsy smiled. Patsy looked at the gun pointed at her; she could feel her heart pounding, and her palms felt sticky and sweaty knowing that these could be the last words she ever spoke.

Hearing Patsy's words made Karen laugh out loud maniacally. 'It doesn't matter does it, you stupid bitch. I will own everything and you're going to be dead.' Looking at Fin, she pointed the gun towards him. 'Him too, but that's no loss. Game set and match, Patsy Diamond, I would say; wouldn't you?' She laughed again. 'You're right though; I gave Karen the overdose. Tom wanted me away from Nick and from her. He'd tried everything else to clean me up and hanging around with her wasn't helping me. He felt she was a bad influence, but that was Tom. It was always someone else's fault, never mine. He loved me no matter what. Denial, I suppose.' Karen shrugged. 'Tom and I hatched a plan. If I took Karen's identity, Nick wouldn't be able to find me and I would have that well needed fresh start. Karen, the fucked up junkie, was dead and buried. I stripped her of everything, just like she would have done me. Junkies are like that – selfish. Everyone knew she had a big mouth. She'd become too clingy, and stupidly while drugged up and pissed, I'd let my guard down and told her everything about myself and Nick. The drugs I used to drop off, the prisoners, and being sacked from the solicitors. No sooner had the words left my mouth I regretted it. She had this look in her eye, like she knew she'd just struck gold. She would have blackmailed me, told Nick where to find me. It's amazing what you're prepared to do for the next hit of heroin or cocaine. I needed rid of her, and in the process, I could get Nick off my back by getting rid of me, Michelle, for good. God, I was pathetic in those days. Karen was the perfect solution. No one would miss her. She was my only hope of freedom. It was Tom's idea that I leave the country; fresh start and all that.'

Bewildered, Patsy stared at her. 'You killed her because of your own stupidity. You gave her the stick to beat you with and then you regretted it and you and Tom decided to murder her. You're a ruthless bitch.'

'Whatever you say Patsy, but you're just as ruthless as I am. In fact, I would probably say you're worse. Your husband supplied women like me and then forced us into prostitution to pay the bills. The money he got paid for those fine clothes you're wearing. *I* paid for those clothes.'

Patsy shook her head. 'Drugs are a choice Karen, Michelle, whoever you are. No one forces you to take them. It's the same as smoking or drinking. It's you that blames everyone else for your short comings. So tell me, what happened next?' Patsy was curious; the more this story unravelled the worse it became.

Karen put one hand on her hips. 'It was easy; we'd drunk a lot of vodka. I sat beside her on the concrete floor by the skips and injected her, watching her foam at the mouth before dying. By choking on her own vomit.' A frown crossed Karen's brow as she thought back to that day. 'It was horrible and that sort of brought me into reality. She looked like a dog with rabies. That could have been my ending and suddenly I realised what Tom meant. Sometimes you have to see it to believe it, don't you? Tom was nearby and it was him who called the ambulance and police.

I took her identity and left the country before they could identify her body. By that time, it didn't matter. No one bothered to look too far into things, especially not France, where I was using her name. I was free.' Karen nodded, almost hysterically. 'She had to die so that I could live. And now, the same goes for you Patsy Diamond. Your time is up.'

Fin cast a glance at Patsy. This Karen woman, or whoever she claimed to be, was completely bonkers and worse than that she was pointing a gun at them. He watched her laughing out loud, with her red painted lips. He'd had enough; it was time to get out of here. He was about to step forward when Patsy stopped him, with her hand. 'Before you kill me Karen, I need to show you something the Milieu gave me. Is it okay if I reach for my mobile?' Fin watched Patsy's ice-cold calmness and swallowed hard.

'If that is your dying wish Patsy, but hurry up because I am fucking sick of you... No tricks now.' Patsy slowly took out her mobile and searched through it for the photo image she was looking for and held it towards Karen. 'Say goodbye to Tom, your thieving lying brother.'

Karen narrowed her eyes to make out the photo and then she realised it was Tom's head! Shocked and horrified, she looked at Patsy.

'They weren't beating up a farm labourer in that basement, they were killing your brother!'

Karen looked again at the image and then at Patsy. Cocking the gun back, she pressed the trigger, but Fin kicked her hard while Patsy lashed out, making her fire into the air.

'You fucking bitch,' Karen panted. 'You killed my brother!' Struggling and lashing out at Fin, Karen flew at Patsy, but Patsy moved aside and Karen fell on top of the grave. Her hollow yell as she cried out made Fin's and Patsy's blood run cold as they looked up at each other then back at Karen. She had fallen into the empty grave with a thud and wasn't moving. Before they had left Paris, Patsy had asked Fin to remove the planks of wood holding up the Astroturf on top of the grave. He had been surprised and shocked, but he had agreed. Fortunately no one had been around to see him and so once Fin had removed the planks of wood, he had quickly thrown the turf down again, almost like a blanket on top of the hollow grave. It seemed to sink a little with nothing to hold it up and in his panic, he had thrown some stones and leaves around the edges to keep it in place. Fin wiped his forehead; he was sweating, and they both glanced down at Karen's lifeless body at the bottom of the grave. Her head was at an awkward angle, and it was clear that she had broken her neck in the six-foot drop.

It had been Patsy's plan to shoot her and bury her in her own grave; it was her headstone after all. But Patsy felt there was such a thing as karma, and Karen had caused her own death.

'What are we going to do Patsy?' asked Fin. He was frightened and kept looking around the cemetery furtively. Time seemed to stand still.

'We need to secure this Fin and get the hell out of here. Where are the boards that were here?'

'Aren't you going to check to see if she is dead? She could just be unconscious.'

'She's dead all right; look at her neck.' Patsy could see Fin was frightened and trembling. He kept rubbing his face with his hands and looking around.

'Don't forget Fin, she would have gladly shot you and left you here. That goes for both of us. We didn't kill her, did we?' Patsy was sweating, and panicking. They needed to get out of there, but Fin was in a state of shock.

Tears brimmed in his eyes when he realised what they had

done. 'You were going to though, weren't you Patsy? You planned this all along and dragged me into it. This is all your fault.'

His accusations annoyed Patsy. They didn't have time for this now. They needed to sort this mess out before anyone saw them.

'Blame me later Fin, but she is dead.' Patsy wasn't so sure; out of the corner of her eye she thought she saw Karen move, but then decided it must have been a trick of the light. She didn't want to look again; she needed to switch her own mind off. Fin fell to his knees, almost sobbing. 'What are we going to do Patsy? We will get life for this. No one will believe she was going to kill us and that it was an accident.'

Standing over him, Patsy slapped his face and shook his shoulders. 'Snap out of it, Fin! Look at that headstone; her name is on it. She is dead already. Who is going to miss her? You heard her confession. She killed the real Karen Duret; she didn't give a fuck about anyone but herself. How do we know her story about what Nick did to her is true? We've only heard her side of it. She was prepared to kill us.' Patsy stressed the fact again to Fin, hoping it would seep into his troubled mind. 'Nick probably didn't know anything about the real Karen. He certainly wouldn't have put a bank account in her name if he did. That was probably Tom's idea. In Nick's hurry to stash money away to live with Natasha and his new family, Nick started up a new bank account in Karen's name and gave her address as the community centre. She even has shares in his business. I don't know what he was thinking but he seriously fucked up this time, didn't he?'

'But Larry knows she's alive. She's signed your documents today. How could she do that if she was dead?' Spit dribbled out of Fin's mouth; he felt sick. 'You lied to me. You said that French lot were beating up a labourer, but you watched them kill her brother, didn't you?' Fin accused. 'Why would they do that?'

'Tom and Karen had crossed them once too often. It was

nothing to do with me and Sheila. We had to get out of there and say nothing to save our own skins. Why scare the others, with what had happened? Also Fin, it was a warning to me if I ever crossed them.' Patsy was trying her best to remain calm, but she could hear herself shouting to get through to Fin. 'Look Fin, as far as Larry is concerned, we dropped her off at her hotel. Don't you remember? The hotel staff can vouch for that if anyone ever asks, which they won't. She didn't want to have a drink with us after all. As far as the paperwork is concerned, believe me, it's not a problem.' Patsy hoped that some of her words would seep into Fin's frightened brain. He wasn't thinking straight.

Seeing Fin crumple before her, Patsy knew the only way to get through to him was through his vulnerability. 'Come on Fin love, we've done nothing wrong. She attacked us and she fell down there. But, you're right Fin, we have to get away from here and no one must ever know, not even James.' She knelt down and hugged him. Inside she felt like screaming at him to get a grip, but the softer touch was what was needed here.

'Okay Patsy, let's do this.' Standing up, Fin walked over to where he had left the wooden boards that had once covered the grave. Grabbing hold of a corner of the Astroturf that Karen hadn't taken with her during her fall, Patsy heaved at it to pull it up. Averting their eyes from Karen's body, they both put the boards in place on top of the grave, securing them. They fitted into their slots Nick had built inside perfectly. They looked as though they had been there years. Quickly they rolled down the Astroturf and stepped on it to bury the corners. Within minutes, it looked like it had never been touched.

'What about the smell Patsy? Won't someone know something is rotting down there?'

Patsy hadn't thought of that, but there was nothing she could do now. 'I don't know Fin. It's very deep and it's covered. Not that many people come here.' Patsy was all out of answers and truth be known, she was tired. They were both dirty, muddy and sweaty. 'Where did that gun go flying off to Fin? We need that and her handbag.'

Within what seemed like hours, but was only fifteen minutes, Fin and Patsy were walking out of the cemetery and back to their car.

They both needed a well-earned cigarette. Seeing Fin's hand tremble a little, she offered to drive, but Fin shook his head and started the engine.

'I have to go away tomorrow, Fin. Not for long. I need to go and see Nancy. No doubt Victoria will want to come.'

'What was that photo you showed Karen? The one that made her think you had killed her brother Patsy?' Fin asked.

Patsy breathed a sigh of relief he hadn't seen it. Taking out her mobile, she scanned through her photos and showed him the one of Nancy and her parents at home. 'She had no intention of letting them live Fin; they knew too much. Seeing that photo, Karen knew Tom must be dead, because they were alive.'

Looking out of the window as the houses and shops passed by, Patsy thought about what a liar she had become. It was becoming second nature these days and part of her hated it.

'Is that the truth Patsy? Karen and her brother had pissed that gang off and they killed him to frighten you and Sheila. Show me the photo you showed her of her brother.'

'For god's sake Fin, don't you think you've had enough night-mares for one day? It's a photo of a beaten-to-death dead man – nothing else. She was just more horrified because it was her brother. It was nothing to do with me Fin, I swear it. Both of them had been ripping that gang off for ages. They were going to kill him with or without me and Sheila there.' Patsy bit her tongue and threw her cigarette end out of the window. She was becoming tired of Fin's interrogations. Mentally, Patsy made a note to herself to get rid of her phone and that photo!

Fin cast her a sideways glance. At that moment, he couldn't make his mind up about which woman was crazier: Karen or Patsy.

'As I was saying earlier Fin, I need to see Nancy, then when I come back to Glasgow we will sort out those bloody Albanians and avenge Spider and Beanie. They were good blokes, and they were our friends Fin and we're going to sort it out.' Patsy knew the only way to keep Fin onside was to appease him and avenge his friends. Seeing the smile appear on his face and a cheeky wink as he looked at her made her feel better. Fin was Fin again.

Consumed with a guilty conscience, Patsy said her goodbyes as they arrived at the estate. Walking through the door of Beryl's flat, she felt drained. All she wanted to do was sleep, but now she had to face Victoria's questions.

'You've been gone ages Patsy. Christ, I thought you were only going to sign some paperwork. What about my granddaughter; is she safe?'

Taking out her mobile, Patsy showed Victoria the photo of Nancy and her parents. 'They are home Victoria. I haven't had a chance to speak to them yet. I thought we might pop down and see them tomorrow.' Patsy's voice caught in her throat and Victoria's expression immediately softened.

She felt like an emotional mess. Victoria knelt down beside her and held Patsy tight. 'It's been a hard few days and you have been strong for us all.' Victoria kissed Patsy on the cheek. 'You really do have a heart Patsy. I must say though sweetheart, you hide it very well.' Standing up, Victoria picked up a piece of kitchen roll and handed it to Patsy. 'Wipe your nose sweetheart, I'll make some tea and to quote Beryl, I'll put something strong in it to make you feel better.'

ONWARDS AND UPWARDS

Victoria was sat watching television, half dozing, when Patsy walked into the lounge. 'What is it about a short nap and a shower that makes you feel better Victoria?' Drying her hair with a towel, Patsy picked up the coffee Victoria had made for her and took a sip. 'Have you eaten? What do you fancy?'

'I think I'll just order something in and have an early night Patsy. I'm shattered. I'm glad you feel better after your nap.'

'Yes, I don't know what came over me. I think it was just knowing that Nancy was safe.'

'That's called being a parent dear. I take it Karen's gone back to Paris with your spoils? Personally, I'm glad to see the back of her and of France.'

Patsy continued drying her hair and hoped the towel would cover her face somewhat. 'Don't forget Victoria, we're now partners in that chateau, so we will have to go back some time. Those truffles are a good investment, and those men assured me there would be no more trouble. To be fair, I think she just annoyed them with her attitude.'

'So why were they beating someone up in front of you then?

Poor Fin was terrified. He's a nice lad, and the more you get to know him, you can't help but like him. Life has dealt him an awful hand.'

Patsy put the towel around her neck and pulled the towelling robe around her. 'They were trying to prove a point Victoria; it obviously sounded a lot worse than it was. Men and power, eh?' She smiled and shrugged. Sitting back in the chair, relaxing and drinking the warm soothing drink, Patsy felt the stress of the last few days leaving her body. When she had closed her eyes on the bed earlier before her nap, she had kept seeing Karen's fatal accident, and assured herself that was what it was. She had simply fallen into that grave, and more to the point, her own grave. It was like fate; that was where she was meant to be. But replaying the scene in her mind, something inside Patsy gnawed away at her conscience. She still wondered if she had seen Karen move, but knew that was impossible. Her head was at an awkward angle. But could she have buried Karen alive? It was a chilling thought and one she didn't want to think about.

Convincing herself it had been a trick of the light or something, Patsy didn't want to dwell on it. As much as she wanted to go back and check, she dismissed it. What was the point? Fin had secured the grave so there was no way she would be able to go back to it and absolutely no way Karen would be able to get out. Anyway, Patsy thought to herself, it could have been herself and Fin in that grave and Karen wouldn't be giving it a second thought.

* * *

They both stared at the film on the television, although not quite taking it in, when there was a knock at the door.

'What now?' Turning the television down, Victoria went to

answer it and was surprised to see Leandra, one of the prostitutes who would be renting Beryl's flat. Victoria showed her into
the lounge. 'Visitor for you Patsy. I'll make some more coffee,'
she said, making herself scarce.

'Sorry about my attire.' Patsy smiled. 'As you can see, I wasn't
expecting visitors. Sit down.'

Sitting on the edge of the sofa, Leandra opened her handbag
and put the rent deposit on the coffee table. 'It's all there Mrs
Diamond.'

Patsy looked at the money spread out before her and then
back at Leandra. 'I'm sure it is Leandra. Thank you. We're almost
ready to leave. This is all yours now. When do you plan to
move in?'

'Would two days be okay Mrs Diamond?' Leandra wrung her
hands nervously.

'That's fine by me. I will be taking the flat above the community centre as a base and an office. I'm only telling you this,
because I don't want you to think I am spying on you. You pay
your rent on time and look after the place and that's all I ask. Is
there anything you need from me?'

'Only what we agreed Mrs Diamond.' Leandra looked
around the lounge. 'I'm sure everything is in order.'

Looking at her tired and weary face, Patsy spied the bruise
on Leandra's cheek, but ignored it, not wanting to embarrass her
by asking about it. The poor woman looked like a scared cat, and
it seemed this flat was going to be her lifeline. 'Well, have some
coffee with us, to seal the deal.'

Leandra refused and stood up. 'I have to get back. Two days
Mrs Diamond.'

Patsy could see she was eager to leave but stopped her.
Standing up, she made her way to the key holder that hung in

the hallway. 'These are the spare keys Leandra, when we leave we will put the others through the letterbox, is that okay?'

The smile on Leandra's face seemed to get bigger as she held the keys in her hand and brought them towards her chest. 'Thank you Mrs Diamond, thank you.' Leandra couldn't say thank you enough as she opened the front door to leave. It was as though a big weight had been lifted from her shoulders. Once she had left, Patsy walked into the kitchen where Victoria had been standing idly over the boiling kettle, listening to everything.

Raising her eyebrows at Patsy, she pursed her lips. 'Christ, she looked worried. It must be awful to live in so much fear all the time. I'm glad she's taking the flat; it's a fresh start. Maybe her and her friends can start living again.'

'It's a big risk though, Victoria and whoever they are working for now, won't take it too lightly when they escape. I'm sure they will come looking for them – don't you? Did you see that bruise on her face? Poor woman. They have all worked themselves to death getting that deposit.'

Patsy thought about Leandra, almost frightened out of her wits, and that made her more determined to sort out the Albanians who bullied them and trafficked them once and for all. She knew she couldn't solve a worldwide problem, but she could help Leandra and her friends and for now, she had to be satisfied with that.

'I might pop and see Larry for an hour or two. Poor bugger; he always seems to be the last in my pecking order. Will you be okay Victoria?'

Victoria smiled and looked at her over her mug of coffee. 'You don't have to make excuses just because I am your mother-in-law Patsy, we've gone long past that. You go and make peace with Larry, and I will see you in the morning – early mind; no drawn out goodbyes.' She wagged her finger in Patsy's face. 'We have a long journey ahead of us. I can't wait to see my grand-daughter.'

Patsy smiled. 'You never know, I could be back earlier if he throws me out on my ear!'

* * *

Patsy felt nervous as she knocked on Larry's door, she hadn't text him in advance to let him know she was going for fear of rebuke. She expected one. He hadn't seemed too happy when she had brushed him off earlier that day, and it felt like she was facing the firing squad. He would fire a million questions at her, and she knew all she could do was lie to him. A feeling of guilt consumed her. He didn't deserve this. He was a good man, with a good heart.

'Well, what's this Patsy, a booty call?' Larry snapped. 'I take it your newfound friend has gone then?'

'She left hours ago Larry; I've been catching up on some sleep. We didn't go for a drink in the end, she wanted dropping off at the hotel she had been staying at; apparently, she had left something there.' Patsy winced inside. That was the first lie of the evening! She didn't want to count the rest.

Larry opened the door. 'Well, I suppose you had better come in. I was just about to eat. Have you eaten?' The smell of food coming from Larry's oven reminded Patsy that she couldn't remember the last time she had eaten. Suddenly her stomach felt empty and hungry.

'No, I haven't.' She grinned. 'What's on the menu Larry?'

'Cottage pie; will that do?' His face was still stern, but he was pleased she had made some effort to come and see him. His stubborn stance showed Patsy she hadn't been let off that easy, then the questions came as expected, as she sat at the table, and he started serving up. It looked delicious, and she wanted to gobble it all up.

'You tricked her didn't you Patsy? She has signed the chateau over to you. But what about her? What about your daughter? Why didn't her brother show up?' Larry carried on serving and opened a bottle of red wine as he spoke.

'Firstly Larry, I didn't trick her; she wasn't interested in reading the contract and bloody hell, you pushed her hard enough,' Patsy snapped. 'What happened to her brother is anyone's guess. I have no idea where he is, but I can tell you now, he won't be working for me again. I'm half tempted to call the police on him for embezzlement!' Patsy felt that was only half a lie, because she didn't know where Tom was now. 'As for Nancy, she is home and safe with my parents. That's why I have come to see you tonight; I'm leaving tomorrow with Victoria.' There, she had dropped the bombshell, that no sooner had she walked into Larry's life again, than she was going to disappear again. She clenched her hands together, pressing her nails into her palms, waiting for that look of despair.

'You can't call the police for embezzling laundered funds and you know it! As for urging her to read the contract, I'm a lawyer and it's my job to advise the clients properly. When you asked me to draw up that contract, I was surprised she had agreed to it, but then I realised she had no bloody idea what she was agreeing to. Was it her you tricked or both of us? Do I look like a gullible fool to you, is that what you think of me?'

Patsy took her reprimand, and sat quietly pouring the red wine. A part of her felt angry that Larry hadn't seen the full picture. He seemed to have forgotten this woman had kidnapped her family and forced her to go to Paris.

'What I've done Larry, is nothing compared to the worry and stress she put me through the last couple of days or are you on her side? No one expected her to turn up out of the blue like Lazarus. We all thought she was dead, including you!' She didn't shout or raise her voice, because the last thing she wanted was an argument.

His voice seemed to soften a little. 'Well, at least Nancy is safe and sound and back home where she belongs. I presume she'll live with you now? I always knew about her Patsy, but you didn't trust me enough to tell me, did you?'

'I know you knew; I remember that day I came to your house and you told me you checked out all your clients and that you knew I had skeletons in my closet. You're far from stupid Larry, we both know that. As for the rest, I haven't thought that far ahead, there has been so much going on I don't know where to start. Why does everyone think I have all of the answers all of the time? I'm bloody human you know.' She grinned and took a mouthful of food; it tasted good and she was eating it much quicker than she should have. She was starving.

'I understand you wanting to go back to London to see your family, I would do the same.' Reaching out, he put his hand on top of Patsy's. 'But then what? Do you have *any* plans?'

'As a matter of fact, I do. My tenants will be moving into Beryl's in two days' time. Victoria will be getting to know Nancy, and then go home to Dorset. And I have decided to move in to the flat above the community centre and use it as a base. But for now, I'm going to finish my dinner and drink your wine and then I am going to rip your clothes off and have mad passionate sex with you. I've missed you, you know. How does that sound?'

A wide grin spread across Larry's face. 'That sounds like a definite plan!' Larry lowered his head and looked down at his food. 'Although there is another alternative; you could move in here with me and let the flat above the community centre. How is that for a plan?'

Shocked, Patsy met his gaze as he raised his head. 'Are you asking me to move in with you Larry? I don't know; what would people say? My husband hasn't been dead a year yet and I'm already moving in with another man.' A frown crossed Patsy's brow when she thought about what Victoria would say about the situation. 'What about your son, how would he feel about it? We haven't known each other long Larry. Why don't we get on an even footing for a while and see how we feel then. But, for now, we could be friends with benefits? I'm not seeing anyone else, and as far as I'm concerned you are the only man in my life, so what's the rush?' She didn't want to disappoint him, but she felt that kind of commitment was too soon.

Smiling, Larry shrugged. 'You can't stop a man from asking. But I understand and I am prepared to go with that. Let's do this properly.' Putting down his fork, Larry wiped his mouth with his napkin and walked over to Patsy's side of the table. 'What about those benefits then?' Lowering his head, he rubbed her nose with his own gently, as his lips gently brushed across her mouth. Their kisses were slow and meaningful and then became more ardent. Feeling a stirring inside of her, Patsy put her arms around his neck, running her hands through his hair as she pulled him closer. The passion of his kisses and his nearness roused emotions deep inside of her. Nuzzling her neck and dropping the thin strap of her dress, Larry kissed her shoulders, letting his tongue trail along her neck, sending shivers down her spine as she closed her eyes and clung on to him. His hands roamed along her breasts, and freed them from her dress, caressing them and trailing his tongue down to the tip of her nipple. Letting out a gasp, she arched her back for more, feeling the excitement in her body grow with each kiss. She could feel his own desire was as heightened as hers as their hands roamed over each other's body.

Taking her hand, Larry led the way upstairs. Patsy's legs felt weak as she followed him willingly. She could feel her body trembling with excitement and expectation as she lay on the bed waiting for him. Slowly, they undressed each other between kisses and strokes, discarding their clothing aimlessly. The moistness she felt as he trailed his tongue along her legs and between her thighs sent fireworks through her body as she reached her peak and clung to him, while her whole body tingled and burned with pleasure. Panting, Patsy pulled Larry towards her, as he slowly raised himself on top of her, his throbbing manhood apparent. He could hold his passion back no longer and thrust himself inside her. They both let out a gasp of pleasure, as Patsy raised her thighs to meet each stroke, their passion and excitement coming to a head as they both cried out.

Their faces flushed, while trying hard to catch their breath, they clung to each other.

'I love you,' he whispered in her ear.

'I love you, too,' Patsy heard herself say, shocking herself. She hadn't meant to say it, but that was how she felt and it had just come spilling out. Lying in his arms and stroking the hairs on his muscly chest, she felt at peace. Their bodies damp with sweat, Patsy let out a satisfied sigh. She felt safe with Larry's strong arms wrapped around her. She wanted to stay in these strong safe arms forever.

'I'll go and get us some more wine, Patsy. You stay here; it's nearly time for round two.' Larry smiled.

Patsy sat up and put her arm behind her head. She marvelled at Larry's naked body as he walked away, noting his very tight, well rounded bottom. 'Do you work out Larry?' she asked quizzically. She had never really looked at him properly before and now she was, it was through different eyes. He was a handsome man, with everything in the right place. A small grin appeared on her face and she giggled to herself like a schoolgirl as he disappeared down the stairs. Yeah, Larry had everything in the right place!

'I swim Patsy. I'm a diver actually, why?' Walking back up the stairs with their glasses and bottle of wine, he poured them both a drink. 'Is that important to you?'

'Not really Larry,' she said. 'It's just that I wanted to know how to get such a firm, tight arse like yours. Now I know I have to take up swimming – god, I hate water!' They both burst out laughing and fell on to the bed again, their lips meeting and their bodies aching for each other. 'I take it this is going to be one hell of a bumpy night.'

'You had better believe it Patsy Diamond. It's been a long few days without you, and I intend to make it up.' Larry's ardour seemed more intense as they made love again, their eagerness bursting into passion. Instinctively they seemed to know how to please one another, and they fit together like a jigsaw puzzle. Exhausted and satisfied, they lay in each other's arms.

'Larry, you know what you asked me downstairs earlier?' Sitting up, she lit a cigarette. It was the early hours of the morning, but she needed to speak, while it was still on her mind.

'What did I ask you Patsy?' Larry snuggled up closer to her body.

'About moving in,' she whispered.

Realising the seriousness of the matter, Larry broke away and sat up.

Seeing him nod his head, Patsy continued. 'You're a good man Larry, much better than I deserve and I'm frightened I would disappoint you. I know I have been busy, and it's going to be a bit longer before I put all of Nick's affairs in order, but it would be nice to come home to you, a home cooked meal and all the benefits you have to offer.' She smiled and ruffled his hair. Patsy also liked that it would be a good cover story if the police ever thought she was spending a lot of time in Scotland. 'Ask me again in a month and in the meantime, I might become a permanent visitor... if you don't mind. But, if at any time, you want to change your mind, I will understand, okay?'

Larry couldn't believe his ears. 'Is this because you're all softened up and satisfied, or is this Patsy talking?' He wanted to be sure she meant what she was saying and it wasn't just the heat of the moment. People said all kinds of things to each other during sexual encounters and regretted it soon afterwards.

Patsy reached for his hand and squeezed it. 'I think you know me better to know I wouldn't say it if I didn't mean it. Give me a month; that's time for both of us to be sure. After all,' she said. 'You haven't seen all of my bad habits and we haven't argued about you leaving the toilet seat up!' She stubbed her cigarette out in the ashtray Larry had placed on the bedside cabinet especially for her, even though he didn't smoke. Turning to face him, she smiled. 'Just give me space Larry and give me time, but remember you're my man.'

'One month it is Patsy.' He beamed. 'Well, if it's my cooking that has swayed you, I'm thankful. After all, they say the way to a person's heart is through their stomach.'

'Really?' Patsy burst out laughing, 'I thought that was an angiogram. Come here sexy.' As they both laughed happily, Patsy turned Larry on his back and started kissing him. She felt better now she had got it off her chest and made some kind of commitment to him. Larry wasn't Nick. Larry was kind, thoughtful and cared for everyone else but himself. There were no sides to him, what you got was what you saw. And at this moment in time, she definitely liked what she saw.

After an early morning start, Patsy showered. She knew Victoria would be waiting for her. Suddenly her phone buzzed, indicating a message. Sighing, she picked up the mobile expecting Victoria's message, but reading it, her blood ran cold and she paled. She sat on the edge of the bed in shock, thankful that Larry was downstairs making coffee. She felt dizzy and sick and read the message again, trying to take it in.

You bitch, did you really think you could bury me alive and leave me to rot. I'm coming for you! Karen.

Karen was alive! Patsy's head spun. Panic rose within her. She had wondered if she was still alive and now she knew she was. Where was she? Wherever she was, Patsy reasoned with herself, she had managed to get her hands on a mobile phone. In her panic, Patsy went to the bedroom window and looked out. She didn't know what she was looking for, but the paranoia that she was being watched and Karen had the upper hand gave her a sense of foreboding.

Her mobile buzzed again and another message popped up from Karen.

Hope you had a nice evening and he was worth it.

Fear gripped Patsy again. Karen knew exactly where she was. She could hardly breathe and sweat formed on her brow. It felt like she was suffocating. She had to get out of here to see if

Victoria was okay; more to the point, she needed to get to her family and make sure they were safe.

Instinctively, she rang her father. Relief washed over her when he answered, and she told him she was just leaving and would be there as soon as possible. Victoria's mobile, on the other hand, was engaged.

Hearing Larry come upstairs, she tried to control her now erratic breathing; it felt like she was having a panic attack and she didn't know what to do. Running into the bathroom to try and compose herself, she rinsed her face with cold water. She needed to leave now!

Once Patsy had gulped some air into her lungs, she opened the bathroom door and saw Larry lying on the bed.

'Breakfast, sweetheart.' He grinned.

Patsy looked at the tray of toast and eggs and wanted to throw up; her stomach was churning. 'Sorry Larry, Victoria keeps messaging me, I have to go.' Her weak smile seemed to hurt her face, but she continued. 'She wants to get on the motorway before all the traffic.' She hardly noticed the disappointed look on Larry's face, but she didn't care. Her own life was at stake, and she needed to sort it out. She cursed herself for not making sure Karen was dead. What a bloody fool! Nick would have made sure, she thought to herself, and he would be laughing his head off at her now. Quickly dressing, she almost ran down the stairs until Larry stopped her.

'Don't I get a kiss goodbye then?' Puzzled, he looked at her worried face. 'Is everything okay Patsy?'

'Yes, sorry Larry. I just have a long day ahead and I'm tired. After all, you did keep me awake most of the night.' She grinned and pecked him on the lips before almost running out of the door.

After stopping at every traffic light in Glasgow, she finally arrived at the estate. Patsy couldn't even remember driving there her mind was so busy.

'Hey, I've been looking for you lassie,' a woman shouted, almost making Patsy jump out of her skin. Quickly turning, she vaguely recognised the woman, but couldn't think straight.

'It's me, Bernie. We met at the community centre with James and a few of the others,' the woman prompted.

Sighing, Patsy now recalled the woman. 'Yes, I remember you now. Sorry, I was miles away.'

'I can see that by the way you've parked your car on a slant.' The woman laughed. 'Me and some of the others have decided to give you a chance and work for you, but I just wanted you to know there is no honour amongst thieves. Stitch me up and I will slit your throat, or someone I know will – okay? Me and the others have organised the stripping of the pizza places with Big Paul, and now there's that community centre, so you owe us wages. I also think you need to sort the mobile shop out again; people need credit and they also want their groceries and drugs delivered to them. You're losing out on a lot of money pissing around like this.'

Itching to get away, Patsy nodded. At this moment in time, she would have agreed to anything. Looking towards Beryl's flat, she could see everything looked in order. 'I'll sort it with James.'

'You look pretty twitchy lassie; have I come at a bad time?' Confused, Bernie could see that Patsy was desperate to leave her. 'If you're not interested, say so. There isn't much work about at the moment. The police are still sniffing about over that Albanian shoot out at the nightclub. I've got bills to pay.'

'No! I just have to go to London, and I want an early start. I have to pick up my mother-in-law, no offence.' Patsy held out her hand to shake Bernie's. Suddenly, a thought popped into Patsy's head. 'Actually Bernie, I do have something else I would like you to do for me.' Patsy looked over at Beryl's flat, and Bernie followed her gaze.

'I have some tenants moving in, and they might have a little trouble. Would you keep an eye on things for me and make sure they're safe?' Patsy thought about the Albanian pimps that would try and harass Leandra and her friends and didn't want the flat trashed in the process.

'You mean the foreign prostitutes? Yeah, I can do that. I heard you were renting it out to them.'

Patsy gave a half smile and thought how quickly word travelled in the underworld. Everyone seemed to know everyone's business, which gave her another idea. One which might solve all of her problems. 'I will pay you 500 pounds to keep an eye on things.'

Instantly she saw the smile appear on Bernie's face, showing the couple of front teeth she had left. The rest of her mouth seemed to look like a black hole. This definitely wasn't a woman to be trifled with.

'I heard some people mention a man called Freddie at the meeting. Is there any way to get hold of him Bernie?' Patsy asked as nonchalantly as she could.

A heavy frown crossed Bernie's face. 'You mean the mercenary? No idea lassie. He's a ghost. No one knows how to find him, but you mention his name in the right circles and suddenly he pops up like a jack in the box.'

'Well, would you do just that for me? Mention his name in the right circles, I mean, and let it be known I would like to speak to him please.' Although Patsy felt desperate and shaky inside, she was doing her best to remain calm in front of Bernie.

'Aye lassie, I will do that for you, although I have no guarantees when and where. Where should I go for my wages?'

'You can go to James. I'm in a hurry at the moment. Sorry to rush you, we'll have a proper chat soon. I'm only going for a couple of days.'

'James and me are not friends lassie, we're colleagues. The only people that are friends with James are the people that don't know him.' Bernie laughed.

Patsy frowned. 'What do you mean by that?'

'You'll find out lassie. The minute things don't go his way, you'll find out.'

Bernie walked away, leaving a stunned Patsy on the pavement. Curiously, she felt that was an odd thing to say about someone she had laughed and joked with. It had been James who had given them all the opportunity to work for Patsy, yet there was obviously some bad blood somewhere. Dismissing it, Patsy went to see Victoria. No sooner had she walked through the door, than Victoria was almost pushing her out of it to leave.

'I've got everything. Fin's going to sort out these boxes for me and take the clothing to the charity shop. We can put some of the boxes with Beryl's personal stuff into the back of your car and I will take them home. I'll use your car and then you can catch the train back here and pick up mine. It's pointless us driving in separate cars,' Victoria rambled on aimlessly, not noticing Patsy's distress.

Suddenly Patsy's mobile burst into life with a message.

Getting that fat lesbian onside isn't going to make any difference. And that dress is badly creased. Karen.

Patsy's mouth went dry when she read the message and furtively she looked around the tower blocks for sign of anyone. Karen was obviously watching her. She was here somewhere. Frightened, Patsy almost threw the boxes into the back of her car. She didn't want to alarm Victoria, but she wanted to get as far away from here as possible. Patsy felt nervous and frightened. She thought about what Bernie had just said, about James. Patsy felt she was being paranoid. Driving off, she took a huge sigh as she headed towards the open road and the motorway, leaving Glasgow and Karen behind.

20

THE COLD LIGHT OF DAY

On the hour, every hour, Patsy's phone buzzed into life with another message from Karen. Patsy's nerves were frayed and in the end she switched her mobile off. She was afraid, and didn't know which way to turn. This was judgement time and although Victoria continued talking about how she would get to know Nancy, Patsy wasn't listening. She couldn't even tell Victoria, because she had lied and told her that Karen had gone home. Only she and Fin knew what they had done.

After what seemed an arduous journey, they arrived at her parents and even though she wasn't in the mood for a family gathering, she knew she had to paint on a smile and listen to her father's interrogation about Karen. Now, as she sat there hugging Nancy and drinking coffee, she wondered if she had brought trouble to their doorstep again. Where was Karen? Patsy felt paranoid, even when a parcel delivery man came to her parent's door she almost jumped out of her skin, spilling her coffee. Victoria was making very heavy hints about taking Nancy to Dorset for a visit to see little Nicky, who was with the nanny.

They all took this to mean that Victoria secretly wanted her granddaughter all to herself for a while.

Patsy suddenly felt very remorseful when she looked at the happy scene of her family and Victoria fussing around Nancy. She had laid a heavy burden on her parents hiding Nancy and she had robbed Victoria of Nancy's early years. Guilt washed over her in folds. She hadn't meant to cause unhappiness, but inadvertently she had, she realised that now. Her mobile had become her tormentor; she daren't switch it back on, but she also wanted to see what Karen had to say.

Switching her phone on, it burst into life and started ringing. Patsy jumped up so quickly she almost dropped it. It felt like a burning torch in her hands.

'Steady on Patsy; are you all right?' Her father came over and sat beside her on the sofa. 'What's going on?' Without looking at the screen, Patsy closed her phone case, ignoring it. 'You've been acting strange ever since you came in, jumping at the slightest noise. Were you that nervous about coming here today?' Her father looked concerned.

Patsy watched as her father opened her phone and looked at her call history. 'It's that James you've been talking about.'

Seeing the number and name attached to it, Patsy breathed a sigh of relief. 'I had better call him back.' Walking into the kitchen for some privacy, Patsy rang James. 'Hi James, sorry about that. How are you?' Putting on an even chirpier voice than she felt, she gushed about being home.

'I just called to remind you that your foreign friends will be expecting a drop off this week. I wasn't sure how long you were staying, but the clock is ticking. Do you want me to sort it out?'

'Yes, I shouldn't be more than a few days, but if you could do that please.' Then she half laughed. 'Why am I saying please? We're partners.'

'We are partners Patsy, but it's your stuff we're dropping off; I don't want to take liberties without speaking with you first. Enjoy your time with the family, speak soon.'

Looking at the phone questioningly, Patsy couldn't understand why James had called her about this. Even before Paris, he had told her himself that anyone could drop a bag off; why did he feel the needed to discuss it with her? She put her suspicious thoughts down to her paranoid state. She was like a cat on hot bricks. She couldn't relax and once again her mobile buzzed, indicating another message. Her heart sank when she saw it was another message from Karen.

Having a nice time with the family? Make the most of it! K

Patsy felt as though she was going mad and was tempted to throw her mobile at the wall. Tears brimmed in her eyes, and she was stressed beyond belief. She hated being out of control and that was how she felt at this moment. She had to be strong, but she didn't feel it. Karen had beaten her. She felt as though she had aged ten years. Looking into the mirror, she saw a haggard, pale woman. No wonder everyone kept asking if she was okay.

Switching off her phone, she went upstairs and applied some make-up and made up her mind to enjoy her visit. There was nothing she could do about Karen. She had no idea where she was or when she would come for her. Putting on a brave face and smiling, she walked back into the lounge. Her dad was arranging for them all to go out for an early meal. To them, life was going on as normal.

'That sounds great Dad. Come on you.' She smiled at Nancy. 'You promised me a hundred hugs and I've only had ninety-nine.' She laughed, picking Nancy up. Looking at Nancy's smiling face, Patsy looked at her eyes. They were Nick's eyes, and at this moment, she felt they were taunting her.

Over dinner at a local restaurant, everyone listened to Victoria as she talked about her house and the sheep nearby and all the wonderful things Dorset had to offer. It was as plain as the nose on your face what she wanted.

At last, Nancy said the words, 'Can I come and see your sheep Nana Victoria?'

Victoria beamed, while everyone else wanted to burst out laughing. She had cajoled and almost bribed Nancy into asking to go home with her. Patsy felt surprised when Victoria hadn't bundled her straight into the car there and then without finishing her meal. So that was settled. Her parents were just going to have some free time to chill out to themselves after recent events. Victoria was whisking Nancy off to Dorset and Patsy was to go back to Glasgow to clean her mess up. Patsy's heart sank at the very thought of it.

'Where are you going to live now that you have sold your flat in London?' asked her father.

'I haven't thought that far ahead Dad. All I know, is I couldn't stay there. I need to start afresh. There's plenty around, I just haven't got around to it. I feel like a traveller these days; all I seem to do is sofa surf!'

'Well, we just wondered about the living arrangements now things have changed.' George, her father, gave a quick furtive glance towards Nancy and then back at herself. It dawned on Patsy what he was hinting at. Now they no longer had to hide Nancy, they presumed she would be living with her. She hadn't thought of that. In fact, she mused, she hadn't thought of anything much lately. Her whole world seemed to be caught up in the underworld these days. She was forgetting how to live life. It did cross her mind that maybe that was why Nick had wanted to get away from everything with Natasha. There was always someone asking questions, or a problem to deal with. She needed to start delegating. Bernie had said that some of the others were prepared to work for her – that was a start.

Almost stammering, she looked at her father and said, 'Erm, you're right. Living arrangements will have to change, I suppose. But I need to find somewhere suitable first and I don't want to disrupt school or anything.'

'There's no rush Patsy. Believe me, it will be a wrench for all of us, especially your mother.'

'Thanks Dad. I don't really want an immediate upheaval. I don't think it would be good, would it?' They were both speaking in code, but everyone apart from Nancy knew what they were saying. 'Did I tell you I have a man friend and although it's early days he's asked me to move in with him in Scotland?'

'Well,' said her mum, 'you don't let the grass grow under your feet do you? You haven't been a widow a year. Who is he and why Scotland? That's a long way away.' Patsy's mum glanced at Nancy. Patsy knew what they were thinking. If she moved in with Larry it would be difficult for them to see their granddaughter. Her father had been right about how heart-breaking it would be for her mother.

'Well, Mum, he's called Lawrence, or Larry as I call him. He's a lawyer and he has a son.' Blushing slightly, Patsy smiled. She felt like a teenage girl telling her parents she had a boyfriend.

Her father shook his head. 'Not another bloody lawyer! Haven't you had a gutful of those?' Then he looked at Victoria and could have bitten his tongue. 'Sorry Victoria, I didn't mean that,' he apologised.

'Yes, you did George and I understand. But I have met Larry, and he seems a very nice family man,' Victoria encouraged.

George's words had made her wince a little, but there was no denying that Nick hadn't been the model of perfection.

Changing the subject, George poured some more wine. 'So when do we get to meet this new man in your life Patsy?'

'Oh, I don't know.' Patsy blushed. 'I'm not ready for tea with the parents just yet. Let's play it by ear, shall we?' Excusing herself, Patsy went to the ladies' loo. Washing her hands, she looked up at the mirror above the basin as the toilet door opened behind her. Patsy's eyes widened, and she swiftly turned around.

'I hear you have been looking for me Lady Diamond.' Freddie stood there with his arms folded.

Patsy felt like falling into his arms, she was so pleased to see him. Freddie put his finger to his lips, to stop her speaking. Then he went into one of the other cubicles and took out a bright yellow triangular sign saying, 'Hazard: No Entry'. Opening the main toilet doors, he propped it up outside. He nodded to a cubicle with his head. Patsy followed him into it and waited until he was ready to listen to her.

'How did you find me?' she asked. 'Even I didn't know I was coming here.'

'That's my job. So how can I help?'

Slowly, Patsy began to tell him all about what happened with Karen at the cemetery. Patsy could see Freddie's chest rise up and down as he chuckled to himself at her story.

'You've been a busy girl missus, but a silly one. You wanted to bury her alive because she was shooting at you? You have a busier life than me!'

'No Freddie, she fell in. Yes, there was a scuffle, and yes she shot at me and Fin, but she fell in. I thought she was dead; her head looked like it was at an awkward angle, but now she's stalking me. She keeps texting me and threatening me!' Tears rolled down her cheeks. She was relieved to be able to tell someone.

'Give me your phone; I'll take it for now. I want a 10,000-pound retainer.' He handed her a piece of paper with his account details on.

Patsy stopped him. 'I already have the details on my phone.'

'Not that account you don't. Be quick now and I'll be in touch.'

Patsy transferred the money and did as she was told. Somehow, she felt much stronger knowing Freddie had the situation in hand. She handed him her phone, wiped her face and applied more lipstick. Walking back into the restaurant, she felt like a weight had been lifted from her shoulders.

'Not more ice-cream Nancy.' Patsy laughed. 'You're going to be up all night with tummy ache.' Everyone was laughing, and even though Patsy glanced at the ladies' loo while her father paid the bill, she never saw Freddie come out. She wondered if he was still in there. Like Bernie had said, Freddie was a ghost!

The next morning, everyone said their goodbyes. There was no point in staying any longer because Victoria was itching to get back to Dorset with Nancy in tow. Kissing her father on the cheek, she could see he looked tired. The last few days had been more stressful for her parents than she realised. 'I'll see you soon Dad, Mum.' She hugged them both; she had so much to be grateful for. They were great parents and had always stood by her.

Stepping off the train in Scotland, Patsy felt strange. Suddenly, there was no Victoria and no Sheila. They had become part of her, and she felt lonely without them. She thought about staying at Larry's as an option for the night. But firstly, she needed to buy a mobile phone and then collect Victoria's car from the estate. She looked around nervously. She expected Karen to jump out of a doorway or something any minute now.

Once she had her phone and had picked up the car, she decided to go and see Sheila to see if there was any awkwardness between them. They hadn't had much chance to speak to each other after that day in the basement of the bistro, and no sooner had they landed at the airport, than Sheila had gone.

Patsy felt a little nervous knocking on Sheila's door, but as soon as Sheila opened it all of Patsy's worries faded away.

'Patsy, lassie, where the hell have you been? It's been days. Come here; give me a hug and I'll put the kettle on.' Sheila came forward and hugged her.

Patsy's grin couldn't have been wider if she'd tried. 'It's good to see you Sheila. Are you okay?'

'Angus is out at work, so we can have a girlie catch up. Where's Victoria?' Sheila kept shouting questions from the kitchen while Patsy flopped into one of Sheila's chairs. It felt like home.

Once Sheila had brought their mugs of teas in, she sat in the armchair opposite and lit a cigarette.

'Victoria's taken Nancy to Dorset. I've been in London visiting my parents. I've only just got back today. I've picked up Victoria's car...' Patsy trailed off. 'Sheila, I've come to clear the air,' Patsy confessed.

Instantly Sheila held her hands up. 'Whoa Patsy. Let's just say now for the first and last time: what happens in Paris, stays in Paris – okay?'

Nodding, Patsy agreed. 'You're right Sheila; I just wanted to make sure we were okay.'

'We're more than okay. We're friends. Anyway, I haven't told you, because I haven't had chance, but my Angus has popped the question.' Sheila beamed. 'Yes, Patsy, he asked me to marry him.

I told him I was going to think about it, cos I don't want to appear too eager.' She laughed. 'God, I have never been a respectable married woman before with a man with a proper job! Don't get me wrong, I loved Steve, but Angus is a different kettle of fish. What do you think?' Sheila's face looked hopeful.

It was clear to Patsy she wanted some form of approval. 'Well, that makes two of us,' Patsy boasted, 'because Larry has asked me to move in with him.' Patsy laughed.

'Oh my god Patsy. Well, go on then, have you made a decision?' Wide eyed, Sheila edged forward in her chair, with her hands around her mug of tea, eagerly waiting for Patsy to give her the spicy details. In no time at all they were laughing like schoolgirls.

'Do you think it's too soon for me Patsy? What would people say?' Sheila bit her bottom lip.

'Too soon for what Sheila? And since when did you care what people thought? What have these so-called people ever done for you? Fuck it, Sheila, if you want to marry Angus, do it.'

'And what about you and Larry?' asked Sheila.

'Sheila, I like Larry a lot. But I've become cynical about love. I used to think I had found love but it seems Nick had female followers everywhere. We probably haven't touched the surface. I respect Larry, but I am afraid I will hurt and disappoint him. You know the business I've found myself in Sheila. I don't have a choice but to see it through.'

'You could walk away from it. You have more than enough money. You had Nick's insurance and the money from his firm plus whatever else is stashed away. Walk away, live with Larry. You do have a choice, Patsy.' Spying Patsy over her mug, Sheila waited. She knew that all of Patsy's insecurities had come to the fore. She had been the little woman, the trophy wife, but now she was Patsy Diamond and she had power in her own right.

People worked for her, and she was in charge, but this new life-style had become an addiction to her.

'Sheila, we have graves full of drugs; why shouldn't we sell them? Who are we going to give them to?'

'Leave them where they are Patsy, dead and buried. If you want to do business, then we will do business, but don't sit there telling me you don't have a choice, because you do.' Sheila gave her a knowing look and pouted. 'By the way, I've been looking at houses. Suburbia Patsy, who would have thought I would live in suburbia with roses around the door?' She laughed. 'Listen to me, like Lady Muck! Angus wanted to know where I had got the money from and I told him Steve was insured, which he wasn't, and I got paid out. I didn't tell him I had all of it and some extra, but Angus wants to go halves. That's my story Patsy, so you see we're both lying, but we're entitled to our own lives too. Fuck me Patsy, why shouldn't we sell those drugs? Apart from the fact we're looking at a ten-year stretch.' Ending the conversation, Sheila pulled out some estate agent leaflets from her magazine rack. Her excited face made Patsy feel better as Sheila showed her the different houses she had been looking at. They spent the day just talking and laughing. Patsy thought this was just what she needed to wash all her cares away. They walked in the after-noon sunshine to collect the girls from school and happily walked home with ice-creams. No sooner had they got in, than Angus came home and Patsy felt it was time to leave.

'Aye Patsy lass, you're not leaving because I'm home are you?' Angus boomed at her in his thick, Glaswegian accent. His domi-neering figure filled the doorway. His temperament did not match his look, Patsy mused. He was like a warm-hearted Labrador, who looked bloody scary but who adored Sheila and her daughters.

'It's nice to see you Angus, but I have somewhere I need to

be. I said I might pop in and see Larry.' She winked, which made him boom with laughter.

'Do you want me to check the oil and water in your car before you go Patsy?' he asked.

Standing with her hands on her hips, Sheila laughed. 'For fuck's sake Angus, take an hour off work! Go on, let him Patsy; he can't stand not being under a car bonnet for long – sad bastard! But you're my sad bastard Angus, and I love you. Go on, check her oil and water if you want to,' Sheila shouted and smiled. 'Do you see what I have to put up with?' Sheila threw her hands up in the air, in mock despair. 'I take second place to your car. Where's my kiss you big lummox?'

'Well, I definitely couldn't stay the night Sheila; I don't have my ear plugs,' Patsy joked while they both watched Angus blush slightly.

'Ochs, you don't need them these days. While the girls are in the house I just bind and gag him so he doesn't shout out,' Sheila teased.

Once Angus had checked her oil and water, Patsy drove to Larry's but she wasn't in the mood for love. She had considered going to a hotel but knew he'd be upset if he found out. She felt like a homeless person, wandering around with a suitcase of clothing in the boot of the car, and decided that come the morning she would sort out the flat above the community centre for herself.

The smile on Larry's face when he opened the door told her she had done the right thing. 'I didn't expect you. I thought you were staying longer at your parents'.'

'Victoria wanted to take Nancy to Dorset so she could have her all to herself, and my parents wanted some respite,' she explained.

He led her into the kitchen, switched the kettle on and asked her if she was hungry. Much to Patsy's relief, Larry's son Paul was there. This would stop any sexual encounter, she thought to herself. Her libido was dead tonight; she couldn't concentrate on anything serious until she knew about Karen. It was a nice evening, homely, just like Sheila's, and seeing all these happy family homes made her feel sad. She had everything, but she had nothing she realised, and now she didn't even have peace of mind. The thought saddened her. When they eventually went to bed, not only did Patsy feign tiredness, she also said that she didn't feel comfortable having sex with Paul in the house. Larry accepted this and so they just cuddled up like two spoons in a drawer. She could hear Larry snoring as she dozed. She couldn't sleep properly, her mind was too busy, but at least she could rest and she felt safe with Larry's arms around her.

The following morning, Patsy went back to the estate. She wanted to check in with James and then sort her flat out. Going back to the estate felt strange; normally, she would have made her way to Beryl's flat, but today was moving in day for Leandra and her friends. Mentally, she wished them well. No one should suffer the way they had. They had been treated like cattle and Beryl's flat was a way for them to fight back; she knew even Beryl would approve of that.

'Morning Maggie, sorry it's so early, is James up yet?' Maggie opened the door wider and went to put on the kettle. Although pleased, Patsy sighed; she was awash with teas and coffees. Why was it every time someone saw her they walked away and put the kettle on?

James seemed shocked to see her so soon and so again she explained about Victoria's plans.

'So you intend hanging around for a while? I thought you might have decided to stay in London longer.'

'I want to see the pizza shops up and running first. When I

drove past, I saw workmen, or rather painters, going inside. Well, I presume so; they were wearing white dungarees with paint splashes on them and they had ladders.'

Maggie came through with the drinks, but moaned that she was running short of milk and would pop out later to get some. That reminded Patsy just how much the local residents relied on the mobile shop. And in its absence, not only was she losing money, but the locals had to travel further just for bottles of milk.

'That's another thing I want to start up again; it's a shame the shop isn't around any more. Although it had its bad points, it also came in handy for the elderly residents.'

'Will you be giving credit?' Maggie piped up. 'They don't always have money until pension day.'

'I suppose so Maggie, as long as they pay what they owe.'

Maggie felt satisfied with that and Patsy knew she would soon spread the word amongst the tenants, and let them know that their lifeline would be up and running again soon.

'Well, you really do have a to-do list, Patsy, don't you?' James grinned.

'Yes James, and the sooner I get started the better.'

'I'll walk over with you; there was something I wanted to talk to you about.'

Patsy felt she knew what was coming; Fin had already put her on the alert. She knew this would be about James's wife and the grudge he held.

No sooner were they out of Maggie's ear shot than James began his speech. 'Do you remember when I said I wanted a favour off you because you owed me?' He avoided Patsy's eyes and continued looking forward as they walked. 'Well, the favour is my wife. I want her gone, her and that fucking boyfriend of hers. They have humiliated me,' he spat out, 'and I'm not letting them get away with it, Patsy. But it would be too obvious if I were to do something. I want you to do it.'

'Do what?' Patsy asked cautiously. She didn't like the sound of this, especially as James had once told her he didn't hit or hurt women. This was a side to him she didn't like.

'Get rid of them. Do whatever it takes. I can lay my hands on a gun; all you have to do is shoot them both.'

Patsy was stunned. Although Fin had told her this, hearing James say it made her blood run cold. 'You want me to kill your wife and her lover? Are you crazy? For Christ's sake James, this is a domestic; just let it go.' She was shocked that he would even suggest her doing it personally. Surely he knew enough people who could sort this problem for him.

'Who else would I ask Patsy, if not my partner? You owe me; I have helped you and even went to Paris with you to sort out your family problems. Well, this is my family problem and I want your help. Anyway, considering we're partners, you didn't have me in on the meeting with that Milieu gang, did you? Or when you signed the partnership with Karen,' he pointed out.

'You know I didn't want to tip the applecart with that gang of thieves,' she lied. It dawned on her that she hadn't told him that she had dissolved her partnership with Karen. And it seemed even Karen hadn't realised that yet; she had certainly never mentioned it in her texts. Things had moved so quickly since she got back, she hadn't had time to speak to him about it.

Patsy didn't like the way he kept telling her she owed him. It made her feel uncomfortable. 'You're asking me to commit murder James and yet you make it sound so simple. I don't even know the woman!'

'It's not the first time you've had a domestic murder on your hands Patsy. What about Natasha? I helped you with that.' James reminding her about Natasha annoyed her.

'She killed my husband and left Beryl to take the blame. That's a huge difference to your wife dumping you after years of putting up with you in and out of prison,' Patsy spat back at him. She didn't want an argument, but wanted to make her feelings clear.

The pressure James was putting on Patsy made her squirm. Her heart was pounding in her chest, but she couldn't deny that she had given the order to kill Natasha, and James had organised the car to explode with Natasha inside it.

Panic rose inside of her. 'Let me sort myself out first James. What's a few more days? You have waited this long. We need to plan this carefully. I don't intend going to prison for killing your wife.' She didn't like it and didn't know how to wriggle out of this, but she was determined she wasn't going to do it.

'Fair enough. A couple more days and then I want the smiles wiped off their faces.' James seemed satisfied with that, even though Patsy felt sick inside. Her hands suddenly felt clammy; the hatred he had inside him shocked her. He had always seemed so reasonable and calm, but this was the other side of him, full of hate and loathing and she didn't like it. James had given her a lot to think about and she was glad to see the back of him for once. She felt angry that he had even suggested she do it and all she could do was play for time.

Wandering around the community centre, Patsy let her hands trail along the dusty canteen counter. Everything else was in order, which surprised her; it just wanted a spruce up and some life breathing into it again. The flat above it was a mess and needed a good clean up. There were empty takeaway cartons and empty cans of lager with ashtrays full to the brim. Clothing and bed linen were strewn everywhere, and the sink was full of dirty dishes. Patsy's heart sank when she saw it. This was going to take days, if not weeks. The paintwork was scratched and there were cigarette burn marks in the furniture. It was a wonder it hadn't gone up in flames, she thought to herself. The hallway floor was covered in flyers and mail. Sitting down in one of the chairs, Patsy put her head in her hands and cried. She had bottled up all her fears, but now she couldn't stop herself. Her body wracked with sobs.

'The more you cry, the less you pee.' The male voice made her head shoot up. Freddie stood in the open doorway with his arms folded. 'In my experience, open doors are an open invitation to burglars.' Ignoring her distressed state, Freddie sat down and crossed his legs in an easy fashion, throwing her mobile towards her.

Brushing away her tears from her red and swollen face, she waited. 'Well? Where is Karen?'

'Well, she certainly isn't in that grave, that's for sure.' Freddie smirked. 'You were right, she wasn't dead. Well, not altogether. You should have shot her while she was in there to make sure.'

'So where is she now? She's going to kill me, isn't she?'

'No, she's not,' said Freddie, 'but I know someone who wants you out of the way.' His nonchalant attitude was beginning to annoy her. She was scared witless and had been for days and Freddie was toying with her.

'I haven't paid you all that money just to sit here while you play games; I've had enough of that already today from James. Do you know he wants me to kill his wife?' she blurted out.

Freddie's interest became more serious. 'Why?'

Patsy explained the situation. All her fears and troubles came tumbling out. She was desperate and had no one to turn to, only Freddie.

'So, as this is a new affair, if James's wife disappeared, he would get the lot if she died. Is that right?'

Freddie's words sank into her brain; she had never thought of that. Suddenly James's hurry in the situation made sense. The last thing he wanted was his wife to divorce and marry again. Now, the truth behind it dawned on her. 'I suppose so,' Patsy stammered and lit a cigarette, inhaling deeply. 'That is why he wants me to do it. If he murdered her, he wouldn't get anything but a life sentence.' The very thought made her feel sick and she paled. This wasn't about love or rejection, it was all about money.

'That sounds about right. Never look beyond your nose for an explanation when it's staring you in the face.'

Patsy's shoulders sank and she sat back in her chair and let out a deep sigh. 'Fuck! Am I stupid or what? Anyway, about Karen; who else wants to kill me if not her? Is it that Milieu gang?'

'Definitely not. They are businessmen. You have paid up and you now have an alliance with them. As long as you pay their half, that's all they are interested in. Someone dragged Karen out of that grave. You can still see the tracks where they pulled her out. They didn't hide it very well in their hurry. Personally, I would say someone followed you to the cemetery as she wasn't in the grave for very long.'

'Why, who? No one knew I was going there,' Patsy interrupted. Then, putting her hand to her mouth, she rolled her eyes to the ceiling. 'Oh my god, do you mean Fin? Did he go back and rescue her!' Patsy shouted. The very thought of being betrayed by Fin outraged her. 'I've done a lot for that bastard, and he is just as much up to his neck in it as I am.' She frowned. 'How do you know she hadn't been in the grave that long?'

'Because there were no scratch marks on the soil at either side of the grave to show where she had tried digging herself out. That's what people normally do. So by my reckoning, she had been in there half an hour at the most, not even that.' Freddie shrugged and lit his own cigarette and waited for another outburst from Patsy, which in turn came.

'But who has sent me those messages, do you know? And where is Karen now?' Firing question after question, Patsy almost ran out of breath and she started panting.

'James.' Freddie's answer was short and sweet. 'Now you have told me about his wife, it makes sense. He doesn't want a partnership, he wants the lot.'

Patsy sat there stunned; her vision became blurred as she stared into space. She felt as if her head was about to explode. 'We're friends; why would he do that?' Patsy shook her head, dismissing it. She didn't want to believe it.

'There are no friends in business where money is concerned and someone has to be top dog.' Freddie stood up to leave. He had done his job.

'Wait!' Patsy shouted. 'You haven't told me where Karen is now.'

'That is anyone's guess.' Freddie shrugged. 'Maybe he wanted her share of your partnership. But James knew you wouldn't go and check on the grave, so why not leave her there? Why drag her out? Had he found another willing partner who would be grateful? Once they had bumped you off or you are carted off for killing his wife, James and his new partner Karen would run the businesses in your absence and reign supreme. Whatever the case, it seems you're a liability to James. You're stronger than he reckoned, and I would say this grateful woman whose life he just saved would be much more amenable to him. And from what I hear, he is pretty pissed off that you didn't introduce him to the French bosses as your partner. You're a cold woman missus, you don't care what you do to get what you want. I like that about you.' Freddie's sarcastic remark felt like a knife in her ribs. She had been taken for a fool. 'He ingratiated himself with you and bided his time. He's the last person you would think of.' Freddie spied her curiously.

Patsy's hands were trembling, and she was visibly shaking from shock. She tried hard to take it all in, but couldn't think straight. She'd trusted James and this bombshell had knocked her for six... 'There is no share of a partnership. I tricked Karen into signing papers dissolving it. She never read the paperwork.' Patsy blushed. 'What do I do Freddie? I don't know what to do.' Tears rolled down her cheeks.

'What do you want to do? Don't cry missus; where is that strong woman I admired from the bistro?' Raising his eyebrows, he gave her a cocky smile. 'Does James know about the partnership?'

'No, I haven't told him yet, I haven't had time. I want him to know that I know he's the Judas in my camp, and that he can't get the better of me. I want revenge Freddie but, I don't know how.'

'Then play the long game. He still thinks he's beaten you. If you still have some money in that account of yours, maybe I could help.' Freddie sat down again. This is what he liked talking about: money and business.

Patsy took out her new mobile phone and started typing in her passcode, then a thought occurred to her. 'Actually Freddie, there was something else I wanted; maybe we could arrange that too.'

Freddie burst out laughing. 'Why is it there's always something else with women! Go on, what's your poison missus?'

'The Albanian ice-cream vendor. No one has taken over his business since he disappeared with the help of James.' No sooner had the words left her mouth than she gasped in horror. 'Oh god, he was James's partner, wasn't he?' she shouted. Her eyes widened. 'Does he deceive all his partners?'

Freddie's face didn't move.

'You must think me a fool Freddie, a bloody stupid fool!'

Ignoring her outburst, he said, 'Tell me about what you want missus.'

Composing herself, she started again. 'I want the business, but I'm not paying for it. I need to avenge some deaths the Albanians have caused to my friends. I want it signing over to me and I want the Albanians out of the picture once and for all. No man is ever going to get the better of me again. I'm in charge and I will rule it properly.'

Freddie rubbed his hands together and smiled. 'Now that is more like it, Lady Diamond. Two million pounds. I want it in sterling.'

Nodding, Patsy tapped away at her mobile banking. Looking over at Freddie, she could see he was thinking. Holding up her phone, she showed him the money had been sent to his account. 'All done.'

'Stay here and clean this shit hole up; I will be back in three hours. You speak to no one and you see no one – do you understand?'

Confused, Patsy nodded; she knew better than to ask. Obviously, Freddie had already worked out a plan. Satisfied, Freddie got up and left. Patsy sat there staring at the walls in despair. James! Of all people, his name rang in her ears. Was he really going to side with Karen to get his hands on half of their partnership? He wanted to be king pin of the lot and he didn't care how many women he killed to get it. It hurt her more deeply than she realised. The more she thought about James terrorising her and betraying her, the more tears brimmed and fell down her cheeks. She had liked him and thought they were friends. She had even encouraged his friendship with Victoria. Maybe, she mused to herself, Victoria was to be another victim of his greed. Victoria really was the golden goose with everything a fortune hunter would want. It made her feel sick to the stomach. She realised now he hadn't helped her by introducing her to the criminals that ran the drug ring, he was proclaiming himself in charge and Patsy as his partner. Angry with herself, Patsy vowed she would never be used and betrayed by another man again. It was becoming a pattern and she wouldn't let herself become a victim. She felt as though she had something tattooed on her forehead proclaiming her a mug to be used. She wasn't sure if she was crying for her friendship or for her own stupidity.

Lighting another cigarette, she wiped the tears from her eyes. 'Enjoy your fun while it lasts James,' she said out loud to the wall, 'because it will end soon enough, you bastard.'

21

REVENGE IS MINE

Pacing the flat, Patsy realised she was talking to herself and cursing James with every sentence. Her stomach churned when she thought about his deceit. This would be a big learning curve in her career of crime. Looking around, she didn't know where to start with the flat; it was a mess. Instead, she sat down and read through all of the horrible messages on her old mobile that James had tortured her with in Karen's name. Before she destroyed it, she wanted them burned on her brain, so that whatever gruesome ending came to James, she would feel no remorse. The bastard! Her anger boiled over into deadly hatred. Only this morning he had smiled at her, while pressuring her to kill his wife, like the wronged husband. Chain smoking, she didn't realise how long she had been sat there mulling over everything, until Freddie came back and she realised she had been sat there for three hours.

'Not got a lot done then?' Sarcasm dripped off his tongue. 'Take these: they are clean and wear gloves when you hand them over to James. Make an excuse that they are for this place or something. Also tell him you have sorted his wife.'

Patsy looked oddly at the plastic bag containing a set of keys. 'What are they for?'

'You will find out soon enough. Now do as I say – no questions.' His voice was stern, and business-like. 'I will be in touch.' With that, he left.

Patsy looked at the keys in the clear plastic bag. She didn't recognise them, but she would go and see James now and hand them over. Freddie's words about James's wife shocked her, but she didn't want to think about it. In her suitcase she had a pair of leather gloves; she would collect them first. This is where her Oscar-winning performance would come in. She would play James at his own game.

'Hi, Maggie, sorry to bother you again; I'm afraid I need your help.' Crossing her fingers and hoping Maggie wasn't going to offer her another cup of tea, she smiled.

'Come in Patsy; what can I do for you?'

Patsy looked at Maggie. No matter what the weather, she always wore the same black cardigan and when there was business to talk about, she wrapped it around her waist tighter. It was strange, but Patsy was getting to know her habits now.

Walking into the lounge, she saw James and her skin crawled. Ignoring him, she turned to Maggie. 'Do you know of a few women that would like to make a few pounds? That flat above the community centre is an eyesore and it needs a good cleaning before anything else can be done to it.'

'I'm sure I can arrange that for you. Are you moving in there then?' asked Maggie.

'Yes, didn't James tell you?' Patsy felt that was odd. 'I'm going to use it as a base for when I come to Glasgow. Thanks Maggie. I won't stop. Oh James, can I have a quick word?' Patsy beckoned him as she was leaving.

Once they were outside, Patsy walked towards her car with

James beside her. She felt confident now, and her loathing of him seemed to double as they spoke. 'That little matter we spoke of earlier. You know, the domestic one. Well, it's done.'

Bewildered, James looked at her. 'When? And how? What did you do Patsy?'

'Does it matter? It's sorted. We're partners and partners look after each other.' She grinned. Opening her car door, she tutted. 'Here, James, take these keys to the flat for Maggie will you? I forgot to give them to her.' Wearing her leather gloves, she handed over the bunch of keys which she had already taken out of the plastic bag. Taking them, James pushed them into his jeans pocket. Patsy drove off, leaving a very puzzled James on the pavement. She parked out of sight around the corner. Her instincts told her he would want to go and see for himself, and she was right. Sitting in her car for a few minutes, she saw him standing on the street corner and hail a taxi. Patsy felt pleased that it hadn't taken long. He hadn't had time to hand the keys to Maggie and so her fingerprints wouldn't be on them. Knowing James as she did now, she knew he wouldn't believe her and would go and check. To be honest, she was curious herself, but didn't follow him. She would follow Freddie's orders.

Driving up to the pizza parlours, she walked through the doors and spotted the very man she was looking for. There was lots of hustle and bustle and already it looked clean and newly painted.

'Paul,' she called over. 'Can I have a word?'

Unsure of what she wanted, he came over slowly, almost dragging his feet. 'Mrs Diamond,' was all he said in acknowledgement.

'Don't worry, you're not in trouble or anything. In fact, I have a proposition for you. Let's talk in my car.'

His huge bulk nearly rocked the side of the car as he got in.

'I'm not going to beat about the bush Paul. I have been thinking about setting up a restaurant in France and I wondered if you would like to run it. You're a chef, aren't you?'

Paul's jaw almost dropped at the suggestion and his wide-eyed pleased expression was followed by a huge smile. 'I am Mrs Diamond, but I can't go to France. I don't have a passport and I am still on the fugitive list,' he explained. Patsy could see his disappointment. She had just offered him what he longed for, but he couldn't take it.

'Yes, you can,' she urged. 'Get that young computer lad to get you a passport. Go to France Paul and start again. More to the point, make my truffles taste beautiful and make me money in the process.' She smiled. As an afterthought, she felt she should be honest. 'I will also be using the restaurant to launder money Paul; do you have a problem with that?'

Paul frowned. Patsy felt there was something on his mind. 'I half expected the money laundering, but what about my brothers? They are chefs too.'

'That is your business. If they want to go with you then so be it. I want a good restaurant, cooking the very best. I have partners in France, so there won't be any trouble. You will get a good wage and a bonus when it does well. In the meantime, there is a chateau nearby that has the truffles, where you can stay. I presume you would want to pick your own. You will also be selling to other venues and the likes. In short Paul, you would be managing the restaurant and the farm, so it's a good thing you will have family with you. You are in charge. I will give you the details once you sort out your passports. Is it a deal?'

Tears welled up in Paul's eyes, and he sniffed to fight them back. This was his dream come true and it was being handed to him on a plate; he couldn't believe it. 'What about these places?' he said, nodding towards the pizza parlours.

'Surely you can show someone how to make a pizza Paul; it's not rocket science, is it? I will be staying at the flat above the community centre; let me know when you're ready and have sorted things out and we will talk more.' Sensing his hesitancy, she laid her hand on his arm. 'There are no strings, Paul. I am not my husband. Do your job, launder my money and run my business. That is all I ask of you.'

Her sincerity touched him, and he sniffed again, overcome with emotion. 'I will make you proud Mrs Diamond, I promise,' he choked. 'I had better get on and sort these places out then sort things out with my brothers.' Getting out of the car, he gave her a weak smile.

Patsy could tell he didn't want to embarrass himself by crying. She had just won his loyalty through friendship. Pursing her lips together, she knew she had also cemented their partnership because she still had a recording of the CCTV footage, should he ever step out of line. Freddie was right, trust no one in business.

* * *

Arriving at his wife's house, James got out of the taxi. Walking up the path, he found it strange that the door was ajar slightly and pushed it open further. Everything was silent and so stealthily he closed the door behind him and walked down the hallway. He didn't know what to expect, or if Patsy was just shooting her mouth off to keep him quiet. Any minute now, he expected his wife to show her face. Everything looked the same, but there was an eerie silence.

As he walked into the lounge, he stopped in his tracks. The gory sight before him, stunned him. His wife was on the floor, lying in a pool of blood. James walked towards her; on closer inspection, he could see that she was dead, even though her eyes were open and her throat had been cut. He couldn't believe it. Bending down, he put his hand over her eyes and closed them. Looking around in panic, he saw that her lover was sat upright in an armchair, although his head was drooping. His shirt and lap were covered in blood. James walked over to him and grabbed his hair and pulled his head back. He too had had his throat slashed. Panic-stricken, James knew he had to get out of there. Looking down, he could see his trainers were covered in blood. Running out in blind panic, he wiped his feet on the front lawn and ran. He was shocked and couldn't believe Patsy had gone through with it, although he was pleased she had. He needed to get home and get rid of his clothing, especially his trainers. Stopping at the top of the street to catch his breath, he cursed himself. He had touched the front door; his fingerprints were on it. He didn't have time to turn back now and when he saw a bus coming, he jumped on it. He needed to get as far away from the crime scene as possible. He was still surprised Patsy had done this. But, smiling to himself, he knew she was impulsive and stupid. She had done his bidding and he was free.

* * *

James got off the bus, and trying to remain calm, he ran as quickly as possible to the estate. He needed to change and burn these clothes – fast! Sweat poured down his face; he wasn't a young man any more and he was panting. He felt a pain in his side from running and he stopped and held it, while gasping for breath. Passers-by looked at him strangely, but said nothing. James was oblivious to them all. He was about to call Patsy to pick him up, but dismissed the idea. He didn't want her to know he had gone to his wife's house to check that she had killed them both. That would look bad, and as though he didn't trust her. No, he had to carry on. Wiping his forehead with the sleeve of his arm, he started to walk slowly at first, then almost marched ahead. His chest felt tight, as he tried gulping breath into his lungs. He was shattered. At last, he saw home. He never thought he would be so pleased to see the place. Once inside, he ran past Maggie, almost knocking her over, and into the bedroom, stripping himself. His breathing was erratic as he tore away at his clothing, and for a moment he had to sit on the bed to catch his breath.

Maggie knocked on the bedroom door, asking if he was okay.

'Yes, I'm fine. I'll be out in a minute,' he called. Trying to think straight, he opened the door in his boxer shorts, much to Maggie's surprise. 'Maggie, I have been with you all morning if anyone asks, and that includes Patsy – okay?'

Suspiciously, Maggie nodded. She presumed she would find out soon enough. He had obviously been up to no good she thought to herself. Suddenly there was a loud banging at her door, which didn't stop. On opening it, Maggie stood back in surprise. Policemen were at her door, asking about James. She tried doing as instructed and told them he had been home all day. But even she could see by the mixture of uniforms and plain-clothed officers that this wasn't something simple.

James had dressed quickly and came out of his bedroom looking puzzled. 'What can I do for you?' he asked as calmly as he could.

Once the plain-clothed detective got him to confirm his name, he informed James he was under arrest for the murder of his wife and her partner and read him his rights, while putting the handcuffs on him. James protested his innocence and tried struggling, but the handcuffs were holding him tightly.

'Make the call Maggie; get her to sort this out.'

Maggie nodded, although she was still in shock. She didn't know what else to do.

'I presume you mean your lawyer James. Well, you can make your call from the station,' said the detective. Maggie realised they had misinterpreted what James had said. James had meant for her to call Patsy.

One of the uniformed officers walked into the bedroom and spotted the pile of clothing on the floor and shouted to the detective. The detective knelt down and with his pen, so as not to put fingerprints on the clothes, poked around the clothing and spied the blood-stained trainers.

'Bag this lot up carefully, will you,' he instructed. Walking back into the lounge the detective looked up at Maggie. 'I think I would change my statement if I were you about where he's been all morning.' With that, they led James out.

Horrified, Maggie ran to the windows. After a short while, she could see James being put into the back of the police car.

* * *

Patsy's phone sprang into life. Looking in her bag, she was surprised to see that it was her old mobile that Freddie had given her back earlier, that she hadn't disposed of yet. She wanted to know if there were going to be any more messages from James. Because this time they wouldn't frighten her; it would only strengthen her hatred towards him.

Answering it, she could hear a panic-stricken Maggie shouting on the other end, asking her to come over. Patsy felt this was something to do with James and so left the pizza shops and drove to Maggie's flat. Fin was there already when she arrived. They were both waiting for her. Fin rubbed his face with his hands and walked towards her. 'They have got him bang to rights Patsy. He's murdered his wife.'

Stunned, Patsy looked at them both. 'What do you mean?' Sitting down, she listened to Maggie as she recalled what had happened.

'They have his clothes Patsy. He was in a terrible state when he came in. I can't give him an alibi; they know he wasn't here and I could go to prison for lying.' Maggie paled. She was in turmoil. Even she knew that whatever had happened, she couldn't save James; the evidence was too damning. 'You have to help him Patsy; get that lawyer of yours to go down there.'

Nodding, Patsy felt there was nothing else she could do for the moment, so she rang Larry and explained what had happened. Once he had agreed to go, she thanked him and ended the call.

'There is nothing we can do now, but wait.' Patsy felt a warm sense of satisfaction. Whatever Freddie had done, she thought to herself, he had done it to perfection. 'Larry will be there soon and he'll be in touch. We need something to take our minds off things. James wouldn't want us fretting, would he?'

Patsy's empathy to James's situation put a smile on Fin's face. James had become a father figure to him of late. Patsy felt it was a shame that he cared so much about a rattle snake like James.

Patsy turned to Maggie. 'Maggie, have you had any thoughts about the cleaners I asked you about?'

'Erm, yes, I have.' Maggie was surprised by how blasé Patsy was being about the whole situation. 'When do you want them to start?'

'As soon as possible, and Fin, I have something for you to do too. As Maggie suggested, we need to sort out a mobile shop, which means we need a van. Any ideas?'

Maggie and Fin glanced at each other, confused, and then

back at Patsy. They were sad and worried about James, whereas Patsy seemed chirpier than ever; they couldn't understand it.

Once Patsy popped to the bathroom, Maggie smiled. 'She's putting on a brave face for our sake Fin. She's as worried as we are, but trying to take her mind off it by keeping busy, and that is what we should do. You heard her my laddie, have a scout around for vans that can be converted and I will sort the women out.' Maggie felt that was the answer.

* * *

James sat in the interview room, thankful that Larry had dropped whatever he was doing and turned up. The detectives opposite him switched on their tape recorder and asked James to give his name. James looked around the interview room nervously. He cursed himself for going to his wife's house; he knew he should have just trusted Patsy. What a stupid prick he was. That was the first rule in the criminal world. You never go back!

Question after question they fired at him, but his answers were stupid, even he knew that. He had no alibi.

'Mr McNally, a neighbour, saw you and is going to identify you in the line-up. Another neighbour heard arguing coming from your wife's house earlier this morning, before your wife and her partner were killed. Why did you kill your wife James?' one of the detectives asked as the other looked on.

'I didn't. I haven't seen my wife in ages, I swear it!' James shouted.

Larry intervened. 'There is no evidence apart from an eyewitness who saw my client leaving the house to say that he murdered them both. Do you have a weapon?'

'No weapon yet Mr Kavanagh, but the area is being searched

thoroughly. The blood is on his clothing and shoes is already being checked for a match against his wife's blood group.'

'Why did you do it James?' asked the other detective in a more reasonable lower tone. 'Were you jealous of her new partner? Tell us what you were arguing about. Why were you at the house today? You can't deny it; you were seen.'

James swallowed hard. 'I did go around this morning, but when I got there, they were already dead. I panicked and ran out of the door.' Even James realised how hollow that sounded. The piercing looks the detectives gave him made his heart sink. If felt like he had fallen into an abyss with no way out. With his track record and the evidence against him, James knew he was looking at a long stretch in prison.

'Why didn't you call the police, or run outside and shout for help? Surely that's the normal thing to do, isn't it? Did your wife answer the door when you arrived James? There is no sign of a break in, so we can only presume that you knocked on the door.'

Larry leaned over, whispering in his ear, 'No comment, James.'

Taking Larry's advice, with each question the detectives asked, James replied, 'No comment.'

The detectives tried tripping him up to say something, but James remained silent.

'I would like to speak to my client privately, if you don't mind,' asked Larry. They were all tired after hours of questioning. Exasperated, even the police felt they should pause the interview. They left the room, leaving James and Larry alone.

'What the fuck am I going to do Larry? I didn't do it. I never murdered anyone. It's lies. You have to get me out of here.'

'Bail isn't an option here James. This is a murder investigation and they have the right to keep you for at least twenty-four hours. Why did you go to your wife's house James?' Larry asked.

James was almost tempted to shout at Larry that he had gone because Patsy had told him she had killed his wife and he'd gone to check, but even that sounded stupid. His only hope was that Patsy might have left something behind. She wasn't an ace criminal, and she would make mistakes, he felt sure of it. Maybe she had blood spots or something on her own clothing. James felt certain that it was only a matter of time before Patsy would be interviewed for the murder.

'I just popped around, no big deal. When I got there they were both already dead. So yeah, I panicked,' James snapped. 'I ran for it. Stupid, I know, but who knows what you would do when faced with two dead bodies covered in blood!'

Larry let out a deep sigh and loosened his tie. The only thing he could do, unless some miracle turned up, was to try and get James's sentence reduced. Then the police came back and the interview started again.

'The blood on your shoes matches that of your wife, Mr McNally, we have just had it confirmed. Why don't we start from the beginning and you tell us exactly what happened when you went to your wife's house.' The two detectives sat back in their chairs and waited while James gave them the same story.

'Why would a murderer leave the door open, James?' one of the detectives asked.

Fraught and stressed, James shouted out, 'Why don't you ask Patsy Diamond? Where was she at the time? What is her alibi?'

Larry almost choked at the mention of Patsy's name and sat up straight, looking James directly in the eyes. The two detectives turned to each other, frowning. One of them stood up and went to the door, opened it, and whispered to an officer outside.

'Tell us more about Patsy Diamond, James; we know you're friends but why would she have anything to do with your wife? Did she know your wife?' the other detective asked.

Larry's mouth went dry and he moistened his lips with his tongue. He felt confused and angry that James was putting Patsy in the frame for this.

'No comment,' answered James, while sitting back in his chair and folding his arms triumphantly. He had already decided that he wasn't going to take the blame. If he was going down, he was damn sure going to take Patsy with him! The smug grin on his face made the detectives call the interview to a halt.

'Take him to the cells; there is nothing more we can do here for the moment,' one of the detectives decided. They both felt there was more to this and wanted to speak to Patsy Diamond about James's accusations.

Frowning and bewildered, Larry asked James what this had to do with Patsy. 'I thought you were friends. Why would you say that?'

James turned and spat, 'Because it's your girlfriend who's the fucking killer here, not me. You're blind mate and she's taking you for a ride!'

As he left the police station, Larry's first instinct was to call Patsy. He had a bad feeling about this and somewhere in his gut he felt she knew a lot more about the situation. He knew the police would be on their way to her soon enough to question her about James's accusations.

'Patsy, it's Larry.'

'Larry darling, how are you? How's James? Is everything all right now?' Patsy asked. She put her phone on loud speaker for Maggie and Fin to hear. When Larry spoke again, it made her blood run cold and she stood there stunned.

'I have just left James at the police station Patsy; we need to talk. I think the police will want to speak to you. James has given them your name, and he's claiming you're involved in this crime...' Larry paused for a moment and bit his bottom lip. He had to ask the burning question on his lips. 'Patsy, do you know anything about this murder?'

Outraged, Patsy shouted down the phone, 'Of course I fucking don't Larry. What are you asking me that for?' Anger boiled inside her, once she realised that James had grassed her up so quickly. He was a rattlesnake and she had classed him as a friend. 'What the hell has James said and why would the police want to talk to me? What's happened to his wife anyway?'

Maggie and Fin both stared at Patsy wide eyed with shock, their jaws almost dropping at Larry's revelation.

'Look, I think I should come to you. Where are you?' asked Larry. Getting in his car, he put his ear piece in so that he could still speak on his phone.

'I'm at Maggie's; we're organising the cleaning of the community centre and the flat.'

Larry let out a huge sigh. 'Patsy, please tell me you don't know anything about this.'

Nervous, but trying to remain calm, Patsy looked at Maggie and Fin. 'You know what Larry, don't bother coming here, because I am on my way to the police station right now!' She ended the call. Avoiding Maggie's and Fin's eyes, Patsy swiftly turned and headed for the door without a backward glance, slamming the door behind her. She was afraid, but felt if she went voluntarily to the police station, it would make her look innocent. All the while she drove there, she cursed James. What the hell had he said, she pondered to herself. Her mind spun in different directions and she tried to rehearse things she would say to the police. And then it dawned on her. She didn't have to make excuses to the police. She hadn't done anything. She didn't even know what had happened or how James's wife had been killed. Her hands felt clammy on the steering wheel as she approached the police station car park. She was nervous and looked around as she got out. She knew she had to remain calm, but inside her heart was pounding, and her legs felt weak. Hearing a noise, she looked up and saw Larry walking towards her.

Scooping her up in his arms, he hugged her. 'I'm sorry Patsy. It's just that James is in there shooting his mouth off, and, well, I'm sorry.' Larry couldn't stop apologising. He had already gone back into the police station and told them that he had located Patsy Diamond and she was on her way. He felt this might clear the way for her.

'Get the fuck off me Larry. You doubted me, didn't you? You think I killed his wife, because James said so. This is your test of love and trust Larry, and you have just failed the exam!' she snarled while pushing him away.

'Stop Patsy! I'll come in with you,' he shouted, chasing after her. 'I'm no longer going to represent James; he can find his own lawyer. I'm sorry for doubting you Patsy, it was just such a shock hearing him mention your name...' Larry trailed off. 'Let me come in with you. Take a breath; we both need to. Don't go in there with all guns blazing. Let's get this cleared up, once and for all.'

'Do as you please Larry; I've got nothing to hide.' Patsy marched ahead into the police station and stood at the reception desk. Once she had given her name, the desk sergeant looked her up and down, asked her to take a seat and then immediately phoned upstairs to inform them detectives she was here.

A side door opened in reception and one of the detectives shouted her name and beckoned her forward. Standing up, she turned to Larry. 'I can do this on my own thanks.'

Larry shook his head, insisting that he should come, but ignoring him, she walked through the door to the waiting detective.

'I'm here to represent Mrs Diamond. I told her you would want to speak to her,' he blurted out.

Puzzled, the detective looked at Larry. 'You've had a busier day than me. I thought you were representing Mr McNally?'

'Not any longer; I am Mrs Diamond's lawyer. When James was arrested, kindly she asked me to come down to see if she could help him in any way. Obviously, she needs my help more than he does. I am her lawyer,' Larry insisted again.

Patsy's eyes were blazing with anger. 'I don't need a lawyer because I've done nothing wrong,' she answered stubbornly. The detectives gave her the option again if she wanted a lawyer present, and Patsy just gave up and nodded to them.

Going through the same procedure, the police informed Patsy it was an informal chat regarding James's allegation. Calmly, the police quizzed Patsy about her relationship with James. 'We're friends of sorts,' she explained. 'I believe he worked for my husband doing whatever.' She shrugged nonchalantly. 'He has been kind, I grant you that, helping me sort out my husband's businesses here. As you know, I have the pizza parlours in the high street and they are being refurbished.'

'Do you have any idea why Mr McNally would incriminate you in the murder of his wife?' asked the detective.

'No. I don't even know his wife or what happened to her. Yes, I've heard she's been murdered, but how, I have no idea. Maybe because I wouldn't lend him that money he was asking for?' Patsy shrugged; now it was time for her bombshell and to stitch James up once and for all.

'He cut her throat, Mrs Diamond. Hers and her lover's.'

The detectives looked at each other when they saw the shock on Patsy's face. Immediately her body language told them she had no idea what had happened to his wife. She paled and sat there silent for a moment, gathering her thoughts, then asked if she could have a cigarette.

'I didn't know that. If it's any help to you, when I saw him this morning, he did say he was going to his wife's house to collect some things. Apparently, he still has his keys.' She shrugged and smiled sweetly, waiting for the detectives to take in what she had just said.

'Keys?' asked one of the detectives, frowning. Casting a furtive glance at his colleague, he asked again, 'Are you saying that Mr McNally still has the keys to his wife's house? Did you see them?'

'Yes, he shoved them into his trouser pocket and said he wouldn't be long. I went to the community centre, which you know I own now. I'm going to take the flat over the community centre as a bolt hole for when I am in Glasgow.' She cast a dirty look towards Larry. 'I was thinking about moving in with someone, but that won't be happening now.'

The detectives spied Larry's disappointed face as he looked down at the table and brushed off a piece of imaginary fluff from his jacket. They both knew exactly who she meant.

They wanted to know where she had been all morning. Patsy explained about the flat and about asking Maggie to help with getting her some cleaners in. 'I know you will check, so go ahead. I have nothing to hide,' she emphasised. Her knees felt weak, as she tried remaining strong. All she could do was tell the truth. And indeed, it was the truth.

The detectives ended the meeting and said they would be in touch and they would need some form of address to find her. 'I will be at the community centre if it's liveable. It's been left in a terrible state.'

'She's staying at my house,' Larry interrupted. 'I will give you the details.' Larry looked at Patsy hopefully and was pleased when she smiled and nodded. Patsy knew she couldn't stay in the flat yet; it was a shithole. Larry had just put himself on the line for her. He couldn't defend her if they were cohabiting, so it was just a means to an end and Patsy would be in Larry's custody for the time being. The detectives thanked her for coming, took the address details from Larry and then they were both free to leave.

A wave of relief washed over Patsy as she breathed in the fresh air of the street. Her stomach had been in knots while being interrogated. She had been through all of that after Nick's death. Day in and day out they had questioned her about his murder; as the wronged wife, she had been the prime suspect. It had been nerve-wracking and stressful. Some days she had just gone into total meltdown and had panic attacks, but she had vowed then as she did now, that she wouldn't become a victim. She would survive.

* * *

The detectives decided to take Patsy at her word and look through James's personal belongings in front of him. Everything had been inventoried when he had arrived at the police station. The detectives displayed his watch and wallet, while James shrugged, not understanding the implication of it all. Finally, they let the bunch of keys fall onto the table and the detectives asked him about them. James swore they were the keys Patsy had given him earlier that day. He had forgotten all about them.

When they asked him to go for a ride in the car to his wife's house, the penny dropped. Patsy had fitted him up. Uniformed police were stood at the gate of the house and forensics were still combing the area for any other evidence. James's heart sank. He could see the curtain twitchers spying out of their windows and felt embarrassed. The police gave James the keys and asked him to see if they fit the lock on the door. James's hands trembled as he held the yale key, knowing it was going to fit. Instantly, the key turned and the door opened. He had just thrust them into his pocket when Patsy had given them to him; his mind had been on other things. Anger burned inside him and his face flushed. He recalled Patsy wearing gloves when she had given them to him and rolled his eyes up to the sky and cringed as a furrowed frown crossed his brows, grimacing at his own stupidity. He had been too blinded by his hatred for his wife to notice the obvious.

'It's Patsy Diamond,' he shouted, again and again. 'She gave me those keys this morning.'

'Why would she have your wife's keys James?' asked the detective. 'Does Patsy Diamond know your wife?'

In blind panic, James tried lashing out and struggled to get away, even though there was nowhere to run. He was held in a bear hug by a uniformed officer, while they put the handcuffs back on him and put him in the back of the police car. Driving away, he hung his head, hardly noticing the blur of the streets as he passed them by. He knew he was doomed and Patsy had set him up. He cursed her into damnation!

Once they got back to the police station, he was officially charged with the murder of his wife and her lover.

22

KARMA

It had been three days since James had been arrested. Fin had been permanently badgering Patsy to go and visit James with him, but she told him she couldn't go yet, given James's accusations about her. The police were still looking into the murders. James had been due to go to the magistrate's court and give his plea, but Patsy wasn't ready to go yet. She would, but in her own time. The police had been on a few occasions and questioned her again. Then they had got her to make a proper statement.

Victoria and Sheila had both been in touch and Sheila had offered her house as a safe haven for Patsy to stay, although she had declined. Patsy didn't want to rock the boat. They had Larry's address and that would do for now.

Patsy had played her trump card with Victoria and Sheila, claiming that as James had no morals about killing innocent women, it could easily have been them or herself. The very thought of it had made them gasp in disbelief and horror. James had been their friend; he had helped them on numerous occasions. Why was he putting Patsy in the frame for this? Again, Patsy had explained to them it was because he needed a whipping boy to reduce whatever sentence he was looking at by giving the police information, and he was using her to wriggle out of an impossible situation. It could have been any one of them, but only she was on Thistle Park Estate on the day he murdered his wife.

Out of the blue, Patsy's phone rang. She didn't recognise the number but with the constant calls the police were making, she answered anyway. Startled, she heard Freddie's voice. 'I need ten thousand transferring to this account Lady D.'

'For what?' she snapped.

'The ice-cream business. You need a paper trail. No one gives businesses away. There are vans and stock here and they want paying for. This is your proof you've paid for it, and you can't argue with that.'

Patsy had almost forgotten about the Albanians with one thing and another. 'Okay, give me the account number.'

Freddie started reeling off an account number while Patsy tapped it into her mobile banking. She hadn't thought about it like that. Of course it made sense. For all intent and purposes and as far as anyone would know, she had bought the declining business and the money would go into the Albanian account.

Nervously, as an afterthought, Patsy asked what had happened to them.

'Ask no questions and we tell no lies,' Freddie replied. 'Has the money gone through?'

'Yes, it has. All done.' On the other end of the phone, Patsy heard two gunshots and the call was ended. Patsy's blood ran cold.

* * *

Fin had walked around sullenly for the past few days and Patsy felt it was now time to play her ace card. She had rummaged through all of the recordings Nick had made when he had spoken to the criminals he employed, and she had found just what she was looking for. Something had nagged in the back of her brain about James's loyalty to his friends, and once she had thought about it, she realised she had the perfect thing to put Fin back on side again.

'I've found a van that I think might do as a mobile shop Mrs Diamond. It will need a few alterations like a serving hatch and stuff, but that's up to you. What do you want me to do about it?'

'Can you get it sorted Fin? Is there a garage or something that can do the alterations? By the way, it's been a week nearly, and so I have decided to go and see James this afternoon.'

Fin's eyes lit up. 'Really? I thought you had forgotten all about him.' Fin looked down at the floor and blushed. He hadn't wanted to admit it, but he thought Patsy was just leaving him there to rot.

'Well, the police would find it very strange that I would visit someone who was accusing me of all sorts wouldn't they? But I said I would go and I will. By the way Fin, I have something that might be of interest to you. I found it by chance and as it concerns your father, I thought you might want it.' Craftily and with a smile on her face, Patsy opened her purse and handed Fin a mobile phone, still with the SIM card in place.

Curiously, Fin looked at it. 'You mean Billy Burke? What is it?'

'How many fathers do you have Fin?' Patsy laughed. She knew it was a hollow laugh and was trying to sound as friendly as possible, but she knew this was the bombshell that would kill all loyalty Fin had for James once and for all.

Fin blushed at her comment and gave a weak smile.

'Listen to the recordings on it, Fin,' was all she said before she walked towards her car. 'I have to go because Paul from the pizza parlour has asked to see me. We'll speak later love.' Patsy felt calling Fin 'love' showed her fondness of him and would hopefully be some comfort to him, as she knew full well she had just blown his world apart.

'I'll get Matt the mechanic to sort out the van; he's cheap enough,' Fin shouted after her as she drove off. She gave him a thumbs up as she drove away.

Walking into the pizza parlour, Patsy was amazed. It didn't look like some old drug den that sold fast food any more; it now looked like a clean, up-to-date fast food place that sold drugs as a dessert, and a going concern to launder money through.

'Miss Diamond.' Paul lowered his eyes as a sign of respect. Patsy thought he was going to touch his forelock and give her a bow.

'Well, I presume this is what you wanted to talk to me about.' She beamed. 'It looks amazing Paul. What about the others; do they look the same?' Patsy was really pleased as she looked around the stainless steel worktops and kitchen area that would pass any hygiene inspection.

Paul nodded. 'We can go and see if you like. If there is anything you want changing, let me know. I have hired some men to cook the pizzas. They worked at the other side of town and the shop they worked at is closing down, is that okay?' His sense of insecurity bubbled to the surface. 'There are also the men who will work the special counter and moped delivery men are two a penny around here – no Albanians though,' he stressed stubbornly. His dark eyes almost pierced Patsy's. 'All trustworthy and know their jobs, rates of pay are up to you. When are you going to open the pizza shops again? Personally,' he rambled on, 'I think you should do a two-for-one offer for open day.' Paul seemed to take a big sigh once he had given his speech. It was clear to Patsy that he had thought all of this out in his mind beforehand and just seemed to want to get it off his chest and say it in one go.

Patsy liked his suggestions; it was clear he was a good businessman, but he had mental health issues that prevented him from doing a lot. Musing to herself, Patsy had always thought people didn't take mental health issues serious enough. Just because you couldn't see it like a broken leg or something, didn't mean it wasn't there. Paul was a prime example, and being blackmailed into Nick's circle of deceit had probably made it worse. Maybe, this would help him.

'Paul, I trust your judgement; you won't let me down. I am positive of that.' Smiling, Patsy felt more than confident. 'When you're ready to go to France, let me know. But I would like that sorted sooner rather than later.' Reaching out her hand to shake his on the deal, she saw Paul twitch nervously and look at her oddly. It saddened Patsy to think that this burly brute of a man was paranoid and afraid of any act of kindness. It just proved he hadn't been shown much in the past. This free hand of management she was giving Paul was a confidence booster to him. Not only would he see things through, he would torture anyone that stepped out of line because he had been given the responsibility to sort it out. This was his personal project and it saved her hiring muscle, because Paul and his brothers were all the muscle she needed. She could see by his body language and the grin on his face that this was a whole new beginning for him and he was as pleased as punch with his new status.

* * *

Fin sat in his flat alone with a can of lager. He had put the mobile phone Patsy had given him on the worn, scratched table in front of him and with each sip of lager he took he spied it. He felt uneasy about it for some reason. He couldn't understand why Patsy had given him this regarding his father. What difference did it make now?

Rolling a cigarette and filling it with marijuana, he took one large exhale, and turned on the recording. He could hear muffled voices and couldn't quite make them out, but, listening again, carefully, he recognised James's voice. Rewinding it, he listened again, paying more attention this time. He could hear Nick Diamond and James talking with Noel, the ice-cream vendor. They were discussing taking over the drug business and the only thing that stood in their way was Billy Burke, as it was his known turf. Stunned, he heard James say that he had been in partnership with Billy, but they had fallen out and James had grassed him up to save his own skin! This was not the story James had told Fin. In total disbelief and wonderment, Fin carried on listening. His heart was pounding, and with each sentence he heard of them plotting to kill Billy Burke in prison, his blood boiled. Fin had had a fair idea that Noel, the Albanian, had had something to do with it, but James? With each inhale of his spliff, his anger and hatred for James grew. Sitting back on his worn, torn sofa with his can of lager, he realised that everything James had said was a lie. Patsy was just another partner James was going to double cross! Well, he decided to himself, he would make sure James never grassed up anyone again. He still had friends in prison, and he knew they would help him, the way he had helped them out in the past. Raising his can of lager in a toast to the nicotine-stained ceiling, Fin stubbed out the end of his roll up. 'Fuck you James,' he said aloud.

A news item on the television caught Fin's eye and reaching

for the remote control, he turned up the volume. There had been some bomb blast and the screen was full of police cars and people rushing around while the presenter was reporting that an Albanian nightclub had been blown up. There was nothing left but rubble and the emergency services were ploughing through it all to see if there was anyone alive buried beneath it all. Black smoke from the building blew in the wind as the reporter tried shouting into his microphone above the sirens and noise while pointing out the burning embers of the club, as the fire brigade were firing their water hoses into the air to control it.

Apparently a second bomb had gone off in the heart of the Albanian ghetto, killing a lot of people. The numbers were unknown, although a lot had been taken to hospital. This was the Albanian side of the town, everyone knew that, and the reporter was saying that it was some form of terrorist attack. Fin watched wide eyed; he couldn't believe it. He knew instinctively that Patsy was behind this, and grinned to himself. He didn't know how she had done it, but she had avenged his friends, just like she had promised. The nightclub his friends had been massacred in, was now just a pile of bricks. Satisfied, Fin stood up and left his flat to organise Patsy's mobile shop. He had things to sort out, including James. Grinning widely, he thought about Patsy and agreed to himself, she was one Diamond lady he could trust.

23

A DIAMOND REIGN

Fin was on his way to Maggie's house when he saw Patsy's car parked outside the community centre. Seeing the side door was open, he ran up the staircase to the flat and almost fell over a couple of women walking down the stairs with bin liners full of rubbish.

'Out the way Fin, you're a bloody nuisance. I've got money to earn and you're in my way.'

'Yeah right Alma; will you be disclosing this money to the benefits people?'

'Bloody cheek! I've paid my taxes in my time, it's just my rheumatism playing me up,' Alma moaned, looking for sympathy.

'Well, your rheumatism isn't preventing you from holding them bin liners and it won't stop you picking up your wages, either.' Fin laughed, dodging Alma's flying hand towards the back of his head.

'I'll get you next time laddie, you bloody waster!' she shouted, as she carried on down the staircase.

'Mrs Diamond! Mrs Diamond!' shouted Fin as he burst into

the flat. Looking around, he saw five or six women with dusters. Some were washing windows and others were hoovering. The whole flat was a hive of activity. Running through each room, he spotted Patsy in the kitchen. She was ordering all of the plates, cups and cutlery to be thrown out. Fin gave a sly grin to one of the women; he knew none of that stuff was going to see the inside of the skip. It would all be shared out, amongst the estate.

'Fin, what are you doing here? Are you looking for work as a window cleaner?' Patsy laughed.

'Have you seen the news Mrs Diamond?' he asked eagerly. His face was flushed and excited. Innocently, Patsy shrugged and shook her head. Fin took out his mobile and googled today's news. Patsy held his mobile; it showed the bombing of the night-club. Both herself and Fin cast a glance at each other and said nothing. She smiled and handed him his phone back.

Patsy looked around at the women in the room waiting to hear the gossip and then back at Fin. Realising his mistake, and understanding her calmness, he nodded. 'Later Mrs Diamond.'

Once he had left, Patsy walked into the bedroom and shut the door. Taking out her own mobile phone, she looked at the devastation from the bombing and sighed. Mentally, she thought about all the innocent people who had been hurt and was saddened by it. None of this turf war was their fault. Switching her screen off, she inhaled deeply. Standing in front of the mirror, she brushed down her pale blue frock coat and straightened her hair. Freddie had done his job and now she would make her claim on the ice-cream business. There had been no news as far as she knew regarding the ice-cream vendor. Taking out her phone again, she trawled through local news items. There was nothing. Perplexed, she carried on and then brought up the local newspaper and after a few minutes she spotted it. A house fire had been reported. Reading the item, it told her what she wanted to know. Two people had burnt to death in their own home. More enquiries were being made; it went on to say it was the home of local businessman and ice-cream vendor.

Patsy read it and smiled. She needed to speak to Larry; now was the time to make her peace with him. Dialling his number, she waited. 'Larry, it's me. I'm not going to beat around the bush. I'm sorry. Can I book a table for us to have dinner tonight?' She paused.

'I'd like that, Patsy. Can I ask what's brought on this sudden turn of events? Am I no longer the enemy?' Patsy could hear his sarcasm and knew she deserved it.

'My bad Larry, and no you're not the enemy, you never were.' Changing the subject, Patsy added, 'Look Larry love, the flat is nearly sorted and after this army of ladies finish, it will be ready to move in to. I could be out of your hair by tomorrow, if that's okay. I'm really sorry Larry – for everything.'

'Patsy! Don't put the phone down. Dinner will be nice. Is this our first kiss and make up?' He laughed nervously. 'Don't move out Patsy. I would rather you hated me in our home, than be without you.'

Choking back the emotional lump in her throat, Patsy could feel tears welling up in her eyes. That was a beautiful thing he had said and it had touched her deeply. It had been years since Nick had said anything like that. Sniffing, and controlling her voice, guilt overwhelmed her over her treatment of him. She hated that she had to lie to him constantly. She wanted to be honest, but she knew Larry wouldn't understand. He was an honest man, and she felt like she was dragging him in the mud. 'Let me buy you dinner Larry. Somewhere with candlelight, where I can fall in love with you all over again,' she whispered. Larry's voice gave her a warm feeling inside and suddenly she wanted to be with him, far away from the criminal world she had fallen into.

'I would love to have dinner with you Patsy, thank you for asking.' He laughed warmly.

'Good, then I will book a restaurant that allows fondling and petting and I'll see you at home. But first I need to shop and buy some underwear,' she teased. Hearing Larry's excited voice mixed with laughter, she ended the call. She felt better now they had made up. She really didn't deserve him.

Sat on the edge of the bed, she daydreamed about her evening with Larry. She could do with some retail therapy. She felt like she hadn't shopped in ages. Musing to herself, she wondered if Sheila would like an afternoon at the shops. Suddenly her mobile burst into life and seeing it was Fin, she answered it. 'Hi Fin, and what can I do for you?' Exasperated, she threw her head back. He'd only been gone a few minutes; what did he want now?

'Hi Mrs Diamond. If you're still going to see James this afternoon, would you mind if I came with you?'

Patsy grimaced and closed her eyes. Shit! She had forgotten all about James. She would have to postpone her shopping trip. Maybe she could get something new to wear on the way back from the prison, although the idea of Fin accompanying her to the shops didn't exactly fill her with excitement. Disappointed, she put on a much braver voice than she felt. 'Yes sure Fin. I will be glad of the company.' Ending the call, she mused to herself about her visit with James. She expected things to get heated.

Victoria had been constantly in touch, telling her all about her time with Nancy. They had gone for long walks and emptied all the shops of dolls and toys. Victoria also told Patsy that social services had been in touch again about Victoria fostering Jimmy,

Natasha's son and little Nicky's brother. It had been clear to Patsy she had been testing the water for Patsy's opinion.

'That's entirely up to you Victoria. It's your choice. It would be nice if the family could be kept together, but, as I say, that ball is in your court.'

Hearing the relief in Victoria's voice, she knew she had said the right thing. Victoria giving him a home took the whole burden of guilt from Patsy's shoulders and Victoria's family was growing by the minute.

* * *

Patsy and Fin stood at the end of a very long queue outside the prison, waiting for visiting time. 'Blimey Mrs Diamond, it's bloody cold.' Fin rubbed his hands together and blew on them, while jigging up and down to keep warm.

'And you want me to do what Fin? Give you my coat, or put my arms around you to keep you warm? Have you ever thought of buying a new coat instead of wearing that jacket?' Turning her nose up, and making a face, Patsy ran her hands along the sleeve of his imitation leather jacket. It felt like cardboard. 'What animal did that leather come off of? A bloody hedgehog?' Patsy flinched as Fin laughed; it made her pause for a moment. The way he put his head back when he laughed was just like Nick. It had never occurred to her before, but they were half-brothers. Suddenly it dawned on her; Fin was her brother-in-law.

'This is a rare animal, like me, Mrs Diamond. Do you like it?' As he showed off his tatty jacket, Patsy made a mental note to herself: maybe she would go shopping after this after all.

'No, I don't, and it smells, like you. When was the last time you had a bath? For Christ's sake Fin, you are going to be running a business with me and you look like some bum druggie off the streets. Time to change Fin and get rid of those bloody mirrored sunglasses! You look like a pimp.' She laughed and reached up and pulled his sunglasses from the top of his head.

Fin stopped messing around and spied Patsy seriously. 'You mean you want me to help you run your businesses? Seriously?'

'Fin, I am like a walking job centre. I need people to run the mobile shop, to help in the shops. Moped delivery men, people to run and work the community centre. I want that up and running again as soon as possible, by the way.' She wagged a finger in his face. 'So you had better pull your finger out and get things sorted. Did you get your mechanic guy onto the van you suggested?' Moving in closer to him, she whispered in his ear, 'We also have to do a night walk and dig up some more stock for the dealers.'

Fin rubbed his hands together. 'Busy, busy busy, that's me!'

Patsy rolled her eyes up to the ceiling.

'Mrs Diamond, I got all the staff you want, straight and bent. Everyone I know is looking for a job but they either have a record or they don't have qualifications. If you give them a chance, they will be grateful of the work. Do you want me to sort it?'

'Of course I do! That's what I'm paying you for, isn't it? But they had better be reliable Fin, because it will be your head on the chopping block if they aren't.'

The noise of the warder opening the side entrance for visitors stopped their conversation.

After being checked, they both walked into the visiting room. Looking around, they saw James sat at the very back and walked towards him.

'You took your fucking time Patsy,' James commented.

'I would have been a lot longer if they had put me behind

bars and thrown away the key like you wanted,' Patsy snapped and sat down.

'You have to sort this Patsy; you know I didn't do anything. You can tell them that it had nothing to do with me. You know I'm innocent!' James slammed his fist down on the table in front of them, making both herself and Fin jump backwards in their seats.

Patsy glared at him, seeing through his façade. All she could see was a desperate, angry old man who was frightened. He was like a caged animal waiting to pounce. 'Fin, pop and get us some coffees and snacks will you?' Patsy handed him a load of change from her purse and once he'd left, she moved in closer towards James on the opposite side of the table. 'You brought this on yourself James.'

'You owe me Patsy,' James snarled. 'You planted those keys on me, you bitch.'

Patsy was seeing James for what he was. His caring friendly side had gone.

'Of course I did. You got what you deserve. Why did you give them my name James? Do you really think I did it?' she spat out. They both looked around as the warders and other prisoners were staring at them. Their hushed argument was beginning to attract attention. They were both flushed and angry and so took a moment to compose themselves and smile at the warders, indicating everything was okay.

James sat back in his chair and mouthed the word 'Freddie' to her. Nodding, Patsy smiled.

'So you see James, I owe you nothing. It cost me a lot of money to get you your heart's desire,' she whispered. Patsy watched him pale and squirm before her. Freddie had never occurred to him. He had been under the impression that Patsy had done it herself.

'Very clever Patsy, but you could have said,' he muttered. 'I went back because I wanted to make sure, that was all. I like to see a job through, and I didn't want you to have left any traces. I was trying to cover your back Patsy,' he lied.

'No, you weren't James. You didn't trust me. How's Karen?' Patsy asked nonchalantly. Seeing that she had put him off balance, she shot a look of hatred at him. 'Where have you put her James? You bastard!' she snarled. 'You're a fucking Judas and I hope they throw away the key. You terrorised me with those messages and for what? You thought you could get your hands on Karen's share of my business; is that it?'

James grinned. 'I followed you. I wanted to know why you'd asked Fin to go with you and not me. I thought we were partners, Patsy. I helped her out and got some air back into her lungs. She'd broken her leg and arm and she was half conscious. In her panic and her frustration when I brought her round, she scribbled a note under my tutoring to state that she bequeathed everything to me, so that you couldn't get your hands on it. The last thing she wanted was to give you everything back. That was when I shot her, pierced her lungs to let the air out and dumped her in the river. That is a good one to remember in your life of crime Patsy. The body is full of gas and air and will always float, unless you let the air out. So you're stuck with me Patsy. I am your partner whether you like it or not,' James spat out triumphantly and folded his arms smugly.

'No, you're not James. At Larry's office, we were dissolving our partnerships. All she's left you are the clothes on her back and the euros in her purse. I already own the lot and you have nothing. You won't even get your wife's life insurance as her murderer. Game, set and match!'

Ignoring her outburst, a frown crossed James's brow. 'What do you mean you dissolved the partnership? She agreed to that?'

Puzzled, he waited for an answer. His mind was swimming. This was not the meeting he had expected. He'd held all the trump cards and expected Patsy to crumble. Instead, like any good poker player, she had held her cards close to her chest.

Patsy burst out laughing. 'She never read the small print James. Now I might not be a criminal mastermind, but I am a businesswoman and I was married to a lawyer for a very long time. And one thing I learnt was, always read what you're signing. Karen couldn't be bothered. She wanted to get back to France. She was no businesswoman James.'

Deflated at this revelation James sat back in his chair and swept his hands through his hair.

'I trusted you James, and you played me. Your wife was your idea – deal with it.' Looking up, Patsy saw Fin heading back to the table, balancing three hot drinks. His pockets were stuffed with chocolate bars and he was carrying a bag of crisps between his teeth. Patsy looked across at James; she could see the hatred burning in his eyes.

Fin sat down. 'Here you go. Sorry I've been a while; this one is yours James.' Fin put the paper cup in front of James, and then his own and Patsy's at their side of the table. James picked up the cup of hot liquid and looked at Patsy. He was tempted to throw it at her.

'Don't even think about it James,' said Fin in a serious tone. 'Because if you do, you won't get what I have put in it for you.'

Patsy was a little taken aback to think that James was going to scald her, but then nothing about James surprised her these days. She was more surprised by Fin. His serious tone and stern look had caught her off guard. Seeing James relax his shoulders somewhat and smile, Patsy felt it was time to leave. They had both said what they needed to say. 'I will wait for you outside Fin.'

James's eyes followed her as she made to leave. 'Enjoy your freedom while you can Patsy. Take a good look at these walls because your prison will look just like it.'

After she'd left, venom spewed from James's mouth as he talked to Fin. He warned him to stay away from Patsy. 'She's evil Fin. She is just like her husband. She was in it with him all along.'

'Drink your coffee James. I've slipped something in the bottom for you.' Fin stood up to leave. 'Enjoy the chocolate, too.'

James winked at him. 'Is it something for me to sell in here?' James breathed a sigh of relief. He knew he could rely on Fin to smuggle some drugs in for him to sell.

Fin's face was deadly serious. 'No, it's the recording of you, Nick and Noel plotting to murder my father in jail. If I were you, James, I would tear up the bedsheets, before everyone finds out you're an informer and does me a favour by igniting you in your cell. Bye James. Sweet dreams.'

Fin walked away as the colour drained from James's face. Fear rose up inside of him and he looked around at the sea of faces looking at him. He knew Fin was well known in the prisons, and a lot of the ex-cons liked him. Some of the older prisoners still liked Billy Burke, too. Any one of these inmates could be planning to murder him in his sleep, even his cellmate. James felt sick with fear. He knew full well that Patsy had given Fin that recording. Fuck that Nick Diamond! Would he haunt everyone forever?

The prison warder stood at the side of him, almost waking him up from his dazed state. 'Back to your cell McNally.' James took a sip of his coffee, and feeling that it had cooled somewhat, gulped it back, almost burning his throat. He wanted to listen to the recording and felt the SIM card slip down his throat as he swallowed.

Outside, Patsy sat smoking in the car as she waited for Fin. She could feel her hands and body trembling with anger. James had shown no remorse. If anything, he still vowed revenge. And for what? He had wanted his wife murdered. He'd got what he wanted; now he was paying the price.

Fin got in the car beside her.

'What did he have to say?' Patsy asked and handed him a cigarette.

'Oh, just what a bitch you are and to steer clear of you.'

Patsy didn't know what to say. 'What did you give him in his coffee cup?'

'The SIM card you gave me. Why didn't you give it to me sooner Patsy?'

'Firstly Fin, I didn't know Billy Burke was your father at the time, and to be honest, I hadn't paid a lot of attention to that one recording until it was pointed out to me that James always seems to fall out with his partners. Then that recording I had listened to came back to me and I recognised James's voice. You deserved to hear it. What you did with it was up to you.' Nervously, Patsy turned on the ignition and started the car. When Fin wasn't acting the fool, he was quite a different person. She had given him a lot to think about, and he was smouldering with anger.

'How did you get the SIM card in?' Patsy asked after a few minutes of silence.

'Shoved it up my nostril, then when I got the coffees I wiped my nose and put it in his coffee.'

As Patsy drove, she winced inside. Fin had stuck a SIM card up his nose and then put it in James's coffee? That was disgusting! 'Thanks for stopping him throwing the coffee at me. It could have scalded me badly.'

The rest of the journey passed in silence. Once they reached Edinburgh, Patsy asked Fin if he wanted to tag along with her while she went shopping. It wasn't the best ice breaker, but it was all she had.

'I'll come if you want,' he replied, and lit a cigarette. 'Can we get a McDonald's as well? I'm starving.' Patsy smiled to herself; she felt better now Fin was his old self again and thinking about his stomach.

Marching Fin around some of the better shops in Edinburgh, Patsy headed for the men's section, which puzzled Fin. 'Do you wear blokes' clothes Patsy?'

Smacking him around the back of the head, she pursed her lips. 'Coats!' She pointed out. 'Get a proper coat. I am going to the underwear section. The ladies that is,' she prompted. 'And when I get back we will see what you have chosen and then put it back on the rail and choose a proper one.'

As Patsy looked around the lingerie section, a leopard-print Basque caught her eye and she smiled. She pictured herself wearing that and her stockings. Now that would cheer Larry up for definite. She grinned and took one off the rail. She also picked out a low-cut black satin dress. Seduction was the key tonight.

Walking back to the men's section, Patsy looked at Fin's choice. 'Absolutely not. Don't even think about it.' Pulling one of the hangers he was holding off him, she put it back onto the rail. 'A blue and white check jacket? You look like a bloody tablecloth! I want a proper coat. Maybe camel, if they have it.'

Fin was also holding a luminous green T-shirt and grinned. 'Okay, I'm putting it back.'

'That's a flashback to the eighties Fin, and you will look like the incredible hulk without the muscles in that. Plain is what we're looking for and let's get you some decent shirts. You're my manager Fin, and you have to look the part.'

'I'm not wearing a tie; people will think I'm going to court.'

Fin laughed. His mood had brightened; he was enjoying his shopping trip with Patsy and purposely picked clothing up he knew she wouldn't approve of. They were both laughing in the end, but eventually Fin came out with a whole new wardrobe, including underwear which he claimed he never wore, which made Patsy squirm even more.

'Before you wear any of it, you have a bath. Do you hear me?' Patsy warned.

Fin nodded, and burst out laughing. 'Do you mean you're not going to scrub my back?'

Patsy laughed. 'No, but I will cut your hair and make you look like a human being again.'

24

HAPPY DAYS

Once Patsy got back to Larry's, she ran a bubble bath; the Chanel perfumed foam made her feel relaxed. Opening the fridge afterwards, she took out a bottle of white wine and was about to take it upstairs when she noticed a brown padded envelope on the hallway table. Looking closer, she saw that it was addressed to herself. Opening it, she saw a set of keys and a note. The note was signed and dated and said, 'Ice-cream business, including vans and stock, sold as seen to Patsy Diamond.' Patsy held the keys in her hand. She now had the keys to the warehouse and a note from the owner saying it had been sold. She looked more closely at the paper; there was a cross under a foreign signature, and Patsy realised that was where she was meant to sign. Quickly scribbling her name on it, she smiled. This definitely called for a glass or two of wine after the day she'd had. It was only 4.30 p.m. and Larry would still be at work, which meant she had time to contemplate her day. The visit with James had shaken her more than she realised. The way that he had turned on her, and joked about killing Karen, made her blood run cold.

Oiling herself in scented oils, she carefully applied her make-up, and blow waved her hair into shape. Opening her shopping bags, Patsy put on her sexy underwear. The leopard-print Basque shaped her waist and rounded her breasts with its black lace. The silk stockings she slid on made her feel sexy. Suddenly, she heard the door open and Larry shout her name. The wine had gone to her head a little, after having only eaten a small burger with Fin.

'Up here,' she shouted. Larry ran up the stairs and stopped in the doorway as she stood there in her underwear. Patsy smiled.

The appreciation of her efforts of the afternoon was already showing in the front of Larry's trousers. His erection was apparent and growing steadily. Pulling off his jacket, he strode towards her and pulled her towards him, kissing her. His hands roamed all over her body, freeing her breasts. Patsy could already feel herself becoming excited and moistening at his touch. Melting in his arms, she arched her back while he licked and teased her nipples greedily. Patsy's body was on fire as she reached forward, stroking his crotch and pulling down the zip of his trousers. Picking her up, Larry laid her on the bed. Instantly mounting her, together they gasped in pleasure as Patsy welcomed him between her thighs. It was feisty and passionate as they clung together, rocking back and forth in unison. A tension built up inside of Patsy, and her head spun as she reached her peak and cried out. Not yet ready, Larry turned her over on to her knees and mounted her again while holding on to her hips. Together they panted and gasped as the fireworks seemed to explode in their bodies. As they lay in each other's arms after, Patsy stroked him again. 'I bought something for you today darling,' she whispered.

Sliding off the bed, she reached for her shopping bag while Larry watched her with a satisfied grin on his face. Patsy took out a set of pink, fluffy handcuffs. Climbing on to the bed, she reached for his wrist and put one on him, closing the clasp on the pine bed post. Taking out another pair, she did the same with his other wrist, causing him to lie spread-eagled on the bed. Larry was helpless and Patsy could see he was turned on by it, which excited her. Stroking his body with her tongue, she felt him twitch and tremble at her touch. Slowly Patsy mounted him; she was excited by the power she held over him, and even when she lowered her breasts in front of his face, she moved aside so he couldn't reach her with his tongue. Impulsively, she slapped him across the face, and felt his body tense inside her as she writhed on top of him, making it more exciting for her.

Getting off the bed, she took out her mobile phone and took a photo quickly before she sent it to Sheila. Laughing to herself, Patsy climbed back on to the bed and freed him from his handcuffs and poured them both a glass of wine.

'Where the hell did that come from Patsy?' Larry asked.

'Did you enjoy it?' Patsy grinned.

Nodding, Larry smiled. 'Christ yes, that was amazing.'

'Well, that's because it's naughty Larry. And everything that is naughty is exciting. Come on, let's get dressed and find somewhere to eat; I presume we've lost our table now, but we can always ask.'

* * *

Over dinner, as they talked, Patsy decided now was a good time to mention she had bought the ice-cream business. Larry was shocked and taken aback a little; after all, she had never even mentioned it.

'Now I really am the ice queen right?' She laughed. 'No, seriously Larry, while I was checking out the pizza shops, this man was talking about his family's dying business. He wanted it taking off his hands, but there wasn't a buyer. It included the vans and some stock they had. Apparently they wanted to sell up and go home to Poland or somewhere.' Patsy shrugged. That was the best excuse she could come up with at short notice.

Larry suddenly put his business head on and wasn't happy when she told him she had a scrap of paper as a receipt. 'How come they sold it to you and not one of their own? Usually they keep their businesses within their own friends and family.' A frown appeared on Larry's brow. 'Didn't that business belong to the people that were in the house fire?' he asked.

Patsy was glad the lighting was dimmed, because she could feel herself blush. 'I don't know Larry. Right place, right time.' Patsy shrugged. 'This man was just having a good old moan about the business being a millstone around their necks. They had lost their patch because the vans hadn't been out in ages and you know me Larry, I do like a bargain. The owner had run that business for years, they just wanted rid of it. And what fire? I haven't heard anything?' Patsy smiled as innocently as she could.

Larry said he would look into the legality of it, which was exactly what she'd wanted. With Larry on board, everything would be watertight. He said he would come and see it with her the next day and she agreed.

'I went shopping today too.' Larry grinned. Reaching into his pocket, he took out a small square box and put it on the table. 'Marry me Patsy. I don't want to play games. I love you, and I want to marry you. I know I am punching above my weight and I don't come into your league.'

Patsy looked across the candlelit table at him. He looked nervous and worried and he was declaring his love with his heart on his sleeve.

'Yes, Larry, I will marry you,' she heard herself say without thinking. She almost shocked herself. Opening the box, she smiled at the solitaire diamond while Larry slipped it on her finger. Everything was fitting together like a jigsaw, Patsy mused, and took another sip of wine. She did love Larry, she admitted. Mainly because he loved her. He wanted and needed her and she didn't feel like a hinderance to him, like she had obviously been to Nick. It gave her a deep warm feeling, knowing that this handsome man before her loved her warts and all. Maybe, she mused to herself, this time it will work out. She mentally envisioned her life at home with Larry, with Nancy by her side. Larry's son Paul would be a frequent visitor and they would be a family. It seemed like the perfect end to the perfect fairy tale.

* * *

Once Larry had visited the ice-cream warehouse and looked around, he saw that Patsy had the keys as well as a document signed and sealed and it all seemed legitimate. Patsy smiled when she thought about Freddie. Her payment into the Albanian woman's bank account was a paper trail and no one could deny it. The fact that there had been a tragic accident after the transaction, didn't make it any less legal. Patsy realised it might look suspicious, but, if she was going to murder them and take the ice-cream business, why would she pay them a large amount of money for it? It didn't make sense.

Paul organised the openings of the pizza parlours and they seemed to be a great success. Patsy had told Larry that she was still keeping the flat above the community centre as an office base and reluctantly he had agreed. He knew the only way to keep Patsy was to not try and clip her wings. She liked her independence. Sheila squealed with delight when she saw her engagement ring, and kept laughing about the photo she had sent her. Instantly she had matched it with her own and showed

Patsy the photo of Angus with his handcuffs on, except she had tied a ribbon around Angus's penis for good measure. Patsy couldn't stop laughing; it was hilarious.

Patsy's heart sank when she drove up to the community centre, and she was greeted by a police car. She felt like they were stalking her these days.

'Mrs Diamond, can we have a word.'

Saying nothing, Patsy walked ahead inside. 'What can I do for you officer?'

'Mr James McNally hung himself in his cell last night Mrs Diamond,' they said and carried on to say there would be no follow up to his accusations against her; it was clear to them he was just a drowning man looking for a lifeboat. As she knew him, they felt she should know. 'Although, Mrs Diamond, your name does seem to pop up a lot these days. You're on our radar.'

'Is that a threat officer?' snapped Patsy.

'No, Mrs Diamond, it's a fact.'

Stunned, Patsy watched them leave. She couldn't believe it. James was dead! Going to Maggie's flat, she informed her first and then asked about Fin.

'He's down at the garage sorting out the mobile shop. It's all finished amazingly; I never knew that laddie had ambition and he looks tidy.' Maggie shrugged. 'God knows how he has managed it this quickly. It's only been a few days.'

'I could say the same about you Maggie. You and your cleaning army are amazing. I am going to open the community centre at the weekend and throw a party of sorts with sandwiches and stuff. I don't suppose your ladies can knock up a few sandwich trays?' Patsy asked.

Patsy still couldn't take in James's death and she could see how sad Maggie was. To be honest, she felt a pang of sadness herself. She had spent a lot of time talking with him, but like Freddie had said: there was no sentiment in business.

'You must be very upset Maggie. Are you okay?' Patsy reached forward and put her arms around Maggie. They held each other for a moment and then Maggie pulled away.

'I'm fine. I went to see him a couple of days ago, and I swore I would never go again. He was abusive and spiteful,' Maggie confessed. Patsy could see by her body language that Maggie felt awkward confessing this. 'He looked like he had taken drugs or something; he laughed about my shitty council flat and called me estate trash. He was quite hurtful Patsy, and I swore I would never go back again. I am sad, but I'm not sorry. He was a murderer.' Making herself busy, Maggie walked into the kitchen and switched on the kettle for something to do. Patsy could see how upset she was and felt it was better if she left.

Patsy's next thought was to ring Sheila and Victoria. It was as though Victoria had already forgotten all about James and her time with him had evaporated into the past. On the other hand, Sheila wanted all the gossip.

'Murdering bastard and he was a coward. He didn't want to face the long sentence he was going to get and took the easy option.' Pausing for a moment, Sheila seemed embarrassed to ask, 'Patsy, do I still work with you?'

Relief washed over Patsy. Since France, she hadn't pushed Sheila into helping her; she'd wanted her to come back of her own accord. 'You're my bloody wing woman Sheila and I need you.' Patsy laughed.

'Well, I just wondered lassie,' Sheila said shyly. She had been thinking over the last couple of days and thought Patsy didn't need her any more; she was running her own Diamond empire and seemed to be going from strength to strength.

'I've left you to your own devices Sheila. I knew if and when you were ready, you would come back to work. We're partners in all of this. We're sisters, as far as I'm concerned.' Patsy felt like punching the air that Sheila would be at her side again. Sheila was the only person she could talk openly with, even Victoria didn't know half of the things they had done together.

'That community centre needs a cook Patsy, and I've been thinking. Why not get on to the local catering college? They always need somewhere to get work experience. You will need someone in charge to mentor them, but you would get paid by the college, or the government. It wouldn't cost you a penny.'

A smile crossed Patsy's face; she liked Sheila's thinking. 'Give them a call Sheila, and put the idea to them. It can't do any harm, can it?' The community centre did need a cook and she would ask Paul about that. She was sure he would know someone who could train the college apprentices and that was an added bonus and the perfect cover. Everything was slotting perfectly into place and Maggie would know some women who wanted a job clearing the tables and pouring the tea and coffee.

'I'll come by later, hopefully with good news. So, when are you and Larry the lawyer having your engagement party?'

Patsy stopped in her tracks. She hadn't thought about that. 'He's only just asked Sheila; I haven't had time to catch my breath!'

No sooner had she ended the call than Fin appeared. God, this place was like Piccadilly; there was always someone walking in and out of the centre wanting her attention.

'Knock, knock.' Fin stood by the open doorway and smiled. Patsy took in his new look. His hair was cut, and he was washed and shaved. His jeans and shirt looked clean and ironed. It was true what they said, clothes maketh the man. Patsy informed him about James. 'I know. I told him to cut his bedsheets up. He wouldn't have lasted long in prison. Even though people hated my dad, he still had friends. James had sided with the enemy, and he knew the price of that.' Fin shrugged in an offhand manner.

Fin wasn't the clown he made himself out to be. He had friends in low places and wanted his own revenge.

'We need to visit some more of the graves Nick marked. They are full of something and we need to know what. This is something I want kept between us. We will do it Fin, us and Sheila, no outsiders. The dealers will want their drop off soon; we need to be prepared.'

'I figured that. I had better get my spade out.' He grinned. 'That mobile shop is more or less ready. It needs stock.'

'Any ideas who is going to work it?' Patsy asked, knowing full well he would have someone in mind.

'Yes, two men I know just out on probation. They need a job and they know the score and will keep their mouths shut. They don't want to end up back inside.'

'I have a few calls to make first, and then we will go shopping for stock Fin... and sort the other stuff of course. How many employees do you think we have?'

'About fifty for now. The nightclub dealers are all ready.'

'Nightclub dealers?' Patsy had heard about this from James, but wanted Fin to fill her in.

'Yeah, they go from nightclub to nightclub selling the stuff until the early hours of the morning. They haven't had much lately and what they have had was crap and they haven't earnt a penny. We need to divide up what drugs there are in those graves and let them make money. They are on a 5 per cent. It might not sound a lot but it soon adds up. If they have enough to sell that is,' Fin informed her.

Satisfied, Patsy looked at Fin with his newfound status. She knew he had a business head because he had lived on the streets with these people for years and they knew and trusted him. He was a good man to work with and in his own way he was honest, if you were straight with him.

'Sit down Fin; we need to have a proper talk.' Seeing Fin's apprehension, she assured him all was well and waited for him to sit down. 'Let's start from the beginning.' Taking a breath and mindfully wondering where to start, Patsy pursed her lips together. 'Victoria was raped many years ago by your father.'

Fin was about to interrupt but Patsy held up her hand to stop him. 'No recriminations; it's long past. But that means you and Nick were half-brothers and that makes you my brother-in-law.'

She saw Fin's shocked reaction, and his shoulders slumped.

'James is dead. Do you want to step into his shoes and take over where he left off? If you don't and want to carry on doing your own thing on the streets, that's fine. You will still work for me I hope. But I want you to carry on and become the businessman I know you can be. Your father was a businessman by all accounts, even though his ways weren't exactly the nicest, but then neither were Nick's. I think you have the same business brain Fin, and I would like you in with me, not just working for me. It's up to you, there is no pressure. Whatever you decide I am happy with.'

'What, like a partner you mean?' Fin was dumbstruck; he hadn't expected this.

Patsy laughed. 'Well, let's just say a shareholder. You will get your cut. Sort your flat out Fin; I want no drug den with the police sniffing around.' Remembering what the police had said, Patsy was aware they were watching her and wanted everything to appear squeaky clean. 'You had no real connection to Nick, and that is good. No pressure Fin.'

Patsy could see Fin's mind working overtime. He was giving it some thought and hadn't just jumped at her offer – she liked that. Fin was weighing up the pros and cons.

After he'd left, even though it was still early, Patsy reached for a bottle of whisky and poured herself one. She decided to ask Larry about any decent accountants he might know. She could cook a lot of the books herself, but having an accountant on your side helped enormously.

Patsy surveyed the community centre; it seemed full of ghosts. Beryl, Nick, Natasha and now James. They had all gone. A lot had happened since Nick's death and she felt a pang inside her and wondered if Sheila felt the same. They had both been widowed on the same day, which gave them that extra bond. It stung her a little to think that this time last year, Nick was having his affair with Natasha, without giving her a second thought. She still thought about him; they had been married a long time and you couldn't just erase those years. Mournfully, she wondered, when his love for her had died, or had he ever loved her at all? She didn't want her relationship with Larry to be anything like how it had been with Nick. He deserved better than that. Soon, everything would be up and running, then she would make time for herself and Larry. They would go on holiday, away from everything and spend some days in the sun getting to know each other properly, she decided. Maybe in time, she would be able to step back from all of this and let Fin and the others take the reins with Sheila's and Maggie's watchful eyes over them. It was a thought, but for the moment, she enjoyed the power, she admitted to herself.

A smile crossed her face when she thought about Larry again. He was her sanity in all of this. Each evening she had gone back to his house, the domesticity of it all made her feel relaxed. But, in the meantime, there was business to attend to.

25

LA DOLCE VITA

Sitting at her desk, in one of the spare bedrooms she had transformed into an office in the flat, Patsy looked at her watch and smiled. It was 3 p.m. and bang on time, she could hear the mobile shop blowing its horn. Sheila had suggested it should go further afield to other estates; everyone wanted credit until their benefits came through, and she was right. Through this, she had inadvertently become a loan shark, and her interest rates were high. Some of the collectors Fin had employed after accepting her offer, had become her 'muscle' and she had left them to their own devices as long as the money came rolling in. She didn't want to think about how they threatened and beat people up to get their payments. It wasn't her problem.

Days had passed into weeks at a hundred miles an hour, and she had hardly had time to catch her breath. Paul and his brothers had left for the chateau, leaving everything in ship shape back in Glasgow and the word from the Milieu gang was good. Posting the community centre on Facebook and Twitter had been a great success and people wanted to hire it for all kinds of events. The money she could launder through those events was unimaginable. She was even booking in fake events that weren't happening to show where the extra money had come from.

Patsy had been to see Nancy who had returned from Victoria's and was back at school, much to Victoria's disappointment. For the time being it was for the best that Nancy carried on her stable life with Patsy's parents at her regular school with her regular friends. Larry had come along to ingratiate himself with her parents and Nancy and they had all liked him. Plus it had given him time to get to know them all properly.

'You okay Patsy?' Fin popped his head around the door. 'You looked miles away.'

'Yes Fin, come in. I was just thinking about stuff. What is it, or is this a social call?'

'Bit of both; here are some of the takings from the mobile shop. I don't like them carrying too much around. There are a lot of thieves out there.' He winked and laughed. 'The lads are tooled up though, so there shouldn't be a problem.'

'They are carrying guns for protection?' Patsy was shocked; she hadn't known about that.

'Bloody right Patsy; have you seen some of the estates they're going to? Bloody hell, some of those bastards would sell their fillings for a gram of cocaine and a bottle of milk.' Fin laughed. 'Don't worry Patsy, my flat is full of unidentified objects. I have all the weapons they need.'

'Talking of your flat Fin, don't you think it's time you bought some curtains or blinds? Two football flags in those dirty windows don't say a lot about you.'

'They say a lot, Patsy.' Fin took on a serious tone and sat down opposite her. 'If I haven't won the lottery and I suddenly have money to decorate my flat, the police will be buzzing around in no time. Seeing my new clothes, people think I've been shoplifting in Next but that doesn't arouse suspicion, does it? They know I'm a thief.'

Patsy nodded and laughed with him. She had to agree with him that his low profile made good business sense.

'Victoria wants us all to go to Dorset for Christmas, and then Larry wants us all in Scotland for New Year. I suppose you do too, being a Scotsman,' Patsy teased.

Fin cocked his head in surprise. 'She's inviting me?'

'Of course, and Maggie if she'll come. Sheila and the kids will be there with Angus and my parents are going with Nancy. We're family Fin. Where else would you spend Christmas but with your family?' Fin's blush made her smile, and she thought she saw his eyes glaze over with tears. He had never been part of a family since his grandma's death and this new sense of belonging touched him.

Sniffing, and brushing it off, he laughed. 'Oh well, I will have to steal her something nice for Christmas then.'

Patsy had realised over the last few weeks that Fin's jokey ways were like a suit of armour to cover his feelings.

Patsy turned and put the bag of money in the safe, giving Fin time to compose himself. 'I'll pop to the bank in an hour. I like to go before closing time and there is the money in there from the dealers. We need to get that distributed amongst the shops to launder.' Patsy burst out laughing. 'Do you remember when we dug up those graves Fin? Even now, I laugh to myself. You, me and Sheila walking through the cemetery looking for Astroturf to roll back and you, you silly bastard, had walked us to the wrong grave. I thought Sheila was going to break her hands trying to pull that grass back!' Tears rolled down Patsy's face as she recalled how they had gone to the cemetery in silence and ended up shouting at each other so much, they had nearly woken the dead!

'Well, it was dark Patsy; it was a simple mistake. Poor Sheila; she fell backwards on her arse tugging at it. She gave me a right kick in the shins for getting it wrong!'

Patsy had suggested emptying all the graves at once and putting everything in a lock up somewhere but Fin and Sheila had objected, arguing that it was too easy for any dealer to find and steal, and a great drug raid if the police ever found out about it.

Suddenly, they both looked up at each other as the ice-cream van tune could be heard into the forecourt.

'It's like a cash register chime every time I hear those horns and daft tunes.' Fin laughed. 'Gotta go Patsy; people to see and pay wages to. Oh, by the way, fat Bernie the lesbian wants a word with you when you're not busy.'

'I wouldn't let her hear you call her that; she'll strangle you with her bare hands. I couldn't believe it when I heard about her chasing those Albanians away from Leandra's and hitting them with a baseball bat. You could be next Fin.' She laughed.

Wondering what Bernie wanted, Patsy made her way across the estate to Leandra's. Bernie spent most of her time there nowadays. The flat was in pristine condition, even though every time Patsy saw them there were different women living there.

Bernie opened the door with a mug of tea in her hands. 'Aye, Mrs Diamond, I presume that scrawny Fin told you I wanted to see you. Me and the lassies here, were wondering what you were going to do with the accommodation above the pizza parlours? The lassies here have some friends who might like to rent it, if you're interested. It's extra cash and you have someone living on the premises.'

Patsy smiled. 'That's fine with me as long as the paperwork is in order. Same price, same deal.' Patsy shook Bernie's hand. 'So, you're a madam now are you Bernie?'

'Just looking after my lassies Mrs Diamond, like you asked. They are too shy to ask for themselves. I've never had that problem.'

'No, I don't suppose you have. You know what I need; once you've sorted it, let me know.' Even Patsy thought it was a good idea to have another income from letting the flats above the shops. Obviously Leandra was happy with the agreement and had spread the word to her friends.

Patsy left, with a cheerful wave from Bernie and Leandra, and walked back to the community centre to find Sheila inside having a cup of tea with Maggie.

'Well, there's a face I'm pleased to see.' Patsy grinned. 'How are Angus and the girls? I actually wanted a word with you about Christmas.'

'That sounds ominous! How's Larry? Is he enjoying being chief cook and bottlewasher?' Raising her eyebrows, Sheila stared at Patsy.

'He likes to cook, and to cook you have to shop, which is something else he likes doing,' Patsy joked. 'He seems happy enough. He says he likes looking after me, because I'm so busy all the time.'

'But he's busy too Patsy. He's a hardworking lawyer. Do you just pass each other in the corridor and on the way to the bathroom?'

'Actually, Sheila, I'm going to take a holiday after Christmas. You're right, we need some "us" time. I'm going to the Maldives for a couple of weeks; can you cope here?'

'What is there to cope with? It runs like clockwork. Everyone knows their jobs and does them properly. I don't know where the weeks have gone to; my life is passing me by. You must feel the same.'

'That's why I need a break.' Patsy sighed. 'On another note,

I'm going to lay some flowers outside the community centre for Nick. It's nearly the anniversary of his death. Are you doing anything for Steve?'

'Yes, I'd like to do something.' For a moment there was a solemn pause between them as they both remembered that day. 'I never dreamed last year I would be owning my home with money in my pocket to burn Patsy. It's been a long year for all of us.'

Nodding, Patsy agreed. 'I think that's why Victoria wants us all there for Christmas. It's her first year without Nick and she wants to surround herself with people to make it happy and light. What do you think next year will bring?'

'Who knows love, but whatever it is, we can face it as long as we have each other.'

* * *

'Merry Christmas,' everyone shouted. The adults yawned, as the sun was just coming up and all of the children ran around in their pyjamas looking under the tree. Victoria had organised a grand affair and the cook and staff enjoyed being used to their maximum ability for once. The huge tree glistened and there were gaily coloured parcels scattered beneath it, just waiting for someone to open them. Surprisingly, even Maggie had come, and social services had let little Jimmy come for Christmas, too. They all spent the day laughing and gorging themselves on the many delights the cook had made. The food was never ending. It was just what Victoria needed, Patsy mused, a house full of laughter and fun, while her heart was breaking inside for the son she had lost. Fin was like a child; he had never seen a Christmas like it and was in awe of the merriment and the gifts everyone had bought him.

'Are you okay Patsy?' Larry put his arms around her waist and held her tight.

'Of course I am; it's a lovely day, isn't it?'

'You're all putting a brave face on, and I haven't wanted to say anything, but I remember last year too. It's a hard subject to bring up.'

Patsy kissed him on the cheek. 'I'm fine Larry. We all are. Who would have thought such a dysfunctional bunch of people like us would find each other out of tragedy. This is our family. Anyway, I have one last present for you. Well, for us both actually.' Picking up her handbag, Patsy took out a large envelope and handed it to Larry.

Confused, he grinned, and then opened it. Inside were two airline tickets. Puzzled, he read them and then looked at Patsy.

'As soon as the New Year is over Larry, we're going to the Maldives, just you and me. Let's get away from the winter and the snow and relax on a beach somewhere.'

'How much has this cost Patsy? I should put something towards it. It's a lovely idea, but I'm not having people thinking I'm living off you.' As pleased as Larry was, he looked at the tickets and saw they were business class and he knew Patsy would have booked somewhere with five stars.

'Equality, Larry. You have a good job and a good living. I'm living in your house, not mine. Who gives a fuck what people think? We're equals and if I want to pay for a holiday for myself and my fiancé, I will.'

Seeing that he had taken the shine off her surprise, Larry apologised. 'Sorry love, I just don't want you thinking that's all I see you for. I love you, thank you. It will be great to be on our own for a while, with no interruptions. Just you and me; that really is something to look forward to.' Leaning towards her, he kissed her lovingly and Patsy duly responded.

* * *

No sooner had Christmas come than it had gone again. Life returned to normality; well, as much as it could in Patsy's world, and Larry was already packed to leave for their holidays.

The airport was full to capacity when they arrived and Patsy was pleased she had chosen business class because that meant they didn't have to wait around in queues. They were both excited as they stood in front of the check-in desk. It was going to be a long flight, but the end would justify the means.

'Patsy Diamond.' Hearing her name, Patsy turned to see a uniformed police officer behind her. The man standing beside him introduced himself as Detective Sergeant Jones, and showed her his badge.

'What's the problem?' Confused, she turned to Larry, who looked just a confused as she did.

'We would like you to come to the station with us; you're under arrest.'

Patsy stared at the detective in disbelief. 'What are you talking about? For what? I haven't done anything. Anyway, I'm going on holiday, this will have to wait.'

The detective shook his head. 'You're not leaving the country Mrs Diamond, and we would prefer to discuss our business with you down at the station.'

'Well, I might be under arrest, but Larry isn't.' Turning to Larry, she gave a weak smile. 'You go on ahead, and this will be cleared up in a few hours. I will join you as soon as I can.'

'No, I'm your lawyer. What is all of this about officer? If you're arresting her, she is entitled to know why.'

'You're not free to leave either, Mr Kavanagh, I'm afraid. Every time we hear Mrs Diamond's name, we hear yours. We need to speak to you as well.'

'What? You're arresting me? For what? Answer the question; why are you arresting Mrs Diamond?' Red faced and angry, Larry put his arms around Patsy protectively.

The detective looked bored. 'Money laundering, organised prostitution, and racketeering. The list goes on Mr Kavanagh. Do you want to speak here, or at the station?'

Larry looked at Patsy and then back at the officer. 'I hope you have proof of these accusations, because you will have a lot of apologising to do when you're proved wrong! Tell him Patsy, tell him you're innocent,' Larry shouted.

Patsy's heart sank and her knees felt weak. Everyone in the airport was watching and listening. She felt embarrassed and blushed to her roots. 'Of course I'm innocent Larry. I don't know what they're talking about.'

Ignoring Patsy, the detective spoke to Larry. 'You're not under arrest Mr Kavanagh, we would just like to talk to you. But neither of you are leaving the country.' The detective nodded to the uniformed officer who produced his handcuffs and told Patsy to hold out her arms. Gobsmacked, Patsy held out her arms nervously, while the handcuffs were put on her wrists. She averted her gaze from Larry, her face burning with embarrassment and shame. He was doing his best to plead her innocence, not knowing what else to do. She was hot and sweaty, almost claustrophobic, and felt as if she was going to faint. Patsy didn't want to prolong this any further. She could see Larry staring at her wide eyed.

Looking up at him, she smiled. 'Do you know any good lawyers Larry?' she quipped. Moistening her lips, she looked directly at the detective. 'Well, we had better get this over with then, hadn't we?' Handcuffed, Patsy was marched out of the airport and into a waiting police car.

Panicking inside, she could hardly breathe, but was determined to keep her composure, while her mind was spinning in all directions. What the hell had happened? Everyone that worked for her kept their noses clean and their mouths shut; although, she remembered the police had told her she was on their radar. Had she done too much too soon? She was trying to think about anything she had done lately that had prompted the police to arrest her. Hearing the things they were charging her with made her cringe. Why had Nick never been arrested? How the hell had he got away with his life of crime for so many years? He had the luck of the Irish, never mind the Scottish.

Patsy knew there was more to this than met the eye, but couldn't think what. Had someone else betrayed her? She felt embarrassed and humiliated in front of Larry. This was what she hadn't wanted, Larry being dragged into her sordid gangland world. He would hate her for what she represented, and that saddened her most of all. She would lose his love by her own doings. Patsy accepted her fate. She knew the pitfalls of the life she was living and if you play with fires you get your fingers burnt, but she'd had a lot of fun in the meantime. She realised that she had sailed a bit close to the wind, but she was more interested in what the police were going to say. What exactly did they have to put her in prison? Suddenly, a smile crossed her face. She could imagine the headlines. 'Patsy Diamond, gangland boss, arrested.' It would build her reputation enormously.

'Say nothing Patsy, say nothing until I get there,' Larry shouted after her. Again and again, his voice rang in her ears, which made her feel even more remorseful. Looking out of the police car as she drove away, Patsy spied Larry getting into another police car. He looked flustered and upset. Shrugging and sighing, she laid her head on the headrest. 'Is it okay if I smoke?'

ACKNOWLEDGMENTS

To Boldwood Books and especially Emily Ruston, my editor, who painstakingly edits and scrambles through my crazy plots.

MORE FROM GILLIAN GODDEN

We hope you enjoyed reading *Queen of Diamonds*. If you did, please leave a review.

If you'd like to gift a copy, this book is also available as an ebook, digital audio download and audiobook CD.

Sign up to Gillian Godden's mailing list for news, competitions and updates on future books.

http://bit.ly/GillianGoddenNewsletter

Gold Digger, the first in the series, is available now.

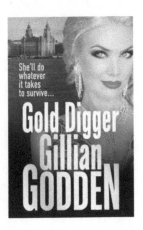

ABOUT THE AUTHOR

Gillian Godden is a Northern-born medical secretary for NHS England. She spent thirty years of her life in the East End of London, hearing stories about the local striptease pubs. Now in Yorkshire, she is an avid reader who lives with her dog, Susie.

Follow Gillian on social media:

 facebook.com/gilliangoddenauthor
twitter.com/GGodden

PEAKY READERS

GANG LOYALTIES. DARK SECRETS.
BLOODY REVENGE.

A READER COMMUNITY FOR
GANGLAND CRIME THRILLER FANS!

DISCOVER PAGE-TURNING NOVELS
FROM YOUR FAVOURITE AUTHORS
AND MEET NEW FRIENDS.

**JOIN OUR BOOK CLUB
FACEBOOK GROUP**

BIT.LY/PEAKYREADERSFB

**SIGN UP TO OUR
NEWSLETTER**

BIT.LY/PEAKYREADERSNEWS

Boldwood

Boldwood Books is an award-winning fiction publishing company seeking out the best stories from around the world.

Find out more at www.boldwoodbooks.com

Join our reader community for brilliant books, competitions and offers!

Follow us
@BoldwoodBooks
@BookandTonic

Sign up to our weekly deals newsletter

https://bit.ly/BoldwoodBNewsletter

Lightning Source UK Ltd.
Milton Keynes UK
UKHW041439031222
413227UK00005B/194